The Swiss Spy

ALEX GERLIS

THE SWISS SPY

CANELO

First published in the United Kingdom in 2015 by Studio 28

This edition published in the United Kingdom in 2020 by

Canelo Digital Publishing Limited
31 Helen Road
Oxford OX2 0DF
United Kingdom

Print ISBN 978 1 78863 996 5
Ebook ISBN 978 1 78863 867 8

Look for more great books at www.canelo.co

Printed and bound in Great Britain by Clays Ltd, Elcograf S.p.A.

List of main characters

Henry Hunter also known as Henri Hesse

Marlene Hesse mother of Henry. Formerly known as Maureen Hunter

Erich Hesse (deceased) husband of Marlene & stepfather of Henry

Louise Alice Hunter (deceased) aunt of Henry Hunter

Captain Edgar British spy master

Hon. Anthony Davis cover name for Edgar

Patrick O'Connor jnr cover name for Edgar

Christopher Porter Edgar's boss

Basil Remington-Barber British spy chief in Switzerland

Sir Roland Pearson Downing Street intelligence chief

Madame Ladnier contact at Credit Suisse, Geneva

Sandy Morgan British spy in Lisbon

Rolf Eder Austrian, working for the British in Switzerland

Franz Hermann Berlin lawyer & British agent. Codename *Hugo*

Frau Hermann mother of Franz Hermann

Werner Ernst Generalmajor in German Army High Command

Gunter Reinhart official at the Reichsbank, Berlin. Married to Gudrun.

Rosa Stern first wife of Gunter Reinhart. Married to Harald Stern

Alfred Stern son of Gunter Reinhart & Rosa Stern

Sophia Stern daughter of Rosa Stern and Harald Stern

Alois Jäger Berlin lawyer

Katharina Hoch British agent in Stuttgart. Codename *Milo*

Dieter Hoch Brother of Katharina Hoch

Manfred contact in Essen. Codename *Lido*

Gertraud Traugott (deceased) 'aunt' in Essen

Telmo Rocha Martins Official in Portuguese Foreign ministry

Dona Maria do Rosario Secretary at Portuguese Legation in Berlin

Viktor Krasotkin Russian spy master

Father Josef Priest at St Hedwig's Cathedral, Berlin

Michael Hedinger official at Bank Leu, Zurich

Anatoly Mikhailovich Yevtushenko Russian émigré in Interlaken, Switzerland

Tatyana Dmitriyevna Yevtushenko wife of Anatoly

Rozalia Anatolyevna Yevtushenko daughter of Anatoly & Tatyana

Nadezhda Anatolyevna Yevtushenko daughter of Anatoly & Tatyana

Nikolai Anatolyevich Yevtushenko son of Anatoly & Tatyana

Prologue

'It looks like it's started. You had better come over.'

It was pitch dark in the room and he was unsure if the vaguely familiar voice next to him was part of a dream or was real and, if so, where it was coming from.

'Are you there Edgar? Can you hear me?'

He realised he was holding the telephone in his hand. He must have picked it up in the middle of a dream in which he'd been surrounded by men even taller than him, all wearing black uniforms with gleaming smiles. The menace that accompanied them had suddenly vanished at the sound of a shrill bell and man calling his name.

'Edgar! Are you there?'

He switched on the bedside lamp and leaned back on his pillow. It was Christopher Porter. Annoyingly, his cigarette case was not on the table.

'Yes sir.'

'At last. I imagine I've woken you up?'

'At two o'clock in the morning? Whatever makes you think that?'

'You'd better come over. Looks like it's all started.'

'Not another false alarm, I hope.'

'I don't think so: you'd better come and see for yourself.'

He dressed quickly, not bothering to shave. Just as he was about to leave his flat he noticed a half full glass of whisky on the sideboard. He hesitated for a moment and then drank it. *If what Porter says is true, this may be the last chance for a drink for some time.*

1

There was a light drizzle as he hurried down Victoria Street and by the time he crossed Parliament Square it had turned quite heavy, causing him to run down Whitehall. The city was enveloped in the darkness of the blackout, causing him to step in a few puddles. By the time he arrived at the entrance to the heavily guarded basement under Whitehall his light summer suit was quite drenched, his socks felt soggy and he was breathing heavily. He joined a small queue of people waiting to be allowed in. The pervading smell was a mixture of rain, sweat and cigarette smoke. He edged his way to the front of the queue, ignoring muttering behind him.

'Who shall I say it is again, sir?' The army sergeant glanced anxiously at the men behind him.

'I told you: I was telephoned just before and told to come here. I really do not expect to be kept waiting. You understand?'

The sergeant hesitated: he had strict orders about who he was to allow into the basement and what accreditation they needed. This man was trying to barge his way in. At that moment the door to the basement opened behind him and a man tapped him on the shoulder.

'Captain Edgar is with me: be a good chap and let him through please?'

Five minutes later they had descended several flights of stairs and passed through a series of guarded doorways. Now they were on a narrow platform overlooking a large and brightly lit operations room, its walls covered in large maps. Men and women in a variety of uniforms were either on the phone, writing on bits of paper or climbing ladders to adjust markers on the maps. Another platform on the wall to their left was crowded with senior officers.

'So this is it, sir?'

'Seems to be: it all started just after midnight – our time that is. The Germans launched air raids against key targets in the Soviet controlled sector of Poland. Soon after that their land forces crossed the border. Hard to be too precise at the moment, but everything we're picking up seems to indicate that this is a major invasion. Some reports say that over one hundred German divisions are involved. Other reports say it could be nearer to one hundred and fifty.'

'Reliable sources?'

'Bletchley say they can barely cope with all the radio traffic: noisiest night of the war, they say. Plenty of good stuff coming through Helsinki too. The Finns are pretty much in bed with the Germans now as you know; wouldn't be surprised to see them joining the party. They're also well plugged into all kinds of sources in Russia, close proximity and all that. Stockholm station is sending broadly the same message. Morgan sent three messages from Lisbon last night saying he thought it was imminent – two different sources apparently, one particularly good one in the Ministry of Foreign Affairs.'

Edgar showed no reaction, as if nothing that he was being told was news to him. He felt in his pockets and realised he had forgotten to bring any cigarettes.

'What does the front look like?'

Christopher Porter pointed to an enormous map of Europe opposite them. 'Starting up there in the north – where that red diamond is – they've certainly crossed into Latvia. Probably the Fourth Panzer Group, we know they were in that area. Then all the way down the border, as far south as the Ukraine. Looks like the Romanians may be involved there, possibly the Hungarians too. See Brest on the map… there? That is where the main thrust may well be though it is a bit early to say for sure. Between there and Lublin: north and south of the Pripet Marshes.'

'Quite some front.'

'Well, if they really have attacked from the Baltic to the Black Sea then that's well over a thousand miles. Extraordinary if they manage to pull that off.'

Edgar stared at the map for a good five minutes. 'He is crazy, isn't he?'

'Who is?'

Edgar looked down at Porter, surprised that he didn't seem to know who he was talking about. 'Hitler. He's left it far too late. Look how far they are from Moscow, over six hundred miles. Talking of which, much noise coming out of Moscow?'

'Nothing official. Apparently there is talk of their High Command having sent out some kind of alert about an invasion some three hours

3

before the Germans attacked, but we can't confirm that. Obviously didn't have any effect. Certainly there was a very noticeable increase in radio traffic in and out of Moscow last night, but then we know that the Soviets are prone to getting quite noisy every so often. All in all, it looks like they were caught by surprise.'

'Well' said Edgar, removing his jacket, 'it was not as if we didn't warn them.'

Chapter 1

A shade after one thirty on the afternoon of Monday 14th August twenty people emerged from the terminal building at Croydon Airport and were shepherded across a runway still damp from heavy overnight rain.

They were a somewhat disparate group, as international travellers tend to be. Some were British, some foreign; a few women, mostly men; the majority smartly dressed. One of the passengers was a man of average height and mildly chubby build. A closer look would show bright green eyes that darted around, eager to take everything in and a nose that was bent slightly to the left. Along with a mouth that seemed fixed at the beginnings of a smile, the overall effect was of a younger face and an older body: possibly around thirty, perhaps a bit older. Despite the heavy August sun he was wearing a long raincoat and a trilby hat which was pushed back on his head. In each hand he carried a large briefcase; one black, one light tan. Perhaps because of his nerves, maybe because of the burden of a coat and two briefcases or possibly due to his natural disposition, this man walked apart from the group. At first he strayed to one side and then lagged some way behind it.

At one point he absent-mindedly veered towards a KLM airliner before a man in uniform directed him back towards his group.

A minute or so later the group had assembled at the steps of a Swissair plane, alongside a board indicating its destination: 'Service 1075: Basle'. A queue had formed as the passengers waited for their tickets and passports to be checked.

When the nervous man with the two briefcases presented his papers, the police officer who was checking the passports looked at his with extra care before nodding in the direction of a much taller man who had appeared behind the passenger. The tall man also happened to be wearing a trilby, although his had such a wide brim that it was not possible to make out any features of his face.

The tall man stepped forward and impatiently snatched the passport from the police officer. He glanced at it very briefly, as if he knew what to expect. He then turned to the passenger.

'Would you come with me please, Herr Hesse?' It was unquestionably more of an instruction than an invitation.

'I cannot possibly understand what the problem might be. Can't we sort whatever it is out here?'

'There may not be a problem sir, but it would be best if you came with me. It will be much easier to talk inside.'

'But what about if I miss my flight? It leaves in twenty minutes.'

The taller man said nothing but gestured towards a black Austin 7 that pulled up alongside them. By now the last passenger had boarded and the steps were being wheeled away from the aircraft. The short journey back to the terminal was conducted in silence. They entered the terminal through a side door and went up to an office on the second floor.

Herr Hesse followed the tall man into the small office, which was dominated by a large window overlooking the apron and the runway beyond it. The tall man sat behind the desk in front of the window and gestured to Herr Hesse to sit down on the other side of the desk.

'Sit down? But I am going to miss my flight! What on earth is this all about? All of my papers are in order. I insist on an explanation.'

The tall man pointed at the chair and the passenger reluctantly sat down in it, his head shaking as he did so. The tall man removed his trilby, but Herr Hesse was little the wiser: the man had no remarkable features and his age could have been anything from his late thirties to his mid-fifties. He had the tanned complexion that someone gets from spending plenty of time out of doors and dark eyes that had a penetrating stare, but in truth there was little memorable about the man's face. Hesse could have stared at it for hours and then have difficulty in picking him out of a crowd. When the man spoke it was in accent that could be described as grammar school rather than public school, with perhaps the very slightest trace of a more refined northern accent.

'My name is Edgar. Do you smoke?'

Herr Hesse shook his head. Edgar took his time to select a cigarette from a silver case he had removed from an inside pocket and went through a lengthy ritual of first lighting it and then concentrating on enjoying the first part of the cigarette. He appeared to be in no hurry. He inspected the lighted end of the cigarette, turning it carefully in his hand, admiring the glow and watching the patterns made by the wisps of smoke as they hung above the desk and drifted towards the ceiling. Behind him the Swissair plane was being pulled by a tractor in the direction of the runway. A silver Imperial Airways plane was descending sharply from the south, the sun bouncing off its wings.

Edgar sat in silence, looking carefully at the man in front of him before getting up to look out of the window and across the airport for a full minute, even timing it on his wristwatch. During that time he avoided thinking about the other man, trying hard to keep any picture or memory out of his mind. When the minute was up he turned round and sat down. Without looking up, he wrote in his notebook:

> *Complexion: pale, almost unhealthy looking, pasty.*
>
> *Eyes: bight green.*
>
> *Hair: dark and thick, needs cutting.*
>
> *Nose at a slight angle (left).*
>
> *Smiles.*
>
> *Build: slightly overweight.*
>
> *Nervous, but sure of himself.*

A colleague had taught him this technique. Too many of our first impressions of someone are casual ones, so much so that they bear little relation to how someone actually looks, he had told him. As a consequence we tend to end up describing someone in such general terms that important features tend to be disregarded. '*Look at them for one minute, forget about them for one minute and then write down half a dozen things about them.*'

A man who at first glance was distinctly ordinary looking, who in other circumstances Edgar might pass in the street without noticing, now had characteristics that made him easier to recall.

You'll do.

'There are a number of things that puzzle me about you, Herr Hesse. Are you happy with me calling you Herr Hesse, by the way?' As Captain Edgar spoke he was looking at the man's Swiss passport, as if reading from it.

'Why wouldn't I be?' Herr Hesse spoke with an impeccable English accent that had a hint of an upper class drawl to it.

'Well' said Edgar, tapping the desk with the passport as he did so 'that is one of a number of things about you that puzzles me. You are travelling under this Swiss passport in the name of Henri Hesse. But do you also not have a British passport in the name of Henry Hunter?'

The man hesitated before nodding. Edgar noticed that he was perspiring.

'I am sure you would be more comfortable if you removed your hat and coat.'

Another pause while he hung his hat and coat on the back of the door.

'So you accept that you are also known as Henry Hunter?'

The man nodded again.

'Passport?'

'You have it there.'

'If I were in your position Herr Hesse, I think that I would adopt a more co-operative manner altogether. I mean your British passport: the one in the name of Henry Hunter.'

'What about it?'

'I should like to see it.'

There was another pause. Hesse hesitated.

'For the avoidance of doubt, Herr Hesse, I should tell you that I have the right to search every item in your possession: the British passport please?'

Herr Hesse lifted the tan briefcase on to his lap, angled it towards him and opened it just wide enough for one hand to reach in. Still taking great care to shield the other contents of the briefcase from Edgar he retrieved a thick manila envelope, from which he removed the passport. He handed it to Edgar who spent a few minutes studying it.

'Henry Richard Hunter: born Surrey, sixth of November, 1909; making you twenty-nine.'

'Correct.'

Captain Edgar held up the Swiss passport in his left hand and the British passport in his right one and moved them up and down, as if trying to work out which one was the heavier.

'Bit odd, isn't it? Two passports: different names, same person?'

'Possibly, but I very legitimately have two nationalities. I cannot see—'

'We can come to that in a moment. The first thing then that puzzles me about you is that you have a perfectly valid British passport in the name of Henry Hunter, which you used to enter this country on the first of August. However, two weeks later you are trying to leave the country using an equally valid passport, but this time it is a Swiss one and in a different name.'

There was a very long silence. Through the window both men could see Swissair flight 1075 edge on to the runway. Captain Edgar walked over to the window and gazed out at the aircraft for a while before turning back to face the man with the two passports, raising his eyebrows as he did so.

'Any explanation?'

Henry Hunter shrugged. By now Edgar had opened the notebook again in front of him and pulled the fountain pen from his pocket. He took some time to write in the book. He was still writing when he spoke again.

'We can return to the business of flights in a moment. Let us look again at your different names. What can you tell me about that?'

'Will I be able to get on the next flight? There is one to Geneva at three o'clock I think. It would be most inconvenient if I don't get back to Switzerland today.'

'Let's see how we get on with the explanation that you are about to give me, eh? You were about to tell me how you manage to have two nationalities and two names.'

Henri Hesse shrugged, as if he could not understand why this would require any explanation.

'Terribly straightforward, really. I was born here in Surrey as it happens, hence Henry Hunter and the British passport. My father died when I was fourteen and a year or so later my mother met a Swiss man and married him fairly soon after. We moved to Switzerland, first to Zurich and then Geneva. When I was eighteen I was able to become a Swiss national and for the purposes of that I used the surname of my stepfather. In the process the name Henry became Henri. So you see, there's really no mystery. I apologise if it turns out to have been in any way irregular as far as the British Government is concerned: I would be happy to clear matters up at the British consulate in Geneva if that helps. Do you think I will I be able to make the three o'clock Geneva flight?'

'There are a few more questions, Mr Hunter. I am sure you understand. What is your job?'

Hunter shifted in his seat, clearly uncomfortable.

'I don't have a career as such. My stepfather was very wealthy and had property all over Switzerland. I would travel around to check on them – keep the tenants happy and make sure they paid their rent on time, that kind of thing: nothing onerous. I also did some work with a travel agency but most of the time I would travel with my mother. I've managed to keep busy enough.'

Edgar spent quite a while flicking through his notebook and the two passports. At one stage, he made some notes, as if copying something from one of the documents. He then consulted a map he had removed from his jacket pocket.

'You said that your stepfather was very wealthy…'

'He died a couple of years ago.'

'And where did you live?'

'Near Nyon, by the lake.'

Edgar nodded approvingly.

'But I see that you now live in the centre of Geneva, on the Rue de Valais I see.'

'That's right.'

'And how would you describe that area?'

'Pleasant enough.'

'Really? From what I remember of Geneva that is rather on the wrong side of the tracks. Overlooking the railway line are you?'

'To an extent, yes.'

'Well, either one is overlooking the railway line or one is not?'

'Yes: we do overlook it.'

'Sounds rather like a fall from grace. Wish to tell me about it?'

Edgar had selected another cigarette and smoked most of it before Hunter began to answer. He appeared to be distressed, his voice now much quieter.

'After my stepfather died, it transpired that he had another family, in Luzern. Of course, with hindsight that explains why he spent so much time in Zurich on business; my mother never accompanied him on those trips. The family in Luzern, it turned out, were the only legitimate family as far as Swiss law is concerned and therefore had first claim on his estate. I do not fully understand why, but my mother's lawyer assures us that there is nothing whatsoever that we can do about it. The property by the lake near Nyon turned out to be rented and the various bank accounts that my mother had access to were more or less empty. We quickly went from being very comfortable to very hard up: hence the flat by the railway line. We have only been able to survive as we have because my mother had some funds of her own – not very much. And her jewellery – fortunately there was quite a lot of that. She has had to sell most of it. I do as much freelance translation as possible at the international organisations, but work is not easy to find at the moment. These are difficult times on the continent.'

'As one gathers. So what is the purpose of your visit back to England – to get away from it all?'

'Family business; friends. That type of thing.'

Edgar stood up and removed his jacket, draping it carefully over the back of his chair before walking to the front of the desk and sitting on the front of it, very close to Henry Hunter, placing his knees just inches from the other man's face. He leaned over, so that he was even closer to him. When he next spoke it was in a very quiet voice, as if there was someone else in the room who he did not want to hear what he was about to say.

'"*Family business; friends. That type of thing...*" What you need to know Mr Hunter is that we already know an awful lot about you. We have, as they say, been keeping something of an eye on you. It would save a good deal of time if you were to be honest with me. So please could you be more specific about the family business that you mentioned?'

'You said "we". Who do you mean by "we"?'

Edgar leaned back, pointedly ignoring the question.

'You were going to tell me about your family business, Mr Hunter'.

'My aunt died in July. She was my late father's elder sister. I was attending her funeral.'

'My condolences: were you close to her?'

'Not especially, but I was her closest living relative.'

'And you are a beneficiary of the will, no doubt?'

'Yes.'

'And how much did you inherit, Mr Hunter?'

The Swissair DC3 was now beginning to taxi down the runway. A tanker was turning round in front of the building, filling the room with the smell of fuel. Henry Hunter shifted in his chair.

'By the sounds of it, I suspect you probably already know the answer to that.'

Edgar had returned to his chair and leaned back in it so that it tilted against the window. As he did so, he crossed his arms high on his chest, staring long and hard at Hunter.

'What I am curious about, Mr Hunter, is whether my answer is going to be the same as your answer. How about if I endeavour to answer my own question and you stop me if I say anything incorrect?'

'Before you do, could I ask whether you are a police officer?'

'No.'

'If you are not a police officer, what authority do you have to question me like this?'

Edgar laughed, as if he found Hunter's remark to be genuinely amusing.

'Mr Hunter, when you find out on what authority I operate you will very much regret asking that question. So, shall I tell you my version of why I think you came over here?'

Hunter loosened his tie and turned around in his chair, looking longingly at the door, as if he was hoping that someone would come in at that very moment and explain that the whole business had been a terrible misunderstanding.

'Louise Alice Hunter was, as you correctly say, your late father's elder sister and you were indeed her only surviving relative.' Edgar had opened his notebook again and was referring to it as he spoke. 'She was eighty-two years of age and had been a resident in the Green Lawns Residential Home near Buckingham for nine years. The matron of the home informs us that you dutifully came over to visit her once a year. You visited her last November and then again in May, shortly before she died. On each of those visits you were accompanied by her solicitor. Am I correct so far?'

Hunter said nothing.

'I shall assume then that you will point out if anything I say is incorrect. Your aunt died in on the 24th July and you flew here on the 1st August – which was a Tuesday, if I am correct. You travelled straight to Buckinghamshire, where the funeral took place last Thursday, which would have been the 9th. So far, nothing remarkable, eh?'

Hunter nodded and loosened his tie.

'But this is where an otherwise very ordinary story does become somewhat less ordinary: sordid, perhaps. I am now substantially relying on a statement kindly provided by a Mr Martin Hart who, as you are aware, is your aunt's solicitor and the man who accompanied you on your last visits to your aunt. According to Mr Hart, your aunt's estate amounted to a not insubstantial 8,000 pounds, all of which was held in a deposit account administered by Mr Hart. You are indeed a beneficiary of that will; the main beneficiary most certainly, but – crucially – not the sole beneficiary. There were bequests totalling some 1,000 pounds to various friends, staff and charities, but after Mr Hart had deducted fees due to him and duty was paid to Exchequer, you would expect to receive a sum of just under 6,000 pounds: certainly a handsome sum. Does this sound correct to you?'

'If you say so. You do seem to know a good deal more than I do.'

'But there is a small problem, from your point of view. That money could only be passed to you once probate was granted, which could take many months, perhaps even up to a year. We have already established that you and your mother have serious financial problems. Your inheritance would restore you to a position of financial security. You would once again be wealthy. However, waiting for probate is bad enough, but with the very likely –some would say imminent – possibility of war, you had a quite understandable concern that you may not be able to get that money out of England and into Switzerland for quite a long time. I—'

'You are making a number of assumptions here, Edgar. What makes you think I have done anything improper? I—'

'Mr Hunter, who said anything about doing anything improper? I certainly did not. However, as you raise the subject, let me tell you what the most obliging Mr Hart has told us. According to your aunt's solicitor, he was prevailed upon by you to "cut a few corners", as he put it and ensure that the entire funds of the deposit account were released straight away. This is not only improper, it is also illegal.'

Henry Hunter shifted in his chair and pulled an improbably large handkerchief from a trouser pocket to mop his brow. Edgar had now removed a pair of reading glasses from a crocodile skin case and after polishing them for longer than would appear necessary, began to read from a document he had extracted from the desk drawer.

'According to the best legal advice available to me, there is no question that both Mr Hart and you committed a crime, namely conspiracy to defraud. My learned friends tell me that on the evidence they have seen, a conviction would be extremely likely and a term of imprisonment would almost certainly ensue. They say that there is ample *prima facie* evidence to show that you have conspired to defraud His Majesty's Exchequer of the duties that would have been owed to it from your great aunt's estate and you had conspired to prevent the other beneficiaries of the will from receiving the money bequeathed to them. Fraud, Mr Hunter, is a most serious criminal offence. Confronted with our evidence Mr Hart has, as I say, been most co-operative. He claims that due to a health issue, as he describes it, he allowed himself to be persuaded against his better judgement to release the funds. He admits that he received a much larger fee than he would ordinarily have expected. Apparently—'

'It is not as bad as it sounds; I have to tell you that.' Edgar was taken aback by how forceful Hunter was sounding. 'I told Hart that if I was able to take the money to Switzerland while I could, then I would be in a position to return the money owed to the exchequer and the other beneficiaries very soon, certainly before probate would ordinarily have been granted.'

'Really? You and Mr Hart cooked up a somewhat clever scheme whereby you were counting on war being declared. Mr Hart believed that in those circumstances, he could apply to be granted a stay of probate until such a time as you were in a position to claim. In other words, Mr Hunter, he would use the war as an excuse: pretend keep the money in the deposit account until after the war, whenever that is. Except of course, the money would not be in the deposit account, it would be with you in Switzerland. Apparently, he – you – may well have got away with it had not the matron at the home overheard some conversation about it between yourself and Mr Hart and contacted the police.'

'It would all have been paid back, I promise you. Once I deposited it in Switzerland I would have transferred what I owed back. It seemed easier to send the money back from Switzerland rather than wait for probate and then have it transferred from London.'

'Really? All we need to do now is find the money eh, Hunter? Do you want me to hazard a guess as to where could be?'

Hunter sat very still and stared across the airport as Edgar stood up and walked round the desk. Once in front of Hunter he bent down to pick up the two leather briefcases and placed them both on the desk.

'Keys?'

Without saying anything or appearing to divert his gaze from the runway, Hunter reached into the inside pocket of his jacket and produced a set of keys which he handed to Edgar.

It took Edgar a full twenty minutes to remove all the bundles of banknotes from the two briefcases, assembling the different denominations in separate piles. Not a word was exchanged during this process, which Hunter watched with some interest, as if he had never seen so much money before. By the time Edgar had finished, there were four piles: one pile comprised the bundles of ten shilling notes, another the one pound notes, then five pound notes and ten pound notes. The pile of bundles of the large, white five pound notes was by far the largest.

Edgar stepped back from the desk and stood alongside Hunter. The entire surface of the desk was covered in money.

'I have only of course been able to do an approximate count, but I would say that there is 7,000 pounds there. Would that be correct, Mr Hunter?'

'More or less. I think you will find it is more like 6,800 pounds. Mr Hart claimed rather late in the day that he needed another 200 pounds – for expenses, apparently.'

'Two hundred pounds does not seem to me to be very much considering the impact this is likely to have on his professional career.'

'It has all been rather rushed, Edgar. As it was such a large sum of cash we had to withdraw it from a main branch of the Midland Bank in the city. We were only able to get hold of it this morning, which is why I missed the nine o'clock flight.'

'Yes, I'm aware of all that Mr Hunter.' Edgar was still standing next to the seated Mr Hunter, with a hand on the others' shoulder.

'In a moment some colleagues of mine are going to come and take you away. I shall look after the money and all your possessions. We shall meet again in a few days.'

—

A few minutes later a clearly shocked Hunter had been escorted from the airport in handcuffs by three uniformed police officers. In the office overlooking the runway Edgar removed his tie, lit another cigarette and dialled a London number from the telephone nestling between bundles of banknotes on the desk.

'It's Edgar.'

'I thought it might be you. How did it go?'

'Very much according to plan.'

'Good. We're on then?'

'Yes. Indeed. We're on, as you put it, Porter.'

'And what is he like?'

'Rather as we were expecting. Not altogether the most agreeable of types, but then that is hardly a disqualification in our line of work, is it?'

'Too true... and, um – any hint at all of... you know?'

'No, none whatsoever. He was rather impressive in that respect, I must say. Had one not been aware, one would really have had no idea at all.'

'Splendid. What now?'

'I think he needs a few days on his own: ought to be easy enough after that.'

Chapter 2

London, August 1939

It was early on a blazing hot Monday afternoon – one of the first truly hot days that August – when Edgar stepped out into Whitehall and paused for a good minute or two on the pavement to enjoy the sun. There was an uncharacteristic bounce in his step as he strolled up Whitehall to Trafalgar Square where he caught the number 12 bus and headed west. He needed some time to think and what, he thought, could be a more pleasant place to do that from than the top deck of a London bus.

He stayed on the bus until Notting Hill Gate and then walked over to Kensington Park Road, taking care as he did so to ensure that he was not being followed. He was about to walk but a number 52 bus came along and he decided to hop on. He stayed on the bus until it was halfway down Ladbroke Grove. He waited a full five minutes at the bus stop to ensure his tail was clear and then headed north west to where the grandeur of Holland Park petered out to a series of plain and forgettable buildings. He passed a grocery shop with a long and excited queue outside it and briefly wondered whether he should join it, as one did these days, but a glance at his watch made him realise he needed to hurry.

Edgar paused outside a small alley, allowed an elderly lady to be pulled past him by a pair of yapping terriers and then entered the alley. At the end of it he pressed a bell and a large iron gate swung open. He was now in a small courtyard: a policeman saluted and unlocked a door and from there Edgar descended three flights of stairs before finding himself in what was, to all intents and purposes, a small police station.

Minutes later he was sitting in a stuffy windowless room in the basement with a police inspector.

'What I would like to know is what his general mood is like. What he does? How he behaves? What he says? That kind of thing, Inspector Hill. I'm sure you know the score.'

The inspector removed a notebook from the top pocket of his uniform jacket and flicked through a few pages.

'Let's see then… in a pretty bad mood when he arrived here on Monday night, shouting the odds, insisting he had a right to a lawyer. Shut up once he'd had something to eat. Next day he was on again about a lawyer. We kept him in his cell until Wednesday afternoon when he was brought in here and I read him the riot act: told him that under emergency regulations he had no right to a lawyer. He asked for a copy of those regulations and I told him it was in the post, which did not seem to reassure him. Thursday: he's still making a fuss so we bring in a couple of the plain clothes boys as you had suggested and that does the trick. They tell him that he's being done for conspiracy to commit fraud and that if he pleads guilty and is terribly lucky with the judge he may get away with five years. Otherwise, he can double it.'

'And how did he take that?'

'Very much as we would have hoped: a few tears before bedtime. He begged to be able to send a telegram to his mother; told anyone who'd listen that there had been a terrible misunderstanding and that he would happily donate the money to charity.'

'And I presume you then did as I asked?'

'Of course: plainclothes boys returned on Friday morning and he provides us with a neat statement, confessing all. I have it here.'

From a drawer in the desk between him and Edgar the inspector produced three closely typed sheets of paper, each signed with something of a flourish. Edgar carefully read and then re-read the statement.

'Signed on Friday 18th August. Good. And since then?'

'We allowed him to stew over the weekend. Other than being brought to this room and into the corridor outside his cell for exercise a couple of times a day, he has been locked in his cell all day. He hasn't seen daylight in a week. Even so…'

'You're hesitating, Hill.'

'It is just that I would have expected someone like him to be even more affected by his ordeal than he appears to have been. According to the guards he doesn't sleep well, is unquestionably shaken and has signed the confession, but despite that he has a resolve about him that I would not have expected. When he was first brought here he was a nervous character: quite jumpy. But I warn you Edgar, there is a certain steel about him.'

'We'll see, shall we? Anyway, well done, Hill. Good work. Better bring him in.'

Despite what Hill had said Henry Hunter looked more worn in the week since Edgar had last seen him, although his smile was still in place. He had lost a bit of weight and dark rings had appeared around his eyes along with two or three day's growth of beard. He appeared to be relieved to see Edgar.

'I thought we may meet again.'

'How has your week been, Hunter? Treated well?'

'Well, I haven't been tortured, if that is what you mean. But they wouldn't even let me have a newspaper and I cannot believe that I am unable to see a solicitor or contact my mother. Is that right?'

'Depends on what you mean by "is that right?", Hunter. While it is *correct*, Hunter, that you have not been able contact either a lawyer or your mother, whether that is *in order* is entirely another matter. You will discover in due course that we have very good reasons for pursuing this course of action. We have, incidentally, taken the liberty of sending her a telegram in your name saying that all is well and she is not to worry.'

'Can I ask, Edgar, whether this a regular police station though? I do seem to be rather… isolated.'

'It is a police station, although you are at present the only person in custody in it. I understand that your predicament has been explained to you by some officers here?'

'Yes. Conspiracy to commit fraud apparently and if I am very, very lucky then I shall get away with five years in prison. I've signed a statement.'

'And did they add that if you are found guilty or plead guilty then all of the money that we found in your possession will be confiscated? After the other beneficiaries have been paid and the duty paid, you will be left with nothing.'

'They did not mention that, no.'

'So all in all, Hunter, a bit of a mess eh?'

'So it would seem.'

A very long silence ensued, during which Edgar lit a cigarette and wrote some notes in his book.

'I am told that the prison regime is likely to be especially harsh during war time. Most prisoners are required to undertake quite onerous physical labour.'

Hunter said nothing, clearly unsure how he was meant to react.

'However, there is an alternative, Hunter. There is a way of avoiding prison and even keeping most of your money. You would be able to return to Switzerland and see your mother again.'

Hunter's eyes lit up and as suspicious as he was, he found it hard to suppress a thin smile.

'Tell me more.'

'Before I can do that I need to know for sure whether you are interested or not.'

'Yes, of course I am interested.'

'Very well then. This is, to all intents and purposes, the point of no return. Once I tell you what the alternative is, then your options really are very limited. Do you understand that?'

Hunter nodded.

'I work for a government agency whose purpose is to gather intelligence. As you are no doubt aware, this country is perilously close to war with Germany. We urgently need to expand and improve our intelligence networks across Europe; they are in a pretty woeful state at the moment. As strange as it may seem, Mr Hunter, you are very well placed indeed. You have genuine Swiss and British passports and are fluent in German and French.'

Hunter leant forward, his hands touching the desk, eager to hear more.

'What would you require me to do?'

'I had hoped I had made that apparent Mr Hunter – Henry. To help us gather intelligence.'

'Be a spy?'

'Correct.'

Outside in the corridor a metal gate slammed shut and there was a murmur of voices passing by. Henry Hunter laughed.

'A spy? You must be joking: what on earth makes you so sure I'm up to this?'

'We aren't: we'll give you some training of course, but our priority is to get you back to Switzerland. That is where we need you to be. For us, your dual identity and your ability to move around what may be enemy territory as a Swiss national are invaluable. And don't forget, we have a hold over you.'

'Which is?'

'If you turn down our offer then the alternative is a lengthy spell in one of His Majesty's prisons. Furthermore, there is the question of the money.'

'You mean my aunt's?'

'Yes: the 6,000 pounds that is legally yours but which you will lose as a result of the court case. However, if you agree to work for us then not only will there be no court case but you will also receive the money: all 6,000 pounds of it. A bank account will be opened in your name at the Quai des Bergues branch of Credit Suisse in Geneva. If you accept my offer then the sum of 500 pounds will be transferred to that account immediately. Thereafter, we will transfer a further 100 pounds a month into that account for as long as you work for us.'

Hunter frowned, trying to work something out. 'Hang on. At that rate, it could take... I don't know, years for me to receive all of my money!'

'Henry, you are not obliged to take up our offer. We cannot *force* you to be a spy. Look, it may be a while before we call upon your services, but if you undertake any specific mission successfully then we can consider advancing further lump sums of 500 pounds. And of course, we will cover any expenses that you may incur.'

'How about if you were to advance 1,000 pounds? My mother and I have considerable debts to clear.'

'Henry: you are really not in a position to negotiate.'

'Will there be any danger – you said something about "enemy territory"?'

Edgar laughed, standing up as he did so, stretching himself.

'Of course there'll be danger: plenty of it, I imagine. What's the point of being a bloody spy otherwise! But if you ask me, even with that risk of danger, it is still a more agreeable lifestyle than ten years hard labour here.'

'Ten? I thought it would be five if I pleaded guilty?'

'Believe me Henry. If you decline my offer and this goes to court, it will be ten years. Come on now...' Edgar was tapping his watch. 'What is it to be? Are you coming with me, or shall I leave you here with the police for the wheels of justice to start rolling?'

Edgar had expected more questions, more hesitation and more signs of nerves, but with what seemed to be barely a second thought Henry Hunter clapped his hands and allowed his thin smile to become a broad one.

'All sounds most interesting Edgar. I'm ready to join you.'

Chapter 3

Henry Hunter's training as a British agent had been entrusted to a classics don who had moved from a crumbling Oxford college to a crumbling country house somewhere north of London for the purpose of training his 'special scholars', as he liked to call them. He never tired of telling them that the transition from teaching classics to teaching espionage was a natural one.

'Classics' he would say, 'is all about war, human failings, chance and intrigue: not so very different to espionage.'

Captain Edgar had visited the country house once a week to check on Hunter's progress. He was taking his time: physical fitness was an issue, as was his radio training but he was regarded as a brilliant map reader and became proficient with a revolver. It was only towards the end of October that the classics don conceded that Henry Hunter was more or less ready.

'My opinion is that the characteristics of a spy are innate. It is a skill one is born with: it is, I believe, part of someone's personality. You see, we all too often make the mistake of taking someone who appears to have all the attributes of a spy and then train them in the specifics of the job. They could fly through the training with an A plus, but that would not necessarily make them a good spy. I have been looking after recruiting and training spies for years, as you well know Edgar. Some of those A plus types make hopeless spies once they're out in the field. A truly effective spy will have some personality flaw or such like which marks them out from most other people. They are used to walking in the shadows, on the other side of the street from most other people, slightly apart from the crowd but not so much so that people would notice them.'

'Very interesting, but will Hunter make it as a spy?'

'Good heavens yes, Edgar. I don't think I have ever come across someone quite so well qualified. The most dangerous moment for a spy is when they make that transition from what one might call "normal society" into the world of espionage. For the vast majority of people that can be too great a wrench: they have too much to lose. But if you feel that you have never really been part of society, that you have always been on the margins of it, then you are a natural spy. I've rarely come across such a good example of this than Hunter.'

–

One week later they Hunter and Edgar were being driven down a lane on a moonless night when Hunter chose to break the uneasy silence that had accompanied them for the two hours since leaving the country house.

'Can't see a bloody thing in this dark Edgar – and what has happened to all the road signs?'

'I appreciate that you have been holed up in that country house for the past three months or so Henry, but it cannot have escaped even your attention that we are now at war with Germany, even if it doesn't actually feel like it. Hence the blackout.'

'And the road signs?'

'No need to help any German spies who are lost, is there?'

'Can you at least tell me where we are, Edgar?'

'No.'

'You are treating me like I am a bloody prisoner.'

'Which, but for the grace of God and my own good offices, Hunter, you actually would be – and for many years. Do not forget that.'

'How could I? You know how grateful I am to you.'

'Less of the sarcasm if you please Hunter. I can tell you that we have been driving south and we are now in Hampshire, which is as much as you need to know.'

'Any particular part of Hampshire?'

'Obviously Hunter, but you don't need to know any more than that. In any case, you'll be gone within a day or two. Look, we have arrived: better go and get some sleep. We'll start the briefing first thing in the morning.'

–

First thing in the morning for Edgar was around two hours earlier than Hunter had hoped it would be. It was still dark when Hunter was woken up by a knock at the door, followed by the sound of a key turning in the lock and a stiff bolt sliding open. The soldier who woke him – the same one who had escorted him to the room the previous night – announced that he would need to be ready in ten minutes.

Edgar was sitting at a long table in a large office, the room already wreathed in smoke. He was wearing a coat and a high window was open, letting in the cold morning air and the distinctive smell of recently turned soil. The table was crowded with files and documents. As Hunter entered the room he was followed in by another soldier who was bearing a tray with a pot of tea, toast and boiled eggs.

Hunter had little appetite, but Edgar tucked in. He ate in silence for five minutes while Hunter nibbled on a slice of toast and sipped the weak tea.

'Right: now we begin! Tonight you will begin your journey back to Switzerland, Hunter. I need to be very clear and you need to fully understand that from now on, you are working for British Intelligence. It is a role that carries few rewards and privileges, other than that of serving your country. On the other hand, you will find that this life that has been chosen for you will have plenty of responsibility and not a few dangers. There will be long periods of tedium and you will find the fact that you can confide in no one makes it a most difficult and stressful existence. I need hardly tell you that the world of espionage is not one of glamour or excitement. The most common emotions are boredom and fear.'

Hunter nodded. This was not the first time he had heard this, but now that his return to Switzerland was imminent he began to feel nervous.

'I will spend the next few hours briefing you. I shall remind you of what is expected of you. I shall tell you everything that you need to know.'

And so it continued for many hours. Within an hour a weak daylight had filled the room, which further filled with smoke as Edgar worked his way through one packet and then another. As noon approached and the sun became brighter, sandwiches were brought in along with a couple of bottles of beer. Edgar began to appear more relaxed than Hunter had ever seen him.

'Usually in these situations, Hunter, one spends a good deal of one's time making sure that someone in your position is absolutely familiar with their new identity. In your case, however, the Henri Hesse identity is so good that there would be no merit whatsoever in seeking to furnish you with a new and false identity. It is far better to stick with this one.

'You leave tonight, Henry. I know that flying is your preferred method of travel around Europe, but I am afraid that now that we are at war there are no more civilian flights to either France or Switzerland, so you're going by boat. A troopship, the SS *Worthing* is leaving Southampton this evening. She is taking a contingent of the Royal Fusiliers over the channel. She'll dock at Cherbourg early tomorrow morning and you will travel from there to Paris. You will stay in Paris tomorrow night and then travel by train the following day to Geneva, using your Swiss identity. Do you understand that?'

Hunter nodded.

'Good. Your mother is expecting you: send her a telegram from Paris giving details of your arrival. Once you arrive, you will tell her as little as possible. All the letters that you wrote while you were being trained have been sent on to her, along with two payments of one hundred pounds into her own bank account. As far as she is concerned you were staying at a guest house in Fulham while you were sorting out your aunt's will. That was the address from where your letters were sent.'

'It is going to be hard to convince her why those financial arrangements took so long.'

'But not as long as it could have been, eh? Do not try and explain too much. Just tell her that it was far more complicated to transfer money out of the country than you had realised and in the end you had to settle for it being paid in instalments. The initial 500 pounds deposit and the 200pounds she has been sent should ensure that you can now lead a more agreeable lifestyle, along with the 100 pounds per month, of course.'

'When will I be contacted Edgar, how will I know what to do?'

'Within a day or two of your arrival back in Geneva you are to go to the Quai des Bergues branch of Credit Suisse, where we have opened an account in your name as promised. You are to ask for an appointment with Madame Ladnier. Under no circumstances are you to see anyone else there. Madame Ladnier is a senior clerk there and, among other matters, she looks after new clients. You are to go through paperwork with her and then she will start the account and you will be able to access the money. Madame Ladnier is, very indirectly, a contact of ours, but you must never discuss intelligence matters with her: she is little more than a conduit, a messenger if you like. However, if you need to contact us urgently, you can do so through her. You can do this either at the bank, which is preferable, or on her home telephone number – she will give that to you. That, you understand, is most irregular so please do be discreet about that. If you need to contact us urgently, simply tell her that you need to change some Swiss Francs into Italian Lira. She will then know to contact us. If there are any changes in your circumstances, such as when you move home for example, you must inform her. Do you understand all this?'

Hunter understood. Edgar got him to repeat it.

'When we make contact with you, it will not be through Madame Ladnier. It could be in anything from a couple of weeks to a few months. Depends on what we need you to do. Chances are that the first job will be something relatively straightforward, probably within Switzerland. Shouldn't be anything too dangerous; a warm up, if you like. What will happen is this: you will be approached in the street by someone asking for directions to the Old Town. What is it you call it in Geneva?'

'The *vieille ville*.'

'This person will be carrying a copy of the previous day's edition of the *Tribune de Genève*. In reply to their question you are to ask them if they would prefer to walk or to take the tram. They will reply that they would prefer to walk if you can point them in the right direction. You will explain that you are walking that way and they are welcome to follow you. Take any route to the Old Town. At some point after entering it they will overtake you. You are not to acknowledge them, you just carry on walking at the same pace, but now you are following them. When you see them place the copy of the *Tribune de Genève* in a waste bin outside a building you are to enter the building and wait. If no one has approached you after five minutes, you are to leave the building and return home. However, if someone joins you and introduces themselves as Marc you are to go with him. He will take you to meet your main contact. At that moment, your new career will have begun. Please repeat all of this to me Henry.'

–

Edgar's briefing had finished just after one o'clock and Hunter was escorted back to his room. Edgar urged him to try and get some sleep: it was going to be a long night and he should not count on being able to sleep on the boat. In his room he saw that a case had been carefully packed for him, along with his two briefcases. A change of clothes was laid out on the bed. Edgar explained that everything had been carefully checked to ensure that nothing incriminating was in his possession in case he was searched.

He was woken at four and the soldier who had been looking after him told him that a bath had been prepared for him. By four thirty he was back in the office where his briefing had been held that morning. The soldier carried his case and Hunter carried his own briefcases. Edgar was nervously fiddling with his leather gloves.

'There is a train from Cherbourg at ten fifteen in the morning, which you're to take to Paris. There is a telegram bureau inside Gare Saint-Lazare: you're to go to it as soon as you arrive and send a telegram with the following message to this address.'

He handed a slip of paper to Hunter. The message read: 'Arrived safely Paris stop regards to all stop'.

'Memorise that and then destroy the paper. Then go and find a hotel and the next morning take the train to Geneva. You know your way around Paris?'

Hunter shrugged. 'I've been once or twice.'

Edgar pointed to the table. 'Here are your British and Swiss passports, which we have been looking after for you. Here is a receipt for the guest house in Fulham to show you were staying there since the middle of August. In this envelope is more paperwork than you could imagine from various firms of solicitors and the Midland Bank relating to the release of money from your aunt's estate, including a terribly helpful letter from the bank explaining that the money can only be transferred legally to a foreign country in instalments. Can I ask, is your mother the inquisitive type?'

'Do you mean, is she nosey?'

Edgar laughed. 'Well, yes.'

'She could not be more nosey, if I was honest. Always poking about in my things.'

'Good. Don't show all these letters and documents to her then, just leave them for her to find. It will be much more convincing that way and she then ought to believe your account of why you were kept here for so long. It is essential that she never suspects what you are up to, do you understand?'

Henry nodded.

'Hang on, before you put all that in your briefcase, here is some more money: twenty pounds worth of French francs which ought to be more than enough for your hotel tomorrow night and the ticket to Geneva, plus meals. And here in this envelope is fifty pounds worth of Swiss Francs, which ought to cover any expenses you may incur in the foreseeable future in Switzerland.'

At five o'clock a car pulled up outside the building and the two men left the office and walked quietly to it. Edgar helped Hunter put his cases in the boot and then joined him in the back.

'I thought you'd like me to see you off.'

Henry Hunter boarded the SS *Worthing* in Southampton before the troops embarked and was taken straight to a tiny cabin in the officers' quarters, which had a bunk bed in it and little else. The captain came in and told him he was to remain in the cabin for the duration of the voyage.

They docked in Cherbourg just after seven the next morning and at nine o'clock the captain came into his cabin. He was safe to leave now, all the troops had disembarked. A taxi was waiting on the quay to take him to the station.

Hunter was shocked at how France had changed. Everywhere there were troops – British as well as French – and people looked pinched, worried and in a hurry, none of which he were characteristics would usually associate with the French. Normally the train journey would have been jolly, with people chatting. Now, it was quiet. People stared out of the windows and said little. It was as if a whole nation was wrapped in its own thoughts, unwilling to share its fears.

The train pulled into Gare Saint-Lazare just before three o'clock: the journey had taken longer than scheduled due to a lengthy and unexplained stop outside Caen. If Cherbourg had been quiet and the train silent, Gare Saint-Lazare was not. Half of Paris seemed to be leaving through the station and the other half arriving into it. He found the telegram bureau and sent the message to London. He had little doubt that he would be watched at the station: requiring him to send the telegram was a good way of ensuring that. He then walked out of the vast concourse of Gare Saint-Lazare and away from Clichy and its temptations.

The further you walk the harder it is for you to be followed.

So he headed south and then east, down Boulevard Haussmann where the elegant shops and straight lines afforded him plenty of opportunity to observe every angle around him. He entered a leather-wear shop to look at wallets and a *tabac* to buy matches and in Boulevard St Martin he joined a long queue in a *patisserie* to buy an almond croissant. The ten minute wait allowed him enough time to be certain no one was following him. He decided to look for somewhere to stay around Republique and found a small hotel by the Canal Saint Martin, where he took a comfortable room with its own private bathroom overlooking, as requested, the front of the hotel and then spent an hour sitting by the window, behind the half open shutters, observing the street below. When he was as certain as he could be that no one had followed him and no one was watching from the street he closed the shutters and drew the curtain. After a bath and a rest he left his room at six thirty.

Had anyone checked in since his arrival, he asked the *patron* at reception? He was not sure if a colleague was joining him or not. The *patron* said no one had arrived. He understood, he said, with a knowing and even conspiratorial look. Hunter was not sure what it was that the *patron* understood, but he slipped him a generous few francs for what he said was an already excellent service and explained that he may be back late, perhaps very late. Would the *patron* be so good as to let him have a key? *Of course.* And would he also be able to perhaps slip a note under his door to let him know if his friend arrived, or indeed if anyone else checked in or even asked for him? 'Naturally,' said the *patron.* '*It would be my pleasure.*' Henry knew that this being Paris, the *patron* would assume that Henry was conducting an affair: in such circumstances it would be his pleasure, indeed his duty as *patron* to do whatever he could to assist.

Hunter walked out into the bitter Parisian night air, where a wind had swept up the nearby Seine and was settling over the city. He waited in the entrance of the hotel for ten minutes and once he was certain that he was alone he headed south, turning up the collar of his coat as he did so.

The real danger of being a spy is that which you court yourself.

He headed in a south easterly direction, away from his destination. On the Rue de Crussol, just before it crossed Boulevard Voltaire, he found a telephone kiosk. The call lasted no more than thirty seconds, much of which was taken up by a pause by the person who had answered the phone.

'*Very well. You know where to come. Give us one hour. Be careful.*'

So he walked down Boulevard Voltaire and then found a tiny cafe in the Passage Saint-Pierre Amelot. There were four two-seater tables in the cafe, crammed into a space where three would still have been a tight squeeze. One of the tables was occupied by a young couple. Hunter took one of the three vacant tables, making sure he faced the door. He remained there for half an hour: dinner was a bowl of soup with bread and an excellent omelette.

It took him twenty minutes to reach his destination from the cafe. The Marais was once swamp-land, then became home to the aristocracy and now, as far as Hunter could tell, was in an advanced state of decay. It was the kind of area where people would say it had known better days, but no one alive could remember those better days. But Hunter liked the anonymity of the Marais, with its obvious edge of danger which meant that people hurried along and avoided each other. It was not relaxed and given over to enjoyment of life, like most other parts of Paris. The area had its different groups; the Jews and their synagogues and little shops around the Rue de Rosiers; those too poor to have their own place and living with others in large crumbling houses; the prostitutes who couldn't make it in Clichy; the gamblers, the drinkers and the anarchists.

He knew the area very well and picked up his pace, darting up and down little alleys, doubling back on himself, pausing in darkened doorways and making it impossible for anyone to follow him. He emerged into the Rue de Bretagne and slipped into the entrance of a large grey building with enormous shuttered windows and waited. On the wall inside the entrance was a series of bells, one for each of the twenty apartments. Under the bells someone had drawn a small circle in pencil. On the opposite wall they had drawn a square. It was safe. He pressed a bell and went straight up to the top floor.

–

'You look very well. You have lost weight.'

'Yes, thank you, Viktor.' Hunter hesitated. He was about to return the compliment but nothing could be further from the truth: the other man was bigger than ever, his face heavily lined and his large nose redder than ever. Viktor had greeted him with an embrace and had held him in it for a while, which made Hunter feel less than comfortable. As he slowly emerged from the embrace the man held him at arm's length by the shoulders – one hand on each shoulder, as if to admire him. For a moment Hunter feared the man was about to kiss him on the cheeks, as he was want to do. He was always nervous in the man's presence, not least after a long gap, as now. Anyone looking at him would have noticed that for a brief moment his thin smiled had disappeared.

'I was not sure that we would ever see you again. Come, sit down. We have much to talk about.'

They were speaking in French, neither man's native language, which added to a formal, even tense air in the room. Two other men stood either side of the window, keeping watch through half open shutters. Another man entered the room and announced that it was all clear: no one had followed him. He was sure of that.

'What will you drink? I seem to have everything here. Whisky?'

'No, not for me thank you.'

'Really? That is the first time I have known you to turn down a whisky. What have they done to you?'

The man's look of concern broke into a broad grin as he poured himself a drink and pulled his chair closer to Hunter's. 'This really has been a most unexpected development, most unexpected. And you are certain that they suspect nothing?'

'I am as certain as I can be' said Hunter.

Viktor shuffled his large frame around in the chair to make himself comfortable. From a side table he picked up a large notebook, expensively bound in brown leather. He produced a pencil from his top pocket and sharpened it with a penknife which came from another pocket, allowing the shavings to gather on the front of his jacket. He made a few notes before looking up at Henry and smiling, as if checking on him once again.

'We have two hours, maybe three. You need to tell me everything.'

–

34

Hunter returned to the hotel just before one that morning. There was no note under the door from the *patron*. Despite his exhaustion, he slept only fitfully and got up at seven o'clock. He checked out of the hotel an hour later, stopped for a coffee and croissant near the hotel and then caught a tram on the Boulevard du Temple down to the Gare de Lyon. He managed to book a good seat on the ten o'clock train to Geneva where he found himself in a carriage with six other passengers: a formally dressed Swiss businessman who tutted loudly if anyone came too near him; an elegantly dressed elderly French lady who spent most of the journey smiling wistfully out of the window and did not remove her leather gloves once during the journey and a couple with their son and daughter who were, as far as Hunter could tell, a year or two either side of ten. They seemed to be overburdened with suitcases and other bags, some of which they had to keep in the corridor. When the children spoke, which was not very often, they did so with strong Parisian accents. The parents spoke to the children in accented French, but to each other in what sounded to Hunter like Polish and also a strange version of High German that he had never heard before. From what he could tell, they were anxious about crossing the border. The wife kept asking the husband if all the paperwork was in order. '*I hope so. Who knows?*' Whenever one of the family spoke the Swiss businessman looked annoyed and disapproving. On more than one occasion he caught Hunter's eye, hoping to share his disapproval with him.

The journey was uneventful until around a quarter to six when the train pulled into Gare de Bellegarde, the last station in France before the Swiss border, just a few miles away. For five or ten minutes, the train just stood still, with no apparent reason for the delay. The businessman looked at his watch and shook his head. The French lady continued to look out of the window, smiling. Then they could hear voices, working their way slowly down the train. Through the window Hunter could just make out the shape of *gendarmes* patrolling along the tracks. The voices grew nearer and the parents looked even more anxious.

'Everything will be all right?' the wife asked the husband, in the strange German dialect.

'I have no idea,' the husband replied. 'Speak in French now: only in French.'

Five minutes later two Swiss border guards and a French *gendarme* entered the carriage.

'Papers please: a routine check: we will have you on your way in a minute.' Hunter showed his Swiss passport. One Swiss border guard showed it to the other and they both nodded. 'No problem, Monsieur Hesse.' Nor was there any problem with the businessman and the elegantly dressed lady. But for the family, it was very different. Both guards looked at the papers in some detail and shook their heads, passing various documents to the bored looking *gendarme* behind them.

'These papers are not in order,' one of them said to the father.

'But I was assured that there would be no problem.'

'Well, there is. You have no valid papers here allowing you to enter Switzerland. It is not possible.'

The husband and wife exchanged glances; the wife nodded. *Do it.*

'Perhaps I could have a word with you in the corridor?' He gestured towards the children. *Away from them, please.*

Hunter could just make out the man pleading with the guards, both of whom looked stone-faced. 'Perhaps I could pay for the visas now? I have the funds?' Hunter could see the man open his wallet and attempt to press a wad of banknotes into the hand of one of the guards, who refused to take it.

'You are denied entry to Switzerland. You have to leave the train now,' he heard one of the guards say. Hunter noticed that the other guard grabbed the banknotes.

'You are in illegal possession of Swiss currency. We are confiscating it.'

The *gendarme* shrugged. *This is not my problem.* The father came back into the carriage, crestfallen and defeated. His wife was doing her best not to cry and the children looked frightened, as if they knew what was happening. The gendarme helped them to remove their cases. The elegant lady looked shocked and the businessman annoyed as baggage was removed from around him. A minute or so later,

Hunter watched as the family emerged onto the deserted platform and the train slowly began to move again. The businessman shook his head and muttered the word '*juifs*'. The lady had stopped smiling.

The train pulled into Gare Cornavin just before seven o'clock. On the short walk home Henry was hit by the icy blast from the nearby Alps, bouncing into the city from the lake. Despite this and despite the burdens he now carried he had the most unusual sensation of arriving somewhere that he could call home.

–

At around the same time that Henry Hunter's train was leaving Gare de Lyon Edgar took a call on a secure line in his office. It was Hurst from Paris station.

'Well done Edgar, you've found a bit of a star there. He didn't half give my chaps the runaround.'

'You didn't lose him, did you, Hurst? There'll be all hell to pay if you did.'

'Come on Edgar, you ought to know my boys better than that. He's very good, but in the end he made the mistake of assuming that one can only be tracked from behind. We managed to keep tabs on him all last night, but only just.'

'Where did he end up?'

'The Marais, as we suspected he would.'

'And the people he met up with: you're sure of who they are?'

'Yes sir, we're absolutely certain. No question about it.'

Chapter 4

from Marseilles to Moscow, December 1939

Early in the afternoon of the first Monday of December a large man wearing a long dark coat and a smart black fedora marched with surprising agility up from the *vieux port* in Marseilles to his *pension* overlooking the port and the Mediterranean beyond it.

The large man was Russian, but for the purposes of his visit he was a Swedish shipping agent from Gothenburg. He had been hanging around the *vieux port* for a few futile days, hoping to make contact with an Algerian who had apparently contacted a Communist Party official in the city with the promise of some secret documents of an unspecified nature. The Party official had now disappeared and the Algerian never showed up. It was the nature of the job he reflected, as the *pension* came into sight: unlike the fishermen he had been watching that morning selling their catch on the Quai des Belges, a spy had to become used the prey only occasionally succumbing to the bait.

He had decided to remain in Marseilles for another day or two; a ship was due in from Greece and Greek crews always offered the opportunity of good contacts. But when he returned to his *pension* there was a telegram waiting for him, sent from the main post office in Gothenburg.

Mother ill stop return home soonest stop

The Russian rarely allowed himself the indulgence of emotion, but he did that afternoon, sitting quietly in his room for a few minutes after he had packed and contemplating what a summons home could

38

mean. He had survived, as he liked to see it, various such calls over the past few years, but feared his luck could not hold out much longer. A sensation of fear swept over him and it took the remains of the vodka by the side of the bed and a cold bath before he came to his senses. *I have done nothing wrong: No one in the service is indispensable, but I am closer to it than many.*

An hour later he had checked out of the *pension* and stopped at the main post office to send a telegram to Gothenburg to the effect that he was so concerned about mother that he was returning home.

love to mother stop

Then he headed to the port office, where he found the captain of a Turkish steamer leaving that evening for Istanbul who was more than happy to take a passenger, especially one who was offering to pay so generously. '*We have a light load: with luck we should arrive on Saturday; maybe Sunday.*'

The steamer duly arrived in Istanbul early on the Saturday evening and the captain took his generous passenger straight to the house of his wife's cousin, who sailed his trawler in the Black Sea. *Yes* said the cousin. *He would be setting off as usual on Sunday morning. Yes, he would be happy to sail to Odessa first. Yes, that is very generous.* '*Thank you sir!*'

Odessa was a day and a half's hard sailing from Istanbul and, encouraged by the Russian's generosity, the skipper made it there late on the Monday afternoon. He went straight to the railway station: the night train to Moscow was leaving at a quarter to midnight. He had time to send a telegram announcing his arrival and then find a cafe where he could eat familiar food and get used to hearing familiar languages around him once again.

It was past midnight when the train noisily pulled out of the station and as the final leg of his voyage began, the fear that had stuck him in Marseilles returned. It kept him wide awake until they reached Kharkov in the early hours of the morning, turning his stomach into knots and making his heart beat fast. Along with the fear came the doubt: *should I have stayed in France? I could so easily have disappeared from there.*

The train was held in Kharkov for three or four hours. As usual, there was no explanation and no complaints from his fellow passengers. He left the train to send another telegram to Moscow: he didn't want them to think he wasn't coming.

By the time dawn broke on the Wednesday morning they were approaching the outskirts of Moscow and the train slowed down. The Russian tried hard to compose himself. The cruellest part of this job was not the loneliness or the danger or the stress of swapping identities every few days and constantly having to be aware of who he was meant to be: that was all to be expected. No, the worst part – the part he could never come to terms with – was that the one place you could call home, the place that that you risked your life for and suffered all the hardships on behalf of – that was the place you feared most. He would have no idea whether the day which had just begun would end with a bullet to his head in the basement. It had happened to so many others, after all. But then he pulled himself together as he remembered what they instilled into all the new recruits: '*Never question; never discuss; never hesitate.*'

The train pulled into Kursky station at eight o'clock and he was met on the platform by two young men who escorted him to a waiting car, which he decided was a bad sign. It was a glorious day in Moscow and he began to feel quite emotional on the short journey. He resolved that if he survived this trip and was sent back into the field he would make plans. Next time he was summoned back, he would disappear. He had worked for the service since 1920; he had outlived all those he had been recruited with and many more that had been recruited after him. He knew that he was good, but he also knew that he was not indispensable. What mattered most was that he outlived his luck and now he feared that this had run out on him.

The car drove straight into a basement, which he decided was another bad sign. He could feel his whole body trembling as he walked with his unsmiling escort to the lift. If it went down into the basement, he knew that was the end. Moments later they emerged onto the fifth floor and he had to bite his lip to stop tears of sheer relief. He was steered into a large office where there were half a dozen of them waiting, all of whom seemed to be pleased to see him. From that group, a familiar figure emerged and hugged the new arrival.

'Viktor, welcome home.'

–

He had been so well received that for a day or two after his arrival in Moscow he wandered whether this was some kind of elaborate trap. But it wasn't: they were clearly very pleased with him but most of all they wanted to know about Henry.

'Who would have thought it?'

'Tell us everything?'

'Does he realise how important he could be – do *you* realise how important he is?'

'We need to handle him carefully.'

After three days in Moscow he was taken to one of the *dachas* outside the city that the service used. For the first time in years he could relax in the silence. A woman came in every day to cook and clean and a younger woman arrived every evening and stayed with him until the following morning. The service could be brutal and cruel, especially to its own, but it knew how to look after those it was especially pleased with.

Viktor stayed in the *dacha* for a week before travelling to Stockholm and from there by sea back to France. But not once during that time was he ever in doubt that he owed all this to Henry. '*Do you realise how important he is?*' they had asked?

But Viktor certainly did not need anyone to tell him how important Henry was. An agent he had recruited had, in turn, been recruited by the British.

Do I realise how important Henry is?

Important enough to have kept me alive.

Chapter 5

Switzerland, 1929-1930

It was a filthy evening sometime in late January 1929 when Henri Hesse emerged from the pink-stuccoed building on the university campus. The rain swept into Geneva from every direction: the Alps, the lake, France. He paused at the end of the flight of steps, already drenched and wondering whether to dash into the Old Town through Les Bastions or go back into the building and wait for the rain to abate.

He was still debating what to do when he felt a hand on his shoulder.

'You are deciding whether to brave the rain? Me too. Who knows when it will stop? When it rains like this in Geneva it feels like it will rain forever.' It was the last speaker at the meeting, a handsome man in his late twenties with piercing blue eyes, thick black hair which touched his collar and a distinctive Parisian accent. Henri had never encountered anyone quite so charismatic and mesmerising. He wore no tie and had a silk scarf wrapped stylishly around his neck and when he spoke it was about the injustices in Europe and around the world and how only the Communist Party had the answer. Henri had felt the hairs rise on the back of his neck; tears had even come to his eyes. 'Europe is in crisis: capitalism is in crisis. The solution is in our hands – your hands,' he had told the thirty or so people sparsely arranged around the large lecture hall.

'My name is Marcel by the way.' The Frenchman's hand was still on his shoulder as he gently steered him back into the building. The meeting had taken place in the Law Faculty and Marcel guided Henri through its corridors until they found a deserted seating area on the first floor. Marcel unfurled his silk scarf, revealing a white shirt with two or three buttons undone. He smiled at Henri, his teeth white and perfectly straight.

'Maybe in ten or fifteen minutes the rain will stop, but it is good to talk. Are you a member of the party?'

'Not yet' replied Henri. 'I am thinking about it.'

'Tell me why?'

It was a while before Henri replied, during which time the noise of the rain beating on the windows and lashing the city beyond them grew heavier. *When it rains like this in Geneva it feels like it will rain forever.*

'I live in a privileged and bourgeois world. I've visited Germany and seen areas which are really poor, where people have no jobs and little food. Even in Switzerland you can go from an area which is very rich to one nearby which is completely different and that just seems to me to be wrong. My mother and my stepfather are always saying that a civilised world relies on having some people making a lot of money and other people working for them. They say that the reason why people are poor is that they are lazy and feckless. They blame unemployment on trade unions and socialists. I always find that I disagree with whatever they say about politics and the people they seem to despise the most are communists. That got me thinking that if my mother and stepfather are so opposed to communism, then maybe it cannot be that bad, but I knew very little about it so I am reading a lot about it at the moment. When I saw a notice for this meeting in the library, I thought I would come along.'

'Really? Tell me, what are you reading?' Marcel leaned forward, genuinely interested in what Henri had to say.

'I have read *The Communist Manifesto* of course and all three volumes of *Capital*, though I can't pretend I found that easy going. Now I am reading *The Origin of the Family, Private Property and the State*, but it is even more difficult.'

'I understand. Engels is not the easiest person to read, but his ideas – they are excellent, do you agree?'

'I do.'

Marcel edged his chair a bit closer to Henri's. 'I can tell from your accent that you are perhaps not from Geneva.'

'No, I lived in Zurich for a number of years. We moved to Geneva last year.'

Marcel switched to German. 'And can I ask what you do; are you a student here at the university?'

'No... not yet. My mother is not keen on me being a student. She thinks I'll end up mixing with people she disapproves of.'

'Like communists?'

'Like communists.'

'I suspect you are not a native of Zurich either? I am not Swiss myself: I am from Paris. I can always tell when someone is not Swiss: they have more... warmth.'

Marcel patted Henri on the knee. *A friend: someone to trust.*

'Actually, I'm originally from England.'

'Really, where?'

'I was born in a place called Woking; it is not far from London.'

'And how do you end up in Geneva?'

'It's a long story and a rather boring one, I'm afraid.'

'No, no – not at all. People's stories are always more fascinating than they realise. Do tell me.'

Marcel had edged his chair even closer to Henri's and looked at his companion in admiration.

'Please tell me, Henri!'

'Well, as I say, it is not terribly remarkable. My father was an accountant and a good deal older than my mother. He died suddenly in the February of 1923; he was sixty when he died. My mother was still in her early forties and although we were not wealthy and my mother had aspirations to wealth. My mother inherited a life insurance policy upon the death of my father and as far as I can recall, she set about spending it – furs, jewellery – that type of thing. We spent most of that summer on the French Riviera and in Antibes she met a Swiss businessman, Erich Hesse. She married him in the November.'

'Rather quick?'

'Indeed: indecent haste was how people described it. But my mother was quite unashamed about it. She disliked England and what she would describe as "a provincial lifestyle". She wanted glamour

44

and wealth and Erich Hesse offered the opportunity of all that. In the short period following the death of my father, she had quickly become accustomed to a certain standard of living. She was aware that there was a limit as to how long this could last; the life insurance policy was unlikely to fund her in the long term, not at the rate that she was working her way through it. So, Herr Hesse was an extremely attractive proposition: financially at least. I ought to add that he was also quite a bit older than my mother. I think he was sixty-five when they married.'

'So you moved here to Switzerland?'

'Yes. To Zurich at first, this is where his business interests seemed to be. We lived in Zurich for around five years and moved here to Geneva last year.'

'Why the move to Geneva?'

'My stepfather has property here, though he does seem to have it all over Switzerland. I think the main reason was my mother: she always said she found Zurich rather stuffy but she loves Geneva and the area around it. We live by the lake, close to Nyon.'

'And how did you become so fluent?'

'I turned out to be something of a natural linguist. I was thirteen when we moved to Switzerland and I had never really fitted in very well in England. I was an only child, rather spoilt, not especially bright academically I suppose and bad at sport. As a consequence, I was constantly bullied. One way with which I could deal with this bullying was through mimicry, which I had something of a talent for. I managed to make myself rather popular by impersonating teachers in particular. I was really rather good at it and the other boys loved it. I was always playing pranks on teachers, phoning them and pretending to be the head teacher, that kind of thing. When I arrived in Switzerland I discovered that talent for mimicry and impersonation was a godsend for learning languages: not so much the vocabulary and the grammar, which I found be easy enough to learn. What I excelled at was imitating the accent and the nuance of speech. In Zurich I became fluent both in German and Swiss German and since moving here my French has really come on.'

Marcel nodded and smiled in the right places. He was sympathetic and friendly, someone Henry instinctively felt he could trust. To his surprise, Henri found himself opening up even more to this stranger about the coldness of his mother; his lack of a relationship with his stepfather; his loneliness; his boredom; his curiosity about the world around him and his frustration at not being able to satisfy that curiosity.

Marcel switched to English, but only after he had looked carefully around the empty room and moved his chair so close to Henri's that the two chairs were touching.

'You are clearly very interested in communism, Henri.'

'Yes.'

'But you have not joined the party?'

'Well, I did pick up this leaflet when I left the meeting.' Henri had removed a damp leaflet from his coat pocket and showing it to Marcel.

'So, are you going to join?'

'Probably. I'm a bit nervous about what my mother and stepfather would think. I know it is nothing to do with them, but they are so opposed to communism that I think they'd throw me out of the house. But they won't need to know, will they?'

Marcel said nothing, as he leaned back in his chair and looked Henri up and down.

'You don't have to join the Party, you know.'

'What do you mean?'

'What matters, Henri, is that you believe in the cause, that you believe in communism.'

'I'm not terribly sure that I follow you.'

Marcel paused while a man and a woman walked by, their shoes reverberating long after they had passed on the wooden floor. The rain now sounded as if it had turned into a storm. Marcel had lowered his head and only raised it very slightly when he spoke again.

'Henri, if one truly believes in the cause then there are many different ways of serving it. Joining the party and attending meetings have their place, but for someone such as yourself, there may be other ways... *better* ways in which you can help the cause more effectively.'

'I am still not really following you. Why are you so interested in me?'

'Because it is clear that you believe in the cause and because you are a man of many parts, not all of them obvious ones. You have a natural caution about you, along with an inquisitive mind. You speak three languages. You have a Swiss passport and a British one. And the only person who knows that you are interested in the Party, and that you came to this meeting tonight is me.'

'There were other people at the meeting.'

'Sure, but do any of them know who you are? Do they know your name?'

Henri shook his head.

'Exactly. For the time being, can I ask you not to join the Party or attend any meetings? In a few weeks, maybe two or three, possibly longer, I will approach you. We will meet and I may be able to introduce you to people who share our views. In the meantime, I ask you not to discuss this with anyone.'

'But how will you know where to find me?'

Marcel patted Henri's knee. 'You are not to worry: finding you will not be a problem.'

–

Marcel found him in late February, around four weeks after they had first met.

He was in the library at the university, which he travelled into on most weekdays. It got him away from his mother and stepfather and from Nyon and the home overlooking the lake. He tended to arrive at the library around eleven in the morning and leave around four. On Marcel's advice he had stopped reading political works – 'There is no need to draw unnecessary attention to yourself' – and was now working his way through the French novelists. On this particular day he was finding it hard to concentrate on Zola's *Thérèse Raquin* so in the middle of the afternoon he went for a stroll along the corridors, past the crowded notice board where he had first spotted the handwritten poster advertising the Communist Party meeting. When he return to his desk he noticed that his copy of *Thérèse Raquin* was closed, with a slip of paper poking out of the last page he had been reading. It was a card from a bar on the Place de la Taconnerie and, in neat handwriting, '*Ce soir. 6.*'

The bar was in the shadow of St-Pierre cathedral and was little more than a dimly lit cellar in which it was hard to make out the identities of the few other customers. Henri had arrived in good time – well before six – and for thirty or forty minutes he sat on a small table facing the entrance and contemplating what he may have got himself into. Up until that evening he had decided that Marcel was just an enthusiast who had perhaps become carried away. He was, in Henri's opinion, unlikely ever to contact him again and he had come to the conclusion that this was very much for the best. Whatever 'serving the cause in different ways' meant, it was not for him.

He did not notice Marcel until he slid into the chair opposite and greeted him warmly, placing two empty glasses on the table and proceeding to fill them both from a bottle of red wine while holding the cork between his teeth. He gestured for Henri to drink and it was only when they had both finished and he had refilled their glasses that he spoke.

'I've come from Paris this morning, which is why I am late. How have you been keeping my friend? Tell me, what you are reading?'

They chatted for a few minutes and by the time they were on their third glass of wine Marcel suggested that, when they finished it, they go for a walk. They left the bar in silence. By now, a grey mist had descended on the Old Town making the cathedral only just visible in front of them. They walked in silence along the deserted streets, as if they were the only people in the city. They followed a road round the back of the cathedral before turning into Rue Verdaine. Marcel placed an arm in front of Henri, gesturing for him to wait. They stood still for a while: ahead of them they could just make out the sound of footsteps. Marcel glanced at his watch, angling his hand to try and catch what light there was from the street lamp. He nodded and then looked straight at Henri.

'You do believe, don't you?' When Henri did not reply but only looked at him as if he did not understand, he repeated the question. 'In the cause, I mean. You still believe in communism?'

'Of course.' *What else can I say?*

'Good.' Marcel started to walk forward again, very slowly. He placed a hand in Henri's back so he would join him. 'You will find that, if you believe, that will help. It is difficult enough even if you do believe, but impossible if you don't. My advice to you is that, even in moments of doubt, you must force yourself to believe; otherwise your life will be intolerable. Do not allow yourself to harbour any doubts. If you force yourself hard enough then it will work, trust me.' Marcel said nothing more, but continued to walk on slowly. They had not gone very far when they passed an alleyway on their left and Henri noticed Marcel peering into it. In the shadows he could just make out a bulky figure standing still at the far end of the alley. They carried on walking, but now Henri could hear footsteps behind them. They reached the corner of Rue de la Vallée and Marcel stopped. When they turned round a large man was standing a few yards behind them. He was wrapped in a long black coat, its collar turned up to conceal the lower half of his face, with much of the upper half hidden by the brim of a large fedora.

Marcel placed a hand on Henri's shoulder: '*Attends!*' Wait. He walked over to and they spoke for a minute, no more than that. Henry knew they were certainly not speaking French or German. As far as he could tell, it sounded like Russian or Polish. When they had finished talking Marcel turned round and beckoned for Henri to join them.

The three of them stood together for a moment, not a word being exchanged. Then, as if on a signal, Marcel turned and walked quickly away, back along Rue Verdaine.

It was the last time Henri would ever see Marcel.

–

As Marcel disappeared into the mist the man in the long black coat and large fedora moved off in the other direction, making it clear that Henri should follow him. Half way down Rue de la Vallée he stopped by a parked Citroen and opened the rear passenger door, allowing Henry to enter first. The driver turned round and nodded and without a word being exchanged, they drove off.

The car drove fast through the Old Town, the speed and the mist making it difficult for Henri to work out where he was. As far as he could tell they were heading south through Champel but then he noticed that they were heading back into the city, driving along the banks of the River Avre. Soon they were in Jonction, a working class district that Henri was quite unfamiliar with. The driver stopped for a while, his eyes fixed on the rear view mirror and then started again. After less than a minute he braked suddenly and then reversed hard into a narrow alleyway, stopping alongside a large wooden door. Henri was guided out of the car and through the door and quickly up a flight of steps into a small attic room which smelt of gas and cabbages.

Once he had closed the shutters and turned on the gas fire the large man looked Henri up and down, his head slowly moving as if checking him out from every angle. He gestured to a pair of chairs in front of the fire and removed his fedora, revealing a lined face that showed no hint of emotion. Once Henri had sat down the man unbuttoned his coat and placed himself opposite Henri and addressed him in French with a heavy eastern European accent.

'English is your first language, yes?'

Henri nodded.

'And you also speak French and German?'

'Yes, although I am more comfortable with French.'

'We shall speak in French in that case, I understand it better than English. Two foreigners speaking French; the French would like that.'

'Henry Hunter,' the man said as he removed his overcoat and pulled a brown leather notebook from one of the pockets. From his top pocket he took out a pencil and sharpened it with a penknife, allowing the shavings to fall on his shirt before he blew them away on to the floor. He squinted as he checked the notebook, the pencil now lodged in his mouth like a cigar.

'I know everything I need to know about you, Henry Hunter.'

'Not too much I hope!' *A nervous laugh.*

Over the course of the next hour the man delivered a quiet mono-logue. He told Henry things about himself which he had thought no one else could possibly know and other things which he had long forgotten or hardly been aware of. He gave him the name of the maternity home where he was born; revealed the names and addresses of family members long forgotten or never heard of; informed him of the name of the accountancy firm for which his father worked and described in some detail his routine, such as it was, in Geneva: when he left home in Nyon, his route into the Old Town and to the library – that kind of thing. He knew the name of every book he had taken out of the library. He knew the names of the bars in the Pâquis that he liked to hang around in, where he cut a lonely figure as he eyed up the working girls without ever quite managing to sum up the courage to approach them. When he had finished, he smiled for the first time, displaying a set of large teeth, half of which seemed to be made of gold. Henry sat incredulous.

'You can call me Viktor, by the way.' A long silence, during which Henri wondered if he was meant to say anything, but had no idea of what to say.

'Marcel tells me that you were about to join the Swiss Communist Party?'

'Not quite: I attended one of its meetings. I told him that I was thinking of joining, nothing more than that. We had a nice chat after the meeting and he mentioned something about not joining or attending meetings. He said that there were better ways in which I could help the cause. I was not altogether sure what he meant.'

'You will work for me, Henry Hunter: that is how you will help the cause. You are a communist, yes?'

'Well, I suppose…'

'You are ideal, Henry. You have two nationalities and three languages. Most people in Europe have just one of each. You are the kind of person who people do not notice too much, if you understand what I mean – you don't stand out.'

'What does working for you entail, Viktor?'

'It means what Marcel said: it is another way of serving the cause.'

From a nearby rooftop a clock struck eight. 'Look, I ought to be getting a move on. I should have been home ages ago and my mother will be getting worried. Perhaps I could think about things for a few days?' Henry said.

Viktor was smiling again, displaying even more gold teeth than before. When he smiled he looked friendly, but the second the smile disappeared his demeanour became cold and menacing. 'No, no, no, Henry Hunter' he said, shaking his head. 'It does not work like that I am afraid. I am not advertising a vacancy at a Swiss bank, I am not looking for a man to deliver Swiss cheese. You are already working for me: you started working for me the moment we met.'

–

For the best part of a year Henry was little more than a messenger for Viktor. At first this amounted to taking an envelope from – say – Geneva to Paris and then stopping off in Lyons to deliver another one on the return journey. Even Henry, normally naïve, came to realise that these errands were probably little more than tests. About once a month the errands would coincide with meeting Viktor, usually in Paris or sometimes in other cities. He was, he realised, being trained: Viktor would talk at length in either English or French about what helping him really meant. He explained the rudiments of espionage: the need to fit in to any environment or circumstance without being noticed; the need for discretion; the ability to see and remember everything; how to assume different identifies to the extent that you became that person for however short a period; the importance of thinking, not just step ahead, but two or even three and at the same time not forgetting what you had been doing before – your cover story.

At no stage did Viktor actually say who he worked for, although over a period of time Henri came to understand that Viktor worked for Soviet intelligence or possibly Comintern, but he was never totally sure which branch it actually was. Henry's instincts told him that the less he knew the better. Viktor began to talk about the 'service' and that became how they referred to who his new employers were.

There was a travel agency in Petit-Saconnex in Geneva that was a front for Viktor's operation and Henri became a courier for them. It provided a perfect cover for his trips and meant that his mother, although curious and somewhat dubious as to whether a travel agency was the right job for her son, did not question his frequent absences.

In the spring of 1930 Viktor introduced Henry to a German called Peter and a week later Henry accompanied Peter to an isolated farmhouse in northern Germany, somewhere between Hamburg and Bremen. There were five other recruits there; two German men; a French woman and a Dutch couple. All of them were a few years older than him.

On the second day at the farm the six recruits were taken to a shed and shown a litter of puppies. '*Choose one each: it can be your companion while you are here!*' Having a dog will make your stay here easier, they were told. Henry chose the smallest of the litter, a black puppy that he named Foxi. He would take Foxi for walks two or three times a day and as with the other recruits and their puppies, they became inseparable.

For the next six weeks they were trained in what Peter described as fieldcraft. They learnt how to create and use secret message drops; how to follow people without being noticed and in turn spot if they were being followed and how to lose the shadow. They learnt unarmed combat and how to use a series of handguns; there was even instruction in making bombs and other forms of sabotage. And in the evenings, there were lectures: 'ideological instruction; was how they termed it. Any hint of doubt about commitment to the cause was spotted and eliminated. By the end of the first week, everyone fully understood that working for the cause in the way which they were meant knowing that there was no room whatsoever for discussion – without total commitment and utter loyalty, they would fail.

Never question; never discuss; never hesitate.

And along with this there were individual sessions. Henri spent hours with first an elderly German man and then a younger Polish woman. They were intent on teasing anything personal out of him. The German man seemed to be a psychiatrist of some sort, asking a series of apparently unrelated questions and making extensive notes. He seemed to be preoccupied with Henry's relationship with his mother.

Everything about the Polish woman looked severe: her manner, her heavy glasses and the way her hair was pulled into a tight bun. She insisted he tell her everything about his personal life. Had he ever had a girlfriend, for instance? Henry had blushed and muttered something about there being one or two, but nothing serious. Had he ever slept with a woman, the Polish woman asked – or a man? Henry was so shocked that he readily told the truth. No; he had never slept with a woman. The thought of sleeping with a man, he said, had simply never occurred to him.

That night he lay in bed, unable to sleep as he tried to make sense of what was happening to him. He felt trapped, drawn into a life he would never have willingly chosen but one which did at least offer some prospect of excitement. He had just drifted to sleep when he was woken by someone sitting on his bed and turning on his bedside lamp. It was the Polish woman, the one who had been asking him all the personal questions. Her hair was now loose, without the heavy glasses and wearing bright red lipstick and perfume that smelt of lemons. Henry found himself unable to say anything.

She leant over and brushed his face with her hand and then gently pulled his head towards hers and kissed it.

'You told me that you have never experienced a woman.' Henry nodded, still unable to speak. She pulled a face, as if to indicate that he had done something wrong and then smiled. 'That is not good, is it. Henry? How can we let you go out into the world and not know what to do with a woman? That would be... risky. You need someone to teach you.' Henry opened his mouth to say something, but the Polish woman placed a finger inside his lips, holding it in his mouth for a few moments before pulling it slowly away. She stood up and removed her dressing gown and then her nightie. She was totally naked. She still for a moment, her eyebrows raised, inviting Henri to look at her. She was standing in front of the bedside lamp, so was lit from behind, in silhouette. Through a gap in the curtain on the other side of the bed the light of the moon lit up the front of her body.

Had she not remained with Henry for an hour after they had made love and indeed made love for a second time, he would have readily passed it off as one of his more pleasant dreams. But they lay there together and every time he tried to start saying something, which he felt he ought to do, she placed a finger on his lips and shook her head – her long hair brushing his bare shoulders. As the first hint of dawn peered through the half drawn curtains, she climbed out of bed and got dressed. 'We never discuss this, you understand? This was something you needed to do: there is a saying that there are more secrets to be found in a bed than in a safe. For your first time you were quite good, Henry, but next time do remember you don't need to rush so much. Try not to think about what you are doing: it will come naturally, it is the most natural thing we do. At least next time will not be your first time.'

Henry was confused, but at the same time quite pleased with himself.

Never question; never discuss; never hesitate.

On his penultimate day at the farm Henry was walking with Peter and Foxi in the woods, when the German turned to him and handed him a pistol.

'Shoot her,' he said, pointing at the puppy.

'What!' The puppy's eyes looked up at him, full of joy.

'The longer you wait the harder it will be.'

Henry fiddled around with pistol, hoping that at any moment Peter would stop him.

'Get on with it. You do as I tell you.'

Henry felt himself drift into a trance and, as if from above, he saw himself call Foxi over and cuddle her, allowing her to lick his face before placing the barrel of the gun behind her ears and pulling the trigger.

Afterwards Peter held out his hand for the gun and Henry did all he could to stop himself crying. *Never question; never discuss; never hesitate.*

When he returned to Geneva after the six weeks near Hamburg he felt emotionally drained: there was now nothing that his new masters did not know about him. They probably knew more him than he did about himself. It was as if they now possessed his soul. He had come to understand, even before Hamburg, that Viktor had been putting him through a process which meant that there was no going back. Whether he liked it or not, he was now committed to the cause. He knew that his views on communism were now quite immaterial.

By the end of 1930 the errands, as Viktor liked to call them, became more serious: clandestine trips to the more dangerous corners of Europe; fleeting encounters with wary women and frightened men; switching identity before hurrying out of the country. There were even some trips to Britain, when he used his Henry Hunter identity to enter and leave the country. He was seeing Viktor at least once a month, probably nearer to once every three weeks. Viktor always allowed plenty of time for their meetings; it was if he enjoyed them. During the course of these meetings it became apparent that Viktor worked for the Comintern and he would reminisce about the Revolution and his early days as a Comintern agent. He would describe to Henri the dangers that he could foresee in Europe. Above all, he seemed to show genuine interest in Henri in a way that neither his mother nor his stepfather did. He clearly cared and Henri found himself being frank with Viktor in a way that he was unable to be with anyone else. Viktor began to refer to Henry as *synok*.

It was the Russian for son.

Chapter 6

Switzerland, 1931

The event which would change Henry's life forever took place in the summer of 1931, but its origins came earlier that year in Paris. At the beginning of the March, Henry had been summoned to the French capital, to one of the safe houses that Viktor used in the Marais. Unlike his usual meetings with Viktor, this one was more charged and stretched over a period of days. Viktor wanted to satisfy himself that no one – 'not a single soul', as he put it – could possibly have any inkling as to what Henry was up to or who he was working for. It took four days and three nights of what amounted to an interrogation for Viktor to satisfy himself of this.

A week later, Viktor was in Geneva – the first time he had been there for some months. Over a long dinner in a private room at the back of a seedy Armenian restaurant in Grand-Lancy, Viktor talked about politics. What did Henry understand about events in the Soviet Union, about the dangerous and counter-revolutionary activities of Trotsky and his mad followers? Henry replied truthfully that he knew little, but that his allegiance was very clearly with Comrade Stalin. Traitors such as Trotsky and his ilk were a distraction.

Viktor had nodded in agreement and then spoke well into the early hours of the morning, fortified by an endless supply of strong Turkish coffee and plenty of vodka. Viktor patiently explained the aims of the Left Opposition, how their arguments may have had some merits in their early days, but that they had deviated seriously from the correct socialist course charted by Lenin. Henry needed to be very clear that there was no room for what Viktor described as a 'bourgeois indulgence'. Henry said he understood and was grateful to Viktor for explaining matters so clearly: he had no doubt that Trotsky and his few remaining followers were enemies of the Soviet Union and of socialism, but surely the matter had been dealt with? Had Trotsky not been expelled from the Soviet Union?

It was one in the morning now and when the exhausted *patron* returned with more coffee Viktor dismissed him sharply in Russian.

'I told him to leave us alone, *synok*; what I am about to say now is most important. Trotsky is indeed living in exile in Turkey and most of his supporters in the Soviet Union have seen the error of their ways – or at least claim to have done so: even Zinoviev and Kamenev. Others have been dealt with. But the danger posed by Trotsky and those of his followers that remain still exists. There are powerful supporters of Trotsky dispersed around Europe and as long as they are able to operate, they pose a threat to us, which we cannot tolerate: we cannot put at risk the achievements of the Revolution. You understand that?'

Henry nodded.

'So dealing with them is a priority for our service.'

Henry nodded again. *Of course.*

A long silence followed, during which Viktor removed his jacket, loosened his tie and looked at Henry in a quizzical manner, as if expecting him to say something. Henri shifted in his chair, unsure of how to react.

'This is where you are going to perform a vital role for the Service, *synok*.'

–

Henry Hunter spent the first two weeks of July 1931 in a large house on the outskirts of Neuchâtel, overlooking the lake. He had been told to expect to be away from Geneva for at least a month, possibly a good deal longer. As far as his mother and stepfather were concerned, the travel agency he had been working for had acquired a new branch in St Gallen and, as Henry spoke good Swiss German, he was being sent there for a while.

Viktor accompanied Henry to the house and remained there for the first two days. Peter, the German who had taken him to Hamburg for his training the previous year was also present. For two weeks, Peter helped Henry assume a new identity. Just before the end of the fortnight in Neuchâtel, Viktor returned and after a couple more days, he finally satisfied himself that Henry had now become William Jarvis.

According to his much used British passport, William Jarvis had been born in Norwich and was, at twenty-six, a few years older than Henry. After graduating from Cambridge University, Jarvis had become a teacher and he had moved to Switzerland for a year thanks to a legacy from a recently deceased and much loved uncle. His aim was to travel and do some occasional teaching, should the opportunity arise.

That opportunity happily arose in Interlaken.

'They've been advertising for an English tutor on and off for weeks: they'll be delighted that a proper Englishman who also happens to be a teacher applies,' Viktor had told him.

'But I am not a teacher!'

'You don't need to be. They want someone to improve their children's conversational English, that's all.'

The night before Henry travelled to Interlaken, Viktor had given him his final briefing.

'Anatoly Mikhailovich Yevtushenko.' The three of them were sat around a finely polished table in the dining room near Neuchâtel and Viktor had almost ceremonially placed a photograph of a distinguished looking man in front of Henry. 'Anatoly Mikhailovich Yevtushenko, born Kazan in 1884: bourgeois family, but became active in socialist politics when he was at university in Moscow. He became a lawyer and was one of the very early members of the Russian Social Democratic Labour Party, which you may or may not know was the forerunner of the Communist Party. He was active in the October Revolution and began to rise through the ranks of the Party. However, in around 1923 or 1924 he became a confidant of Trotsky and since then the two have become very close. In 1924 Yevtushenko took up a position in the finance department of the Party. In early 1928, not long after Trotsky was sent into internal exile, Yevtushenko and his family disappeared while on holiday in Crimea. We lost track of them, but a few months ago we discovered that they were living in Interlaken.'

Viktor nodded at Peter, who opened a folder and produced a series of photographs which he laid out in front of Henry as if dealing from a deck of cards.

'This is Yevtushenko's wife, Tatyana Dmitriyevna' said Peter. 'We understand that she suffers from a debilitating lung condition, which may well be the reason why they are living in Interlaken. This is, Rozalia Anatolyevna, she is seventeen. Nadezhda Anatolyevna is fourteen and this is the son, Nikolai Anatolyevich. He is eleven.'

'And that is their house?'

'Indeed. A very fine house as you can see, but also a very secure one. This wall runs all around the house and is twelve foot high. It is not altogether unusual for houses to have such security in Switzerland: people like their privacy and Interlaken is a wealthy town.'

Viktor moved the photographs away from Henry. He wanted him to concentrate on what he was about to say. 'We have been watching Yevtushenko very closely. We have come to the conclusion that he is an important source of finance for Trotsky and his movement, something the Service had long suspected. We know now that in the few months before he escaped from the Soviet Union, Yevtushenko channelled large sums of money from Moscow into Swiss bank accounts. Only he has access to them. We do not know exactly how much money is in these accounts, but we believe it could well be in the region of eight hundred million Swiss Francs. As well as the family, these three men live in the house – Peter...' On that command the German produced a series of photos, blurred shots of three different men. 'They are guards, all Russians. They stay in the house and vet whoever comes in or even approaches it. A local woman and her daughter act as housekeepers: they arrive early in the morning and do the cleaning, cooking and shopping. They leave in the middle of the afternoon. The family very rarely leave the house and when they do, they are always accompanied by a guard.'

Viktor took over speaking now. 'Approximately once a fortnight, Yevtushenko leaves the house and travels first to Bern and then to

Zurich. He always leaves very early in the morning and arrives back late in the evening. He is always accompanied on these trips by two of the guards. We know that in Bern he visits the Swiss Volksbank and in Zurich he goes to the Union Bank and to the Eidgenössische Bank. Our assumption is that once there he is able to transfer money from the accounts he controls to the accounts of Trotsky's supporters around Europe or even to Trotsky himself. Our aim is very simple: that money was stolen from the Party and we want it back. In the process, we can starve Trotsky of the funds that are keeping his miserable movement going.'

'And my role is…?' Henry sounded confused.

'To become the family's English tutor, *synok*, and become trusted by them. That may take weeks. Once that happens, we will be able to move to our next stage.'

'And what does that involve?'

'You will find out then, *synok*,' said Viktor.

Never question; never discuss; never hesitate.

–

It had all gone according to plan, as things tended to do in Switzerland, especially when they were organised by Viktor. William Jarvis had taken the trouble to write from England to reserve a room in an inn in centre of Interlaken. He was on the top floor with a small balcony, from which he could see Lake Thun to the west, Lake Brienz to the east, the mountains of the Jungfrau and the Grindelwald to the south, with the Harder Kulm and Emmental beyond it to the north. Henri, who now had to think of himself as 'William', had decided that this could turn out to be a pleasant enough task.

He waited until his second day in Interlaken before enquiring in the bookshop about the discreet sign in their window seeking an English tutor and that afternoon he telephoned the number the bookshop owner had passed on to him. Two days later he walked through the town and crossed the River Aare, and there on the north bank found the house on the very edge of the rising forest. It was a perfect position, separated from neighbouring houses by trees and surrounded by a high wall, with the front gate set into it. Next to the gate was a small window. Two large men searched him after he rang the bell and he was then led through to a library.

Both Anatoly Yevtushenko and his wife, Tatyana, were in the room, but the interview was conducted by the husband in passable German. His wife, he explained, did not speak German. Tatyana Yevtushenko was a thin woman, with skin so pale that it was the colour of chalk and, although it was a warm July day, she was dressed for winter. Anatoly Yevtushenko told William Jarvis that the family had moved around Europe but had settled here in Switzerland. 'Because of my business,' he said, in a tone that made it clear that he did not need to elaborate. For the most part, they educated the children themselves he explained, but they did require the assistance of tutors from time to time.

'Please tell me about yourself, Mr Jarvis.'

William Jarvis remembered what Viktor had told him: '*Tell him just enough, not too much… He will be clever, he will spot any mistakes… Concentrate on how much you would enjoy tutoring his children rather than talking about yourself. Avoid sounding too fluent: be slightly hesitant with dates.*'

Anatoly Yevtushenko spoke to his wife every so often in Russian, evidently giving her the gist of what he had been told.

'Are you interested in politics, Mr Jarvis?'

'I am afraid not sir. I do hope that is not a problem?'

'No, not at all. And what about foreign affairs, do you follow those?'

'Only what one reads in *The Times* sir, but I have to tell you that my main interest is literature. I would rather read a good book than a newspaper!'

And so it went on. After a brief conversation with his wife, Anatoly Yevtushenko offered William Jarvis the position of English tutor to his children. They agreed the fee and that he would come for two hours every morning. They would review his position after two weeks.

At the end of the first week William Jarvis was summoned into Anatoly Yevtushenko's study.

'How long do you plan to stay in Interlaken for, Mr Jarvis?'

'A few months, possibly. I hope to learn to ski so I suppose I am in the right place. It depends on whether I have work to help pay for my stay'.

'Well that is why I have asked to see you. The children adore you: they absolutely insist that we keep you for as long as possible. For reasons that are too complicated to explain, our life is an isolated one and my wife and I worry about the effect of that on the children. Already we can see how you have been able to help brighten their lives. From now on, we would like you to spend an hour every day with each child and to stay for lunch, which will be a further opportunity for you to converse with them in English.'

This was the routine for the next month. William Jarvis would arrive at the house at eleven o'clock every morning apart from Sunday and ring the bell on the wall. The heavy metal gates would eventually open and one of the guards would search him before another would lead him through to the library. He would spend the first hour with Nadezhda, who was by far the brightest of the three children. Nikolai would have the second hour, which was hard work as the boy completely lacked discipline, but seemed to be pleased to have William read simple stories to him in English. Then he and the three children would eat lunch together, speaking only English during the meal.

After lunch, he would teach Rozalia for the final hour. Very quickly, he came to appreciate that this was the part of the day he most looked forward to. At first he had seen Rozalia as little more than a child, but on her own, away from her parents and her sister and brother, she was more of a young woman. Her thick, long brown hair fell well below her shoulders and she was constantly sweeping it away from her face. Her skin was not as pale as her mother's, but she had certainly inherited her complexion more from her than from her father. What she had inherited from him were dark brown eyes, with an almost unblinking gaze.

They would spend much of the time in the garden, wandering around, talking in English but more often than not slipping into German. Her German was not too bad and she did her best to ignore his attempts to speak in English. She was, Henri realised, desperately lonely. She had fled her home country and was now trapped in a house surrounded by high walls. So she confided in Mr Jarvis, as she called him. He found it hard to do other than lend a sympathetic ear and assure her that if she was patient her life would change for the better. He told her about life in England and what he seen of Europe on his travels.

'Call me Roza.'

'Very well – and do call me William.'

'What is a short form of William?'

'Bill, I suppose – or Billy.'

Roza preferred Billy and so she and Billy became friends. When they did read from books she would sit very close to him so that their bodies touched. Roza had a habit, a mannerism even, of touching his arm and allowing her fingers to briefly hold him by the wrist. He had noticed her doing this to the others too so he did not imagine she meant any special affection for him, but once or twice he tried to return the gesture –placing his hand on top of hers. She would smile and would sweep the hair from her face before gently removing her hand. He knew that what Roza wanted more than anything else was companionship. William's story was that his mother had died when he was young and his father had remarried. This struck some kind of chord with Roza, whose eyes would fill with tears when he told her about being sent to boarding school at the age of six and how his stepmother did not like him. Henri worried that he may be getting too close to Roza, but then Viktor had told him to make sure that he became trusted.

He knew that he was developing feelings for Roza, but he also knew that he was unlikely to be in a position to do anything about them. She would never be allowed to leave the house without a guard and the house was always busy. One morning, after he had been there for a month or so, the downstairs toilet was being repaired and he was told to use the bathroom upstairs, which he would normally never do. When he opened the bathroom door he was met by the sight of Roza, who had clearly just stepped out of the bath. Despite the steam and the fact that she was mostly covered by a towel he could clearly see her breasts, smaller than he had imagined them to be but almost perfectly shaped, with locks of her dark, wet hair hanging down them. There was a very brief moment when neither of them said anything or moved, then he said 'Sorry,' and swiftly shut the door before hurrying downstairs. Neither of them ever said a word about it, but that afternoon she was even friendlier than on Sundays – the only day on which he did not go to the house – Henry would take the bus from Interlaken to Thun, where he would meet Peter in a park. They would walk while Henry would recount what had happened during the week and Peter would ask a series of questions, occasionally pausing to write something in his notebook. Once he took Henry to a small apartment above a shop in the centre of the town, where Henry was told to draw detailed plans of the house.

In the middle of August he arrived in Thun on a Sunday to be taken straight to the apartment by Peter. When they arrived, Viktor was waiting with three Frenchmen, who were introduced as Lucien, Claude and Jean-Marie: the conversation that followed – which lasted well into the evening – was conducted in French.

'*Synok*, Peter tells me that you told him last week that sometimes you and Roza are allowed to leave the house?' Viktor was sitting directly across a narrow table from Henry, watching him carefully. Despite the stifling August heat the Russian was wearing a heavy jacket. The three Frenchmen were lounging back in their chairs and one of them had a revolver in a shoulder holster.

'Well, yes and no. Roza has a lot of spirit, she feels like a caged animal in that house, but her parents will not allow her to go into the town, certainly not without a guard. However, behind the house is a small wood which is private, just for the residents of the houses around it. It has a fence around it.'

Peter handed a map to Viktor, pointing to a circled area.

'Here?'

Henry picked up the map and studied it. 'Yes, here. You can get into it from a door set into the wall in the garden. Her father agreed that we can go for a walk in there, as long as it is just for a few minutes and we promise not to leave the wood. The guards have the key: At first they would come along to let us out and then in again, but now they don't bother. I have to collect it from them and return it afterwards. I am trusted.'

'And tell me, *synok*, when do the housekeepers leave – is it still in the afternoon?'

'Yes. They make the lunch and then prepare the evening meal. They are usually gone by three o'clock'.

The Frenchmen and Peter all asked questions and Henry must have described the layout of the house a dozen times. Viktor then outlined his plan. It was clever and audacious and by the time he had finished, Henry felt quite sick.

–

Two more weeks. Viktor had decided that another two weeks would help ensure that William Jarvis was even more trusted by the Yevtushenkos and this was important, because if they did not trust him then the plan would not work. The two weeks was also important because Anatoly Yevtushenko's last trip to Bern and Zurich had been just a few days previously. The timing had to be right.

The agreed date was the 1st September – a Tuesday. On the Thursday before that Peter had arrived in Interlaken and rented an apartment on the east side of the town, close to Lake Brienz. Henry checked out of the inn and moved into the apartment with Peter.

William Jarvis arrived at the house just before eleven o'clock on the Tuesday morning. By now the guards were more relaxed with him, even quite friendly. He went through to the library and had his lessons with Nadezhda and Nikolai. By the time they went into the dining room for lunch he was feeling sick with nerves and anticipation. He hardly ate anything, but no one seemed to notice. He managed to keep the children distracted by playing 'I spy'. After lunch he went to guards' room at the front of the house to collect the key. The guard who spoke the best German handed it to him, with a warning to make sure he locked it properly.

He and Roza wandered into the garden, with Roza struggling to count to one hundred in English. That was the way it worked:

complete a task such as counting or naming the days of the week or months of the year and they could go into the woods as a reward. Roza became marooned in the seventies but Henry announced that was good enough. He unlocked the garden door and they spent the rest of the hour walking around the wood. Henry kept glancing around, expecting to see people hidden amongst the trees or beyond the fence, but it was as deserted and as silent as always, apart from the sound of water rushing on the Aare below them.

'Are you all right, Billy?'

'Yes thank you, Roza. Why do you ask?'

'You are very quiet'. She had switched to German now. 'You keep looking around and you did not eat any lunch.'

'I am fine thank you, Roza. I slept badly last night that is all. Look, you really must speak English. Please try.'

'Why? What is the point? We will never visit England. We will never leave this house. I am a prison, Billy' she said in English.

'I am a *prisoner*, Roza. That is what you meant to say. A prison is a building in which the prisoners are kept. I am sure you will get to visit England one day.'

They spent much of the hour with Henry doing his best to sustain some kind of conversation in English. As ever, Roza was wrapped up in her thoughts. When they went back into the garden Henry told Roza to go on ahead while he made a play of locking the garden door. The door appeared shut, but he kicked a stone against it just in case the wind blew it open. After he returned the key to the guards' room he went into the library, pausing on the way to remove the bolt on the side door that opened into the garden. His hands were shaking so much that he feared the sound of the bolts being removed echoed around the house.

They'll need to move: I told them the guards usually check the garden door soon after I lock it.

Roza and Nadezhda were in the library. He would hang around for a few minutes, as he had come to do. He could hear Nikolai playing upstairs and the two local women leaving the house. Anatoly was in his study and he imagined the mother would be asleep upstairs. From the corner of his eye he imagined he caught a movement in the garden, but he did not want to look up. A few moments later and there were some sounds from the front of the house, nothing too noticeable at first but then it became more of a commotion and first Nadezhda and then Roza looked up. Seconds later and the sound of shouting down the hall and then three loud popping noises followed by a scream and the sound of Anatoly shouting and then scuffling in the hall. Seconds later, the door to the library burst open. The first person in the room was one of the Frenchmen, followed by Peter and behind him Viktor and another of the Frenchmen frogmarching Anatoly into the room. The girls screamed and Viktor shouted at them in Russian, waving his revolver at their father's head as he did so. The message was clear: '*Shut up or I shoot.*'

Viktor pushed Anatoly into an armchair and gestured for the girls to sit on the floor. They could hear movement upstairs. 'Go and see what is going on' Viktor told Peter in French. Shortly after that one of the other Frenchman appeared in the room, dragging Nikolai in with him by his hair. Tatyana followed as if in a trance, followed by Peter. Nikolai was shoved on to the floor next to his terrified sisters while their mother was guided to a chair opposite her husband. Viktor addressed the family in Russian and then in French told Peter to see what was happening at the front of the house. When he reappeared it was with the third Frenchman and the two of them were dragging along one of the guards. He appeared to be badly wounded: he was groaning and his chest was covered in blood.

'What about the other two?' asked Viktor.

'Dead,' said the third Frenchman.

'And him?' He was nodding at the injured guard.

'Took one in the chest.'

'Finish him off.'

The Frenchman had been holding a revolver by his side. Now he knelt down by the guard and yanked up his head, forcing the barrel of the gun into his mouth. As he did so, the guard seemed to become fully conscious, his eyes opened wide – clearly terrified. The three children screamed and were only silenced when Viktor shouted at them. When the Frenchman pulled the trigger the guard's head slumped, followed by a long silence and then the sobbing of the three children. Tatyana sat very still, clearly in shock and seemingly unaware of what was going on. Henry noticed that Anatoly was staring at him.

Viktor spoke to the family in Russian, pointing at Anatoly and waving his pistol around. They all nodded. *We understand.* Then he spoke in French: 'I'm going to separate them now.' He pointed to the three Frenchmen. 'I'll take Anatoly into the study; he and I have much to talk about. One of you will come into the study with me, the other two had better keep an eye on the rest of the house – make sure one of you stays in the guardroom, we need to keep an eye on the front. Peter, you stay in here. William, you too: try and keep the children distracted. You'll need this.'

It was only when Viktor handed a revolver to Henry that it dawned on the family that he had betrayed them. From the shocked look on the faces of the children and the glare of hate on the face of their father, Henry realised that up until then they must have thought that he too had been caught up as a victim in this nightmare.

Anatoly was hauled up by one of the Frenchmen, who then hand-cuffed his hands behind his back before marching him out of the room. As he passed Henry, Anatoly stopped and looked Henry straight in the eye before spitting out '*Du Bastard!*'

None of the children wanted anything to do with their English tutor. They ignored all his attempts to talk in English. Nadezhda spent most of the time quietly sobbing, sitting on the floor by her mother's chair. Little Nikolai looked confused and terrified, while Roza stared at him with blazing eyes. 'You were the one person I thought understood me. You were someone I trusted,' she said in German, in a quiet but angry voice. 'You know what will happen to us now, don't you?'

'Everything will be all right, Roza, don't worry.'

'You think so do you, Englishman? In that case you have no idea who is paying you.' She shuffled over to him, lowering her voice even more. 'They will kill us all, you realise that?'

Peter leaned over from the nearby chair where he was sitting, 'Shut up' he shouted at Roza. He turned to Henry and spoke in

69

French, 'Don't talk with her anymore.' From the study there was the sound of raised voices in Russian, mostly Viktor, but Anatoly too. The afternoon turned into evening. One of the Frenchmen brought food into the library but, apart from Nikolai, none of the family ate anything. When it began to turn dark, Viktor called Henry and Peter into the kitchen.

'He finally understands that we mean business. I think he realises that he has no alternative but to do what I say. There is a train to Bern at seven twenty tomorrow morning: Lucien and Jean-Marie will go with him. He will be at the Swiss Volksbank when it opens: I have agreed that he can telephone here to be assured that everyone is safe. Then he will transfer all the funds from the Swiss Volksbank. After that, they will travel to Zurich and repeat the procedure at the Union Bank and the Eidgenössische Bank.'

'How do we know he will transfer all the funds under his control?' asked Peter.

'We cannot be totally sure, but we know from following him that these are the only three banks he has ever visited. I managed to persuade him to show me what documentation he had and the accounts amount to just over nine hundred million Swiss Francs: that is more than we estimated. They will be very pleased. By tomorrow night that money will be in accounts controlled by the Party.'

'And what happens then, Viktor?' The German looked nervous, playing with his watch strap and biting his fingernails, glancing first at Henry and then back at Viktor.

'We'll see. I have told him that he will be brought back here and that, a few hours after we leave the town, we will phone the local police to release them.'

'Roza told me that they are all going to be killed. Why would she say that?' Henry asked.

'Don't worry about it, *synok*. We know what we are doing.'

'But—'

Peter leaned over the table and grabbed Henry's forearm, very tight. 'Don't you remember anything? We just do as we are told. This isn't that stupid game you play for days at a time in England, understand?'

Never question; never discuss; never hesitate.

Viktor told them both to shut up. They would keep Anatoly apart from the rest of the family that night. Two of them would guard him while the others stayed with Tatyana and the children in the library, taking it in turns to sleep. Anatoly was made to telephone the housekeepers: '*You are not required tomorrow, please take the day off — we will see you as usual on Thursday.*'

Anatoly was woken up at six in the morning. Henry had been with him in his bedroom along with Peter for the past few hours and was surprised that the Russian had slept at all. They watched while he washed, shaved and dressed. When he was ready he turned round and addressed them.

'Tell him I want to say goodbye to my family before I leave.'

They called Viktor up and there was a short exchange in Russian. The result was that as Anatoly came downstairs he went into the library and hugged each member of his family, but said nothing other than a word or two in Russian to each one. When he had finished hugging the last one, Nadezhda, he turned sharply and swiftly left the room. As he passed him in the hall Henry noticed that the Russian's eyes had filled with tears.

–

Viktor spent much of that Wednesday in the study, behind Anatoly's desk. The first phone call came at nine thirty: it was Lucien at the Swiss Volksbank. Peter brought Roza through from the library and put her on the phone to her father.

'Yes, we are all all right. When are you coming home? What are they—?' The phone was snatched back from her. Thirty minutes later and Lucien rang again. The money had been transferred. They were now on their way to Zurich. The next phone call came at a quarter to one. It was Jean-Marie to say that they had arrived in Zurich and were about to go into Eidgenössische Bank. This time Nadezhda was brought in from the library to assure her father that all was well. Henry was in the study when Jean-Marie rang again at one thirty to say that the transfer had been made; they were on their way to the Union Bank.

'Wait. Ring me back in half an hour. I need to make a call first.'

Viktor dialled a Zurich number and after a short conversation, in which he said no more than a few words, a large smile filled his face, displaying the familiar gold teeth. 'Good news, *synok*. The funds from both banks have already been transferred to our account in Credit Suisse. Before the close of business today they will have been spread among various untraceable accounts across Europe. We are better at capitalism than the capitalists!'

By three o'clock the business had been done. Nikolai had spoken to his father before the transaction at Union Bank and then Lucien rang to say it had been completed.

'Is Yevtushenko in the room with you?' Viktor was speaking with Lucien. 'Right then, don't say anything, but when I have finished say out loud that you will be on the four fifteen train from Zurich and that you expect to be back in Interlaken by eight o'clock, you understand? You know what to do, Lucien… I will see you in Paris.'

Viktor paused while Lucien responded and then placed the phone back on the receiver, holding onto it for a while after putting it down. He sighed and loosened his tie.

'All good, *synok*. The transfers have taken place. Moscow will be delighted. Now, Trotsky has no more money.'

Henry nodded. 'Is Anatoly on his way back here, Viktor?'

The Russian peered at him as if the sun was in his eyes. 'Tell Peter to come in. You stay in the library with Claude.'

–

The longest half hour of Henry Hunter's life began very soon after that.

He was in the library with Claude, keeping an eye on Tatyana and the three children when Viktor appeared in the doorway. He spoke in Russian and Roza and Nadezhda both raised their hands. Viktor pointed at Nadezhda and gestured upstairs. 'I've asked if they want an opportunity to use the bathroom' he said to Henry in French. Viktor closed the library door as Nadezhda went upstairs. Viktor said nothing but glanced at his watch and then up at the ceiling, his back against the closed door. After five minutes he spoke to Roza. *Your turn.* She brushed past Henry, looking though him as she went past him, pulling her cardigan tightly around her shoulders and across her front.

Ten minutes later, with no sign of either of the girls, there was a knock at the door. Viktor opened it slightly to reveal Peter on the other side. The German nodded briefly but said nothing. 'Viktor nodded his head approvingly and briefly gripped Peter's shoulder in a friendly manner.

'Go into the guardroom' he said to Henry, 'and tell Claude to come here. You remain there. Keep an eye on the road. Don't leave until you're told to.'

From the guardroom Henry could see the front gate and the quiet road beyond it. The silence was pierced by a scream, one that was loud but stopped short by a loud popping noise and then the sound of something falling. Henry wondered whether to go and see what was happening, despite Viktor's instructions. Next came the sound of Nikolai shrieking and another popping noise, followed by two more. After that, more silence.

The door to the guardroom opened. Peter was standing there. 'You're to go to the library.' When he got there Viktor and Claude were standing in the middle of the room, revolvers in their hands. The body of Tatyana was thrown back in her chair, her eyes and mouth wide open and a large wound on her forehead. Prostrate on the floor in front of her was Nikolai, two wounds visible on his back and a large pool of blood emerging from under him.

Henry was too shocked to move and for a while could say nothing, until he noticed Nikolai's back moving.

'He's breathing, Viktor! Nikolai's breathing.' Henry felt himself swaying. Claude walked over to the boy and with his foot turned him over. Nikolai was breathing very slowly. His face was white, but his eyes were moving as if he was having trouble focussing. Claude looked up at Viktor. *What do you want me to do?*

Viktor held up a hand: wait. 'Henry, you finish him off. It is a tradition in our service: everyone on a mission should take part.' The

Russian pressed his own revolver into Henry's hand: the barrel was still hot. Henry's hand was shaking so much that the gun was waving around.

'Be careful with that thing please, Henry. You'd better use two hands,' said Viktor. 'And be quick. We need to get out of here.' Henry breathed in deeply. *Never question; never discuss; never hesitate.* He calmly walked over to Nikolai and knelt down by him. The boy's head moved slowly towards him, his eyes locking onto Henry's as his mouth opened, allowing a trickle of blood to form down his chin.

'Come on, quick' said Claude. Henry released the safety catch and placed the revolver against Nikolai's temple. He noticed that he was trying to say something: hearing him say something – anything – would be more than he could bear. When he pressed the trigger he felt the splatter of blood and flesh on him before he heard the sound. It had been no harder than shooting his puppy. Claude hauled him up.

'Good. Well done. We need to move now.'

–

They left the house just before four o'clock, after trying to make it appear as if a robbery had taken place and gone dreadfully wrong. They opened the safe and made the study look as if it had been ransacked. Henry went upstairs with Peter to help find any jewellery. As they walked past the bathroom Henry stopped suddenly. A girl's leg was poking out of the door. Its shoe had fallen off and was upside down on the carpet in front of him. Peter pushed in front of him as he tried to open the bathroom door, placing himself between Henry and the door.

'You don't need to go in here.'

'I want to see,' said Henry, barging his way past the German.

The bodies of both Roza and Nadezhda were sprawled out on the floor, on top of a pool of dark blood that had spread around the room. The heads of both girls were jerked at an unnatural angle, facing each other, their eyes open and full of fear and very still. Roza's hand had reached out to her sister's, her fingers clutching one of Nadezhda's wrists.

'What…?'

Peter had now pushed past him and was drawing the curtains. He smiled at Henry and pointed at the girls and made a cut-throat gesture.

Henry stood in the doorway for a minute, watching as Peter hauled the bodies of the two girls into the bath and then started throwing towels onto the floor to soak up the blood. He was shocked to realise how un-shocked he felt. His main concern was that he should be careful not to step in the blood.

Henry left the house as normal through the front gate and headed into town, crossing the river and towards Interlaken West train station. He was halfway down Bahnhofstrasse when the car pulled up. Peter and Claude got out and walked towards the station. Henry climbed into the passenger seat next to Viktor.

They drove north towards Bern, but were well past Thun before either of them spoke. 'You realise there was no alternative, don't you, *synok*?' Viktor turned briefly towards Henry, who shrugged. 'We could not afford to have any witnesses.' Henry said nothing. *Never question; never discuss; never hesitate.*

Instead of driving into Bern they stopped briefly in Köniz and then took the road towards Lausanne. It was only then that Henry spoke. 'What happened to Anatoly?'

'I think you can guess, *synok*.'

'Did he know what was going to happen to him?'

'I would imagine so: he has been an *apparatchik* all of his adult life. He knows how we work. He would have known what to expect.'

'So why did he co-operate then?'

'Because I promised him that if he did, we would spare the children.'

'And he believed you?'

Viktor said nothing for a while as he thought about Henry's question. The headlight of an approaching bus caught the Russian's gold teeth as he turned to reply.

'Probably not, but what choice did he have? He wanted to believe that I – we – would spare the children and his wife. Look, you are

75

asking too many questions, *synok*. You did well, just leave it at that. You are one of us now. You should be happy.'

Later that night, once he had arrived home in Nyon and he lay in his own bed for the first time in weeks, what most shocked Henry was the realisation of how much he agreed with Viktor. He was now one of them. He was happy. But he knew that it had come at a terrible, terrible price. When he had returned from Germany the previous year he knew that they had taken possession of his soul.

Now they had destroyed it.

That night, he had the dream for the first time.

Chapter 7

Berlin, January 1940

On a foggy winter's afternoon in the middle of January a tall man with a stooped bearing that afforded him a misleadingly academic air left his office at the Reichsbank on Werderscher Markt in the centre of Berlin, by the canal. It was five thirty, somewhat later than most other people he worked with. The later he left work, he reasoned, the later he would arrive home and that suited him fine.

Gunter Reinhart had developed a habit of leaving the enormous complex through different exits on different days. Had someone been observing him, which they would have no cause to do, they might be suspicious. But he did not vary his routine for reasons of security; the truth was far more prosaic than that. It afforded him the opportunity to take different routes home and on each of those routes lay various bars, where he could further delay his arrival there. At least it gave him something to think about during the afternoon.

There was no point in leaving through the Unterwasserstrasse exit because beyond that was the canal. He liked the anonymity and slightly rougher edge to the bars round Leipzigerstrasse, but that was further from home. Leaving through Französischestrasse meant heading towards the Unter den Linden, which one could never accuse of offering anonymity. He would, he decided, leave through Kurstrasse and find somewhere to stop off around Jägerstrasse.

These days, stepping out into the street after dark was like descending into a pitch black tunnel. Gunter Reinhart had very mixed feelings about the blackout that descended upon Berlin at dusk. On the one hand, it conferred an atmosphere of privacy on the city. You felt you were in your own world. On the other hand, there was no question that it made life more difficult. There were no streetlights, buildings were dark and the trams moved around like ghost trains. Cars had just a small strip of paper over their headlights. Any lights that were allowed were covered in blue paper, while low-level red lamps marked danger spots, such as road works. Then there was the phosphorous paint: gallons of the stuff liberally sloshed on the pavements and road surfaces to give pedestrians and drivers some chance of knowing where they were. The effect was quite eerie and unsettling. Berlin at night looked as if it was deserted. There were reports of numerous traffic accidents and people being killed from walking into things or falling over in the blackout. The sister of one of the secretaries in his office had been killed when she stepped off the platform at Kaiserhof station. And then there were the rumours. Berlin thrived on rumours anyway; they had been part an essential part of its pre-war diet. Now, rumours were disseminated in more hushed and guarded tones. The latest rumour was that a murderer was taking advantage of the blackout and had already killed a dozen young women. There had even been oblique references to it in the newspapers. Naturally, the police said they suspected the person responsible was Jewish; or Polish; or both.

The few people who moved around the city at night did so tentatively, as if wading through water. Some people had taken to whistling or coughing constantly so as to alert others to their proximity and thus hoping to avoid bumping into them. But that was something of a forlorn hope: it was impossible to avoid other people.

Even though this was a route that he knew very well, on nights like this, when there was no moonlight, Gunter Reinhart could not find his bearings.

Just after the intersection with Friedrichstrasse he came across a group of men silently beating up a man on the ground. He paused for a moment, taking in the surreal nature of what he was witnessing before he decided to cross the road. He had learned to keep well away from trouble. Suddenly, a long black car swept past him and stopped. Very quickly, the man who was being attacked was bundled into the car.

Six months previously he would have been shaken to the core by what he had seen, but now it was quickly forgotten. He was more concerned with finding somewhere to drink. Looming out of the dark he spotted the dim blue-covered sign for Das Potsdamer Taverne, a bar that he used to visit at least twice a week, although recently it had become something of a favourite haunt for a group of young SS officers. Given that the whole point of going to the bar was to relax, they were the last people he'd want to find in there.

He walked slowly down the steep steps to the basement, clutching on to the iron railings and keeping a careful eye on the dabs of phosphorous paint on the steps. The bar was quiet and there was no sign of the SS, or indeed anyone else in uniform. The bar had a low ceiling which caused him to stoop. Through the blue-brown cigarette smoke he could see perhaps half a dozen other customers spread out: all of them alone, all smoking, all drinking quietly, all sitting as far as they could manage from each other. Like him, they were avoiding going home.

The barmaid caught his eye as he waited to order a drink.

'How are you, I haven't seen you for a while?'

'A week perhaps? No more than that. I was in here last week.'

That kind of conversation, the kind repeated in bars around the world, between barmaids and husbands who would rather not go home.

The barmaid was a friendly girl with broad shoulders and hair that looked as if it had been dyed yellow. His wife, in her usual waspish manner, would describe her in the unlikely event of her ever meeting her by saying that she had 'seen better days', but she had friendly eyes and a seductive voice, with a distinctive Bavarian accent. She kept glancing at him as she pulled the beer, her eyes darting around her. He started to move away, hoping to find a seat on his own. She held up her hand. *Wait a moment.*

When she had finished serving another customer she leaned over to talk quietly to him.

'A man was in here asking about you.'

Eight words no one wanted to hear in Berlin in 1940.

'What man?'

'I don't know, I have never seen him here before. He was very polite and well spoken. A Berliner definitely: wore a nice coat.'

'When was this?'

She leant back as if trying to calculate the answer.

'Last Thursday, I think: and then again yesterday – Monday.'

Gunter Reinhart pulled up the stool next to him and sat on it. This was bad news. Who could possibly be coming into a bar to ask about him? People knew where he worked and where he lived.

'And what did you say?'

'He seemed like a nice man, Herr Reinhart, but I did not want to say much. On the other hand, I did not want to lie. I just said that you come in here every so often: about once a week these days. Was that all right?'

Not really.

'Did he say anything else?'

'Wait.' The barmaid knelt down and emerged with her handbag, which she rummaged through. 'Here, I've found it. He said that if you come in, I'm to give this to you.' She handed him a book of matches with Das Potsdamer Taverne on the front. He looked at it for a while, puzzled.

'Open it.'

Neatly written inside were two dates.

Den 8 Juni 1901

Den 4 Oktober 1929

'Are you all right Herr Reinhart?'

Gunter Reinhart was evidently not all right. The hand that was holding the book of matches was shaking and the other hand was gripping the bar tightly. Beads of sweat had formed on his forehead. He could feel his chest tightening.

'Pardon?'

'Are you all right Herr Reinhart? You look shaken.'

He put the matches in his top pocket and drank most of the glass of beer in one go and pushed the empty glass towards her and nodded for her to refill it.

'I am fine, thank you. Did this man say how I could contact him?'

'He said that he would be here at six o'clock every Thursday and Monday night until he was able to meet up with you.'

Gunter Reinhart stayed in the bar for another hour and three more glasses of beer before he decided to walk all the way home to Charlottenburg. It was a long walk, but he needed that time to compose himself. He crossed Hermann Goring Strasse, which people would quietly joke was almost as wide as the man himself, and into Charlottenburger Chaussee, the Tiergarten an enormous void on his left.

Despite the brisk night air and absence of British bombers, he found himself becoming increasingly tense rather than composed. He had continuously checked the dates before leaving the bar. There was no question about them.

Why on earth would someone write the down the birth dates of his first wife and his eldest son, especially when they were no longer in Berlin?

The following morning he took extra care on his journey into work to ensure that he wasn't being followed, not that he was sure what he was meant to do. He was a banker: his knowledge of subterfuge was limited to the world of finance. He could move funds from one bank account to another without leaving a trace, but he had absolutely no idea how to walk from one place to another without being spotted and, in any case, he towered above most other people. It would not be hard to follow him. When he arrived at the Reichsbank he casually enquired of his secretary – maybe a bit too casually – whether anyone had been asking for him: '*Perhaps over the past few days?*' His secretary assured him that no one had been asking after him. She looked appalled at the very thought that someone might have enquired of him and she would not have passed the information on.

His head of department informed him that Funk wanted to see them both the next morning: he wanted an urgent and up-to-date report on some of the new Swiss bank accounts. 'You are not to worry,' he assured his head of department, 'the information will be ready.' Pulling it all together was at least a distraction for Reinhart, but it did mean that his head of department fussed around him for the rest of the day. He was a rotund man with bad breath whose suit was always too tight and reeked of mothballs. He had been promoted from his natural level as an assistant bank manager somewhere near Magdeburg simply due to a long standing loyalty to the Nazi Party and as a consequence was now utterly out of his depth.

The next day – Thursday – followed a sleepless night: the meeting with Walther Funk proved to be but a two hour distraction, even something of an amusement. The President of the Reichsbank, who doubled as Hitler's Minister of Economics, was someone else who had been promoted because of service to the Nazi Party rather than any kind of financial competence or knowledge. Reinhart produced a series of complicated balance sheets and lengthy lists of transactions: Funk was impressed and confused in equal measure, but unable to own up to the latter.

The afternoon went slowly and, as the sun disappeared over Berlin, Reinhart wondered whether he was being led into a trap. Maybe he had been a bit too clever by half. Maybe he had upset one too many of the Nazi Party bosses at the top of the Reichsbank, who felt they had cause to distrust him. *Gunter Reinhart, the man who knows everything about the Swiss accounts: time to put him in his place.*

Das Potsdamer Taverne was as quiet as it had been the previous night. He nodded at the barmaid and she smiled, slightly shaking her head: *not yet.*

There was a tiny table wedged into a corner behind the bar, where no one else could fit and he waited as the bar became quieter. He was just wondering how long he should remain in the bar when he caught sight of a man who looked vaguely familiar and who seemed to be glancing in his direction. The man remained at the bar, toying with a glass of beer. A few minutes later he appeared at Reinhart's table.

'Do you mind if I sit here?'

Reinhart was almost certain that this man was a friend of his first wife's family, a lawyer – specialised in banking and finance, rather intelligent and a bit too liberal for his liking: Catholic. First name Franz, if he remembered correctly. He doubted though that this was the man who had gone to such lengths to meet him. After all, bumping into an acquaintance in the centre of Berlin was hardly the most remarkable of coincidences. The man produced a packet of cigarettes, took one out and placed it in Reinhart's hand.

'Would you like a light?'

Reinhart hesitated. The man reached into his pocket and found a book of matches, one with Das Potsdamer Taverne on the front. As he opened it he casually angled the packet so that Reinhart could clearly see it. Again, two dates were handwritten on the inside of the packet.

Den 8 Juni 1901
Den 4 Oktober 1929

This time it was in the unmistakably familiar handwriting of his first wife. The man shifted his chair even closer to Reinhart and when he spoke again it was in a quieter voice.

'You remember me, Gunter? Franz Hermann. Just act normally, don't speak too loudly or too quietly. Smile occasionally.'

'I remember you, Franz. I guess it was you who's been asking about me here?'

Franz nodded.

'What is it all about? You've given me a couple of sleepless nights.'

'I fear that I am about to give you many more. You see...'

He paused. A couple of Luftwaffe officers had come into the bar and had moved noisily towards them, looking for somewhere to sit. Franz waited until they moved away.

'Good, this is not a conversation that we would want them to overhear. Stop looking so worried Gunter; you'll draw attention to yourself. Just relax and smile: we are friends who have met in a bar. Don't look like you're being interrogated by the Gestapo. When did you last hear from Rosa?'

Gunter frowned, trying to remember.

'There was a letter from Paris in October. She sent it at the beginning of October but I didn't receive it until the end of the month: it came via a friend of hers in Switzerland and then through my brother.'

'How come?'

'I don't know if you're aware, but I remarried soon after Rosa and I divorced. Far too soon, as it has turned out. It has not turned out to be a happy marriage, but we have children and it is a situation I am stuck with – I only have myself to blame. Gudrun – my second wife – will not tolerate me having any contact whatsoever with either Rosa or our son, Alfred. As far as she is concerned, I have nothing to do with them. It is safer that she thinks that. She has become a devoted Nazi, like the rest of her family. The fact that I was once married to a Jew and had a son with her is a terrible thing in Gudrun's eyes. I have had to promise her that I have no contact whatsoever with Rosa and Alfred, that I have disowned them. Have you heard from her, Franz: is everything all right? What about Alfred?'

'Gunter, unless you keep your voice down and act normally we are going to have a serious problem. Do you understand? Drink some of your beer. Try and look relaxed.'

Gunter nodded and composed himself. 'I understand, but is there any news?'

'For time being, they are safe.'

'And they're still in Paris?'

Franz Hermann lowered his head and talked a little more quietly.

'A smile please, Gunter, you need to smile. We are old friends meeting for a relaxed drink. Good, that is better. You need to prepare yourself for what I am about to say. They are safe, for the time being: Rosa, Alfred and little Sophia. But I don't know for how long. They are in hiding you see. Here in Berlin.'

–

Gunter Reinhart had to wait three days before he could see his son and his ex-wife, along with her young daughter. Having to wait that long was bad enough, but visiting them on a Sunday presented added problems. Sunday was the day on which his wife demanded his undivided attention, but he insisted that he had work commitments that were none of her business and he was able to slip out of the house once they returned from church.

'They are living with my mother in Dahlem, Gunter: near the Botanischer Garten,' Hermann had told him at the bar. 'My mother has become quite unwell, unable to look after herself. She insists on staying in the old family home. She needed someone to live in and look after her and luckily with her qualifications and experience, Rosa is ideal. She will tell you the full story. On Sundays, my brother-in-law drives over from Brandenburg and takes her back to their house for lunch. She leaves at eleven in the morning and they bring her back at around four, so you see that will not leave much time.'

Not much time.

'There is no reason to think that anyone will suspect what you are up to, Gunter,' Franz had warned him 'but be careful. Assume you are being followed and take basic precautions: walk at an even pace, don't keep looking behind you – that kind of thing.'

So he walked at an even pace across Spandauer Strasse and caught the S-Bahn at Westend. He did as Hermann had advised: making sure he got onto the busiest carriage and watching out for anyone getting on at the same time as him. The train worked its way south at a Sunday pace. At Schmargendorf he changed to the U-Bahn and then headed south again, getting off at Podbielski Allee.

He was not far now: he had not seen his son or Rosa for nearly six months. He had assumed they were out of the country. His excitement at seeing them was mixed in with the shock that they were still in Germany.

From Podbielski Allee he headed down Peter Lenne Strasse towards the Botanischer Garten. He had memorised Hermann's instructions. '*Write nothing down Gunter.*'

At the end of the road he turned left into Königin-Luise-Strasse, across the square and then continuing along Grunewald Strasse. 'You know Kaiser Wilhelm Strasse, Gunter? Runs off Grunewald Strasse. Turn into there: first right is Arno-Holz Strasse. The white house on the corner is where my mother lives. I will be there from twelve. If the curtains are drawn in window directly above the front door, it is safe to approach the house, but please only do so if you believe you have not been followed. Otherwise, head on down to the Botanischer Garten at a leisurely pace.'

He did as instructed. In other circumstances he would have enjoyed his walk on what had turned out to be an unseasonably warm afternoon. The house was as Hermann had described it, the front garden deep and heavy with trees, the walls white and in need of repainting and above the front door, a window. The curtains were drawn.

He looked around him once more, but the streets were deserted. He had not been followed. He unlatched a noisy iron gate and walked down the path. As he approached the porch the front door opened and behind it he could see Franz Hermann, silently ushering him in.

They stood together in the dark hall of a silent house.

'Are they here, Franz?'

'Upstairs. Take your shoes off.'

Gunter ran up the stairs. On the landing, waiting for him in the gloom was his ex-wife and their son. Behind them, peering out from behind a door was Sophia, his ex-wife's daughter from her second marriage.

Alfred flung himself at his father, holding him tight and burying his face in his chest. Gunter could feel his warm tears seeping through his shirt and vest. Rosa came up to him and held his face, kissing him tenderly on each cheek, one hand cupping the back of his neck. He could feel tears welling up in his eyes. Little Sophia waved at him. He waved back.

He held both Rosa and Alfred, unsure of what to say. *The only family I ever wanted*.

It was two thirty when Gunter and Rosa sat alone in a small room on the top floor of the house. Franz had told them he would wait with the children and keep an eye on the front. Gunter would need to be away by a quarter to four to be safe. He and Rosa sat quietly for a while, holding hands.

'I thought you were in Paris, Rosa?'

He was trying hard not to sound angry.

'We were in Paris, Gunter. I wrote to you at the beginning of October. Did you get the letter?'

He nodded. She shrugged.

'Harald was meant to join us in the middle of October: he had remained in Berlin because he needed to make a few arrangements. The idea was that he would get what money he could out of the business – which was not much – and transfer it to Switzerland. Then we would have something to live on and, together with the money you gave us, we may be able to get on to America.'

'That was the idea.'

'I promise you that was the plan. As you know, Harald had been forced to sell the business to two of his managers for a fraction of what it was worth. Both of them were men who were friends of his, who he had always helped in the past. They had always said that they would help him and one of them did, but the other refused. I don't know exactly what happened, but from what I can gather Harald was reported to the Gestapo for trying to get money out of Germany, which is illegal for a Jew to do. I suspect that the manager he had fallen out with was the person who reported him to the Gestapo. So Harald was arrested and taken to Sachsenhausen – it's a special camp for prisoners of the Nazis. Have you heard of it?'

'Of course I have – near Oranienburg. Are you sure he is there?'

'Believe me, I am sure. Terrible things happen there. I don't like to think about what he must be going through. I know that he is still alive, or at least he was two weeks ago, but I don't know what state he is in.'

'So why on earth did you come back here? What were you thinking of, Rosa?'

'I don't know what I was thinking, Gunter. Please don't be angry with me. I thought that if my husband was in prison here then I should come back to help him. I thought I could get him released.'

'But, Rosa, what about Alfred – and Sophia?'

'I know, Gunter. But remember, we left Germany for France in July. I had no idea how bad things had become. In Paris I borrowed some money from my cousin and I sold all of my jewellery. I thought I could pay a fine or a bribe or something like that and get Harald released. But when I went to the police station they confiscated my passport and wanted to know where I was living. I gave them the address of the old flat in Pankow that we were staying at and they only let me go because I had papers showing I was registered there. I knew that they would come for us, but fortunately, I had left the children with my old colleague Maria in Kreuzberg while I went to the police station. When I left I went straight to Kreuzberg, picked up Alfred and Sophia and then contacted Franz. He took us to his house which is also in Dahlem for a few days and then came up with this plan for us to move here in with his mother. It has worked out well: the old lady is almost deaf and cannot climb the stairs, so as long as the children are quiet and stay upstairs then they are all right and she has no idea that they are here.'

'And she doesn't suspect you?'

'She has been told that I am a nurse from Bremerhaven whose husband is in the Navy. Of course, I don't let on that I am a doctor. I can use all my skills to keep her alive. If she dies then we will have to leave the house. I have some papers that Franz managed to get hold of showing that I am from Bremerhaven, but they are not good enough to travel with. Franz comes round most days. The old lady has very few visitors other than that: one or two friends who pop in for an hour every so often, but they always call first. Franz's sister does not know the truth about me but I think she is just grateful that someone is looking after her mother which means she doesn't have to.'

'And the children?'

'It is terrible for them here; they just have to stay upstairs all day. Poor Sophia has no idea what is going on, other than that her father is in prison and she has to keep quiet all of the time. Alfred knows what is going on, of course. That makes it worse, I suppose. He misses you terribly, Gunter.'

Gunter sat for a while with his head in his hands, deep in thought.

'Why didn't you contact me before now – I mean, once you got back to Berlin?'

Rosa looked at him long and hard. *You don't know why?*

'Gunter – you always said that I was not to contact you directly. You said Gudrun would not allow it. I did not know what your situation is, whether it was safe. I also thought you would be angry with me. I was hoping that we would find a way back to France. Franz was going to see if he could find false papers, but it is impossible. We are trapped here in Berlin, Gunter.'

Rosa was weeping now, her trembling hand holding Gunter's.

'I should never have divorced you Rosa, I was—'

'Don't blame yourself, Gunter. We agreed it was for the best.'

'No, I was being selfish. The three of us should have left after that damn law was passed…'

They sat in silence for a long while.

'It is three fifteen, Gunter. Franz says you are to leave soon. Please spend some time with Alfred before you go. He misses you so much.'

'I don't know what to do, Rosa. Do you need food or money?'

'Yes, but what we really need is to get out: even if you can just save Alfred. As far as the Nazis are concerned, he is only a half Jew. Could you take him? Would Gudrun not understand?'

Gunter laughed. 'Understand? Even if I said that you had abandoned Alfred and I had found him in the middle of Berlin, she would not want to know. When we got married she made me promise I would never, ever have anything to do with the two of you again. Frankly, I would not put it past her to turn him in. Her brother Norbert, who has all the intelligence of a field mouse but with less of the personality – he's now a big shot in the Nazi Party in Bergdorf, which says everything you need to know about him. The fact that I was once married to a Jew is a terrible secret in that family. Gudrun insists that the children are not allowed to know about it.'

'But what are we going to do, Gunter?'

'I don't know Rosa. Give me time, I'll think of something.'

Chapter 8

'*Do nothing unusual and certainly nothing that is likely to draw attention to yourself.*'

For eight long months Hunter had followed Edgar's advice, leading an unremarkable existence. The waiting to be contacted was tedious and living with his mother even more so. The fact that he was now in control of the purse strings was more than she could bear. It was 'intolerable', she announced during a dramatic argument on the night he returned. She could not understand why he had returned with so little of the aunt's money.

He explained their predicament once more, very clearly and very slowly.

'Remember it was your clever idea to bypass probate and for me to attempt to bring all the money back here as soon as possible. That proved to be simply impossible – and illegal: I could have ended up in prison. I have told you what happened: I had to go to London and stay there for all that time to sort out the money. I was tangled up in reels and reels of red tape and then war was declared at the beginning of September, which made matters almost impossible. The British Government simply do not want to release money to go overseas, they say they cannot be sure whose hands it will end up in. You ought to be grateful that I managed to get anything out at all and return in one piece.'

'But it is our money, Henry!'

'*My* money actually mother and not all of it, as it turned out. In the end the authorities accepted my explanation that there had been a misunderstanding over the will. I was fortunate. Then it took a few more weeks for probate to be granted. After that, I had to obtain agreement that the money could be released but, as I told you, I don't get it in one sum. You were advanced 200 pounds, I will be able to access a further 500 over the next few days and the rest of the money will then come through at the rate of 100 pounds per month. It is not the amount we had hoped for, mother, but it is enough for us to be able to live far more comfortably.'

Since the death of her second husband, Marlene Hesse's perfectly formed world had steadily unravelled. She now accepted the changed situation with the minimum of grace. At least they had been able to afford to rent a larger apartment in a much more respectable location just off Quai du Mont Blanc, which was some consolation.

But the wait to be contacted was considerably more trying than his mother. Two days after his return he had gone, as instructed by Edgar, to the Quai des Bergues branch of Credit Suisse and made an appointment to see Madame Ladnier later that morning. In a small office in the basement she went through the details of the account, before handing him a folded piece of paper.

My home telephone number: I only give this to special clients and then only to be used in particular circumstances. You understand?

After that, nothing. As soon as they moved into their new apartment he went to see Madame Ladnier to give her the details. She assured him the matter would be dealt with. He was desperate to ask her if there was any news, but managed to restrain himself.

He began to follow a routine, in the hope that would make it easier for whoever would approach him: leaving the apartment at a certain time, returning to it at a certain time, an afternoon walk, the shops…

Christmas came and went, celebrated mostly in silence with his still embittered mother and January brought the snows down from the Alps, but still no contact. By the end of the month he started to wonder if he would ever be contacted and wondered if this would be no bad thing. Perhaps had forgotten about him: at least the money was still appearing in his account. There was the occasional contact from Viktor and he always told him the same: no news. Loyalty was proving to be a most complicated business.

At the end of February he received a phone call from Madame Ladnier. Could he come into the bank to sign a document? 'You are not to worry,' she assured him. 'They have told me to tell you that you will be contacted in due course, but it may take a few months. Remain patient – and discrete.'

The same happened at the end of April: 'They want me to assure you that you have not been forgotten. Be patient. It should not be too long now.' Viktor was not surprised when he told him – 'There's no rush, *synok* – that is how people like us operate.'

On the last Tuesday in June, Henry left the apartment off Quai du Mont Blanc as usual at nine thirty. It was already a warm morning, with light breeze skimming over the lake. As he headed south for a brisk walk before breakfast a woman swept past him before slowing down and studying a map. As he drew alongside her she looked surprised and then spoke in French with a Provençal accent, much faster than the Swiss.

'I am sorry, sir, I appear to be lost! I am looking for the Old Town. Do you know the way?'

It was so natural, so matter of fact that Hunter was taken aback and thought that this could not possibly be the contact, who he had assumed, would be a man. It must be a coincidence he thought, but then he noticed that she was carrying a copy of Monday's *Tribune de Genève*. It took him a moment to compose himself.

'Of course. Would you prefer to walk or take the tram?'

She smiled. 'I would prefer to walk if you are able to show me the way to go.'

Another smile and a slight hesitation before Henry replied, 'Well, I am walking to the Old Town myself now. If you wish, you are most welcome to follow me.'

She smiled and theatrically held out an elegantly gloved hand. *Lead on.*

'*Take any route to the Old Town.*'

Henry tried to walk at a normal pace as he headed to the Old Town, unsure what a normal pace felt like. He crossed the Rhône at the Pont des Bergues, allowing himself a glance behind to check that the woman was still following. He crossed the Rue de la Rôtisserie into the Old Town and soon after that the woman overtook him: it was now his turn to follow her. She walked through alleyways, crossed roads, waited on corners and eventually they emerged onto Rue de l'Hôtel de Ville. Her pace did not change, other than when she paused briefly at a shop window. Henry was wondering how long this would go on for, but then they crossed into the Grand-Rue and there on the corner was the Brasserie de Hôtel de Ville and outside it a waste paper bin, into which she dropped her copy of *Tribune de Genève*. She carried on walking, but Henry knew that his rendezvous would take place here. He entered the cafe.

'*You are to enter the building and wait. If no one has approached you after five minutes, you are to leave the building and return home.*'

He glanced at his wristwatch and the clock on the wall. Within two minutes a man entered the cafe, smoking a cigar and greeting two people sat at a nearby table. He shook hands with the barman and walked straight over to Henry.

'I am Marc. Would you care to join me?'

'*If someone joins you and introduces themselves as Marc you are to go with him. He will take you to meet your main contact. At that moment, your new career will have begun.*'

Henry nodded. Beside the bar was a door which Marc opened. *After you.*

A narrow staircase twisted and turned to the top of the building. When they reached a small landing Marc gestured for him to wait and then knocked three times on a polished oak door.

'It is me, Marc. I have the delivery.'

Henry heard a bolt being drawn and then the door opened. It was a corner room, expensively furnished with an ornate fireplace and a thick carpet: one wall was taken up with a floor to ceiling bookcase, many of the volumes leather-bound. On a French-polished sideboard there was an exquisite cut glass decanter with matching glasses on a silver tray. Next to that was another tray, with a teapot and various cups.

The door was opened by a dapper man in his sixties who was wearing a three piece suit. His iron grey hair, going white at the sides, was slicked back, slightly longer than Hunter would have expected.

'Ah, Hunter: welcome! At long last. Welcome indeed. Sorry about all this John Buchan stuff. Not really my idea: seems to be the form these days. Apparently we can't be too careful.' It was a distinctly upper class drawl.

'Now do come in and make yourself at home. My name is Basil by the way, like in the Swiss city.'

'Pardon?'

'Basle, Hunter. The Swiss seems to find it amusing, or at least they would do if they allowed themselves the indulgence of a sense of humour. Basil Remington-Barber. There's an "Hon" that goes in front of the name if you're a stickler for that kind of thing. As far as the Swiss are concerned I am a commercial attaché at the British Embassy in Bern. As far as you are concerned I run the station out here in Switzerland. And, if you are still confused, that means I look after all intelligence matters from our place on Thunstrasse. Thought it would be a quiet place to wind up my career. Had rather expected to have retired by now but I am told there's a war on and someone in London has decided that I am indispensable: helps that I speak the lingo I suppose, all of them as it happens. Had hoped to be hacking my way round some of Scotland's easier links courses by now, but there we go.'

With that, he switched to Swiss German, alternating between it and German. 'Now tell me, Hunter: are you raring to go or had you been hoping that we'd forgotten all about you?' That sentence had been delivered in Swiss German. Hunter replied in the same language.

'Well, I can't really say. I imagine that—'

'Bit of both probably, perfectly understandable – not knowing is the worse part. Sorry about the delay, but the good news is the waiting's over. The fall of France has rather spurred London into action as far as I can gather. We have a little errand for you. But first of all, let us have some tea: milk and sugar?'

Hunter relaxed a bit now. The civilised serving of tea and the promise of a little errand sounded quite acceptable, perhaps even fun.

What was it Edgar had promised? '*Chances are that the first job will be something relatively straightforward, probably within Switzerland. Shouldn't be anything too dangerous; a warm up, if you like.*'

The Hon. Basil Remington-Barber took a while to serve tea, fussing over Hunter's and then his own tea to check that it was neither too weak nor too strong. When he was satisfied that everything was just right he leaned back in his armchair and addressed Hunter through the steam rising from his china teacup. Hunter was beginning to enjoy his morning. His pleasure was to be short-lived.

'We understand that you are very familiar with Stuttgart, Hunter?'

'I beg your pardon?' Hunter felt his throat tightening.

'Stuttgart, the German city?'

Hunter placed his teacup down on the side table next to him. His hands were beginning to shake and he needed to cover that up, so he folded them on his lap, crossing and then un-crossing his legs as he did so.

'Yes, I know it.'

'Been there often?'

'Once or twice.'

'Really?'

Henry shrugged. *Not sure.*

'*Quite* a few times, we understand, Hunter.'

'Well, possibly...'

'Something that you omitted to tell any of my colleagues back in England?'

Hunter hesitated for longer than he knew he should. 'Forgot rather than omitted I would say.' He was not convinced by his own answer. Nor was Basil Remington-Barber, who shook his head in mild disapproval. 'I rather know the feeling. I seem to forget the odd thing these days. My wife tells me I'm starting to remind her of how her father was just before he went completely potty! The old boy had to be locked up after he shot one of his gamekeepers: thought he was a pheasant, apparently. The point is though, Hunter, that not mentioning Stuttgart is a rather important omission. Perhaps you would like to tell me about it now?'

Hunter tried to sound as casual as possible, hoping to convey the impression that his knowledge of Stuttgart was really nothing very important, the kind of thing that one could so easily forget.

'There is not an awful lot to say. My stepfather had some property in Stuttgart. I used to pop up there every so often to keep an eye on things for him.'

'How often would "every so often" be, Hunter?'

'I really couldn't say. Once or twice a year, maybe.'

'My very strong advice, Hunter,' Remington–Barber had dispensed with the bonhomie, 'would be that you are totally honest from now on. You see, your first mission is to go up to Stuttgart and the more that we know about your familiarity with the city, the better. I do hope you understand that.'

'*Shouldn't be anything too dangerous; a warm-up, if you like.*'

'Edgar implied that my first mission would be within Switzerland.'

'Did he now? Well, that is Edgar for you: an officer but not quite a gentleman. Grammar school, I am told. Now, tell me all about Stuttgart.'

'My stepfather had a fair amount of residential property in Stuttgart, in the best areas: quite a lot in Gänseheide to the east of the city centre and more in the north, Azenberg and Killesberg mostly. He had local agents that looked after them, but he liked me to go up there once a quarter to check everything was in order and to oversee the transfer of his rental income back to Switzerland.'

'So you visited Stuttgart four times a year?'

'Yes.'

'For how many years?'

'Seven or eight, possibly more.'

'Mathematics was never my strongest subject, Hunter, but I make that somewhere in the region of thirty visits to Stuttgart.'

'If you say so.'

'I do. So you are very familiar with the city?'

'I suppose so.'

'Speak the local dialect?'

'No, though I do understand it.'

'And where did you stay?'

'Usually at Hotel Marquardt in Schlossplatz.'

'That is certainly quite an omission, Hunter. Don't worry too much; I am sure that you are about to more than make up for it.'

–

Henry Hunter could never quite see the point of Bern. It was a pretty enough place, with an undoubted medieval charm and the River Aare leant a certain picturesque drama to the city as it twisted through the centre. But in a typically Swiss way it was rather too aware of its virtues; a little bit too smug. For the past ninety years or so the city had been the capital of Switzerland and now all roads led to it and in the case of Hunter's journey there on a windy Wednesday morning, so did the trains.

At the end of their briefing the previous day the Hon. Basil Remington-Barber had told him to get a move on. Hunter had rather imagined that this meant by the end of the month, possibly within a fortnight.

'A fortnight? You must be joking, Hunter. No, this week. Get up to Bern tomorrow, sort out your visa and then I'll give you your precise instructions.'

He explained to his mother that he was visiting friends in Basle for a few days and took an early morning to Bern, arriving at the station in Bahnhofplatz just in time for lunch. Hunter had been pleasantly surprised when Remington-Barber suggested he book into the Schweizerhof, the best hotel in the city and no more than a very short stroll from the station.

'Rather goes against the grain, Hunter and certainly pushes the expenses, but the point is that you have to stick to your role: as far as the Germans are concerned you are an affluent Swiss gentleman who wishes to travel to Stuttgart on business. Such people stay at the Schweizerhof, I am afraid. Make sure you're seen out and about in the hotel. There's something like one hundred and fifteen thousand people in this city and I think that if you took the spies away, it would be less than one hundred thousand. Most of the spies hang around the Schweizerhof, so it's good to be seen, just being yourself. Book yourself in for two nights. I just hope London buy it.'

'*Make sure you're seen out and about in the hotel.*' Once he had checked in and changed he went down to the restaurant. The restaurant manager asked him to wait at the bar, where he found himself alongside two very formally dressed middle-aged men speaking in German. The two Germans greeted him correctly, almost standing to attention as they did so.

'What brings you to Bern?' they asked. Henry explained that he was from Geneva but was here in Bern to arrange a visa: he was hoping visit Germany soon on business.

'Whereabouts?'

'Stuttgart.'

'Very good.' *Was Herr Hesse likely to be in Berlin at any time in the future?*

'Maybe. You never know!'

'You will look me up if you do. There are so many misunderstandings about Germany these days. I am sure that you are not one of those people, Herr Hesse who thinks nothing but bad of Germany; we are, after all, of the same race, yes?'

Henry nodded enthusiastically. *Indeed.*

'But if you are ever in Berlin I could introduce you to people. You will be pleasantly surprised. I would be happy to be of service.'

With that he presented Henry with a card, bowed slightly and then left. Henry looked at the card:

Alois Jäger
Rechtsanwalt
181 Friedrichstraße
Berlin

A Berlin lawyer; you never know.

The next morning, he visited the German Embassy on Willadingweg. As he planned his journey there he remembered Remington-Barber's instructions.

'Whatever you do, Hunter, keep well away from where we are in Thunstrasse. There's a good chance you may be seen, the Germans pretty much keep a permanent watch outside our place. You know how you are to get hold of me.'

He breakfasted at the hotel, returned to his room briefly and then strolled casually through the Old City, past the Münster – the enormous Gothic cathedral, over whose main entrance the sculpted participants in *The Last Judgement* gazed down at him, trying to decide whether he was wicked or virtuous.

He crossed the river on Kirchenfeldbrücke and soon found a taxi which took him to the German Embassy, located in a residential street in the east of the city. A large swastika hung limply over the entrance, which was guarded by half a dozen armed German soldiers. In the street outside were two Swiss policemen.

He had expected a short delay, but not the queue which greeted him. The visa office, the man in front of him explained, did not open until eleven. It would close for lunch at one, re-open again at three and then close at five. The man looked up and down the queue. They do not hurry, he told Henry, but with some luck you may be seen sometime around four. Then you will have to return tomorrow to collect the visa.

He had been standing in the queue for an hour and a half when he heard a familiar voice behind him; Jäger, the Berlin lawyer.

'My dear Hesse, what are you doing in the queue? Come with me.'

To the obvious annoyance of the people in front of him, Henry was removed from the queue and escorted straight into the Embassy.

Wait here.

It was one fifteen now and the visa office had closed for lunch. Ten minutes later and Jäger emerged from it with a clearly reluctant man in tow.

'Hesse: Herr Soldner himself will look after you. You could not be in better hands. He has volunteered to curtail his lunch break in order to deal with your visa.'

It was evident that Herr Soldner was no mere clerk, as much as he looked like one. As they marched through the ground floor of the embassy to his office on the third floor on the third floor colleagues greeted him with a '*Sieg Heil*', which he returned enthusiastically. His office was well appointed, overlooking the gardens at the rear of the embassy. There was a portrait of Hitler on the wall and a large photograph on the desk of Herr Soldner shaking hands with some officers in black uniforms. Next to that was a smaller photograph of Herr Soldner with what he assumed was Frau Soldner and their children. On his lapel was a swastika badge. He gestured for Henry to sit down, removed his spectacles and then read through Henry's form, nodding at times, making notes in the margin in places.

'Please explain the purpose of your visit to Stuttgart, Herr Hesse.'

Henry spoke in standard German, repeating the story that he and Remington-Barber had agreed.

'My stepfather had some business interests in Stuttgart – property mostly. Unfortunately, he died two years ago and I want to ensure that there are no outstanding liabilities. Tie up loose ends, if you like.'

'Do you have any bank accounts in Germany, Herr Hesse?'

'No.'

'Do you have friends in Stuttgart?'

'More like acquaintances – business contacts.'

'Their names please.'

Henry gave the names of the two lawyers they dealt with, along with the three property agents who handled the various properties.

Herr Soldner wrote each name down. He then put down his pen and put on his spectacles.

'The last name you gave me, Herr Hesse – one of the agents.'

'Bermann?'

'Yes: first name please.'

'Heinz: Heinz Bermann.'

'A friend of yours?'

'As I say, more of an acquaintance, a business associate.'

'When did you last see Bermann?'

'Last time I was in Stuttgart, some three years ago.'

'And were you planning to see him this time?'

'Possibly.'

'Do you realise that if you did so Herr Hesse that would be in breach of the conditions of your visa?'

'Really... why is that?'

'The very strong likelihood is that Bermann is a Jew – an enemy of the state.'

With only the briefest hesitation, Henry slapped his thigh in annoyance.

'You don't say! Well that would explain a lot, Herr Soldner. I did not want to say too much before I went there but we never totally trusted this Bermann. We always suspected that he was being less than honest with us. That was one of the reasons for my visit, to find out whether he owed us money. Typical.'

'If he is still in Stuttgart, Herr Hesse, he will no longer have any assets in his own name.'

He wrote on a plain sheet of paper and attached it to the visa application, placing the complete document in a tray.

'Your passport please, Herr Hesse.'

He handed his Swiss passport over to the German.

'Please wait in the reception on the ground floor. I will call you when I am ready. You will understand that I need to make some enquiries.'

–

'The one thing we could get unstuck on, Henry, is if they delve too far back,' Remington-Barber had told him. 'The only problem would be if they found out that either you or your mother also has British nationality.'

'That would be most unlikely. My mother hated being Maureen Hunter, she thought it sounded common. She has always regarded becoming Marlene Hesse and taking on Swiss nationality as the height of sophistication. She changed her name and her nationality when she married Erich Hesse in 1923 and I am certain that she has not used her English name or British identity since then, which is nearly seventeen years ago. Also, remember we moved from Zurich to Geneva after this happened. I became a Swiss national in 1927 and as far as the Swiss authorities are concerned, I'm Henri Hesse.'

'Well, the Germans would have to dig very deep indeed to find all this out and they're only going to do that if they suspect anything. Obviously, we hope that they don't.'

Obviously.

–

An hour later Adolf Hitler was once more staring at Henry Hunter, who was attempting to remain as calm as possible after being summoned back to Herr Soldner's office.

'Your visa is valid for thirty days from next Monday, which is the 1st of July. It expires on the 30th July. You will be in breach of your visa if you are in Germany after that date: do you understand?'

Henry nodded. He was hoping to be back in Switzerland long before then.

'You are only permitted to stay in Stuttgart. While in Germany you must not take part in any political activities; you are prohibited from meeting or consorting with Jews, criminals or other enemies of the state; you will register at a hotel within two hours of your arrival and are not permitted to stay anywhere else during your stay. You are not allowed to approach any military establishments or observe any movements of the armed forces. You are not permitted to take photographs. The only currency that you allowed to use in Germany is Reichsmarks: upon your arrival you are to go to a bank and exchange your Swiss Francs for Reichsmarks. I should warn you that using the black market is regarded as a serious criminal activity. It should not be necessary for me to warn you that should anyone approach you and ask for your help, particularly in regard to bringing information or messages back to Switzerland that is also regarded as a very serious criminal activity. You should immediately report any such approach to the authorities. Do you understand?'

Henry did.

'Good. I do hope that you enjoy your visit to Germany, Herr Hesse.'

—

An hour later Henry Hunter entered a cobblers on an arcade on Kramgasse and explained to the bearded man just visible behind a mound of shoes on the counter he had caught the heel of one of his shoes in the tramline by the station. The cobbler nodded and lifted the counter top, beckoning for Henry to come through.

'Go up the stairs to the very top: He is waiting for you.'

The Hon, Basil Remington-Barber greeted Henry warmly.

'Beauty of this place is that I can get into it through the back of a cafe about five doors along. Now, tell me how you got on.'

Remington-Barber checked the passport and the visa. 'All in order: good.' He was, he said, as certain as he could be that the Germans suspected nothing. For the next hour he gave Henry a detailed briefing on the Stuttgart mission.

'You've got everything, Henry. All clear?'

'Yes, although you say that I am going to be contacted by this Milo. I'm still not sure how I will know that it is him?'

'And I told you – don't worry. Milo will find you: you have memorised the codes so you will know. The less you know before you meet up, the safer it is.'

'In case I am caught?'

'Exactly, in case you are caught. Remember, you do whatever Milo tells you, you understand?' Henry said he did.

'There's plenty of Swiss Francs in this envelope here: change them into Reichsmarks as soon as you arrive – don't risk hiding any on you. Go back now to the Schweizerhof and check out: there's a direct train to Geneva at six thirty. Before you leave the Schweizerhof ask them to make you a reservation at the Hotel Victoria in Stuttgart, arriving Tuesday the sixteenth, leaving on the Friday – the nineteenth.

It looks better if you leave a couple of weeks between the visa being granted and you actually travelling there: makes it appear that you're not rushing. Understand?'

Henry nodded.

'One other thing: be careful at night in Stuttgart. There is a curfew on and few places to eat so you are to eat in the hotel. On the first night certainly you should order room service: in my experience that tends to draw less attention to yourself.'

'And how would you like me to get to Stuttgart?'

'On the Monday morning you take the train from Geneva to Zurich: tell your mother you will be there all week. Give her this address; we'll cover any contacts there. Stay overnight at the Central Plaza hotel by Oetenbachgasse, it is very near the station: a room has been booked for you there. On Tuesday morning there's a Swissair flight from Zurich to Stuttgart. It should only take fifty minutes, here's hoping the RAF doesn't shoot you down!'

Chapter 9

Salzburg Airport, July 1940

Early in the afternoon of the last Tuesday in July, at the height of the Austrian summer, half a dozen men were doing their best to avoid each other in a stuffy room overlooking the runway at Salzburg Airport. The men were all dressed in uniforms denoting high rank in various branches of the German armed forces: two stood by the large window but well apart from each other; another appeared to be asleep; two others were leafing through their copies of *Völkischer Beobachter* and another was pacing the room, drawing hard on a cigarette as he did so.

A short while after the clock struck two, a nervous young Luftwaffe officer entered the room. 'A delay: many apologies. The plane was delayed after refuelling in Munich. Departure will now be at three o'clock – four at the latest.'

Much muttering and shaking of heads around the room: the young Luftwaffe officer paused in the doorway just long enough to remember to give a hurried '*Heil Hitler*' salute which was ignored by all the others.

The man who had appeared to be asleep stood up and carefully straightened his Kriegsmarine uniform before leaving the room. Outside was a small lawn with flowers planted neatly around its edges. He strolled up and down and was soon joined by an army officer, one of the two men who had been by the window. The admiral and the general walked in step alongside each other in silence for a while. The general took his time lighting a large cigar before addressing his companion.

'I see we cannot even rely on the Luftwaffe to get us back to Berlin on time! I imagine that Jodl's plane was not delayed.'

'He flew back last night, I understand: soon after the briefing,' said the admiral, looking around as he spoke. 'He probably did not want to hang around too long.'

'Indeed. I assume he wanted to avoid our questions,' said the general, speaking in a louder voice than his companion.

The admiral nodded and looked over each shoulder before he spoke. 'And how is your son?'

The *Generalmajor* paused, slightly surprised by the question. In the circles he moved in, in Berlin, asking questions about an acquaintance's family, especially sons in the armed forces, was a form of code – a way of broaching the sensitive issue of what one really thought about the war. It was the same as discussing food shortages with people. These were questions only asked to people you could really trust.

'Karl is well, thank you; he's an *Oberleutnant* now, based in Poland. And yours? You have two don't you?'

'One son, one daughter. Ernst joined the Kriegsmarine naturally, but unlike his father, uncles and grandfather he seems to prefer to be under the water rather than on its surface! He's with the 7th U-boat flotilla based in Kiel.'

The two men paused to watch a Luftwaffe Junkers passenger plane pass low overhead from the south, neatly framed against Untersberg mountain. The plane banked to the left and began its noisy approach to the runway.

'That must be our plane; we could well be back in Berlin this evening after all. Tell me Ernst: what do you make of what Jodl had to say...?'

Generalmajor Ernst turned to face his companion, carefully studying his face. He wanted to be sure he was not being led into a trap.

'You mean about...?' It was clear he wanted the admiral to say it first.

'The invasion plans: what else were we there for?'

'He only wants us to *plan* for an invasion of the Soviet Union, Hans. That is probably prudent don't you think – to make contingency plans, in case...?'

'Come on Ernst: we have known each other for many years! I was watching you yesterday during Jodl's briefing, you hardly looked enthusiastic. It's madness, you must know that better than me. Just imagine for a moment that you were a British general rather than a German one and you had found out that the *Führer* had ordered his high command to turn up in Bad Reichenhall yesterday to be instructed to plan for an invasion of the Soviet Union. You'd be delighted, wouldn't you?'

The *Generalmajor* shrugged. Behind them a plane was noisily taxiing in front of the building where they had been waiting. 'I think our flight will be ready soon, Hans.'

'Come on Ernst, answer my question. If you were a British general you would be very pleased to hear that Germany was planning to break its alliance with the Soviet Union and fight on two fronts, would you not?'

'I think that more than anything, Hans, I would be surprised. So surprised in fact that I would struggle to believe it.'

Chapter 10

'I was only asking what business it is that you have in Zurich, Henry. Surely I have a right to ask? One minute you're off to Basle, then Zurich… wherever next?'

Marlene Hesse had little choice but to accept her son's imminent and largely unexplained departure with her customary lack of grace. Henry had come to learn that these days all he needed to do was tell her what he was doing and then leave it at that.

He arrived in Zurich on the Monday and spent that night in a hotel on Oetenbachgasse where his flight tickets were waiting for him. He left the hotel early the next morning and took the airport bus from Hauptbahnhof station at seven o'clock.

The flight left on time at eight fifteen, the Swissair DC3 banking heavily to the east before climbing noisily through the cloud and then appearing to float as they headed north and crossed the border. The plane landed at Stuttgart Echterdingen just after nine thirty; a few minutes before they had begun their descent the two stewardesses had come round and drawn all the curtains. Henry was in a single seat, but he heard a man sitting in a double seat across the aisle from him explain to his neighbour in French that they always did this. 'It is a military airport now. They don't want us to spy on the Luftwaffe!'

The captain welcomed them to Germany, with a noticeable lack of enthusiasm. 'Please respect all the special security rules in place at airport. Please follow all instructions. Passengers for the onward flight to Berlin should remain in their seats. Passengers disembarking here in Stuttgart should ensure they have all their belongings with them.

We hope that you have enjoyed flying with Swissair. We wish you a pleasant stay in Stuttgart.'

The plane taxied to a remote part of the airport: outside they could hear shouting and the noise of engines. The passengers were led down the steps to a bus with blacked out windows that had drawn up alongside it. Henry had no more than thirty seconds to glance around as they were led onto the bus: he could see very little, other than a ring of troops around the plane and a couple of oil tankers nearby.

There were few other passengers in the vast terminal building, although at the far end Henry could see groups of men in uniform hurrying along. At the other end of the terminal were the airline desks, most of which appeared to be abandoned. There were a few people waiting by one of the Deutsche Lufthansa desks but the only other airline desks that seemed to be operating were Swissair and Ala Littoria. While he waited there were a few announcements made by a woman just managing to suppress her Swabian accent: *'Arriving passengers should wait until they are called; any passengers for the Swissair flight to Berlin are to proceed to the departure gate immediately; a further delay is announced on the Deutsche Lufthansa flight to Lisbon, Portugal.'*

Henry was questioned by two men stood behind the desk; one in SS uniform, the other in a cheap suit with a swastika badge on each lapel. Behind them was a large clock with enormous swastika banners draped on either side.

They each checked the visa, silently. The man in civilian clothes left the desk at one stage with Henry's passport, but returned a minute later.

'How long are you intending to stay in Stuttgart, Herr Hesse?'

'Until Friday.'

'You have a return ticket?'

Henry handed it to them and they both studied it before returning it.

'And the purpose of your visit?'

'Where are you staying?'

'With whom will you be meeting?'

'Are you aware of the restrictions of your visa?'

All questions that had already been asked at the embassy in Bern: Remington-Barber had warned him of this. *Routine. They will just trying to catch you out. They'll be looking to compare your answers. Nothing to worry about. Just play a straight bat. Don't smile too much. Don't get impatient.*

'We would like to know more about your business affairs in Stuttgart, Herr Hesse' said the civilian.

An unnecessarily detailed and complicated account of how his stepfather's business affairs in Stuttgart followed. Henry told how he suspected they had been mishandled by a man called Heinz Bermann – at the mention of which there was a knowing look between the two Germans – and how following his stepfather's death, which was probably hastened by the activities of this Heinz Bermann, it was taking time to unravel everything but he felt it was his duty to come here and see what was going on… and so on. It had the desired effect of making the two officials look bored. Henry hoped to God that poor old Heinz Bermann had managed to get out of Stuttgart: he was a decent man and had always been very charming. It would be a shame if Henry had just added to his woes.

After ten minutes, Henry was taken through to a small side room where he and his bags were thoroughly searched by two policemen. His copy of that morning's *Neue Zürcher Zeitung* was removed from his briefcase and thrown away. Everything else was carefully examined. Nothing else aroused their suspicion, other than the Swiss Francs.

'Are you changing all of these here?' the official in charge of the search asked.

Henry nodded.

'Wait here while I count them.'

The official left the room, returning with the francs five minutes later. Later, Henry would discover that the official had helped himself to some of the money.

He emerged from the side room into the queue in front of yet another desk, but this was a much quicker process. His passport was stamped again and he was now in Germany.

'You are now permitted to cross the border, Herr Hesse. Please go the cashier's window over there and change all money into Reichsmarks. Welcome to Germany.'

Henry changed his money and then joined a queue which had formed just outside the terminal for the bus into the city. The journey took half an hour: again, the curtains were drawn and it was difficult to make out where they were, other than through occasional glimpses through the front window. Henry thought he recognised one or two familiar sights and as far as he could tell, there were few signs of the war, other than a good deal of military traffic on the road. They passed through two road-blocks, at the final one of which three policemen climbed on board and checked everyone's papers.

'*Stuttgart-Mitte*,' announced the driver: The bus pulled into Fürstenstrasse, just off the enormous Schlossplatz.

It was no more than three or four minutes' walk to the hotel and Henry knew the area well, but somehow the city centre did not feel familiar, although it was hard for him to put a finger on precisely why. The buildings were the same and he recognised the street names and knew exactly where he was. But for him any city had always had a unique atmosphere to it, which was hard to describe but he knew it when he was there. Despite its familiarity, Stuttgart did not feel like somewhere he had ever been to before, as if he had only ever seen it on film. The city now had an undoubted military edge to it; so many of the people on the streets seemed to be wearing a uniform of one type or another and there were anti-aircraft batteries on the Schlossplatz. Most of the buildings had large red and black swastika flags draped from them.

By the time he had reached the Hotel Victoria on the corner of Friedrichstrasse and Keplerstrasse and walked through its ornate entrance he had a better idea why Stuttgart felt so unfamiliar. It was the people and how they behaved, moving around in silence, hardly anyone speaking to anyone else and all of them appearing to avoid eye contact. A city that he had once found friendly now had a distinctly menacing air to it. Germans had always struck him as being smartly dressed but now, compared to the relative sophistication of the Swiss, they looked drab.

The man behind the reception desk did, at least, look him in the eye. 'Yes, we have a reservation for you, Herr Hesse,' he said, holding up the telegram from the Schweizerhof in Bern. 'You are staying for three nights, correct?'

Henry said that was indeed correct and completed the various forms handed to him by the receptionist. He was then escorted to his room on the third floor by an elderly and evidently arthritic porter. Once he had unpacked, he decided to go for a walk in the afternoon. As tempting as remaining in the relative safety of his room was, he knew that would draw attention to himself and also would not allow Milo the opportunity to approach him, though he was still none the wiser how that was going to happen. Remington-Barber had been decidedly cryptic with regards to that during their meeting in Bern.

'You will be approached by someone using the phrase "We usually have some rain in Stuttgart at this time of year",' Remington-Barber had said. 'You are to reply "That must be the case all over Europe". In response they will say "Surely there must be rain over the Alps". You will reply "There is always rain around the Alps even in summer" and when they say "How wonderful" then you know it is Milo speaking to you and that it is safe.'

Remington-Barber had asked him to repeat that, many times.

'Good: you are to do precisely what Milo tells you. If they send you somewhere, you go.'

So Henry wandered around the centre of Stuttgart for the best part of an hour and a half and as far as he could tell, he was not being followed. From Schlossplatz he walked down the Planie, which had now become Adolf Hitler Strasse and then into Charlottenplatz, which was now Danziger-Freiheit. *A different city.* He sat on benches, paused by shop windows – noticing that there seemed to be far less in the stores than on previous visits. He crossed the road and back again, allowing anyone wanting to approach him plenty of opportunity to do so. He was beginning to get a sense of what a country at war felt like: it was as if the horizon was diminished and there was less air to breathe. Less colour, so much quieter and the ubiquitous slogans on buildings and flags hanging from them. From Danziger-Freiheit, he headed north to Neckarstrasse, where one of his stepfather's property agents had their offices. He decided to go in there and then, just in case he was being followed – it was good to be able to show that the reasons he had given for visiting Stuttgart appeared to be genuine. Herr Langhoff took him into his office and was happy to talk for a while: times were very hard; many people had joined the military; Jewish property was being given away which meant less business for them. No, as Herr Hesse was surely aware, all of his stepfather's properties had been disposed of.

He left the office after half an hour, satisfied that anyone watching would feel that he had indeed been in there to conduct business. A few doors along he found a small basement bar. The barmaid knew better than to ask too many questions, especially when she realised he was Swiss. After a drink he left the bar and walked back across the Schlossplatz to the hotel, concerned at how and when Milo was going to approach him: he could hardly spend the next few days doing little more than hanging around the hotel, going for the occasional walk and eating in his room.

He wandered around the lobby for a while and then returned to his room. He closed the heavy curtains with their view over Keplerstrasse and then ran a hot bath, rested, read a little before telephoning reception to order his evening meal. There were three dishes on the menu, only one of which was available: sausages and potatoes.

After his meal he left the tray, as instructed, in the corridor outside his room. It was only eight o'clock but he began to think about settling down for the night. He was beginning to think that this trip was no more than a test by British Intelligence to see how he coped – whether he could get in and out of Germany and no more than that. The more he thought about it, the more sense it made. After all, hadn't Edgar more or less told him that his mission would be something relatively straightforward? Whichever way you looked at it, he told himself, travelling into Germany and meeting with another agent was hardly straightforward. The British were unlikely to risk a novice agent's first assignment on anything too dangerous. Surely they would simply want to see whether he had the nerves to go there and return in one piece?

But what was it Viktor had told him at the weekend? '*Don't think too much, synok: they will know what they are doing.*'

There was an easy chair near a radiator by the window and he sat on it, kicking of his shoes and putting his feet on the small table. He began to recall another conversation with Edgar, when he had implied that they may advance 500 pounds of his aunt's money on successful completion of a mission. Would this count as a successful mission? Maybe he could now afford a car. He watched the patterns forming on the ceiling by the lampshade by the bed when a firm knock on the door disturbed his train of thought. He was annoyed, assuming that they had come to collect his dinner tray when in fact he had left it in the corridor.

'The tray is out there for you,' he called out.

A female voice replied. 'Thank you, Herr Hesse. Please could I come in? We have managed to locate your missing case.'

'I think there must be some mistake, I...'

A car door slammed on Keplerstrasse followed by the sound of a lorry moving down the road.

'There is no need to worry sir, I am the duty manager: if you could open the door please?'

The woman who Henry let into his room was wearing the dark formal uniform of the hotel staff. On her lapel was a badge: Katharina Hoch, Night Manager. She closed the door carefully behind her and then looked him up and down, as if checking him out. 'It is good news that we found your case, Herr Hesse.' She was carrying a small leather suitcase.

'There has been a mistake I am afraid. I have my case here. I only brought the one with me.'

'Are you enjoying your stay at the Hotel Victoria?'

'I am but—'

'And in Stuttgart: you are enjoying Stuttgart? We usually have some rain in Stuttgart at this time of year.'

Henry felt unsteady on his feet. *Milo?* 'I beg your pardon?'

She replied in a pleasant, conversational manner.

'We usually have some rain in Stuttgart at this time of year.'

114

Henry sat down on the edge of the bed, aware that he was shaking violently. He took a moment or two to remember his correct response.

'That must be the case all over Europe.'

Was it safe to have a conversation like this in a hotel room?

'Surely,' she said, checking behind the curtains and then glimpsing into the bathroom, 'surely there must be rain over the Alps?'

'There is always rain around the Alps even in summer.'

'How wonderful,' she replied, like she really meant it.

There was a long silence. Another car door slammed on Keplerstrasse; the sound of distant laughter. The woman smiled at him in what in other circumstances he would have taken to quite a seductive manner. Her mouth was quite beautiful, without any trace of lipstick.

'So you are Milo?' He was speaking in barely more than a whisper.

'I am Milo, yes – don't look so shocked. Look, I am on duty so I do not have too long and we have much to talk about.'

'Is it safe in here?'

'Do you mean are we being listened to? You do not need be concerned. We provide the Gestapo with a list of all new guests and the ones that they have some interest in we have to put in special rooms on the fifth floor, so you don't need to worry, not for now at least.'

She lifted the suitcase onto the bed and opened it. It was full of men's clothes, along with a hat and a pair of black shoes. 'Have you ever been to Essen, Herr Hesse?'

'Where?'

'Essen. In the Ruhr: north of Cologne.'

'No, I can't say that I have.'

'Tomorrow will be your first visit then.'

'But... surely not? My visa does not permit me to travel outside of Stuttgart.'

'That is what all this is about.' She pointed at the suitcase on the bed. 'Henri Hesse will not be travelling to Essen. You will travel as Dieter Hoch.' She had removed a wallet from the suitcase and emptied its contents onto the bed.

'Dieter Hoch is my brother. Dieter is four years older than you but the photograph in his identity card here is not a good one and so we are confident that your identity documents will pass a basic examination. It will work as long as no one has any reason to suspect you. You will only wear these clothes here: they all belong to my brother. Everything that you wear will be German made. There must be nothing on you that could identify you as being Swiss. You will take this suitcase.'

'And your brother is in on this?'

'Of course: we both do what we can to help the British. We are not Nazis, you may have gathered that. Dieter is a manager with the railway here in Stuttgart, which means that he is able to travel more freely on trains. He has worked for the past seven days and finished this evening, so now he is off work until Friday morning. He will remain at home until then and will not leave the house: he will tell my parents he is unwell. That gives you two clear days to get to Essen, complete your mission there and return here. We want you back in Stuttgart before the curfew on Thursday night.'

'But what about the hotel? Won't people spot that I'm not here?'

'I am the duty manager for the next two nights. I will ensure that all the paper work is in order. I will also come up during the night to ensure that the room looks as if someone has slept in it. As I say, no one suspects you. The Gestapo is kept very busy enough with people that it does suspect.'

'And what do I do in Essen?'

'Do you know anything about Essen?'

Henry shrugged. *Not really.*

'Essen is a major producer of steel and coal. The Krupps family own much of the industry in the town. The steel that is produced there is vital to the Nazi war effort. The British wish to destroy the factories, but their intelligence is poor. Some of the locations that the British are aware of are no longer in use, others have been opened. They are in the process of compiling a much more accurate map of Essen. That is your mission, to assist in that.'

'So I just wander around Essen drawing maps?'

Katharina Hoch looked irritated. 'I will give you the details of how to make contact with someone in Essen. But this is going to be a dangerous mission: you will be required to move around Essen, memorise what you see and then compile a grid of locations which you will then bring back to Stuttgart. Throughout Germany life is dangerous, but in Essen especially so.'

Chapter 11

Essen, July 1940

He was woken at five in the morning by Katharina Hoch; a gentle rap on the door so as not to disturb other guests. He washed and shaved, dressed in her brother's clothes and double-checked the minutiae of his new identity: address, date of birth – the details that could trip him up.

He left the room as quietly as possible and descended through the fire exit stairs at the end of the corridor to the basement level, where Katharina was waiting for him.

She looked him over, like a parent checking that a child was properly dressed for school. She asked him to empty his pockets to be sure that he was carrying nothing incriminating: everything was in order.

'This is your ticket here for the rail journey: the train leaves at six o'clock, in twenty five minutes. The train is scheduled to arrive in Frankfurt at ten o'clock: Dieter says that this train tends to run on time. It is carrying troops so is less likely to be subject to delays. At Frankfurt you should purchase a ticket to Essen: there is a direct service that departs at a quarter to eleven and is due to arrive in Essen at a quarter past two or fourteen fifteen, that's how they like us to refer to it these days, presumably they think it makes everything sound more efficient. Dieter says he knows less about that part of the DR network, so you may encounter delays. Now you remember I told you last night about the purpose of your visit to Essen, in case anyone asks you?'

'Visiting an aunt?'

'Correct: Gertraud Traugott recently celebrated her eightieth birthday and as you have not seen her in a while this is a surprise visit. She lives in an apartment in the west of Essen, in Altendorf. This is her address, please copy it down now in your own handwriting and put the piece of paper with the address on it in your wallet.'

She waited patiently while Henry copied down the address, folded the piece of paper and placed it in the wallet.

'But you are not to go straight to that address. When you arrive at Essen station you are to go to the lost property office, which is located behind the main ticket office. You will find that it is well signposted. In the unlikely event that you arrive in Essen before two o'clock, don't go in any earlier. If you arrive after four o'clock, wait outside the office. You have a contact in Essen who is going to help you and he works in the lost property office. His codename is Lido. He is always on his own there between two and four. Go into the office and enquire if anyone has handed in a gentleman's umbrella, which you mislaid that morning. He will ask you to describe it and you will say that it is black with a carved wooden handle engraved with the initials "DH". He will then ask you to come into the back of the office to inspect the umbrellas. Once there, and when it is safe, Lido will brief you on what is to happen during your stay in Essen.'

'And what if he isn't there?'

'If he isn't there or something goes wrong you should try and get out of Essen as soon as possible and head back to Stuttgart. Lido has very limited information about who you are or even where you are coming from, so your security should not be compromised if he is arrested.'

Henry tried to take all of this in: the detail was one thing but the sense of fear quite another. He was beginning to shiver, despite the warmth of the basement.

'It is nearly a quarter to six; you need to get a move on. Wear your hat; it will help mask your identity. Carry the raincoat. The next thing I have to say is very important: in the event of you being arrested, your story will not stand a lot of scrutiny. It will not take the Gestapo long to find out that you are not Dieter Hoch or that Gertraud Traugott is not your aunt. Hopefully, it will not come to that, but if you do find yourself being interrogated by the Gestapo you must do your best to hold out for twenty-four hours. That will give us enough time to dismantle our cell here in Stuttgart and try and escape.'

Katharina put her arm around his shoulder and leaned close to him. Her mouth looked even more astonishing close up. Her eyes did not blink as she stared straight into his.

'Twenty-four hours, that is all that we ask. Tell them you are a Swiss citizen and your passport is here in the hotel to prove it. They will probably not kill you – the Germans cannot afford to upset the Swiss. But if you keep your wits about you hopefully you will not arouse suspicion. You must leave now.'

'There is one final thing that you should know: there is a pencil case in the suitcase, in a zipped compartment in the lid. Under no circumstances should you take it out of the case or open it. You are to give it Lido. That is very important. Do you understand?'

He nodded that he understood. Katharina led him up a steep flight of concrete steps to a door that led directly onto Keplerstrasse. She motioned for him to wait while she looked up and down the street, and then waved him to come up. She pushed him along with a whispered 'Good luck'.

It was already light and it was a quick five minutes' walk down Friedrichstrasse to the main station, which was reassuringly busy. He had just enough time to stop at a kiosk and buy a bread roll with cold sausage and a copy of that morning's *Völkischer Beobachter*.

He spotted the Frankfurt train on platform six, with long lines of troops in black forming to board it. Small clouds of steam floated across the station and the smell of engine oil and the sounds of metal and whistles and people calling out all felt oddly reassuring. He showed his ticket to the man at the barrier and then a policeman asked to check his papers, but was quick to wave him through. Just as he was about to board the train, he felt a hand on his shoulder and when he turned round it was an officer in black uniform. He noticed the distinctive Death Head symbol: SS. He felt like laughing. He had not even managed to board the train to Frankfurt. It had all been a trap.

'Do you have a light?' The officer was holding an unlit cigarette and smiling. 'I seem to have found myself with a unit where no one smokes. Imagine that!'

Henry apologised profusely. 'I don't smoke either.' *Perhaps I ought to take it up*, he thought as he climbed into his carriage.

–

He was both surprised and relieved when the train from Frankfurt pulled into Essen Main at twenty minutes past two that Wednesday afternoon. The journey could not have gone more smoothly; the Stuttgart train had arrived in Frankfurt at ten o'clock, allowing him ample time to buy his ticket for Essen and still be able to sit in a small cafe on one of the platforms where he sipped a cup of bitter ersatz coffee and glanced at the *Völkischer Beobachter*. He was able to board the Essen train at half ten when the barrier opened, with the policeman on duty giving his identity card no more than a cursory look. The train was packed all the way to Cologne, so he closed his eyes to avoid being drawn into conversation during the journey up the Ruhr. Inevitably, as he began to doze, Roza appeared before him: gentle at first, as always. Her fingers lightly touching his wrist and a shy smile as she tossed her hair back from her face. And then the fingers grasped his wrist so tightly that he could feel the pain and that was followed by her looking at him with more hate than he could imagine: 'You know what will happen to us now, don't you?' He was about to explain when she began to fade away, asking one further question as she did so: 'Where are you going?' He sat up with a start, concerned he may have said something, but no one in the carriage so much as looked at him. *Where am I going? Where indeed?*

As the train reached Essen, enormous factories loomed either side of the track, with thick plumes of filthy smoke reaching far into the grey sky. The station was not nearly as large as the ones in Stuttgart or Frankfurt and there seemed to be less security. There was a noticeable smell of coal and industrial fumes and the large swastika flags draped above the platform were streaked with grime. He decided not to go to the lost property office straight away; he needed to get a sense of his surroundings. He studied the timetable on the side of the ticket office. If he needed to leave Essen quickly there was a train to Dortmund in ten minutes and one to Cologne in twenty minutes. There was a cafe on the platform but he felt too sick with nerves to even enter it.

He waited until two thirty and then entered the lost property office. A man in DR uniform was behind a long, low counter, attending to an elderly lady.

'I can assure you that I have looked very carefully and more than once, as you ask. There is no sign of your gloves. They may still be elsewhere in the station: I suggest you try again tomorrow. I will keep a special eye out for them.'

Henry waited until she had left. The man behind the counter looked to be in his late fifties at least and moved in a slow and quite deliberate manner. The man looked tired, his hair a steely-white. His most noticeable feature was an impressive pair of eyebrows that seemed to join up above is nose and curved up at either end, lending him an owl-like air.

'Can I help you, sir?'

Henry glanced around to ensure that they were on their own.

'I appear to have lost my umbrella.'

No pause, no flicker of understanding, no sign of anticipation from the man behind the counter.

'And when did you lose it sir?'

'This morning: it's black with a carved wooden handle. My initials are engraved on the handle: "DH".'

The man behind the counter shook his head.

'I cannot recall it but perhaps you would like to come behind the counter and have a look? We have quite a collection of umbrellas here sir: I could open a shop!'

The man lifted up a section of the counter and slowly led Henry to a room at the back of the office. He closed the door and removed his cap, turning to face Henry.

'I'm Lido, by the way.'

'I gathered that: Dieter.'

Lido grasped Henry's hand and shook it warmly, holding his wrist with his left hand as he did so.

'There are some umbrellas over there, pretend to be looking through them. I'll look out of the window in case anyone comes in, but it is very quiet at this time of the afternoon. It is very quiet most of the time now. People don't seem to lose things in the war, apart from their lives.'

Lido spoke quickly and quietly, looking out of the little office window towards the counter as he did so.

'Just wait a moment.'

A woman with two young children had come in and Lido went over to the counter and after a very quick conversation she left. He came back to Henry.

'Every other person who comes in here thinks we are the left luggage department. It says very clearly that we are lost property. Stuttgart explained that your cover for visiting Essen is to visit your aunt, yes? Let me tell you then that Gertraud Traugott is an elderly neighbour of mine. I live in an apartment block in Altendorf; her apartment is two doors down from me. However, Gertraud Traugott has not been in her apartment for three or four months now. She started to lose her mind a year ago, although she seemed capable enough of looking after herself. In November they took her into a sanatorium near Oberhausen. I went to visit her last month: she tells everyone there that she is engaged to the Kaiser and she is waiting for him to come and take her away. I am not sure how long she will be there – one hears terrible rumours these days about what they are doing to people like her, but that is another story. Now, you need to listen very carefully and I will tell you what you need to do.'

–

At ten to three Henry left the station by the north exit and headed into the centre of Essen. 'I finish work at four,' Lido had said. 'Wait for me by the Hindenburg Strasse exit. I will come out just after five past four. Follow me all the way to Altendorf – I will make sure that I take a route that takes you past as many factories as possible. Make sure you memorise everything. And don't forget to follow me at a safe distance, not too close, not too far. Can you remember all that?'

He could remember all that. He also remembered his training and the need to avoid wandering around a place without any apparent purpose. He used the hour and a bit he was going to spend in the centre of Essen had a purpose to purchase a gift for his aunt: he was there to celebrate her eightieth birthday after all.

Lido had agreed that this was a good idea. 'Go past the Handelshof Hotel and the Opera House and you'll reach Adolf Hitler Platz. The best places to go shopping are to the north and the west of that – around Verein Strasse and Logen Strasse. Any idea of what kind of gift you are going to buy?'

Perfume, they had agreed. 'Any woman appreciates perfume; no one is going to think that is an odd gift.'

He followed Lido's instructions: he had plenty of time, so he made sure he did not rush. Lido had said he thought there may be a perfume shop somewhere past Logen Strasse. It wasn't something he ever had occasion to shop for these days, he had said. In an arcade off Limbecker Strasse he found exactly what he was looking for, a quaint *Parfümerie*: all wooden beams and leaded windows, reached by climbing down a couple of worn steps. There was a sign on the door to ring the bell and when he did so it was a minute or two before the elderly owner shuffled along to unlock the door.

'My apologies: when I am preparing perfumes at the back I lock the door, I have had people stealing bottles in the past. Perhaps I should be more trusting these days. After all, it is not as if Jews come into the shop any more.' Henry noticed that the owner was wearing the distinctive round Nazi Party membership badge on his lapel, a black swastika stark on a white background. The shop was tiny, with all the walls and counters covered in bottles of perfume in every imaginable size and colour. The smell was close to overpowering.

'Now, how can I help you?'

Henry explained that he was looking for a perfume for his aunt, for her eightieth birthday. The owner perused the shelves. 'Maybe something with lavender in it? That is always popular with older ladies – or perhaps bergamot? What kind of a lady is she?'

Henry explained that he had not seen her in a while, this was a surprise visit.

'You do not sound as if you are from this area?'

'No, I am from… the south.'

'I see: whereabouts in the south?'

'Stuttgart,' said Henry, regretting his answer straight away.

'You do not have that dreadful Swabian accent, thank God! You have travelled a long way to see your aunt. Where does she live in Essen?'

'Altendorf.'

'Altendorf? I know it well. I lived there myself for many years, before my wife died and my children left Essen. What is your aunt's name?'

Henry hesitated. There was something about the owner that he found unsettling. It was not the Nazi Party badge, half the population of Germany seemed to wear one of those these days as far as he could tell and it was probably good for business. No, the questions seemed to be pointed and persistent rather than friendly. It was as if he distrusted Henry.

'Maybe I will come back later. I need to do some more shopping.'

'Your aunt's name, you were going to tell me her name?'

'Gertraud. Gertraud Traugott.'

'Gertraud? But I know Gertraud Traugott, I know her very well! Tell me, how are you related to her?'

Henry momentarily considered leaving the shop, but had already revealed too much; Gertraud Traugott's name and Stuttgart. *Trapped*.

'I told you, she is my aunt.'

'But on which side?'

'My mother was her sister.'

The old man nodded as if he was satisfied with the answer. Henry felt a sense of relief. He had overreacted.

'Ah, so you are Hannelore's son?'

'That's right, yes.' He managed a weak smile and felt faintly relieved. The old man leant against the counter, so close that Henry could smell the garlic on his breath.

'Gertraud has no sister. She had a brother but he was killed in the Great War and had no children. And she has not lived in Altendorf for months. You cannot be her nephew. Who the hell are you?'

The old man's hand move along the counter towards the telephone. Henry moved fast. He reached over the counter and pushed the man as hard as he could against the shelves behind him. His head struck one of the large glass bottles and he slumped to the floor. A few of the bottles fell on top of him, the glass shattering and the perfume spilling over the old man, who was now groaning. Henry darted over to the door and locked it, turning the sign round so that it would show that the shop was closed. *Geschlossen.*

He climbed over the counter and dragged the limp body into the small room at the back of the shop where the man had been preparing the perfumes and closed the door into the shop. The old man was bleeding from the head and soaked in perfume. Henry could hear someone trying to open the door, the handle turning against the lock and then a knock. The shopkeeper stirred, as if trying to call out. Henry held one hand firmly against his mouth and then gripped his head with the other. The man struggled, so Henry knelt on top of him, one knee pressed hard into his chest, his eyes bulging and his face turning bright red. The knocking stopped and it was quiet outside, but Henry continued to hold the man down. The struggle lasted for what seemed like an age. He could feel something hot and wet against his hand over the man's mouth. Blood was trickling out of his nose.

And then it stopped. The body suddenly slumped, all the resistance had flooded out of it and Henry knew he was dead. For a few minutes he sat on the floor, catching his breath and gathering his thoughts, watching the old man for any sign of life. The broken bottles of perfume filled the room with the smells of citron, sandalwood and rose. He went back into the shop and drew the blinds on the door and windows. From the till he removed all the notes that were there and left the till open. He turned off the shop lights and went back into the room, taking care to shut the internal door and lock it. He had already noticed that there was another door from the room which he assumed would lead outside. He undid the bolts and carefully opened it just a few inches. Outside was a narrow, enclosed alleyway, the buildings opposite almost within touching distance. He went back inside the shop and removed the old man's wristwatch: this needed to look like a robbery. He was about to leave when he had another thought. From the old man's lapel he removed the Nazi Party membership badge, checked that nothing was engraved on the back and then put it on his own jacket. As he did so, he noticed that his raincoat, which had been on the floor alongside the man, had some bloodstains on the sleeve and reeked of perfume. He bundled it up, hoping to find somewhere nearby to dispose of it.

He carefully opened the door to the alleyway once more. It was dark and, as far as he could tell, deserted. He pulled his trilby low over his face and hurried down the alleyway, eventually emerging into Webster Strasse. Just before he did so he noticed a large bin that was nearly full. He looked around him and then leant into the bin, pushing his coat as far into it as he could manage, covering it over as best he could with the other rubbish.

Lido was shocked to see him when he appeared in the Lost Property Office. It was five to four and he was preparing to close for the day. Fortunately, there was no one else there. Lido gestured for him to come to the office at the back.

'What the hell are you doing here?' he hissed. 'I thought I told you to meet me in Hindenberg Strasse?'

Henry explained what had happened. Lido sat with his head in his hands.

'I am sorry, but I had no alternative. For some reason, he suspected me. I should never have given him Gertraud Traugott's name of course, but how on earth was I to know he knew her...? What were the chances of that? If I hadn't given a name, that would have looked suspicious too. At least I did my best to make it look like a robbery.'

'That is the problem with this town, everyone knows everyone. Did anyone see you enter the shop?'

'Not as far as I know. It was very quiet.'

'At least you got rid of the coat. That could identify you too. Here, choose another one, there are a dozen or so on the rack over there. It was a dark brown rain coat you were wearing, is that correct?'

'Yes.'

'Choose one of the black ones then. And change your hat too. Choose something different from that trilby. You'd better give me the watch you took from him.'

Lido examined the watch with a professional interest.

'Shame, it is a good watch, but too distinctive. I'll lose it down a drain. My guess is that it will be a few hours at least before he is discovered. You are sure you locked the door?'

'Yes.'

'Let's hope so. We had better go back to the original plan. You leave now and start following me once I emerge in Hindenburg Strasse.'

Lido called him back just as he was leaving the Lost Property Office.

'Did you remove everything from the pockets of your coat?'

'I didn't have anything in them, as far as I was aware.'

'Are you sure?'

Henry left the office without replying. If only he was sure.

–

Lido emerged from the station into Hindenburg Strasse at ten past four. Without pausing, changing his pace or looking around him, he walked on, turning left at the Krupps Hotel and then left again into what, to all intents and purposes, looked like a factory. Towering above him on either side of the road were vast industrial buildings, whose sheer height shut out much of the daylight. He could feel the fumes fill his lungs, but the most overpowering sensation was the noise: it was not simply the volume, that was to be expected, but more the physical effect it had, sending tremors throughout his body. The buildings on the south side of the road seemed to be denser and every so often Lido would remove his hat and scratch his head for a moment or two before putting it back on. That was the signal for Henry to take special note, which may be the entrance of another factory, usually with a board outside. Most of the entrances had sentries outside them, their gaze following him as he walked past.

It soon became obvious to Henry that goods were moved around the factories and the town by rail: at frequent points on their journey the road was bisected by railway lines and bridges. They had to wait at one or two of these for trains to pass, which gave Henry a good opportunity to look around. He was making mental notes; of where different factories were in relation to one another, their names, where the railway lines went, where any power plants appeared to be located.

After a while he noticed that Lido had slowed down his pace and kept removing his cap, scratching his head. A factory to their left was more or less open to road and in it he could see half built tanks and what appeared to be heavy artillery lined up in a yard. A bit further on they had to pause: a soldier was ordering pedestrians to stand back while a group of workers, all under close guard, were led past them. There were about thirty gaunt men in the group, all dressed in a rough grey uniform. He heard them talking quietly as walked past him: he was sure that they were speaking Polish.

Soon after that, they emerged from the complex of factories although the smell and the noise lingered on. They were now in the Altendorf district. Lido stopped to tie a shoelace, which was the signal for Henry to drop back further: they were nearing the apartment. Just after a school, Lido turned right into Rullich Strasse and at that point Henry slowed down even more to allow Lido to get out of his sight. He knew to turn from Rullich Strasse into Ehrenzeller Strasse and then into the apartment block towards the end of the street. It was a large block; four stories high with the apartments opening out onto an external corridor.

'There are six apartments on each floor, all sharing the same corridor. I am in number nineteen on the second floor. Gertraud Traugott's apartment is just along from mine, number twenty two.'

Henry reckoned that Lido had the five minutes he said he needed to get inside his own apartment, so he climbed the steps to number twenty-two. In common with all the other apartments in the block it was shabby with paint peeling to reveal warped wood. He knocked on the door, but there was no sign of life. He knocked again and waited. He knocked once more and at that the door of the apartment next door opened.

A woman in her forties came out. She was wearing a filthy apron with two equally filthy children huddled behind her.

'Who are you after?'

'Frau Traugott,' he replied.

'She's not here and with some luck she'll never come back. I'd had enough of her frightening the children. Who are you anyway?'

'A relation, from out of town: I'm in Essen on business and thought I'd pop in to see her.'

Lido had now emerged from his apartment and joined them. He nodded politely at the woman and asked if he could help. Henry explained his story again. Lido also informed him that Frau Traugott was not there.

Henry managed to look suitably disappointed. 'I counted on her being here. I was hoping to stay with her tonight. Do you know of a hotel nearby?'

'You'll have to head back into town' the neighbour said, ushering her children back into their apartment. She was sensing she may be called on to help out and her reluctance to do that was marginally outweighed her innate nosiness.

'Manfred will help you. He is an old fashioned gentleman!' With that she laughed and disappeared into her apartment, but not before hearing Lido ask him to join him in his apartment.

Number nineteen was neat and cosy inside. Once Lido had locked the door and checked that all the curtains were drawn he showed Henry into a small sitting room. There was a table, bookshelves, an easy chair and a sofa: he gestured for Henry to sit on the sofa.

'Let's wait ten minutes. If they were following us they will come by then. If not, we can relax, if such a thing is possible these days. You can call me Manfred by the way. I don't need to know your real name, as far as I am concerned, you are Dieter.'

After a silent ten minutes, Manfred removed his jacket, then took Henry's and then went into the kitchen, emerging a few minutes later with two steaming mugs.

'It's what we call coffee these days. Coffee was my passion. I am assuming that I will never drink proper coffee again.' He sat there shaking his head, sipping at the drink and pulling a face as he tasted it. He removed a bottle of Asbach Uralt brandy from a shelf and poured some into their coffee cups, without asking Henry.

'You will find that makes it more palatable. I will make us something to eat soon. Now you must start making notes of what you saw. There is a false lining to your suitcase. When you have finished with the notes, we'll seal them in there. Before I forget, you have something for me?'

'Pardon?' said Henry.

'Stuttgart should have given you something for me... in a pencil case?'

'Oh yes, sorry. I forgot.' Henry opened the suitcase and removed the pencil case from the zipped compartment in the lid of the case.

Manfred held it carefully with two hands and placed it on the table. He left the room and returned with a small towel, which he folded in half and placed next to the pencil case, which he then slowly opened. From it, he extracted three brass pen-like objects, one by one. He gingerly placed them on the towel, which he then carefully wrapped up. He left the room with it and returned a minute or so later. He handed the pencil case back to Henry.

'What are they?' he asked.

'Those? Oh, they are pencil detonators. For explosives, you understand. I will pass them on quickly to the people who know what to do with them.'

'You mean I carried these detonators with me all the way from Stuttgart?'

'Indeed you did. I am most grateful.'

'But what about if I had been searched and they found them?'

'Then you probably wouldn't be here now, would you? We take such risks all the time.'

Henry sank back in the sofa.

'Are there any other surprises?'

'You are the man for surprises, Dieter, eh? You had hardly been in Essen for two hours before you killed one of our citizens. With some luck, the police will assume it is one of the foreign labourers or a Jew. It is very handy that they blame them for everything. It makes it easier for decent Aryans to commit crimes.'

They both laughed. Henry spent the next hour writing in pencil what he had seen and then they sealed the paper into the lining of the suitcase. Manfred prepared an evening meal and they sat down at the table to eat: a hot stew with more potatoes than anything else.

'How long have you lived here, Manfred?'

'I moved to Essen in 1935. I was a teacher in Dortmund when the Nazis came to power and as I was a social democrat I lost my job. Soon after that my wife died and, as you can imagine, I was in despair: on my own and with no job and an apparent enemy of the state. However, my sister-in-law had a fairly senior position at the local authority in Dortmund and she was able to alter my records. My surname was Erhart and she changed it to the alternative spelling of Erhard. All of my paper-work showed my Christian name as Hans, but she replaced it with my middle name, Manfred. So Hans Erhart became Manfred Erhard: very simple, but very effective. The thing about us Germans you see is that we can be too efficient, too methodical. Had I been Hans Erhart then the authorities would have tracked me down, but as all the paperwork is in order for Manfred Erhard, he has no problems. I moved to Essen, got this apartment and a job at the station. As far as people are concerned, I am what I appear to be, a rather lonely railway worker who lives on his own and bothers no one.'

'So how did you get involved in this business?'

'By chance: a couple came to Lost Property who were clearly terrified. They were trying to get out of Essen but the Gestapo were after them. Without having time to think about it, I allowed them to hide in Lost Property office overnight. The next morning they gave me the phone number of a contact of theirs. He arranged to collect them and managed to smuggle them out of the town. A few days later that contact came to see me and asked if I would like to stay involved, to help from time to time. I had no option of course, what could I do? I was already involved. Our main role now is to help gather intelligence for the British so that they can bomb the Krupps factories. With some luck the intelligence we give them will be so good that they hit Krupps rather than this apartment block. There are some mining engineers at the Krupps Maria mine in the north of Essen who are communist sympathisers: they can get hold of dynamite and who knows, with the detonators you brought maybe we can do some damage to the factories ourselves, without having to rely on the RAF.'

'Maybe that will be safer.'

'We are a small cell and it is very dangerous work, which goes without saying. So far we have been very lucky but that cannot last. I am sixty-three now, Dieter, I have little to live for. Helping to resist the Nazis gives me some purpose, but I know I will not survive long. I have a suicide pill: I just hope that when the Gestapo come for me I have time to take it.'

After Manfred had cleared the dinner plates he returned to the small room and checked the curtains once again.

'Are you ready for some entertainment?'

Henry nodded, uncertain what Manfred had in mind.

Manfred was by the bookcase, on top of which was a Bakelite cabinet.

'This is a *Volksempfange*: a triumph of German engineering. When the Nazis came to power they were so proud of their ability to communicate with us ordinary folk that they had this radio receiver built. It was cheap, this one cost me something like seventy marks and it works well. It is important for them that we catch all the speeches and fall for their propaganda. For me, I enjoyed listening to the jazz, but they soon banned that. Apparently they felt that it was all Negroes and Jews. So now they expect us to listen to their nonsense, but they failed to take into account this...'

Manfred was moving the dial to the left, stations momentarily bursting into life and then fading away as he went through them. He them settled on one station and turned the volume very low, beckoning Henry to join him crouched by the speaker.

'The BBC,' Manfred was pointing at the dial on the radio. 'We'll listen to their German language service. It is excellent. If they catch you listening to a foreign radio station you can end up in prison. Goebbels clearly does not like his own propaganda to be contaminated, so now I spend part of my evenings knelt by the radio, with the volume so low that I can only just hear it.'

Henry did not sleep that night, wracked as his body was with exhaustion and fear. Every time he began to drop off he saw the bulging eyes of the shop owner or would hear the resigned tone of

Manfred, a man who knew his fate. It was another face that would now haunt him, along with Roza who inevitably appeared before him in the very early hours, her fingers holding his wrist, slowly tightening over the course of what felt like many hours. There was a strong wind that night and the windows in the sitting room, where Henry was trying to sleep on the sofa, rattled viciously. Worse than that was the front door, which shook heavily when caught by the wind: each time that happened throughout the night he imagined that the Gestapo had come for them.

The next morning Manfred was up at six thirty and they sat together eating black bread and jam and drinking ersatz coffee.

'I start work at eight o'clock. You should aim to catch the quarter past nine train to Cologne. We are going to go on a more roundabout route to the station but it is one which will enable you to see much more of Essen. It is very busy at this time of the morning, so we should be all right, but who knows? Keep an eye on me and make sure you memorise well what you see – and, remember, if you see me remove my cap and put it in my pocket, we are in danger. If that happens, just ignore me and get away as soon as you can.'

Henry watched as Manfred packed his lunch neatly into a tin box, leaving space for the detonators wrapped in the towel. 'I had better be careful I don't eat them!' Both men laughed nervously, grateful for the brief diversion of humour. They left the apartment just after seven and Henry followed Manfred to Altendorf station. They travelled north, allowing Henry ample opportunity to see yet more Krupps factories and the Maria and Amalie mines. At Altenessen they changed trains and took one south: anyone following them would have been immediately suspicious that they were taking such a circuitous route when a more direct one existed, but it was busy and Henry was convinced no one was watching them. Essen was like Stuttgart: people avoided eye contact with each other. The next stage of the journey had the added advantage of being painfully slow, as the train crawled down the track past yet more factories to the North Passenger and Goods station. It was now a quarter to eight and, as arranged, Manfred headed straight to the main station. Henry had more time and walked slowly, taking a slightly longer route so as to take in the power station and the electricity station around Viehofer Strasse.

As he headed towards the station, pleased with his morning's work and relieved to be beginning his journey back, he became aware of a commotion ahead of him. Too late he realised that he was very near Limbecker Strasse, where the *Parfümerie* was. There were police everywhere, stopping all pedestrians and coralling them into different lines. He thought of turning around, but soon found himself being pointed to a queue. Ten minutes later he was at the front of it. A policeman directed him towards a man in a long trenchcoat, who beckoned him. *Come here.* The man held out an oval, metal warrant disc: there was the Nazi eagle on one side and the words *Geheime Staatpolizei* on the other. Gestapo.

'Papers.'

He handed over his identity card.

'Where are you heading?'

'The station.'

That seemed to satisfy the man, who did not press him.

'Open the suitcase.'

He rooted around in it for a moment or two but again was satisfied.

'Your watch.'

They'd be looking for the old man's watch. His was fine.

The Gestapo officer seemed satisfied.

'One last thing: let me see your wallet.'

Henry handed it over. He and Manfred had agreed that it would be best to dispose of the Reichsmarks he had taken from the till. 'You never *know*,' said Manfred, 'some shopkeepers mark their notes or there could be specks of blood on them.' Henry was certain that there was nothing to worry about in the wallet – nothing that would arouse suspicion. He did have the slip of paper, with the name and address in Altendorf of his aunt, but that would appear as innocuous as all the other contents.

But it was as the Gestapo man handed the wallet back to him and told him he could go on his way that Henry had the most terrible thought. He remembered that the slip of paper was not in the wallet:

he had transferred it to his coat pocket just before he arrived in Essen the previous day. For some reason he had decided it would be safer there. And now it was in the blood-stained and perfume soaked coat that he had abandoned and which there was every chance would be discovered. They would find the piece of paper and go to the apartment block in Ehrenzeller Strasse and start asking questions. The lady with the filthy apron in the next door apartment would happily tell them about the man who had knocked on Gertraud Traugott's and who had been taken in by Herr Erhard in number nineteen.

His legs were shaking as he hurried to the station. The large station clock had edged past ten past nine and he could see steam billowing from the Cologne train on platform three. There was a good chance they would find the coat any moment now – maybe they had already found it and had already spoken with the woman at the apartments. Maybe they were on their way to the station. He knew he should go to the Lost Property office to warn Manfred, but he also knew that if he did so then he would almost certainly miss the train.

There was movement around platform three, the guard was about to close the gate. Henry ran along and managed to squeeze through in time. He hopped on board as the brakes were noisily released and the train began to ease along the platform.

Every time he closed his eyes on the journey back to Stuttgart he saw Manfred: he knew he could have warned him and given him a chance to escape, but that would have delayed his own departure from Essen and put himself at risk.

Poor Manfred, he thought: a decent enough man whose remaining ambition in life was that he could take his suicide pill before the Gestapo got to him.

I just hope he manages it.

Chapter 12

Lausanne, Bern, August 1940

Henry travelled to Lausanne on Monday 5th August, following the long weekend to celebrate Swiss National Day the previous Friday. He took the early morning paddle steamer from Geneva and when the *Montreux* docked in Lausanne a gleaming black Traction Avant was waiting for him.

On the twenty minute drive to Lutry, the Alps rose high to his left, the lake sweeping below him to the right. That summed it up, he thought: caught between two powerful forces. Not unlike serving two masters.

It took the Citroën a further ten minutes to climb the steep road out of Lutry to an isolated villa high above the town. Henry was led through to a magnificently appointed lounge, with large windows offering sensational views of the lake. The furniture was of the best quality, along with magnificent carpets and cabinets with enough silver in them to fund a war a slightly smaller than the current one.

As with all his meetings with Viktor, it began with an embrace. As Henry extricated himself from it he turned round to admire the room.

'Bit luxurious isn't it, Viktor?'

'The location is very discreet: that is what matters.'

'Do you lot own this?'

'We borrow it from a good friend, *synok*. We have very little time for questions; we need to get to work.'

Henry ignored him and walked around the room, genuinely admiring it. A pair of chairs on either side of the fireplace appeared to be genuine Louis XV: Viktor told him he was not permitted to sit on them. Someone had brought in a tray of what smelled like proper coffee and he helped himself to a cup and before sinking into a large armchair opposite Viktor, who had his brown leather notebook on his lap and was sharpening his pencil with a penknife, the shavings scattering on the precious carpet.

'You have not heard from your Mr Remington-Barber yet?'

Henry shook his head. So did the Russian.

'Strange. I would have thought he would have contacted you by now. As far as we can tell, you're not being watched. You certainly weren't followed today. He doesn't seem to be very suspicious, does he?'

'I have no idea, but maybe they are unhappy about what happened in Essen.'

Viktor raised his eyebrows momentarily and looked up. 'And what did happen in Essen, Henry?'

Henry took a deep breath. He had been dreading this moment. He was not sure who he feared telling most: Remington-Barber or Viktor. He closed his eyes and carefully recounted the details of his trip to Germany. He had decided to leave nothing out: the killing of the old man in the shop and the fact that his carelessness had almost certainly compromised Manfred. Viktor allowed him to speak uninterrupted, carefully taking notes. When he finished, there was a long silence, broken only by the sound of Viktor sharpening his pencil. Henry had leant forward in his seat, his elbows on his thighs, staring down.

'What is the matter, *synok*? You look bothered about something.'

'He'll be dead now, won't he?'

'Who?'

'Manfred – Lido: do you think the Germans would have found him?'

Viktor shrugged. 'I would imagine so. Whatever we think of them, we cannot accuse them of not being thorough, can we? I would be most surprised if they did not find the coat and that would have led to Manfred.'

Henry shook his head.

'You seem to be upset?' Viktor looked confused.

'Well, I am actually, yes. He was a decent chap and it was my mistake that probably did it for him.'

'He was a social democrat, Henry: their fate is to end up dead. And now he is a victim of war. How do you feel about killing the man in shop? Has that upset you as much?'

'Of course not: he was clearly a bad sort – a Nazi. I had no alternative.'

'Indeed. I imagine that it was somewhat easier than with the boy in Interlaken, or the puppy. That is why we train you like that Henry, so you are used to killing. As far as your Mr Remington-Barber is concerned, it is your first killing.'

'You think I should tell him then?'

'Of course! It is always good to have an agent who has killed in the field. I am not sure whether an English gentleman will approve or not, but he ought to be impressed with it. In any case, he may already be aware of it and it will not look good if you don't tell him.'

It was six o'clock now. Viktor checked back through his notebook, nodding his head at various points. He seemed pleased, though Henry knew better than to expect him to actually say he was. It was now Viktor's turn to speak, in his deliberate and concise manner.

'Listen carefully Henry: this is what is expected of you... We are satisfied so far Henry, but there are many difficult days ahead... It is too risky for us to meet on a regular basis... We can keep an eye on you but we must keep these meetings to a minimum... You must learn to operate on your own but to do exactly what we want you to.'

It was a quarter to seven when Viktor finished.

'I think we can risk driving you back to Geneva, *synok*. We now need to wait until Remington-Barber contacts you: I imagine that will be soon.'

Viktor stood up and embraced Henry once more. The two men who had brought Henry to the villa had come back into the room. *Time to go.*

'Before I go, Viktor, there is something I need to get off my chest.'

Viktor raised his eyebrows and looked at his watch, clearly irritated. *If you must: go on then.*

'I just wanted to say that I am risking my life now. I've told you what happened in Essen. I am not playing games. I know what I let myself in for, I realise all that. But there is something that has made me very unhappy and I need to talk about it.'

Viktor shifted uncomfortably and looked at the two other men in the room. He nodded at them and they both left.

'Go on, but make it quick, Henry.'

'I agreed to work with you – for you – because I believe in your cause: I see it as my cause too. You know that.'

Viktor nodded in agreement, unsure what was going to come next. Henry paused to compose himself.

'I agreed to work for you because I was ideologically committed.'

'We know that.'

'And I still am. But now that I have started to lay my life on the line, I cannot understand why we signed that bloody pact with them last year. I mean, they were meant to be our sworn enemy, they stood for everything we despise and now I have to get used to the fact that they're our allies, our friends even. That seems wrong to me. Whose side am I meant to be on now?'

Viktor sank back into his chair and motioned for Henry to do the same. He leant forward, placed his enormous hands on Henry's knees, gripping them quite tightly.

'What you must understand, *synok*, is that they are not our friends. There is no question of that.'

'But our allies? That is bad enough... perhaps even worse!'

'Hardly even that. It is a non-aggression pact, Henry, that is all – a matter of expediency. I shouldn't quote Trotsky of course, but a couple of years ago he said that "the end may justify the means as long as there is something that justifies the end." That end is the victory over fascism and the triumph of communism. The pact is meant to buy us time to enable us to achieve that. Our feelings about them have not changed, but we need to be ready and this pact allows us to do that. It is not meant to make us feel comfortable; it is meant to protect us.'

'Well, I do feel uncomfortable, Viktor.'

'And do you think you are the only one?' He gripped Henry's knee so hard that he winced in pain. His raised voice meant that one of the men who had been sent out of the room popped his head round the door to check that all was in order. Viktor stood up and leant over Henry, his hot breath was moist and smelt of alcohol.

'We are not permitted the luxury of personal feelings or opinions: they are mere indulgences. Do you understand that?'

Henry edged back in his chair.

'We do as we are instructed, all of us. Maybe we permit you too many bourgeois indulgences, *synok*. Have you forgotten? Never question; never discuss; never hesitate. You would do well to remember that more often than you evidently do. Otherwise, *synok*, you'll be in a lot of trouble.'

–

Henry's journey from Essen to Stuttgart had been uneventful and when he arrived at the Hotel Victoria late on the Thursday afternoon Katharina Hoch had not yet come on duty. She came up to his room later that night to collect her brother's clothes and papers. She insisted that he was not to tell her any details of the Essen trip. 'I don't need to know anything else. Save that for Bern. They will want to know everything.' He couldn't decide whether she had any inkling of what had gone on in Essen, but if she did she gave no hint of it.

He had removed the Nazi Party membership badge he had taken from the dead man in the perfume shop from his lapel before arriving at the hotel. *You never know*, he thought. He hid it in the lining of his wash bag.

She was right – Bern would want to know everything, although he could not understand why it was taking quite so long. Before the mission, Remington-Barber had told him that he was not to initiate any contact when he got back to Switzerland. 'Just wait, I'll be in touch. Be patient. Apparently it is a virtue.'

Henry had taken the Swissair flight from Stuttgart which landed in Zurich just before four thirty on the Friday afternoon and had managed to catch a train straight back to Geneva. He was utterly exhausted. He had hardly slept for the past week: his plan now was to catch up on sleep that weekend. He assumed that Remington-Barber would be in touch on the Monday, if not before.

But nothing: nothing on the Monday nor the following day or the rest of that week nor indeed the following one. His visit to Viktor in the hills above Lausanne came and went, and it was the middle of August when returned from his morning walk to be told by his mother that a messenger had come round from Credit Suisse. There was a letter.

'Whatever can be the problem, Henry?'

It was from Madame Ladnier. Henry tried to read it away from the prying eyes of his mother, who was trying to move behind him.

> *I would like to meet with you today to review recent transactions. Two o'clock this afternoon, Quai des Bergues. Giselle Ladnier (Madame).*

At last. He felt relieved. His mother was looking at him anxiously, her eyebrows raised high.

'What is the problem, Henry?'

'There is no problem, mother, none at all. I have a meeting to review my account. It is routine.'

Madame Ladnier was calm and business-like. Henry had arrived at the branch in Quai des Bergues at five to two and as the clock struck two above the cashiers' counters Madame Ladnier emerged from an office door and ushered Henry into a small office down a long corridor.

'How are you, Herr Hesse?'

'Very well, thank you.' *Do I ask about the delay? Ask why I have not been contacted? Do I mention anything about Germany?*

'Good. Your account is in order. Please now take a few minutes to check your statements and initial each page to indicate you have read them.'

He scanned through the statements, initialling each page. There was no message for him on any of the pages as he thought there may be. He kept glancing up at Madame Ladnier, hoping for a smile or a nod or some acknowledgement of the situation, but she remained as impassive as one would expect of a Swiss bank official.

When he had finished, he returned the papers to her. She checked them and placed them neatly in a folder marked with his name.

'Thank you very much for coming in, Herr Hesse. I am pleased that your account is all in order. I would also ask you to take this pamphlet with you: it explains the various options should you wish to invest any of your funds with Credit Suisse.'

She had stood up now, preparing to leave the room. As Henry stood up she came round to his side of the desk and bent to pick up a piece of paper from the floor.

'You appeared to have dropped this paper, Herr Hesse.'

'I don't think so,' Henry replied.

She handed him the small piece of paper, her gaze making it clear that it was for him. It was a receipt from the cobblers in Bern where he had met Remington-Barber before the trip to Germany. Scrawled underneath the price of a shoe repair were the words: 'Collection Friday 16th August, 1pm.'

Madame Ladnier held a long manicured finger over her mouth in case Henry was inclined to speak.

He left Geneva on the nine thirty train on the Friday morning and was in Bern in good time for his appointment at the cobblers in Kramgasse. There were no customers so he entered the leather emporium, where the cobbler glanced up and nodded, holding a few tacks between his lips and a hammer in his hand. He lifted the counter top and pointed the way up the stairs with the hammer. Basil Remington-Barber was standing by the window.

'Good trip?' He sounded as if he was enquiring after a holiday.

'Well, all things considered, yes.'

'All things considered?'

'Well, considering that I was sent into Nazi Germany and then into the heart of the Ruhr carrying detonators concealed in my baggage, yes it was fine thank you.'

'I am not terribly sure what you were expecting, old chap.'

'I was expecting that it would be a bit more of a "testing the water" mission: you know, see how I got on.'

'Which, in a sense, it was. Having said that, we are hardly going to go to the trouble of getting you into Germany and take the risk of exposing some of our very few remaining agents there just as part of a simple training exercise for you, are we, eh?'

'And the detonators?'

'One of the purposes of your trip, Henry: I am told that we British make first class detonators. We managed to get a few into Stuttgart at the end of last year, but we needed to move some to the Ruhr, which is where you came in. Evidently Lido did manage to pass on the detonators to another member of the cell the morning you left, so that is rather good news: with a bit of luck we may be able to do some damage there. Aerial bombing tends to be a bit hit and miss, but if we can plant actually something inside a factory or a coal mine – well, who knows?'

'I think I ought to have been told a bit more about my mission before I was sent on it.'

'Not sure it works like that, old chap. Not to put too fine a point on it, you do as you are told. You remember what Tennyson said? "*Theirs not to reason why.*" You are one of the "theirs", if you catch my drift.'

'Yes, but what worries me is what he said in the next line: "*Theirs but to do and die*".'

'Let's hope it doesn't come to that. No reason why it should. Now then, old chap, care to tell me about it?'

'About what?'

Basil Remington-Barber stared at Henry for quite a long, not in an altogether unfriendly manner, his eyebrows raised quizzically.

'About what led to Lido being arrested and killed: and be a good chap and leave nothing out, eh? It would be safe for you to assume that you were – how shall I put it – observed while you were in Essen. We have a good idea of what happened, even with that shopkeeper chap – but not all of it.'

Henry already decided to explain what had happened, but confirmation that Manfred was dead caused Henry to swallow hard. When he regained his composure he began to recount the story in much the same way as he had with Viktor. Unlike the Russian, Remington-Barber interrupted him frequently with little questions to help him on his way or clarify a point. When he finished, he asked Remington-Barber what had happened to Lido.

'You left Essen on the Thursday. As we understand it, that evening he was pulled in by the Gestapo. Apparently they had arrived at his apartment in the afternoon, turned the place upside down and were waiting for him when he got home. Thank heavens the detonators weren't there. From there he was taken to the police headquarters in Virchow Strasse.'

'How do you know this?'

'One of his neighbours – most likely the one you met. Half the neighbourhood heard what happened from her and one of our chaps there overheard it. As far as the police are concerned, they've pulled in a number of retired detectives while the younger ones are in the army and another of our contacts heard all this at the bar that they frequent. Manfred was at Virchow Strasse right through the weekend: the Gestapo gave him their standard working over. Not pleasant stuff Henry: they're bloody barbarians. He was a bloody pulp when they took him to the provincial prison across the road on Zweigert Strasse. The Gestapo had another go at him on the Monday and then, by all accounts, he died that night. Apparently they were due to give him another working over the next day. I suppose in one sense they didn't kill him as such, but of course...'

'Of course...' Henry felt bereft. 'Do you think I should have warned him?'

'Well from what you say, you didn't have time, did you? If you had done that then you would have missed the Cologne train and you weren't to know how long it would take them to find the coat and the trail which would lead to Lido.'

'Good Lord... I don't know what to say.'

'Whatever they did to him, he didn't utter a word. He gave nothing away. If he had sung straight away they may even have picked you up in Stuttgart – possibly even before you got there, but turns out he was a brave man. We always tell our chaps to hold out for twenty-four hours, although to be frank, even that is pushing it with those animals. But he held out for far longer than that. Remarkable how resilient people can be.'

'And brave.'

'Indeed.'

'And the shopkeeper?'

'What about him?'

'I'm sorry if that turned out to be rather… messy.'

Basil Remington-Barber looked confused. 'Messy? Not at all! You did absolutely the right thing. It would have been messy had you attempted to extricate yourself from the situation in any other way. No, we have all been rather impressed: it was desperately unlucky that the shopkeeper knew Gertraud Traugott. Not your fault. Important thing is that you acted decisively. Don't look so worried, Henry!'

'I rather thought that you'd be… I don't know… angry with me?'

'I'd have been angry had you not told me what happened. And as I said, you were observed in Essen: what you told me tallies with what we already knew. And there's no harm whatsoever in having an agent who knows how to kill, not to put too fine a point on it, eh?'

Remington-Barber clapped his hands and ushered Henry over to a table by the window, on which a large map of Essen was spread out.

'You have brought your notes with you?'

Henry had.

'Good. What we need to do now is fill in all the information you picked up on the ground against this map. It will be like doing a jigsaw: should be rather fun.'

Henry would not have described it as fun. They spent an hour going over the large map of Essen, Henry doing his best to point out the location of factories and other key buildings. For all his bonhomie and apparent diffidence, Remington-Barber turned out to be highly adept at teasing information out of Henry. By two thirty, the map was much more detailed.

'RAF ought to be chuffed with this' he announced, carefully rolling it up and slipping it into a metal tube. He then stood up and rubbed his hands, as if in excitement.

'Right then! If you hurry you'll catch the six o'clock train to Geneva: saves us another hotel bill, eh? And talking of money, London are very pleased with the mission. Edgar says to tell you that 500pounds will be put into your Credit Suisse account next week: says you'll know what all that is about. I hate anything to do with money.'

'And what happens now?'

'Go home and wait for us to contact you, which we will do through Madame Ladnier.'

'And when might that be?'

'Good question, Henry. The truth is, I have no idea. Could be next week, could be next year. The only thing I would say is that if London are this pleased with this mission, the next one could be a lot more interesting. Something to look forward to! So don't worry, I'm sure London will want to see you soon.'

Henry was alarmed. 'London! You want me to go to London?'

Remington-Barber frowned. 'Good heavens no! London will come to you.'

Chapter 13

Berlin, August 1940

Berlin in the first full summer of the war was a city of secrets and hushed conversations; a city at the centre of the conflict but a long way from the sounds or more obvious effects of it. The closer to the centre of power the more secrets there were and the more hushed conversations became. Unless you knew someone very well and were absolutely sure you could trust them, even a routine conversation was guarded and required a circuitous route to reach its point.

For Franz Hermann, such a cautious approach was by no means an alien one. As a lawyer he was used to being careful and non-committal; discretion came as second nature to him. But late in the afternoon of an extremely pleasant Tuesday in the middle of August he was mindful of the need to be even more careful than usual. Franz Hermann was on his way to meet a very important client, a general in the Army High Command.

The lawyer had left his office in Friedrichstrasse to visit this client at his home in Moabit. Hermann headed west, along the north bank of the River Spree and at Lehrter Station turned into Alt Moabit, past the Post Stadion. Four years earlier he had been at the Post Stadion watching Norway unexpectedly beat Germany two nil to knock the hosts out of the Olympics football tournament. His initial disappointment at the defeat had been more than compensated for by the fact that Hitler was at the game and was reported as being furious. He decided that if Hitler was so upset by the result then maybe defeat was not so bad after all. *Your enemy's enemy...*

Halfway along Strom Strasse he reached his destination: a handsome apartment block, overlooking the Kleiner Tiergarten. A maid, who looked as if she was still in her teens, let him into the apartment on the top floor of the building.

Generalmajor Werner Ernst was in his study, still wearing his uniform. He moved his large head slowly, as if he had a bad neck. His eyes were noticeable for how small they were in comparison to the rest of his face. He smiled politely and pointed to one of two armchairs that were angled towards the window, a small coffee table between them. Behind him were enormous picture windows over the park. A breeze which had not been apparent on the street was causing the tops of the expanse of trees to sway gently from side to side.

'Please do sit down, Herr Hermann. You'll have to excuse me, I have only just returned from work and have not had time to change.'

They paused while the young maid came back into the room, carrying a tray which she placed on the coffee table. Hermann could smell real coffee, an increasingly rare sensation in Berlin.

'Thank you, Anke, don't you worry, I will pour the coffee. And Frau Ernst reminded me that it is your night off. You may leave early if you wish.'

The *Generalmajor* busied himself pouring the coffee and offering freshly baked biscuits to his guest. He waited until he heard the front door of the apartment close before signalling to his lawyer that he could proceed.

For the next half hour Franz Hermann went through various documents with his important client.

'A signature here please... An explanation necessary there... Another signature here, thank you... Just an initial here will suffice... Let me explain this sheet... I have taken the liberty of having this form already witnessed... One more signature there... All is in order. There we are sir. I think you will find that the business of finalising your mother's estate is now complete. I would estimate that the funds will be in your bank account within the month.'

'Thank you, Herr Hermann. You have deal with this matter most efficiently. I realise that it has taken some effort to sort everything out. I am most grateful to you.'

'A pleasure, sir.'

Hermann began to gather the papers and place them in his brief-case.

'Will you join me for a drink, Herr Hermann? My wife has gone to stay with her sister in Potsdam and it is a pleasure for me not to be ruled by the stopwatch at home for once.'

Without waiting for an answer the *Generalmajor* produced a bottle of Armagnac and poured a large measure for his guest. There was a long silence while he surveyed the drink before putting the glass to his lips and leaning back in his armchair, his tiny eyes first studying Franz Hermann carefully and then closing. It was a while before he opened them.

'Do you have children, Hermann?'

'No, sir.'

'I hope that you do not think it is impertinent of me to ask, but it is something I have been thinking about recently. This may be a strange thing for an army officer to say, but I have noticed among my colleagues that the ones without children seem to have a very different attitude to the war than the ones with them, especially those with sons. My own son is based in Poland, Herr Hermann. He is an *Oberleutnant* and just twenty-two years old. As an army officer I have never held any fears for my own safety. Of course, I have always done my best to avoid making rash judgements that could cause harm to men under my command. But now that my own son is a soldier, I have found that is having an unexpected effect on my attitude to the war: I am more cautious, I worry about the course of the war. It has had a much more profound effect on me than I had imagined. I had hoped that my son would become an architect...'

The *Generalmajor*'s voice tailed off, he seemed to be preoccupied with his own thoughts.

'Hopefully he will not need to remain in the army for too long, sir. Victory will be ours soon!'

The *Generalmajor* looked long and hard at the lawyer.

'You think so, Herr Herrmann? What makes you so sure of that?'

The lawyer shifted uncomfortably in his seat. 'One reads in the papers how well the war is going, that it is just a matter of time before Britain surrenders and—'

'And you believe everything you read in the papers, do you, Herr Hermann? I had thought that lawyers were trained to question things, not to accept matters at face value.'

Franz Hermann shrugged, unsure of what to say and wondering how he had allowed himself to become drawn into a conversation like this.

'Tell me, Herr Hermann: are you a member of the Nazi Party?'

'I am a lawyer, sir. I am not involved in politics.'

'Many lawyers are members of the Nazi Party.'

'I am not one of them, sir.'

Generalmajor Ernst stood up and unbuttoned his jacket, then walked over to the window. The trees in the Kleiner Tiergarten had stopped swaying. The *Generalmajor* shut the window and turned round to face the lawyer.

'Well, if it makes you feel any better, Herr Hermann, nor am I.'

Franz Hermann started to get up, relieved at the opportunity to finish the conversation at that juncture. The *Generalmajor* gestured for him to remain seated and sat down next to him, pulling up his chair alongside the lawyer's.

'You are a clever chap, Herr Hermann.'

'Thank you, sir.'

'You are not just a very competent lawyer, but you are good at managing to appear to be what you are not.'

'I am sorry, I am not sure…'

'You do an excellent job of giving the appearance of being a mild-mannered lawyer, with no interest in politics. You are quiet and you are discrete. You do not draw attention to yourself. But I also know that you have – how can I put this – that you have contacts.'

Franz Hermann could feel his breathing tighten and the room become hotter. He did his best to sound relaxed.

'I suspect, sir, that there must be a misunderstanding here. I am as you originally describe me: a lawyer with no interest in politics. But please be assured that I am a loyal—'

'Please, please, Herr Hermann. I am sure you are all of these things. But you see, I know that there is more to you than that and you will find that I am not altogether unsympathetic. I know that you have certain contacts and I wish to avail myself of your contacts.'

Franz Hermann said nothing. The *Generalmajor* leaned towards him, so that their faces were just inches apart. He could smell the brandy on his breath and see the tiny red lines in Ernst's eyes.

'Three weeks ago, on the twenty-ninth of July to be precise, I was in Bad Reichenhall. Have you heard of it?'

'Of course: a very pleasant spa town in Bavaria, not too far from Salzburg. My parents spent their honeymoon there.'

'Indeed. But I was not there to use the spa, I can assure you. Do you have a good memory, Franz?'

'Yes sir.'

'Werner: please call me Werner. You will make sure to memorise what I say now. Write nothing down.'

Hermann nodded.

'My area of expertise in the army is logistics. It is not a glamorous job, but few people in the high command know better than me how to move our troops around in an efficient manner and then to ensure that they are well supplied. That is perhaps the most underestimated part of warfare. It is one thing to advance fast, especially against a weak enemy, but it is quite another to ensure the integrity of an advance is maintained by ensuring that our forces have good supplies of food and fuel and ammunition. That is what I excel at. But I am not telling you all this to make me seem important. The reason why I was in Bad Reichenhall was because the Chief of Staff, General Jodl, was holding a top secret meeting there on the express instructions of the *Führer* himself. You will have some more Armagnac, Franz? It is quite excellent, one of the more tangible benefits of our conquest of France.' He poured two more large measures. 'Jodl is a busy man, he does not gather senior officers around him in pleasant Bavarian spa towns without very good reason. And the reason gathered us last month was that now that France has fallen, the *Führer* has turned his attention to who we attack next. The common belief is that Operation Sea Lion is our priority and that we will soon launch an invasion of Great Britain. As you know, we started our aerial assault against them over a month ago. But the Kriegsmarine has serious doubts that we will ever be able to successfully invade the British Isles. Our hope is that we win what they are calling the "Battle of Britain" – gain air supremacy – and this leads to victory, but that does not appear likely. The RAF is proving to be a resolute opponent and Churchill shows no inclination whatsoever to surrender.'

With the window closed, the room had now become quite stuffy. The *Generalmajor* stood up to remove his jacket and loosen his collar.

'The *Führer* has instructed Colonel General Jodl to explore other options, in the eventuality that we do not invade Britain. The option that we discussed in Bad Reichenhall was that of invading the Soviet Union.'

During the shocked silence that followed Hermann heard the loud ticking of a clock from the hall. The tops of the trees in the Kleiner Tiergarten had begun to sway again. The *Generalmajor* reached over to a side table and opened a box of cigars, offering one to the lawyer – who declined – before slowly lighting one for himself.

'Invade the Soviet Union? But surely that would be madness! We have a pact with them?'

'It is not as outrageous a thought as you appear to think it is, Franz. That pact was designed to keep our eastern borders quiet while we dealt with Western Europe. Now, I have no love for the Soviet Union but for many of us, Franz – those of us who approach matters from a professional military point of view as opposed to an ideological one – the prospect of invading the Soviet Union is a nightmare. To attempt to invade the Soviet Union would be to ignore the lessons of history. Bismarck himself said that the secret of politics was to "make a good treaty with Russia", which is of course what we did. From a military point of view, invading the Soviet Union has all the potential to end in disaster. Even Field Marshall Keitel is trying to dissuade Hitler from the idea and he is well known for never disagreeing with the *Führer*.'

'When will this invasion take place?'

'Too early to say, Franz: it may never happen. The purpose of Jodl gathering us in Bad Reichenhall was to get us thinking in theoretical terms about how we might prepare for such an invasion. Such an invasion is so sensitive and so secret that we can do little more than think about it. The final decision will rest with the *Führer*. After the conquest of the Low Countries and France, he is convinced that he is a military genius. He thinks that we older Wehrmacht officers are too cautious, too conservative.'

The *Generalmajor* was now wreathed in cigar smoke, the colour of gun metal. He leant back in his chair, staring up at the ceiling.

'However, Franz, even Hitler knows that the timing of an invasion would need to be very precise if we are not to be caught out in the Russian winter. If we have not achieved our objectives by the start of the winter then we are doomed. So we would need to attack by mid-May at the latest. Then we have a chance of success, although not a very good one.'

'Why on earth are you telling me this?'

'Many of us believe that to invade the Soviet Union would be suicide for Germany. There are groups of us in the Bendlerblock who are of a like mind. We believe that we are acting in the best interests of Germany. As you may be aware, the Abwehr has its headquarters in the Bendlerblock. A few days ago, I was talking with an old friend who is a very senior officer in the Abwehr. His mother died a month ago and he asked if I could recommend a good lawyer to take care of everything. I told him about you and that was that. The next day he asked me to go for a walk with him along the banks of the Landwehr Canal. He confided in me that you have come to the attention of the Abwehr...'

'This is preposterous sir. It is simply untrue. I must insist that—'

'Franz, you must not worry.' He patted the lawyer on the arm in a reassuring manner. 'Just be very, very grateful that it is the Abwehr that you have come to the attention of and not the Gestapo. According to my friend, they are aware that you are able to channel information to the Allies. They have permitted you to carry on doing this because they believed that there may come a time when they wished to use this channel. That time has now come.'

Franz Hermann held out his hands in 'what can I say' gesture. 'I am not a traitor, sir. I consider myself to be a loyal German. I happen to believe that Germany should be a democratic country and that this war could ruin us.'

'No one is saying that you are a traitor. Nor am I, for that matter. We all have our different motives. Will you pass on this information, about the meeting at Bad Reichenhall and the possibility of an invasion of the Soviet Union?'

'Of course.'

When he left the apartment there was a cool evening breeze which was a welcome relief from the stuffiness of the apartment, but this had no calming effect on Hermann. He felt the huge trees closing in on him and imagined that the people around him on the pavement were looking at him. He would have to move fast, he could not afford to think about things.

–

When Franz Hermann was sixteen or seventeen, it had been briefly fashionable among his group at school to root out ancient Chinese proverbs, which they would then quote to each other as if they had stumbled upon words of wisdom which unlocked the secrets of the universe. It was all rather pretentious and it was a phase which did not last long. A couple of their group had continued to grasp at various ancient beliefs long after they had left school and they were the ones who had become early members of the Nazi Party.

One of the sayings that they had passed around sounded at first like a Chinese good luck wish: 'May you live in interesting times.' The twist was that it was actually a curse. He had never quite understood why hoping that someone lived in interesting times was a curse. All his life he had wished that his life had been more interesting: an obedient student; not fit for military service; a childless marriage and a worthy but dull career.

Now he was trapped between the gates of heaven and the banks of hell. A chance remark during an unguarded conversation at a dinner party a month after the start of the war was followed up by a clandestine meeting at the zoo a week later. He and the elegant woman with a Viennese accent, who had had slipped him the note as left the dinner party, had stood alongside the elephant enclosure watching the animals spray each other with water.

'I noticed you made some remarks about the regime. You had best be careful where and to whom you say such things,' she had said, softly. He nodded, he realised he had been careless; his wife had told him as much, in no uncertain terms on their way home. Too much good wine had been his excuse. '*But you also said something about tensions in the Nazi Party leadership in Berlin?*' the Viennese woman had whispered. 'Where did you get that from?'

He had waited for two of the elephants to finish calling to each other.

'From one of my colleagues,' he told her.

'And what is his name?'

He had hesitated before replying. The elegantly dressed lady with the elegant Viennese accent was evidently not quite what she seemed. Franz Hermann could have walked away at that point. He could have said that he wanted to take matters no further and would appreciate it if they could both forget they had ever met. She was hardly likely to report him to the Gestapo. But there was something almost seductive about her manner. He found it impossible not to reply to her.

'Alois Jäger: we work at the same law firm. He is some big shot in the leadership of the Nazi Party in Berlin. As far as he is concerned, I am completely apolitical. I pick up a lot of his legal work while he is on Nazi Party business, so he has reason to be grateful to me. And he cannot help gossiping. I hear him talk about Goebbels: he cannot stand him, they just don't get on. But from what I gather, there is a feeling shared among a number of senior Nazis in Berlin that Goebbels cannot be an effective *Gauleiter* of city and Minister for Propaganda. They think he should concentrate on one or the other.'

'This is very interesting,' she had replied. 'You are clearly in a position to pick up such information. I would like to tell you how you can pass it on to people who need to know this kind of information. Are you willing to do so?'

Franz Hermann said that he was. They walked round to the tiger enclosure and then over to the aquarium. The elegant lady with the Viennese accent had slipped her gloved arm through his as she explained in detail how he could make contact with the right people.

And then his position became even more precarious in December when Rosa had turned up on his doorstep. What could he do: turn her away? It made sense to lodge her and the children with his mother, and he was sure it would only be for a few weeks, but that was eight – nine months ago. Now he was a British spy and harbouring a Jewish family so now he understood why 'May you live in interesting times' was indeed a curse.

–

He would have preferred to walk and give himself some opportunity to compose himself, but time was against him so he took a tram from Alt Moabit into the Unter den Linden, getting off a stop earlier than he needed to at the junction with Friedrichstrasse.

Despite being so near to it, he decided against popping back into his office: had anyone been following him or had spotted him in the street it would have looked normal for him to return to work, but he was in a hurry. He walked along the Unter den Linden for another two blocks before turning left into the Opernplatz.

Although he came to the pretty square at least twice a week and had done so for years, it nonetheless left him with an uneasy feeling. He could never forget what happened there seven years before, in May 1933, when the Nazis had burned tens of thousands of books. The smell had lingered for days and for weeks afterwards people would come across tiny piles of ash throughout the area. Even months later it was not uncommon to come across scraps of paper that had somehow escaped the flames, floating around the city in a defiant manner, daring passers-by to steal a look at a word or two that may corrupt them.

His sense of apprehension increased as he entered St Hedwig's, the cathedral he had worshipped at since he was a boy. Although they lived in Dahlem and there were plenty of Catholic churches near to where they lived, his mother seemed to be of the opinion that their piety was increased by praying at the seat of the Archbishop.

Now, the cathedral served a very different purpose for him.

The mass was just coming to an end and most of the congregation were leaving the church. In the old days, people would gather in small groups and chat, but that was not the done thing now. You never knew who may be watching, or listening.

Franz Hermann sat on his own towards the back of the cathedral, watching the small group of priests at the high altar as they began to disperse. Sure enough, the tall and slightly stooped figure of the young priest he was looking for emerged from the little group and walked in long strides towards the confession box that sat on its own to the side.

'*I always take confession after mass on Tuesday and Thursday afternoons. On those days I use the confession box that is on its own, the one near the high altar. Only come to me then. No one can overhear us there. It is safer. Or at least, not as dangerous.*'

Franz Hermann left his seat at the back of the cathedral and walked towards the altar, where he knelt and crossed himself before walking over towards the confession box that the young priest had gone into. An old man with scruffy trousers had just entered the confession box, muttering silently to himself as he did so. The lawyer sat down next to an elegantly dressed lady who had a blue silk scarf wrapped around her neck. She was clutching a photograph of what looked like a boy in Luftwaffe uniform and dabbing her eyes with a crisp white handkerchief.

The old man shuffled out, still muttering silently to himself and the elegantly dressed lady replaced him, her high heels echoing sharply on the old tiled floor. The confession box was in a perfect position: unlike the ones grouped together on the other side of the cathedral, this one was isolated in a quiet cloister and the chairs were some way from the box: it was impossible to overhear anything, not even the sound of voices in the box, let alone the words.

A few minutes later the lady emerged from the confession box, still dabbing her eyes with a crisp white handkerchief. Franz Hermann walked over to the box, crossed himself, closed the heavy velvet curtain and knelt down.

'In the name of the Father, and of the Son, and of the Holy Spirit. My last confession was two weeks ago.'

He had not been sure if Father Josef was aware he was there, but he looked towards the grill and at the sound of his voice he could see through young priest sit up sharply. As Father Josef glanced towards him he caught sight of the priest's bright red nose, as if he had just come in from the cold.

'Go on, my son.'

'I have sinned Father. I fear I have been treating our maid too harshly because I suspected she may have been stealing some small change left around the house, although I now think it was not her. And I have been guilty of the sin of envy: a friend has been able to find some best quality cloth material and has had it made into fine suit. You must know how hard that is in these times and I find it has been the cause of feelings of jealousy in myself.'

'And any other sins, my son?'

'I am afraid that I took the Lord's name in vain: I used it in a disrespectful manner. I am sorry for these and all the sins of my past life.'

'And that is it?'

'That is it, Father.' The lawyer thought he had done quite well to muster three things that he could pass off as sins.

The priest would be decoding his message. The confession of treating the maid too harshly was for security: '*all is well, I am not being followed*'. The sin of envy indicated that he needed to meet his contact. Taking the Lord's name in vain meant that it is urgent.

'I see.' The priest coughed, pausing to take everything in. Through the grill he could see the priest's head bob up and down, the bright red nose most clearly visible in the gloom. 'Say a "Hail Mary" and pray for your sins. She will next be in on Thursday, my son. I will pass on your message. Meet her at the usual place at the usual time on the Friday. Can you manage that?'

'Yes Father.'

'If she cannot manage that or does not turn up, return here on Tuesday. You had better say an Act of Contrition, my son.'

'I am heartily sorry for having offended you my Lord and I detest all my sins, because I dread the loss of heaven and the pains of hell. I firmly resolve with the help of your grace, to confess my sins, to do penance and to amend my life. Amen.'

The priest replied with a prayer of forgiveness. 'Give thanks to the Lord for He is good.' Franz Hermann crossed himself and replied 'for His mercy endures forever.'

He left the confession box. The waiting chairs had now filled. He paused in the main body of the cathedral, said his 'Hail Mary' and a few other prayers and then hurried out and headed home to Dahlem, his reply to the absolution repeating in his mind throughout the journey.

'*For His mercy endures forever.*'

He certainly hoped so.

–

The military attaché at the Portuguese Legation in Berlin was well aware that his secretary attended Mass whenever she could. Although not as devout as he would like to be, this rather impressed the Colonel as he found religious observance in others somehow reassuring. At least it was a sign that his Dona Maria do Rosario, a reserved woman who shared little of herself, must be trustworthy. He sometimes liked to imagine what sins his secretary had to confess to. She led a pious life: she did not drink or speak out of turn; she was a hard worker and a loyal servant of the Portuguese Government, with a framed photograph of Salazar on her desk.

Berlin was, the Colonel was fond of reminding whoever would listen, not an easy posting and perhaps the most important of all of Portugal's overseas missions. A neutral country had to lean one way and then the other, depending upon the wind of war. It required him to be fleet of foot and have the utmost discretion, and the Colonel in turn demanded that of his staff. So it was neither unusual nor even unexpected when Dona Maria do Rosario entered the Colonel's office with a neat pile of documents just after five o'clock on the afternoon of Thursday 15th August.

'These letters need to be signed, sir; each one is appended to their relevant file. If you can sign them before you leave I can ensure they are in the diplomatic bag on Friday evening. I am leaving now to go to the cathedral but happy to return later if you require me, sir. Otherwise I will be in first thing in the morning.'

'That is fine,' the Colonel told his secretary. 'I will sign the papers and see you first thing in the morning.' In truth, she arrived at work sometime before he did. She was invariably in the office by seven thirty, when few other staff were around. He was unsure why she came in quite so early, but he had every reason to be most grateful to her for doing so. He would arrive at work between eight thirty and nine to find all his papers in order and everything neatly set out on his desk, his day already organised for him. Of course, he was technically in breach of protocol by allowing her access to secret documents, but it made life so much easier and, of course, how could such a devout Catholic not be trustworthy?

Dona Maria do Rosario hurried out of the Legation at a quarter past five and arrived at St Hedwig's Cathedral in time for the early evening Mass. It was close to seven o'clock when she finally entered the confession box, a slight early evening chill now around in the cloisters, causing her to pull her light jacket tight around her shoulders.

'In the name of the Father, and of the Son, and of the Holy Spirit. My last confession was one week ago.'

Father Josef looked at her urgently, his face pressed tight against the grill to check it really was her.

'What are your sins?'

She gave the code: a sin of gluttony to indicate that all was well and a sin of speaking ill of someone behind their back to ensure she had nothing to report. The priest spoke urgently.

'Hugo's been here – two days, ago. He needs to see you as soon as possible. I told him it would be tomorrow, the usual place and the usual time. I hope you can make it?'

Dona Maria assured the priest that she could. 'How are things?' the priest asked her.

Very busy, she told him. 'So much material comes through the Colonel's office that I work late most nights and I'm starting earlier every morning just to find the most important papers. It is getting more and more risky though. I fear that sooner or later someone will suspect me.'

'Maybe moderate your hours. The material you are sending back is so good, I am told, that you should not risk too much. Don't forget, you need to meet Hugo tomorrow and report back on what he tells you.'

'I know.'

'Do you want to pray? Shall I grant you absolution?'

Dona Maria do Rosario was already up and preparing to leave the confession box.

'No thank you, Father.'

As she hurried out of the church she only just remembered to cross herself and pause for a very brief prayer.

–

The following day, Friday, an unusual wind whipped around the centre of Berlin. For some reason, it appeared to linger about four feet off the ground, creating the strange effect of leaves and small bits of litter fluttering around in mid-air. The strange wind was still at play when Franz Hermann hurried out of his office at one o'clock. He was going for a walk, he told his secretary, reassuring her that he would be back in time for his two o'clock meeting. He turned into Behrenstrasse and then left into Wilhemstrasse. In between Wilhemstrasse and Hermann Goring Strasse was a small park, taking up no more than a block, where office workers and civil servants – but not too many of them - liked to take their lunch.

He entered the small park and walked towards the north west corner where a series of old benches surrounded an enormous tree. Perhaps because the benches appeared so uncomfortable or perhaps because the size of the tree ensured that this little spot was permanently in the shade, this area was deserted, apart from an olive-skinned woman in her late thirties poised demurely on the edge of one of the benches. Her jet black hair was pulled back from a face that could have been prettier, but for the absence of any make-up and the presence of what looked like a disapproving look. She was eating an apple and an open book was resting on her lap. He sat on the next bench and removed his jacket, taking out a packet of cigarettes from the jacket as he did so. He offered one to the lady.

'No thank you, sir. I do not smoke,' she replied in a foreign accent.

'Very sensible: my wife does not approve.'

'I can offer you an apple in return.'

And so the exchange continued. In the unlikely event of anyone overhearing the conversation it would have sounded like two strangers passing the time of day. But soon they had established that each other was safe; that they had not been followed and that he had information to pass on.

Franz Hermann shifted to the end of his park bench, so that he was now nearer to the one that Dona Maria do Rosario was sitting on. She had opened her book and was giving the appearance of avidly reading from it. The lawyer was bent forward, his elbows resting on his lap and busy smoking. He was facing the ground, occasionally looking up to be sure that no one else was around. He spoke very quietly, but at a volume that ensured Dona Maria could hear everything he was saying.

'How quickly can you get a message to Lisbon?'

Without looking up from the book she replied. 'It depends how long it is, but there is a bag going this evening. If I can type it up in time then I could get it in.'

'You'll have to, it is urgent. This is what you need to tell them. Colonel General Jodl held a meeting at Bad Reichenhall on the 29th of July. My informant, who is a senior officer in the OKH, was present. I am not giving his name, not at the moment. Apparently they are now entertaining the possibility that Britain may not capitulate after all and Hitler wants to have alternative plans in place. The purpose of Jodl's meeting was to get senior officers to start thinking about plans for the invasion of the Soviet Union.'

He looked up at Dona Maria. Her eyebrows had risen very slightly and momentarily, as if she had read something interesting in her book, which she was still looking at. She took a dainty bite from her apple.

'My informant says that a lot of the professional army officers are against the idea of invading the Soviet Union as they think it will end in failure,' he continued. 'The thinking is that any invasion will have to start by the middle of May because it would need to be over by the onset of winter. Have you got all that?'

Dona Maria said she had. Franz noticed that her face had relaxed now and she had even allowed herself a slight smile as she briefly turned towards him. He asked her to repeat what he had told her. Her repetition was impressively word perfect. She would return now to the Legation and type it up in code in time for that evening's diplomatic bag, she said. Was there anything else?

'I think that's enough!'

Chapter 14

Berlin, January 1941

'And finally one other matter, Herr Hermann.'

These days, Franz Hermann's secretary always seemed to have 'one other matter' that needed to be dealt with. Before the war there had been enough work for the nine senior lawyers in the firm at 181 Friedrichstrasse to be kept busy and well paid, but not so much that they were overstretched. That had all changed now: one of the senior lawyers had retired and not been replaced and two others had joined the armed forces, along with half of the junior lawyers. As if that was not bad enough, Alois Jäger now seemed to spend more than half of the time he was meant to be at work on Nazi Party business, which meant that the remaining five seniors had to pick up more and more of Jäger's work. It was not as if they could complain; they just had to go along with it. As far as Franz Hermann was concerned, as distasteful as it felt, at least it afforded the firm a degree of political protection.

'Do you remember *Generalmajor* Werner Ernst, Herr Hermann?'

He had heard nothing from the General since their meeting in August. He had hoped never to hear from him again. He did his best to look as if he was having a lot of trouble remembering who the General was.

'You'll have to remind me, Ilse. Was it something to do with a dispute with his bank?'

'No, sir. That was another army officer. You were sorting out the affairs of *Generalmajor* Ernst's late mother. It was all tied up in August.'

'Yes, of course. I remember now. Doesn't he live near the Kleiner Tiergarten?'

'That is correct sir. He rang today while you were in a meeting. He says that one or two issues have arisen regarding his mother's estate that he would like to see you about.'

'You have my diary Ilse, please arrange the meeting.'

'He said it was urgent, Herr Hermann.'

He knew that Ilse would expect him to protest: matters arising from the estate of the General's mother all these months on could hardly be construed as urgent. He also knew though that if the General said he needed to see him urgently then it was urgent. He could feel himself getting very hot again and was aware that he was drumming his fingers loudly on the desk.

'Very well then, Ilse. He can either come in here during the day tomorrow or I can go to his apartment tomorrow after work.'

'He said that you are to go to his apartment tonight, sir.'

–

Franz Hermann waited impatiently for Ilse to leave work, spending the half hour before she got round to doing so optimistically trying to think of a possible genuine problem with the *Generalmajor*'s mother's estate, which he knew was highly unlikely. Had there really been a problem it would have emerged some time ago. He feared that the *Generalmajor* was about to entrust him with another secret.

He allowed five minutes to pass after Ilse's departure and then left, managing to find a rare taxi on the Unter den Linden to take him as far as Storm Strasse, from where he walked the short distance to *Generalmajor* Ernst's apartment block. The same teenage maid let him into the apartment, which was now in a state of chaos.

There were packing cases piled up in the hall, suitcases assembled by the door and furniture and paintings covered in dustsheets. A large lady who he took to be Frau Ernst briefly came out of the kitchen to check who the visitor was but went straight back into the kitchen, where Hermann could see at least one other maid busy scrubbing the sides. *Generalmajor* Werner Ernst came to meet him in the hall.

'Hermann: thank you for coming so soon. I have to go away very soon and need to sort out some annoying paperwork before doing so. Anke, please ensure that we are not disturbed. Follow me, Hermann.'

The study was in a similar state of upheaval to the rest of the apartment, but there were two uncovered armchairs towards the window, which Ernst led his lawyer over to.

'I am sorry to hear that there are problems with the estate, sir. I had assumed that everything was concluded in a satisfactory manner back in August.'

The *Generalmajor* had been rooting around in a nearby packing case, from which he produced a bottle of Armagnac and two glasses. He poured a large measure for Hermann and a considerably larger one for himself. As he sat down he shifted his heavy armchair very close to Hermann's, so that the two armrests were touching. When he spoke, it was in a quiet voice.

'Of course everything was satisfactory, Hermann. You did an excellent job. However, I am afraid that for the sake of appearance, I have had to make a bit of a fuss: I have told Frau Ernst that you have been less than efficient and I wrote as much in a letter to my son. He has now been transferred to Norway and I assume that the censors may be reading his letters.'

The *Generalmajor* stood up and stretched himself and then walked over to the curtains, pulling them together. Hermann noticed that the *Generalmajor* looked more drawn than before, his tiny eyes slightly bloodshot. He appeared to have lost some weight and his face was more lined. He twisted a half-finished cigarette into an ashtray and took a cigar from a box on top of a packing case, not bothering to offer one to the lawyer.

'Things are not good, Hermann. The atmosphere in the Bendlerblock is terrible. The atmosphere in the whole of Berlin is terrible. Everyone suspects everyone else of conspiring against them – it is hard to know who to trust. The professional soldiers in the High Command and the leadership of the Abwehr are the most distrusted, I fear. Even if you join the Nazi Party it does not seem to make any difference these days. I felt obliged to join in November but I still think that people are suspicious of me. The reason for all this upheaval in the apartment is that I am being transferred to Warsaw. In my view, it is quite unnecessary; I can do my job just as well, if not better, from Berlin. But I think Hitler and Himmler and the rest of them want to dilute any possible sources of opposition to them. Maybe opposition is too strong a word – perhaps what I mean is disagreement.'

'Do you think they suspect you of having passed on information?'

The *Generalmajor* shook his head slowly, at the same time as lighting his cigar. He paused a while as he inhaled deeply.

'No, no, no! Look Hermann, if they did, I would not be here – and nor, I suspect, would you. I was very careful and I assume that you have been too. The thing is, ever since the meeting at Bad Reichenhall at the end of July, a number of the senior officers like myself who were asked to start thinking about the possibility of invading the Soviet Union have been advising caution. Not everyone, by any means. Too many people feel that they have to say what the *Führer* wants to hear, so they enthusiastically go along with planning for the invasion. A number of others, it should be said, actually agree with invading the Soviet Union. But for people like myself, well we have done nothing that could be construed as treason. In my case, I have been able to produce very detailed papers about the difficulties in keeping our forces properly supplied during an invasion of the Soviet Union. Tell me, Hermann: do you know how far it is from our border in Poland to Moscow?'

The lawyer shook his head. *No idea.*

'Over 1,000 kilometres. To put that in perspective, from our western border, say near Saarbrücken, to Paris is around 340 kilometres: so an invasion of the Soviet Union would be three times that distance and let me tell you, the roads in France are considerably better than those in the Soviet Union. And as well as the terrain you also have to take into account other factors like the weather and you can see how risky an invasion becomes. That is what I have been saying in my reports – I am very careful to stick to the facts. But it has not done me any favours. They are keeping an eye on people like me. They do not completely trust me, hence my move to Warsaw.'

'So why are you packing up the apartment?'

'My wife does not want to remain here on her own. She and her sister in Potsdam are talking about moving to their family's old hunting lodge near Magdeburg. She says that she will feel safer there. Look, Hermann, there's something else I need to tell you, one other piece of information for you to pass on through your contacts. This will have to be the last information that I give you. It is too dangerous for us to meet again and, in any case, in a few days I will be in Warsaw.'

The lawyer nodded and leaned closer towards Ernst.

'I happen to know that a week before Christmas, Hitler issued a detailed directive about the invasion of the Soviet Union. The *Führer* is very sparing in the number of directives that he issues, no more than one or two a month. This directive is so secret that I was only able to glance at it in the presence of others, certainly not allowed to take a copy away – which is perhaps another reason why I know that I am no longer trusted. I am only vaguely aware of what is in this directive, though I do know that it talks about the invasion taking place in the middle of May. You must pass this on: will you do that?'

'Yes, but they will want to know more detail, surely?'

'I am sure that they will, they may even want to see a copy of the Directive no doubt, but it is very, very restricted. From what I gather, there were only nine copies. If you only get across that the invasion is still on and scheduled for the middle of May, that is important. You had better leave now, Hermann. I am glad that we have finally been able to sort out my mother's estate!'

As they left the study he placed his hand on the lawyer's shoulder.

'I doubt that we shall meet again, Hermann. Maybe one day, if circumstances are very different, we will. But who knows, eh? Good luck.'

As Franz Hermann headed home that evening he could not recall ever having felt more miserable, or so afraid.

–

'And that's the message…? No more?'

Dona Maria do Rosario and Franz Hermann were walking around the enormous tree in the small park between Wilhemstrasse and Hermann Goring Strasse, aware that this was more exposed than sitting on the benches around the tree, but it had been raining and the benches were sodden: sitting on them would have looked suspicious.

'I know it is not long but it is very important. Remember, Hitler issued the Directive a week before Christmas: they are still planning to invade the Soviet Union and they are talking about the middle of May. That's four months away.'

'Yes, I would have hoped even the British would be able to work that one out, thank you.'

–

Franz Hermann had met Dona Maria do Rosario on Friday the seventeenth of January. The following Tuesday Ilse came into his office just before lunch. There had been a phone call.

'The man said that he understood you specialised in sorting out estates, especially complicated ones. His uncle recently died in Bremen and he wanted to know if we had an office in Bremen. I said "no" and he said not to worry and that maybe he would call back.'

'Bremen you say?'

'Yes, Herr Hermann. I am not sure why he would think we had an office in Bremen, but there you are. Now, these letters…'

This was only the second time that Father Josef had called him like this. The very fact of telephoning him at the office meant that something was up. The 'Bremen' reference meant that it was very urgent. He was to attend confession that night.

–

'In the name of the Father, and of the Son, and of the Holy Spirit. My last confession was one week ago.'

Father Josef pressed his face against the grille separating the two men. 'We need to be quick. I have a message from her: she passed on your message and has been contacted urgently. Apparently you talked about a document… don't tell me anything about it, just wait my son… and they are saying they need to see it. That is the message. Do you understand?'

'I understand Father but I have not got it. I will see what I can do, but they need to understand that my source has left Berlin. This is going to be very difficult.'

'I am only passing on the message. She said you needed to know before you could meet at the usual rendezvous, in case you can get hold of it. Do your best, my son: I am sure that God will guide you. Do you want to take confession?'

Franz Hermann shook his head.

'No thank you, Father. I wouldn't know where to begin.'

–

In the twelve months since he had been reunited with his first wife and son, Gunter Reinhart had done his best to visit them at least once a week at the house in Dahlem where they were living with Franz Hermann's mother. In one respect the arrangement had held up very well. Franz Hermann's mother could not have been better looked after and therefore the talk of her having to move into a nursing home or even a hospital was long forgotten. Frau Hermann had no idea that her excellent nurse was actually a doctor and certainly had no idea that she was Jewish and that she had two children with her. Her hearing was so poor that she never heard the footsteps in the floor above her or the subdued sound of the children's voices.

But in every other respect, their predicament was an increasingly hopeless one. The situation for Jews in Berlin worsened by the day: although it was still possible for some to emigrate, in reality this had slowed to a trickle and that was just for people who had all the right paperwork and who could afford the punitive taxes being charged. And even then, they needed to find somewhere that would take them. Most of Europe was occupied. There were rumours about Sweden, even Spain. The place most people aspired to go to was Switzerland, but those borders were sealed tight, on both sides.

Gunter, Rosa and Franz had come up with countless schemes to get the three of them out of the country but all of them had too many risks and too many flaws. Gunter usually visited after work on a Wednesday. That was the day that his wife took their children to their piano lessons in Reinickendorf and afterwards they stopped for tea at a favourite cafe on Holtzdamm. They rarely arrived home before seven thirty, so Gunter found that if he left work at five he could go down to Dahlem, spend an hour and a half there and be home in plenty of time.

He did his best to take some food and money with him and Franz's wife, Silke, always tried to be there at the same time so that she could sit with Frau Hermann while Rosa went upstairs to be with Gunter and the children. On the last Wednesday of January, Gunter arrived at the house to find Franz Hermann sitting in room upstairs that Rosa used as a lounge. Rosa followed him into the room.

'Where are the children? Is Alfred all right?' asked Gunter.

'They are fine, Gunter. You will see Alfred in a minute. I need to talk with you first.' Franz Hermann was leaning forward on the low sofa, opposite Gunter and Rosa. His head was bowed low. As he talked, he continued to look down at the patterned carpet.

'I am afraid that I have some bad news, Rosa.'

There was an audible intake of breath from her and she gripped Gunter's knee.

'Harald?'

'I am afraid so.'

Rosa Stern lifted her head high and turned to the window, her head resting for a while against the thick curtains. When she turned round again her eyes had filled with tears. Gunter put his arm round her and pulled her close. She let her head fall on his shoulder.

'Tell me everything, Franz.'

'I'll tell you everything that I know, Rosa. As you are aware, we could hardly make a direct approach to Sachsenhausen – "Please can you tell us how Harald Stern is getting on?" – I had begun to hear that when people died at Sachsenhausen, or any of the other camps that they've taken Berliners to, the police turn up at the home of the next of kin. They bring their ashes with them in an urn, along with a bill for the cost of the urn.'

'Do we need all this detail, Franz? Is it really necessary?'

'No, Gunter, don't be concerned on my part. I need to hear all of this.'

'Of course, you are Harald's next of kin, but fortunately the authorities do not know where you are. You remember a few months ago I managed to track down an address for his elder brother, Paul – in Spandau? I visited him and told him that as far as I was aware, you are in Paris. If he is questioned by the Gestapo about you then he cannot tell them what he doesn't know. He had heard nothing from Harald either but he did say that he would contact me if he did. I did not give him any of my details; again, it is too risky. But I said I would try and visit him every few weeks and if he had any news, he would then be able to give it to me. I visited him yesterday and he told me the news.'

Franz Hermann paused to remove a handkerchief from his pocket and he noisily blew his nose. His voice was trembling when he next spoke. 'They brought the urn round last week containing Harald's ashes. They say he died of a heart condition – natural causes. Apparently that is what they say with everyone. I am so sorry, Rosa...'

The ensuing silence lasted a lifetime and as happens in such circumstances, even the quietest, least obtrusive sound reverberated around the room. Rosa cried solidly for the next ten minutes, and then she stood up and walked around the room, deep in thought. When she spoke, her voice sounded resolute. 'I have made a decision Gunter. Do what you can to get Alfred out. It will be easier if it is just him, no?'

Both men nodded: this is what they had been saying for months.

'We're all doomed if we stay. Alfred will be the easiest to smuggle out. Can you do it?'

Franz Hermann nodded his head up and down and from side to side, weighing up the chances of success. *Maybe; there's a chance.*

'We can try, Rosa, I promise you' said Gunter. 'And then we will get you and Sophia out.'

It was seven o'clock before Gunter Reinhart left the house on the corner of Kaiser Wilhelm Strasse and Arno-Holz Strasse. Franz

Hermann said he would walk with him to the station while Silke looked after his mother, allowing Rosa to stay with the distraught children.

They walked in silence until they were on Königin-Luise-Strasse, each man wrapped in his own thoughts and seemingly overwhelmed by the enormity of the situation closing in on them.

'We must get Alfred out before it is too late,' said Gunter. 'But it is going to be so difficult, Franz – so dangerous. The boy has no papers. If there was any way I could get him to Switzerland then I have a good friend in Zurich who would take care of him, but how can I get him there?'

Franz Hermann said nothing for a while, but Gunter noticed that first he was shaking his head and then nodding it, as if he was having a heated debate with himself. *Pros and cons.* Podbielski Allee station was in view by the time Hermann spoke, although only after he had carefully looked around to ensure that no one was within earshot: that was how people spoke in Berlin these days. 'This is about your son's life, Gunter, so I can absolutely trust you, yes?'

'That goes without saying.'

'Let me ask you a question first: how senior are you at the Reichs-bank?'

'Senior enough: I run a department.'

'And how close are you to Walther Funk?'

'We aren't friends as such, but I am good at my job and he relies on me for certain matters: I handle our transactions with the Swiss. That is very important to him—'

'And the economies of countries we have occupied, do you get involved in them?'

'To an extent, certainly if we need to move money and gold from those countries to Switzerland. Why are you asking this?'

'I want to know how much you are trusted at the Reichsbank. After all, you were married to a Jew.'

'That was many years ago, Franz. And remember, I divorced her. It is no doubt on a file somewhere, but it is not an issue. I even made sure I joined the Nazi Party. In answer to your question, I am trusted.'

'I have some… contacts, Gunter: people who may be able to help get Alfred out of Germany. But they would want something in return, something that you may be able to get your hands on.'

The two men had now moved to the side of the pavement, standing next to the railing and under a tree whose branches fell to just above their heads. Franz Hermann paused and took a deep breath, about to take the plunge.

'Go on, Hermann, what is it?'

'I am going to ask you about something: if you have not heard of it, please forget I ever asked the question. Do you understand?'

He nodded. The two men waited while an elderly couple and their dog strolled past, nodding in reply to their greeting.

'Have you ever come across a document called Directive 21?'

Gunter Reinhart stared at Franz Hermann long and hard, his eyes terrified. He looked more shocked than when he had met the lawyer in the bar and been told that Rosa and the children were back in Berlin.

'Are you being serious?'

'Yes. Are you aware of it?'

'I am. But how on earth have you heard about it?'

'For heaven's sake, Gunter, keep your voice down. You do not need to know that. Have you actually seen it?'

'I have. Do you know how top secret this is?'

'Tell me how you have had access to it?'

'There is one copy in the Reichsbank. It is kept in a safe in Funk's office but I have been able to see it because he is very concerned that if this… hang on, Hermann: you tell me what this Directive is about – you tell me that before I say anything else.'

'It is about plans to invade the Soviet Union.'

'Very well then: Funk and no doubt many of the others are nothing if not greedy. They are concerned that if – when – this invasion takes place we should have plans in place to get our hands on what assets we can and get them into our Swiss bank accounts. That is why I am allowed access to the document.'

'Presumably you can't take it out of Funk's office?'

'Yes and no: if I need to see it I have to put a request in writing to his private secretary and if he approves then I am allowed to see it in a secure room next to Funk's office.'

'Are you alone in that room?'

'Funk's private secretary is meant to stay in with me, but he is an impatient sort: he will usually stay in the room for five minutes and if it looks like I am going to be any longer he will go and sit at his desk, which is just outside the door.'

Very slowly the two men walked towards Podbielski Allee station, talking as they did so. It was gone eight o'clock before Gunter Reinhart returned to his house in Charlottenburg and the inevitable wrath of his wife. He was, however, oblivious to it.

He had to make a plan.

Chapter 15

On a blustery Tuesday afternoon at the beginning of February, Captain Edgar was summoned to Christopher Porter's office on the top floor of a building best described as functional rather than in any way elegant. Edgar stood at the narrow window overlooking St James' Square, his back turned to his superior who appeared to be even more ill at ease in Edgar's presence than normal.

'I do wish you'd sit down Edgar.'

Edgar turned round, leaning against the window ledge.

'You said this was urgent... sir.' There was a pause before the 'sir'.

Christopher Porter cleared his throat and nervously straightened the fountain pen holder on his desk. 'I have to tell you, Edgar, that I am getting all kinds of flak from Downing Street. It is most trying.'

'I am sorry to hear that, sir. Is this in connection with anything in particular?'

'In connection with our intelligence that Germany may be planning an invasion of the Soviet Union. You insisted on it being a complete secret, but now Downing Street have caught wind of it and they are not happy, to say the very least. Their view – and I am informed that this is very much the view of the Prime Minister – is that from the outset we should have shared our intelligence that such plans existed more widely.'

'But we are not obliged to share every shred of unconfirmed intelligence, surely?'

'Indeed Edgar – but this is more than a "shred of unconfirmed intelligence", isn't it? We knew about the meeting in Bad Reichenhall last July and we know about this Directive that Hitler issued in

177

December, don't we? The Prime Minister is of the view that this is the single most important area of intelligence at the moment and we must do everything we can to get our hands on it. It has been made very clear to me that our failure to share this intelligence is viewed most seriously: the one way in which we can redeem ourselves is by getting our hands on this wretched document. If—'

'*Get our hands on it?* Are you joking? If that is seriously the view of Downing Street then one has to be most concerned at their grasp on reality. We have been told that there are no more than nine copies of this Directive 21. The idea that we can obtain one of them is ridiculous. How do your chums in Downing Street propose that we go about this?'

Christopher Porter was now busying himself moving the large blotting pad around on his desk.

'You will need to go out there, Edgar.'

'You mean go to Germany?'

'Not if we can avoid it. I was wondering about that chap Hunter?'

'Henry Hunter?' Edgar began to pace the room, turning once again to stare out of the window overlooking St James' Square, deep in thought. 'That is not a bad idea sir, I'll grant you that. His trial run in Germany last year went well. He's still in Switzerland so has perfect cover to go into Germany.'

'The best bet would be for you to get to Switzerland through Portugal and Spain – can't see another way at the moment. Once you're safely there we can take a view.'

Edgar stared at Porter in disbelief as it dawned on him that he was being serious.

'Any other country you'd like me to drop into while I'm over there? Italy perhaps, Poland? And how do you propose that I get out there?'

Porter smiled as he unlocked a drawer in his desk and removed a small pile of envelopes.

'That, Edgar, is where I think I can surprise even you!'

'You are being serious then are you?'

'Indeed I am, Edgar. Not only serious but also resourceful. You may or may not be aware that there is a scheduled daily air service from

Bristol to Lisbon. You won't know how hard this has been, but I have managed to secure you a seat on the flight to Lisbon on Thursday.'

'This Thursday?' Edgar looked surprised. 'And when I get to Lisbon?'

'Well, Lisbon station is very much Sandy Morgan's show. He'll arrange for you to meet up with Telmo and three of you can see where we are with regards to our lady in Berlin. After that Morgan will get you into Spain and over to Barcelona: there are scheduled Swissair flights from there into Switzerland. From Barcelona you're going to have to go into Switzerland with your American cover: no alternative, I'm afraid: the Swiss are terribly jumpy about us at the moment.'

–

Captain Edgar was acutely aware that he appeared to have been cast as a character from one of those Agatha Christie crime novels of which his wife was so fond.

It was midday and he and the other characters were assembled in a draughty room at Whitchurch Airport, just outside Bristol. There were fifteen passengers including a priest, two elderly women wrapped in furs, a woman accompanied by a young boy and two men speaking Portuguese. Edgar was half expecting to be joined by a Belgian detective with a waxed moustache.

It had been an hour since Edgar had checked in for the flight. For the purposes of the trip Edgar was travelling under a British diplomatic passport in the name of the Hon. Anthony Davis. The 'Hon.', Edgar assumed, was an example of Porter's public school humour. The Hon. Anthony Davis had various letters with him to the effect that he would be spending an unspecified period of time at the British Embassy in Lisbon dealing with 'consular services'.

A few minutes after midday the passengers were led out of the room and across the apron to the DC-3 that would be flying them to Lisbon. Within minutes they were airborne, heading west along the Bristol Channel and out towards sea. When the southern tip of Ireland peeked out of the low cloud the plane changed course, at which point the captain spoke to the passengers:

'*Welcome aboard this BOAC flight from Bristol to Lisbon, where we expect to arrive just after four pm local time. Due to wartime flying regulations we will be flying at a maximum altitude of 3,000 feet.*'

Edgar closed his eyes and tried to rest as the captain continued to speak. He recalled being told that the pilots on these flights were all Dutch: they had managed to fly most of the KLM fleet to Britain just before the German invasion of the Netherlands and they and their planes now serviced the few remaining BOAC flights.

To his surprise, Edgar must have fallen asleep straight away because he was woken up by a stern looking stewardess who was shaking him by the elbow. They were beginning their descent into Portela Airport.

The plane was flying low, hugging the Portuguese coast, the sky cloudless and the remains of the sun lighting up the land to their left. Edgar glanced to his right: across the aisle the priest was fervently praying, the rosary gripped tightly in his hands. The plane banked sharply over the city, buildings rushing by underneath them. Within a minute, Portela Airport appeared below them. The pilot made one pass of the airport, turned one hundred and eighty degrees and then began the final approach.

–

At the British Embassy just off the Rua de São Domingos Sandy Morgan greeted him like the old friend that he was. He hurried out from behind his desk in a crumpled white suit and after grasping Edgar by the hand and warmly shaking it, removed a large bottle of Bells from a cabinet by the window. Two glasses were on his desk, one of which he pushed towards Edgar.

'Now then, old chap, bet you can do with one of these? Good flight, I hope? Beats me how we can get away with it: can't understand how they just don't take a shot at our planes. Mind you, I suppose we'd do the same to theirs, eh? Handy though, can't tell you how much useful stuff we pick up at the airport. We have people watching it the whole time. Germans do as well, so I suppose we cancel each other out. Even pick up their newspapers, which London is rather keen on. Anyway, cheers!'

Sandy Morgan downed his whisky, which had clearly not been his first of the afternoon, in one go and quickly refilled his glass from a new bottle he had produced from behind his desk. Edgar held his hand over his glass and shook his head.

'Now then, quick run through the plan. Idea is that you stay in my place, which is in an annexe of the embassy, so no need for you to be seen out and about. We'll sort you accreditation with the Ministry of Foreign Affairs tomorrow. Correct me if I am wrong, but the story is that you're here to check our consular system?'

'Something like that.'

'Funnily enough, they could do with sorting out but I can't imagine you're interested in that. That gives you the cover you need: the PVDE keep a careful eye on us, but it is not too difficult to fool them. Idea is that after a couple of days you will come down with something nasty which will keep you in bed for a couple of weeks. The doctor we use is a rather helpful chap; he'll back up any story. That will give us enough time to get you to Barcelona and Switzerland and then back again, and home without the PVDE spotting it. Sound reasonable?'

Edgar nodded, slightly unsure. Sandy Morgan, despite his manner, was a good operator. He was one of the few station chiefs whom he trusted.

'We will meet with Telmo on either Saturday or Sunday: it's quieter then, easier all round. I'll only know for sure late tomorrow. Assuming that goes well, you will head off to Spain on Monday. Madrid station will look after you and get you over to Barcelona and a flight from there to Switzerland. You'll be using an American cover, I understand?'

–

Sunday was warm; it almost felt spring-like. Edgar and Sandy Morgan sat on the balcony of Morgan's small apartment in the Embassy annexe, sipping fresh coffee. Edgar had been aware that Morgan had left the apartment very early in the morning, before six as far as he could tell.

'I wouldn't say that Telmo has got cold feet but he's nervous, Edgar. Things aren't quite right in this city. Portugal is meant to be our oldest ally, but Salazar trusts no one – not us, not the Germans and certainly not Spain. He seems to have got it in his mind that Spain has plans to invade this place. Upshot of all this is that everyone is very twitchy. The PVDE are watching everyone and Telmo is worried that they're watching him. He tried to cry off on Friday night and then again last night, which is why I had to sneak out this morning. He's agreed to meet you, Edgar, but be gentle with him. He is one of us, after all.'

'When and where?'

'This afternoon. Hope you like football.'

Morgan and Edgar left the Embassy later that morning, half an hour apart and met as arranged at a bar on the Rossio an hour later. They then travelled by tram, taxi, foot and tram again. By the time they had finished their second tram journey they were part of a crowd heading in one direction. They were, Morgan announced, in Lumiar.

'We're in the north of the city, not far from the Airport.'

Twenty minutes later, Edgar was inside a football ground for the first time in his life.

'Quick briefing, Edgar: you're now in the Campo do Lumiar which is the home of Sporting Clube de Portugal, which is always called Sporting. They're one of the top clubs in the country; some would say the top club though I daresay Benfica and Porto might disagree. Their opponents this afternoon are Barreirense, so it is something of a local derby.'

They were walking down the stand now, Morgan looking carefully along the rows.

'Just so you don't have to appear too ignorant, Sporting play in green, Barreirense in red.'

'And who do we want to win, Sandy?'

'Doesn't matter, does it? Personally I have a soft spot for Benfica, so I don't mind. Barreirense are quite a good side this year so it could be a close game. Perhaps best if you don't shout too much anyway. Clap in the right places. Ah... good, there's Telmo; so he turned up after all. Now remember to be nice to him – make him feel wanted. We don't want him turning cold on us, do we?'

At the very end of a row Telmo Rocha Martins was standing up, waving casually at them. *Here I am.* He was short – about five foot five, bald, with a neat moustache and round, black glasses. A large crowd had already formed in the Campo do Lumiar and Telmo, wrapped in a large, slightly shabby jacket, was just one of them.

It was the first time that Edgar had actually met Telmo Rocha Martins, one of the most important British agents in Portugal. Telmo was a middle-ranking civil servant in the Portuguese Ministry of Foreign Affairs – not regarded highly enough nor ranked so senior as to be considered a diplomat, but the kind of civil servant who ensures that everything runs smoothly while other people grab the glory. This had been a source of increasing resentment to Telmo, one that had led him to approach the British when the war started with an offer to pass on the kind of information for which money changed hands.

Now, his status and his low profile suited him perfectly. No one suspected this mild-mannered, bespectacled man for a moment. The quality of intelligence that he passed on to the British improved all the time. He had been given a miniature camera and at first it was copies of Ministry briefing papers and some telegrams from overseas embassies that were passed on. Then, in early 1940, Telmo asked Morgan at one of their regular meetings whether he would be interested, by any chance, in more material from Berlin?

'*Rather*,' had been Morgan's response, careful to show that he was not too desperate. London had been crying out for *anything* from Berlin, such was their paucity of sources in the city. *And we mean anything: even bloody bus tickets!*

What Telmo came up with was much better than 'bloody bus tickets'. There were briefings from the German foreign ministry, minutes of meetings with German officials, assessments of the strengths and weaknesses of the armed forces, telegrams: half the contents of the diplomatic bag, as far as Morgan could work out. And from what London was telling him, it was all first class stuff. '*Well done. Plenty more of that will do nicely thank you!*'

But Morgan was a cautious chap. He was well aware that this intelligence coming out of Berlin could turn out to be too good to be true and if that were the case, he did not fancy getting the blame for it. So, one Saturday afternoon, he took Telmo out for a drive to Cascais and they went for a long walk along the seafront.

'London want to know how come you're getting such good material out of Berlin?'

This was not strictly true: London were so grateful they were not questioning the material as much as Morgan was. They had walked for quite a while with Telmo saying nothing, evidently weighing up whether or not to come clean.

'I had been considering raising this with you. If there is ever a problem, will you promise that you will ensure that you could get me to England, maybe on one of your convoys?'

'I'd do my very best, Telmo: what kind of problem were you thinking of, though?'

'If they ever suspected me – that kind of problem. I would like to go to England. I would like to have a house in London. Maybe near to Buckingham Palace.'

'I'd certainly see what we can do. Not sure how near to the Palace, but there are some other lovely parts of London.'

'And if my source in Berlin was to accompany me, would that be a problem?'

'No! Not at all. I'd need to know who this person is, of course...'

'Even if we were not married?'

Which was how Telmo Rocha Martins came to tell Sandy Morgan all about Dona Maria do Rosario. He told him how Dona Maria had been a secretary to his head of department in the Ministry of Foreign Affairs; how they had become close and eventually became lovers; how it would be impossible for him to leave his wife and remain in his job and stay in Portugal. He told Morgan about how Dona Maria had become proficient in German and had been transferred to the Legation in Berlin, but not before he had confided in her and she had agreed to supply information. In her case, the motivation was personal and political. Her fiancée had been imprisoned during the 1926 coup and had died soon after. Following this she had left Porto and moved to Lisbon, working her way through the various government ministries around the Praça do Comercio.

Telmo had chosen a good spot. They were at the end of the front row of their block, so there was no one sitting in front of them or to the right. Morgan sat between Telmo and Edgar, acting as interpreter.

'We are very grateful to you, Telmo,' said Edgar quietly, pausing while Sandy Morgan translated. 'Very, very grateful. I want you to know how much we appreciate your help. I can assure you that if there is ever a… problem here in Portugal, we will do our very best to get you to London.'

Telmo smiled and nodded his head, not taking his eyes off the pitch. 'I am very grateful. But can you promise me that this assurance will also apply to Dona Maria?'

'Of course…'

They paused as the crowd rose around them: a Sporting player was fouled on the edge of the penalty area. They continued to stand while the free kick was taken and then sat down after it soared over the bar.

'I need to ask you about Dona Maria. She is sending a lot of material. How is she able to do this…? Is she not suspected at all?'

'I assure you she is careful. Because of my job, I am in a position to see the diplomatic bag soon after it arrives at the Ministry, before anyone else has seen it other than a clerk. I am then able to take the material, which is all in code. It is not possible for other people to spot the material or be aware of any code. If we were suspected, they may be, but no one suspects us. But I have something important to tell you.'

There was another delay as a Barreirense winger beat a succession of Sporting defenders but then shot wide. 'Our defence is too slow today, far too slow. Listen carefully, please: Dona Maria passed on your message to Hugo, about getting hold of this document. A message came through on Friday. Hugo wants you to know that he may be able to get hold of the document: it seems that he has a source who has access to this document. But there is a price to pay.'

'How much?'

Sporting scored and the crowd leapt up around them. Everyone was patting their companions on the back, as if they'd played a part in the goal. Telmo looked delighted.

'Fortunately our attack is much better than our defence. It's not money. It is a lot more complicated. You had better listen carefully.'

Edgar did listen carefully. It was complicated. He would need to get to Switzerland as soon as possible.

He was only shaken out of his thoughts by Sporting's second goal.
The game finished two nil. If only everything in life was so clear
cut Edgar thought as they left the ground and Telmo melted into the
crowd.

Chapter 16

London, February 1941

By noon on Wednesday 12th of February, Christopher Porter had been kept waiting in a narrow corridor in a draughty and heavily guarded basement under the Admiralty building in Whitehall for well over an hour past the time of his appointment. When he was finally called in to the office outside which he had been waiting, there was neither apology nor explanation, just a mildly exasperated look from Sir Roland Pearson.

'How can I help you, Porter?' Sir Roland Pearson had once been a colleague but now worked in Downing Street and currently had the ear of the Prime Minister on all matters to do with intelligence. He gave the impression that he was now far too important for his time to be wasted.

'As you know, Sir Roland, we met on the third when you made clear the Prime Minister's feelings regarding our intelligence from Berlin and the Directive regarding a possible invasion of the Soviet Union. I subsequently dispatched Edgar to Lisbon, where he met our source, Telmo, on Sunday.'

'Telmo. Remind me?'

'Telmo Rocha Martins: he works in the Portuguese Ministry of Foreign Affairs in Lisbon and has proven to be an extremely useful source of information for us. His main informant is Dona Maria do Rosario, who is secretary to the military attaché in the Portuguese Legation in Berlin. As well as passing on information through Telmo she also serves as a contact for Hugo – he is Franz Hermann, the Berlin lawyer who is working for us. Any information that he has, or messages that we have for him, comes through Dona Maria in the Portuguese diplomatic bag.'

Porter had now opened a notebook and put on a pair of reading glasses.

'When Edgar met Telmo on Sunday he passed on the latest from Hugo, via Dona Maria. We were aware that Hugo has been sheltering a Jewish family, which we thought was an unnecessary risk and therefore did not wholly approve of. However, it transpires that this family may be critical in terms of our obtaining a copy of this Directive. The family Hugo is helping to shelter is a Jewish woman called Rosa Stern and her two children: an eleven-year-old boy called Alfred and a five-year-old girl called Sophia. Rosa's husband is a businessman called Harald Stern, who was arrested by the Nazis sometime in late 1939 and subsequently died – or was killed – in one of their prison camps. Harald Stern was the father of Sophia but not of Alfred. Alfred's father is one Gunter Reinhart, Rosa Stern's first husband. Reinhart is not Jewish: he and Rosa divorced in 1935 after Hitler's law which prohibits marriages between Jews and non-Jews.'

'I hope this is family saga is leading somewhere important, Porter.'

'It is, sir. From what we understand, Gunter Reinhart and Rosa Stern remained on good terms and Gunter did what he could to help them. Rosa and the children had moved to Paris, but returned to Berlin when Harald was arrested – it seems that he may have remained there to try and sort out some business matters. Now they are being hidden in the home of a relative of Hugo's. However, Gunter Reinhart works for the Reichsbank, where he occupies a fairly senior position. Part of his job is helping to move money out of countries occupied by the Germans. In this respect, it appears that he has access to a copy of this Directive 21.'

'Good heavens.'

'Good heavens indeed. You see why I needed to give you the background.'

'And this Reinhart – he can supply us with Directive 21?'

'Yes, but...'

'He wants money, I imagine. How much?'

'I only wish it were that simple. His condition is that we smuggle his son Alfred out of Berlin. Reinhart has a friend in Zurich: once Alfred has been safely delivered to that friend, he will release a copy of Directive 21 to Hugo.'

Sir Roland had leaned back in his chair and was staring at the ceiling, as if the solution may be hidden in the cobwebs he had spotted above the coving.

'So how do we get Alfred to Zurich?'

'Even as we speak, Sir Roland, Edgar is on his way to Switzerland. We have an agent there called Henry Hunter. Hunter also has a genuine Swiss identity and he is able to travel into Germany with it. A year ago we sent him into Germany on a test mission of sorts, which went well. I have said to Edgar that he and Basil Remington-Barber must come up with a plan to get Hunter to Berlin and out again with Alfred.'

'Which will not be straightforward.'

'Indeed, Sir Roland. But we have to get Alfred out – the prize is too great not to attempt it.'

Sir Roland stood up and walked away from the table and over to his desk, from which he picked up a silver box and lit up a cigarette he had selected from it. He removed his jacket and hung it over the back of his chair. On the wall behind him was a map of Europe and for a while he studied it, reacquainting himself with the various locations. With his forefinger he traced an angled line south from Berlin to Zurich.

'And once this Alfred is safely delivered to this friend in Zurich we get the report?'

'Once the friend has confirmed it.'

'And I presume that Hugo then hands the report over to Dona Maria whatshername and she pops it into the diplomatic bag and we pick up the report in Lisbon?'

Porter closed his notebook and folded up his reading glasses. Twice he started to speak, but hesitated. He was clenching and then unclenching his fists and clearly finding difficulty in knowing where to start.

'Can I be most frank and most honest with you, Sir Roland?'

'I had rather hoped that had been the case up to now anyway, Porter.'

Porter's hands were now clasped as if in prayer. He drew a deep breath before speaking.

'The most obvious route to bring the Directive out of Berlin would indeed be through the Portuguese diplomatic bag, I quite agree. But if there is an overriding purpose to us obtaining this document it is to help prove to the Russians that their supposed allies are not what they seem and in fact have plans to invade them. Correct?'

Sir Roland nodded.

'Up to now, the Russians have chosen to ignore all of these warnings, most especially the ones that can be attributed to us. Frankly, they do not believe what we tell them. They are convinced that our motives are to stir up trouble between them and the Germans. They choose to believe that whatever intelligence we are passing to them is false. Our concern is that if we – the British – show them the Directive or tell them about its contents then they will similarly ignore them, as they have all the other warnings. All the considerable effort of obtaining the Directive will have been wasted.'

'What do you suggest then, Porter?'

'This is where I have to be very frank. Henry Hunter, our agent in Switzerland who is able to travel into Germany, is not quite what he seems… I think I will have that cigarette after all, Sir Roland.'

Sir Roland rejoined Porter at the table and slid the silver cigarette box across it, followed by a box of matches. He noticed Porter shook slightly as he lit his cigarette.

'We had our eyes on Hunter for some time. He is ideal in many ways: very good Swiss identity, speaks all the relevant languages. Even the Swiss believe he is Swiss, if you get what I mean. We picked him up here just before the start of the war: he was trying to smuggle out some money he had inherited and we gave him the choice of working for us or spending a few years breaking rocks or whatever we make people do in prisons these days. He chose to work for us.'

'Good.'

'However, what he did not know and still does not know is that we know something else about him. That he had already been recruited as an agent: by the Russians.'

Sir Roland had been moving his cigarette towards his mouth. Now he stopped, holding it is mid-air. He leaned towards Porter.

'Really? When did this happen?'

'We think it was around 1930 or 1931, Sir Roland – a couple of years after he moved to Geneva from Zurich with his mother and stepfather. Basil Remington-Barber had an informant in the Geneva branch of the Communist Party of Switzerland. He thought we'd be interested because Hunter had dual British and Swiss nationalities. He had seen Hunter at one or two meetings and then disappeared from view. Normally we would not have attached a good deal of importance to that: plenty of young chaps go to these type of meetings and then lose interest. But Remington-Barber's informant thought that he had seen Hunter chatting to a French chap who was rumoured to have links with the Comintern and we do know that it is a very well established recruitment tactic of the Soviet intelligence agencies for them to keep an eye open for likely recruits who have joined or try to join their local communist parties. What happens is they spot someone and then persuade them that the best way to serve the cause is not to be a party member but to work for them. They leave the party, all records are destroyed and they display no outward affiliation with or interest in communism – often the opposite, in fact. We assume this is what happened with Hunter.'

'And how and when did you get to know that he was a Soviet agent?'

'Not until early thirty nine. We think he must have been told to lay low until they needed him and certainly the way he was living in Geneva no one would have had any reason whatsoever to suspect him We became very interested in a Soviet spymaster, chap called Viktor Krasotkin. Very bright chap: based in Paris but moves around Western Europe as if he owns the place. Quite brilliant actually, but our people in Paris were aware of him and for a while had someone quite close to him. This person tipped us off about an English chap with Swiss nationality who was one of Viktor's agents. Once we knew this, we tried to recruit him and he rather fell into our hands.'

'But what has this to do with the Directive?'

'Once Henry delivers Alfred to Zurich and Reinhart gets the green light, Henry can return to Berlin and he can bring the document back to Switzerland.'

'The point of that being…?'

'He will be made well aware quite how important the document is – top secret, et cetera. We know that as soon as he gets back to Switzerland he is bound to show it to Viktor Krasotkin, even before he hands it over to Edgar. That way, the Russians will know it is genuine. It will have come straight from the horse's mouth, so to speak. They will have to believe it then, won't they?'

Chapter 17

Under the identity of Patrick T O'Connor Junior, a U.S. citizen, Edgar left Muntadas airport in Barcelona just before ten in the morning on Swissair flight 1087. The flight landed on time in Locarno at a quarter past one. Five hours later he was in a small apartment above a hardware shop on Basteiplatz. He was let in by an Austrian called Rolf Eder, who worked for Remington-Barber.

'No need to worry about Rolf,' Remington-Barber had assured him. 'Completely trustworthy: he's an Austrian social democrat. Whitlock recruited him in Vienna sometime around thirty six. Nazis rolled into Vienna in March 1938 and Rolf rolled out soon after that: hates the Germans more than we do, if that is possible. His fiancée's a prisoner of theirs. When Whitlock had to leave Vienna and he found out that Rolf was here in Switzerland he recommended him to me.'

–

Basil Remington-Barber and Henry Hunter arrived in Zurich late on the Thursday afternoon and checked into the same hotel on Oetenbachgasse where Henry had stayed the previous February on the night before he travelled to Stuttgart. The next morning Remington-Barber left Hunter in his room to rest and met Edgar as arranged on Bahnhofquai. Together they watched a noisy barge make its way up the Limmat.

'Hunter all right, is he?'

'After a fashion, yes: picked him up yesterday morning in Geneva during his morning walk and told him to pack his bags, bid his farewells and we're off to Zurich. It's a year since he was in Germany and I rather think that he assumed we had forgotten about him. Not very happy that I haven't told him what's going on, but then I hardly know myself, do I?'

'And did you give him an opportunity to make contact?'

'Naturally: I told him that we would catch the one o'clock train to Zurich and I would meet him by the platform with his ticket at a quarter to one. That gave him ample opportunity to get a message to his other people that something may be on. Good to dangle bait of some kind in front of them.'

'Good, well done, Basil. Sorry to be somewhat elusive, but I need to track someone down. Come along later this afternoon to the apartment with Hunter.'

—

All things considered, it had not been a good day and a half for Henry Hunter, and it showed no signs of improving.

On the Thursday he had been whisked away from Geneva by Basil Remington-Barber, with little by way of an explanation other than 'We're going to Zurich: pack for a few days. Don't forget your passport.' The subsequent train journey had passed mostly in silence, Remington-Barber declining to answer any of Hunter's questions.

Then Remington-Barber had ordered him to remain in his stuffy little hotel room for most of the Friday morning. He had no idea what was going on or what was going to happen, so he was feeling increasingly anxious. There was a small part of him – a very small part, admittedly – which was relieved that, after a year of hearing nothing from the British, at last they now seemed to have plans for him. An even smaller part of him was excited at the prospect of what those plans may involve. He had spent the past year reflecting on the fact that although the trip to Stuttgart and Essen had been fraught with danger, but the excitement of having completed the mission so successfully had surprised him. The months since then had been a mixture of boredom and nervous anticipation of when he would next be called upon: added to this was the pressure of serving two masters. At least the 100 pounds was being paid into his Credit Suisse account each month, which was one consolation.

Now Remington-Barber had sent a rather friendly Austrian called Rolf to bring him to a small apartment above a hardware shop on Basteiplatz. It was three thirty in the afternoon and they had been waiting in the sparsely furnished lounge for the best part of an hour. Henry Hunter was sitting on an uncomfortable sofa while Remington-Barber nervously paced the room, darting over to the window overlooking Basteiplatz every time he heard footsteps below. The diplomat had said very little since they had arrived there: 'Sit over there Henry... Yes, we are waiting for someone... Please be patient.'

Eventually, a bell rang and Remington-Barber sent Rolf downstairs to let whoever it was in. Hunter heard two pairs of footsteps ascending the stairs. At first he did not recognise the tall figure wearing a trilby hat who had to stoop as he entered the door. But then he removed the trilby and said 'Henry' – no more than that, just 'Henry' – before taking off his raincoat and slinging it over a chair and then angling the single armchair so that it was directly facing the sofa.

'Sit down, Basil, you're making me nervous. No need to keep looking out of the window: no one has followed me; I can assure you of that. Make yourself useful – pass me that ashtray and then go and sit next to Henry. Either of you chaps fancy a cigarette?'

Edgar lounged back in the armchair, stretching out his long legs so that they almost touched the feet of the two men opposite him. Not bothering to stifle a series of yawns he closed his eyes momentarily and for a while it looked as if he was about to fall asleep. Then he sat up straight, slapped his thighs and then rubbed his hands.

'Right – down to business. Henry, you look rather shocked to see me: understandable I suppose. I imagine you rather hoped that you'd never see me again, eh?'

Henry said nothing.

'And are you keeping well, Henry?'

'I'm well thank you. And you?'

'Basil tells me that your little trip to Germany last year went well.'

Henry was about to reply but Edgar raised a hand to stop him.

'And the money going in to your account every month as promised, I presume? Along with the 500 you received after your trip.'

Henry replied that it was.

'Which, in a sense, is why I am here. It's time for you to do something more to earn that money. How about if I was to tell you that you're going back to Germany?'

Henry was drumming his fingers on his knees and very slowing nodding his head. 'To Essen?'

'Good heavens, no! We can hardly have the murderer returning to the scene of his crime, can we?' Edgar laughed heartily and Remington-Barber joined in nervously.

'We thought Berlin would make a nice change.'

Henry gazed quizzically at Edgar, as if he was trying to work out whether the man opposite him was being serious.

'Berlin?'

'Yes, Henry, Berlin. Capital of the Third Reich.'

'Really?'

'Yes, really. Look, I could tell you all about it now, but I'd just end up repeating myself later on. We have a chap coming to see us in an hour or so and we'll put all of our cards on the table then. Talking of tables, Basil, how about some tea, eh?'

Basil Remington-Barber headed over to the small kitchen, pausing in its doorway.

'You certain this chap is going to turn up, Edgar?'

'Don't worry Basil. I am certain of it. He really has no alternative.'

–

Captain Edgar had finally approached the man at lunchtime that Friday. It felt as if he had spent half of his life following people, waiting for hours in the shadows of doorways for them to appear, calculating when they would emerge and what would then be the best time and place to approach them. He had learnt through years of experience that most people tended to be unpredictable in their habits but he could have guessed that if anyone would be a man of precise routine it would be a Swiss banker and Michael Hedinger did not disappoint him.

According to the message that Hugo sent through Lisbon, Gunter Reinhart's friend in Zurich was a man called Michael Hedinger who worked for Bank Leu. Hedinger was apparently aware 'in principle' – whatever that meant – that his friend Gunter in Berlin wanted him to help look after his son, but he would have no idea that he was about to be approached.

Edgar had watched the bank over the past couple of days. It had been founded in 1755 and some of the employees he watched coming in and out looked as if they had been there that long. Now it was one of the 'Big Seven' Swiss banks: not one of the largest, but still big enough to have its snout in the German trough, along with all the others. With the help of a porter at the bank who had been paid generously in return for doing no more than giving a signal when Michael Hedinger entered the building, Edgar had been able to spot his quarry.

Herr Hedinger left the head office of Bank Leu on Paradeplatz at precisely one o'clock, presumably on his way to lunch. He turned into Bahnhofstrasse and Edgar decided that now was the time he had to make his move.

'Herr Hedinger, may I have a word with you?'

Edgar had approached the banker from behind, having got as close to him as possible and making sure he placed himself between the man and the road. It was a well-practised technique, as was the friendly but firm hand on the man's elbow and the enforced shaking of his hand. *Hold one arm, shake the other arm: take control.* That way, anyone watching would assume that it was a chance encounter between two acquaintances.

'I beg your pardon?' Hedinger had replied in German and sounded surprised rather than annoyed. This was encouraging but Edgar could not assume this would last for long.

'I need to talk you about a rather important matter, Herr Hedinger. Is there somewhere quiet perhaps we could go?' Edgar was speaking German too.

'I don't know who you are. What is this about?' Now Hedinger was beginning to sound annoyed and a man and woman turned to look at them as they passed by. People were not accustomed to raised voices on the streets of Zurich.

Edgar edged even closer to Hedinger. 'It is in connection with Gunter Reinhart in Berlin, Herr Hedinger.'

Edgar was not prepared for the reaction that followed. He had hoped that, at the mention of Reinhart, Hedinger would relax and want to know more: quite possibly he had expected to be contacted and may even be relieved. What he had not expected was to see the look of sheer panic and fear that spread across Hedinger's face. Edgar could not be sure, but it looked as if his eyes had filled with tears. The banker appeared unsteady on his feet.

'Come with me.'

Michael Hedinger meekly allowed Edgar to shepherd him across Bahnhofstrasse and then onto Kappelergasse where they settled on a bench overlooking the river. Edgar could see that the man next to him was terrified, a reaction he had not expected. Edgar took his time lighting a cigarette and held the packet in front of the other man. Hedinger shook his head. 'No, I don't smoke.'

'What is your name? What is this about? Please tell me!'

Edgar ignored the first question. 'I told you: it is in connection with Gunter Reinhart. You know Herr Reinhart – from the Reichsbank in Berlin?'

'I am not sure. Why do you ask?'

'It is a very straightforward question, Herr Hedinger. Either you know him or you don't?'

'We are acquaintances, in a professional capacity.'

Edgar had prepared his next line: *Herr Reinhart has asked for help in bringing his son Alfred out of Berlin and he tells us that you are prepared to look after him in Zurich.* But before he had an opportunity to say that Hedinger gripped his forearm and turned to face Edgar. He was a man of medium height, but with the kind of shrunken appearance reserved for those of especially nervous disposition. With his unhealthily pale complexion, watery blue eyes with scarcely a trace of eyebrow above them and his few remaining wisps of hair dancing in the wind he reminded Edgar of an English country clergyman, the type sent to only the most undemanding of parishes. Now he looked like a clergyman who had been caught in a compromising situation and was about to be defrocked. He was utterly terrified. Edgar could smell it on his breath.

'I have always feared this moment and had resolved that if – when – it came about, I would immediately be honest.' Hedinger's voice trembled as he spoke. 'It has all been a terrible misunderstanding... a most unfortunate misunderstanding. Herr Reinhart wanted to divert some of the funds from Germany into a private account in his name and in a moment of weakness I agreed and in a moment of even greater weakness I accepted some money from Herr Reinhart for myself... for my efforts. I regretted it immediately and in fact my money is held in a separate account. I can arrange to have it paid back to you within a matter of days. I can see to it this afternoon in fact.'

Edgar loosened the grip that Hedinger had on his arm and stood up to face the river. In a world of surprises, it was very rare for one to shock him, but this one had. By the sounds of it, Hedinger and Reinhart were involved in a scheme to smuggle German state funds out of Germany into their own private accounts here in Zurich. Hedinger must have assumed assuming that Edgar was a German official. He turned round: Hedinger was trembling, his feet tapping on the ground.

'I have a young family and I am a good man: I go to church every week. Please understand that I did not intend to keep your money. I am sure that I can have it all returned to you this afternoon – along with the money in Herr Reinhart's private account.'

'Are these accounts with Bank Leu?'

'Naturally.'

'Do you have the account numbers please?'

Hedinger obediently removed a slim black notebook from his jacket pocket and turned the pages with trembling fingers that had the appearance of having been manicured. From what Edgar could see, the notebook was full of numbers, figures, initials and dates. Edgar opened his own notebook and turning to a blank page wrote 'Reinhart' and then 'Hedinger'.

'Write the account numbers underneath each name please. Don't forget to put down how much money is in each account. I am sure we can resolve this matter in a satisfactory manner. If you co-operate, Herr Hedinger, then there should be no need for us to take further action.'

Hedinger grasped the bait like a hungry fish, eagerly copying down the account numbers. When he had finished he handed the notebook with its incriminating lists of bank accounts back to Edgar.

'Can I ask you sir, are you from the Gestapo?'

Edgar laughed: the outcome to the encounter with Michael Hedinger had been far better than he could have hoped.

'Well that is where I think I am going to surprise you, Herr Hedinger.'

–

'How can you be so sure he'll turn up, Edgar?'

'Because he will: because it is not in his interests not to turn up.'

Basil Remington-Barber shook his head and moved away from his spot by the window overlooking Basteiplatz which he had occupied on and off throughout the afternoon.

'Well, I wish I were able to share your confidence. In my experience, things don't always turn out quite as planned.'

'Basil, do stop pacing around and sit down quietly, as Henry is doing. It is now five o'clock. At this moment, our visitor will be leaving his office on Paradeplatz and commencing his short walk here. It will take him six minutes; I timed it myself earlier this afternoon. In fact I walked the route three times and it takes six minutes and twenty seconds, but I would not want you to think that I am a pedant. He will be with us by ten past five at the very latest, mark my words. What is it they say about the Swiss and clockworks?' And just one warning: he may tell us things we are already aware of – like the boy, Alfred. Pretend it is the first time we've heard it, eh?

At seven minutes past five a knowing smile crossed Edgar's face as the bell rang. He gave Remington-Barber a 'told you' look and went downstairs to let their visitor in. Two minutes later Michael Hedinger had joined the three Englishmen around the table.

For a moment the four of them sat in an uncomfortable silence. The newcomer was in a state of considerable nervousness. He had declined offers to remove his coat and had only reluctantly taken off his gloves and hat. He was clutching his bright brown briefcase to his chest and was clearly edgy, jumping at the sound of a car engine backfiring and at a door slamming in an apartment above. Edgar had placed himself at the head of the table: Hedinger was sitting to his left, opposite the other two men.

When Edgar began to speak it was initially to Hunter and Remington-Barber.

'Henri, Basil – this is Michael Hedinger. I will speak in German by the way: Herr Hedinger's English is very limited. Herr Hedinger works for Bank Leu, of which more in due course. Perhaps I should explain that when Herr Hedinger and I first met, some four hours ago, there was something of a misunderstanding. It was perhaps a fortunate misunderstanding from my point of view, less so from Herr Hedinger's. Is that not correct, Herr Hedinger?'

The banker looked up in an absent-minded manner, with a 'what me?' expression. He nodded meekly in reply to Edgar's question.

'Not to put too fine a point on it, it turns out that Herr Hedinger here in Zurich and Herr Reinhart in Berlin have been operating a – how can one put it? – a scheme whereby a proportion of the funds that were being transferred from the Reichsbank to the safekeeping of Bank Leu were diverted into private, numbered accounts: one belonging to Herr Reinhart, the other to Herr Hedinger. Is that correct, Herr Hedinger?'

Hedinger began to speak but was stopped by Edgar. 'You will have ample opportunity to talk in due course, Herr Hedinger. A very risky but at the same time very lucrative scheme: Herr Hedinger tells me that of the millions of Reichsmarks transferred through Herr Reinhart's operation at the Reichsbank to Bank Leu, some twenty five thousand have ended up in the two private accounts – that is around two thousand pounds sterling. Is that not correct, Herr Hedinger?'

He nodded, avoiding eye contact with anyone around the table.

'And the money is split equally, is it not?' Again, Hedinger nodded.

'Now this is where Herr Hedinger must be kicking himself. When I approached Herr Hedinger earlier today, I knew nothing of this scheme. However, the private enterprise with Herr Reinhart has obviously been on Herr Hedinger's conscience and he assumed that I was an official – a *German* official would you please – who was investigating the matter. Before I even had an opportunity to explain what I had approached him about, he confessed. Have I accurately summed up what happened, Herr Hedinger?'

The Swiss coughed and spoke in a soft voice. 'I never intended to keep the money but Gunter – Herr Reinhart – is a very persuasive man. He insisted that with the amount of money that was being transferred and the fact that some of it was obtained from private accounts by the Reichsbank, well… he said that it would be impossible for our accounts to be traced. He may well have been correct, but I have been terrified that I would be caught and that I would lose my job and my house – so much so that I have been a nervous wreck in recent weeks. I felt that it was just a matter of time before I was caught. When you approached me on Bahnhofstrasse I assumed that I had been caught: I was almost relieved, hence my rather too hasty confession.'

He shrugged his shoulders and spread his hands out in a 'so there we are' manner.

So there we are.

'As I told you earlier, Herr Hedinger, I could not care less about the money. Keep it, as far as we are concerned, better that it is your account and that of Herr Reinhart than in one belonging to the Reichsbank. The money is not our concern. Neither Bank Leu nor the Reichsbank need find out about it: you will keep your job and your fine house. But a happy outcome of that misunderstanding is that our knowledge of it has ensured your complete co-operation, Herr Hedinger, am I correct?'

'Indeed.'

'So now we come to our main business, of which we spoke briefly and of which Henry here is unaware. Herr Hedinger, for the sake of my colleagues here, please tell me again about your relationship with Herr Reinhart.'

The Swiss cleared his throat and paused for a while, clearly giving careful consideration to what he was about to say. His soft voice and the careful way in which he spoke reminded Edgar even more of an English country clergyman – someone more suited to talking to elderly ladies than spies.

'Gunter and I have known each other for some five years. As you are aware, Gunter occupies a senior position in the foreign department of the Reichsbank. He is been involved with the transfer of funds from the Reichsbank to foreign banks and Bank Leu is, in this respect, one of their main clients. I have been working in the international division of Bank Leu for a number of years and am currently its deputy head. You should be aware that there is a very close relationship between Germany and the Swiss banks. Germany is an important client for us and we are very important to them – an efficient and discreet way of moving funds in and out of the country. Not all of their funds, it has to be acknowledged, may have been obtained in entirely legal ways. As part of my job I oversee our relationship with the Reichsbank, so over the years I have visited Berlin on a very regular basis and I think it is reasonable to say that Gunter and I have become good friends. We found that we have much in common; it took us a couple of years to really trust each other but, once we did, we found we could confide in each other. We have been able to talk frankly about our private lives and our worries. About a year ago, when I was in Berlin, he took me into his confidence and told me a secret which he said, if it came out, would cost him his job and quite possibly his freedom. What I am about to say will stay within these walls?'

Edgar laughed. 'We're hardly likely to inform the Gestapo, are we?'

'I realise that, but I am divulging something that was told to me in complete confidence. What Gunter told me was this: he had married a woman called Rosa in 1924, when he was twenty-nine years of age. Rosa, I think, was two or three years younger than him. He describes Rosa as the love of his life. She happened to be Jewish but was not practising and Gunter said that their differences of religion were simply not an issue, or at least, not for them. Their son Alfred was born in 1929, so he's now eleven or twelve. Gunter absolutely dotes on Alfred. Gunter describes their life together as idyllic, but that began to change when the Nazis came to power in 1933. Until then, not many people knew that Rosa was, in fact, Jewish, but life became increasingly uncomfortable. Then the Nazis started to bring in all of these anti-Jewish laws and one of them – in 1935 I think it was – banned marriages between Jews and non-Jews. So they had a choice, either leave the country or get divorced. May I trouble you for a drink please?'

There was a pause while Remington-Barber disappeared into the kitchen, emerging a few minutes later with a tray of tea, a jug of water with glasses and a bottle of whisky. Hedinger poured himself a glass of water.

'Gunter says that their original plan was to emigrate: they would have had to leave everything behind, pay a hefty tax and then find somewhere that would give them an entry visa. Nonetheless, they were prepared to do that. But then it was made very clear to Gunter that unless he divorced Rosa immediately he would lose his job at the Reichsbank. From what I understand, they both still loved each other and saw the divorce as a temporary measure: Rosa and Alfred would try and go to England or France and then Gunter would join them there and they would remarry. But for reasons of which I am unclear, Rosa delayed leaving Germany: I think it may have been that she really wanted to go to England but she could not get an entry visa. Gunter, meanwhile, was finding life difficult. He met a woman called Gudrun and they married – I think he felt that until he remarried, there would always be suspicion about him, but I believe he has always regretted it. He remained in contact with Rosa, but it was difficult and in 1936 she remarried – a Jewish man called Harald Stern. They soon had a daughter, Sophia. My understanding is that this was all done with Gunter's blessing, because Harald's plan was for them all to move to France and Gunter just wanted Rosa and Alfred to be safe. Gunter was even helping them financially and also to try and obtain the right papers.'

'Could he not have had custody of Alfred himself?' asked Basil Remington-Barber.

'A good question: Gunter told me he could have done and if he had contested custody he would almost certainly have won, although Alfred's status would be a difficult one. The Nazis say that anyone who has three or more Jewish grandparents is a Jew. Someone like Alfred, who has two Jewish grandparents, is what the Nazis call a *mischlinge*, which means a "crossbreed" – like a dog. Nonetheless, Gunter felt he could have taken in Alfred and dealt with that – there are ways, you know. But Gudrun, his second wife, would have nothing of it. As far as she was – and is – concerned, he is to have no contact whatsoever with his first family. Now what I am about to say is complicated and highly sensitive: forgive me if I am unclear as to the exact dates. Essentially, what I believe happened is that soon after war was declared Rosa did go to Paris with the two children and Harald was meant to follow them. However, he was arrested and taken to a camp for Jews and political prisoners, called Sachsenhausen. For some foolish reason, in an act of utter madness Rosa retuned to Berlin with the children in an effort to get Harald freed. She failed and had to go into hiding, and a few months later she heard that Harald was dead – either he died of natural causes or was killed, who knows?'

'And has Gunter been in touch with them?'

'Yes, since January or February 1940. There is a Berlin lawyer called Franz Hermann who is an old friend of Rosa's. He is hiding Rosa and the children in his mother's house in the city and Gunter is able to visit them. They are trapped there. Hermann is the connection between Gunter and Rosa and the children.'

'And you say that Gunter told you all this last year?'

'Yes.'

'Do you remember when last year?'

'Maybe March… possibly April. In fact, that was when he started diverting the money into our private accounts – he said that the reason he was doing this was that he needed the money was to help Rosa and Alfred. I was last in Berlin at the very end of January, just a couple of weeks ago. It was a very brief visit and I only saw Gunter on his own very briefly. He said to me that if he was able to arrange for Alfred to be brought out of Germany, would I promise to look after him in Switzerland? I said yes... what else could I say? That is why he told me about the lawyer, Hermann. He also said that he may even need my assistance in helping to get Alfred out, but that he would be in touch. That was the last I heard – until we met today.'

Michael Hedinger looked less nervous now, as if he was pleased to have got things off his chest. His pale head was wet with perspiration, his strands of hair now plastered to it. Edgar was nodding his head, taking everything in and thinking, while Henry looked bemused, unsure of what his role in all this was meant to be. It was Edgar who spoke next.

'How often do you go to Berlin?'

'Perhaps every other month.'

'And other Bank Leu officials, how often do they go?'

'Hard to say exactly, but on a very regular basis. Look, the Reichs-bank is one of our most important clients, but it is a very sensitive relationship. The money that they are placing with us comes from sources that require utmost discretion on our part.'

'What do you mean by that?'

'They have confiscated millions of Reichsmarks from Jews and also plundered money from the countries they have occupied. They need to move that money around; so much of it comes to banks like ours to be converted into Swiss Francs, which is probably the safest currency in the world at the moment. They are also sending us a lot of gold, not just us – all the Swiss banks. The business we get from Germany is extremely profitable, so we prefer to deal with the Reichsbank in person. We ask very few questions and we leave nothing to chance.'

'Do you send couriers to Germany?'

'Of course! Every week, if not more frequently than that. Documents need to be signed, letters need to be delivered. Couriers are a very important part of our relationship with them.'

'And these couriers are...?'

'Employees of Bank Leu or people who do this on a regular basis – people that we know and trust.'

Edgar was thinking and looking around the table as he did so. He looked at Henry and smiled while addressing the Swiss. 'Tell me, Herr Hedinger, do you have the authority to decide who can be a courier on your behalf?'

'Yes, in fact only in November I used my own brother-in-law as a courier.'

'I see.' Edgar was still looking directly at Henry as he spoke. Henry was beginning to feel uncomfortable. 'So Henri here could become one of you couriers?'

'I'm not sure, maybe he—'

'You don't need to worry. Herr Hesse is a Swiss citizen and a regular visitor to Germany himself. I have no doubt that he would be a most capable courier on behalf of Bank Leu.'

Michael Hedinger left the apartment at six thirty. Before he left, Edgar pressed him on how soon he could arrange Henry's accreditation as a courier for Bank Leu.

'It is now Friday evening so obviously I cannot do anything before Monday. It will take me a few days from then. We have a procedure at the bank, you see. Fortunately I am in a position to organise my own couriers, but the paperwork has to be done properly, otherwise we will arouse suspicion. If Henri can give me his passport now, that will speed things up. Also, remember that I will need to sort out paperwork for Alfred. That will not be easy.'

Edgar nodded at Hunter, who looked as shocked as he had done when he first heard about the plans for his trip to Berlin. He removed his passport from his jacket passport and handed it over to Hedinger.

'How soon then?'

'By the end of next week, I am sure I can have it sorted by then.'

'End of the week! I thought it could be done in a day or two.'

The Swiss shook his head vigorously. 'No, no, no – I told you, we have our procedures. I need to fill in the form, send it to the correct department, they need to process it, then the form has to be counter-signed by a director and then I need to arrange Herr

Hesse's registration as an official courier of Bank Leu with the German consulate here in Zurich. I can assure you that it will take a week. Hopefully by next Friday morning it will be sorted.'

They agreed that they would meet again at the apartment the following Friday lunchtime. As well as his accreditation, Hedinger would bring along documents that Henri Hesse would be taking to Bank Leu's clients in Berlin. They waited for Michael Hedinger to leave the apartment and all three of them stood at the window watching him cross Basteiplatz.

'I thought that went rather well, Edgar. Good work.'

'Thank you, Basil. This scheme of his and Reinhart really is most helpful. I was able to tell him that unless he fully co-operated with us then we may be obliged to inform the Swiss authorities. It means that we have him over a barrel. So, Henry, you're going to Berlin. Looking forward to it I hope?'

Henry had poured himself a glass of whisky which he drank in one go. 'It is madness. You seriously want me to go to Berlin pretending to be a courier for a Swiss Bank and then return accompanied by an eleven-year-old half-Jewish boy? It will never work.'

'Why shouldn't it? Your Swiss identity is perfectly genuine and your visit to Stuttgart last year would have been all in order as far as the Germans are concerned. After all, they have no idea that you went to Essen. If you get questioned you simply say that you now have a job as a courier for a bank.'

'And the boy?'

'We will see what paperwork Hedinger comes up with, but it is in his interests for it to be good.'

'It will have to be more than good, Edgar. I'm not sure whether you're aware of it but the Swiss are doing their level best to stop Jews crossing the border from Germany. They'll be looking out for the likes of him.'

'Yes, I am aware of it, thank you, Henry. But they'll not be looking out for the likes of you, will they? And the fact that he is with you, in whatever capacity… well that ought to ensure a safe passage. Anyway, that is only half of the story.'

'What do you mean?'

'Obviously don't want to say too much in front of Herr Hedinger, but going to Berlin and coming back with the boy is only half of your mission. Once the boy is safely brought to Zurich, Herr Hedinger will send a coded message to Gunter Reinhart. Herr Reinhart has an extremely important document which he will hand over to us once he knows that his son is safe. It is a document that could determine the future course of the war, so it is vital that it is brought out of Germany as soon as possible.'

'How is it going to be brought out, Edgar?'

'By you, Henry!'

Chapter 18

Switzerland, February 1941

After the meeting in the apartment on the Basteiplatz, Henry was instructed to return to Geneva for a few days while Michael Hedinger sorted out all the paperwork.

'Basil will come and collect you on the Thursday. Just act normally until then,' had been Edgar's advice.

As soon as Henry arrived at Gare Cornavin on the Saturday he walked to a phone booth in a quiet area at the back of the station. The phone call was brief and, as a result of it, he found himself on the Monday evening in the private room at the back of a seedy Armenian restaurant in Grand-Lancy where Viktor had first taken him in 1931.

'So, Edgar himself was in Zurich was he, *synok*?' Viktor sounded incredulous, so much so that he had poured himself another glass of something that, to Henry, tasted like liquorice-flavoured acid. 'I don't suppose he told you how he got to Switzerland?'

Henry shook his head. 'I presume he came on some roundabout route, Viktor.'

'I am not interested in presumptions, *synok*. I am interested in facts. It is quite a feat to travel from England to Switzerland these days, so it was obviously by a roundabout route: he was hardly going to fly direct, was he? I would be curious to know what that route is. You know, it would be a pleasure to meet your Captain Edgar. I think we would have much in common, despite everything. Tell me Henry, this must be important if Edgar himself has come to Switzerland.'

'I have to go to Berlin next week. I'll be using my own identity and acting as a courier for Bank Leu. I have to bring a boy back from

Berlin, a Jew, or a half-Jew to be precise. Once I deliver the boy to Zurich I am supposed to return to Berlin, where I will be given a document to bring back to Switzerland.'

'That's it?'

Henry laughed. 'That's it? Surely, smuggling a Jew out of Germany and then returning to collect a document is enough isn't it?'

'What I meant was whether you can tell me anymore.'

'Edgar said that the document is so important that it could decide the future course of the war. I asked him what he meant and he was reluctant to tell me at first, but I told him that if I was going to put my life on the line by going into Berlin twice then I had the right to know. So he told me that it is a document from the very top of the Reich – those were his words – about a proposed German invasion of the Soviet Union.'

Viktor had removed a pencil from his top pocket and had been in the process of sharpening it when Henry said this. He stopped, the knife poised in mid-air, pointing towards Henry.

'Say that again.'

'The document is to do with a proposed German invasion of the Soviet Union.'

Henry could have sworn that the deep lines on the Russian's face grew longer as he took in what he had just been told.

'Edgar told you this?'

'Yes. He seemed to regret having told me as soon as had done so, but I was quite persuasive, don't you think?'

'When you return from Berlin the second time – with the document, that is – did he say where you go?'

'Zurich, because that is where I am supposed to be based – it would look suspicious to the Germans if I went elsewhere in Switzerland. However, once I get to Zurich I'm to hand the routine bank papers over to the contact at Bank Leu and then head straight to Bern to give the document to Edgar.'

Viktor looked worried, lowering his head in thought and then looking up to the ceiling for inspiration.

'Plans for a German invasion of the Soviet Union, you say?'

Henry nodded.

'You don't know what day you will be back in Zurich with the document, do you, *synok*?'

'No. Edgar said that all being well I go on the first trip to Berlin a week today, which I think is the 24th. Depending on how things go, I'll probably be back there the following Monday, which would be the 3rd of March, I suppose. So I guess I'll be back in Zurich sometime that week. Maybe the Wednesday: the sooner the better.'

'We'll be waiting in Zurich for you: don't head to Bern until we have made contact with you. Do you understand?'

'Of course: but how will you know when I'm there? Edgar says I'm not to hang around in Zurich: I'm to go from the station to Bank Leu, hand over the bank's papers and then go straight back to the station and travel to Bern.'

Viktor removed his heavy coat and paced around the room. From an inside jacket pocket he took out a small notebook and leafed through it. When he found what he was looked for he wrote on a piece of paper which he then handed to Henry.

'Here, memorise this number. When you arrive back in Zurich from Berlin, ring it and say "Peter is coming round for dinner". That is all. "Peter is coming round for dinner." They will reply by asking if you are bringing wine with you. If you say yes, we will know you have the document. We will meet you at Zurich Hauptbahnhof exactly one hour after the phone call, you understand?'

—

The journey to Berlin began in Zurich, in the borrowed apartment above the hardware shop on Basteiplatz. A shade after a quarter past one on the Friday, Michael Hedinger arrived, breathless and busily explaining how he had been waiting on one extra document.

'I have to be back at my office by two o'clock for a meeting. I have everything here.'

From his bright brown, leather briefcase Hedinger removed a number of items which he placed neatly in front of him on the table.

He took Henri Hesse's Swiss passport from the top of the pile and handed it to him.

'All is in order, Herr Hesse. Thanks to our excellent relationship with the German consulate here in Zurich your passport now allows you to travel freely between Switzerland and Germany a maximum of six times over the next six months – until the 20th of August to be precise. That is a routine arrangement for our couriers.'

Edgar and Remington-Barber both studied the visa, emblazoned with a swastika and a rampant eagle and made approving noises.

'And here are the documents that you are carrying from Bank Leu to the Reichsbank in Berlin, for the attention of Herr Reinhart: they are, of course, the purpose of your trip as far as the German authorities are concerned. You will see that they are all in sealed envelopes. I would ask that they remain that way until they are handed over. In this envelope...' he passed a long white envelope with the bank's crest to Henry 'is your letter of accreditation from the bank and here are your rail tickets from Zurich to Berlin: you change at Stuttgart. It is a long journey but you will travel first class which is very tolerable. I have taken the liberty of booking you on the train that departs Zurich at six o'clock on Monday morning. You should be in Berlin by six o'clock in the evening.'

Another envelope came over to Henri Hesse.

'In Berlin you will stay at the Kaiserhof: our couriers either stay there or at the Excelsior on Askanischer Platz, but the Kaiserhof is rather charming and is slightly closer to the centre. It is certainly more discreet than the Adlon: everyone stays at the Adlon, it is not private enough I think – too many journalists and possibly spies. Here is the letter of confirmation from the Kaiserhof. The bill will be settled directly by the bank, you do not need to worry about that. Your room will be en suite.'

Henry checked the contents of the latest envelope to come his way across the table.

'Very efficient, Herr Hedinger' said Edgar. 'I trust you have addressed the somewhat more complicated issue of young Alfred?'

Hedinger nodded. 'I am proposing that he travels under the identity of my own son, Andreas.'

213

The banker pulled a large white handkerchief from a pocket and used it to wipe his forehead. He hesitated a while before he replied. 'I have to be honest with you, this has been most difficult. I have had sleepless nights over it. I have never met Alfred but Gunter has shown me photographs of him. Alfred is eleven, or twelve. My own son, Andreas, is ten, but is tall for his age. I would not say that Andreas and Alfred look alike, but I think with a bit of imagination, you could ensure that at the very least they do not look too different, if you see what I mean. Here is his passport.'

The three men studied the passport photo of Andreas Hedinger. His black hair was straight and had a distinctive parting low down on the left side. He wore a pair of round, wire-framed glasses.

'Here are the very glasses that Andreas is wearing in that picture.' Hedinger had brought a spectacle out of his briefcase. 'We bought him a brand new pair yesterday. I think that if you make sure that Alfred's hair is like Andreas' and he wears these glasses, then you have a chance.'

'Have you told your wife about this?'

'I had to. If this works, we will need to keep Andreas off school until Alfred arrives in Zurich. Also, I have had to tell her about Alfred: he will be coming to stay with us, after all this is done.'

'What does she think of it?'

'Fortunately, Helga is braver person than I am. She is a very devout woman. She believes that this is her Christian duty. As long as there is no danger to Andreas, then she will go along with it.'

'That's all very well, but why on earth would Andreas be in Berlin – and with me?' Henry was holding the boy's passport. 'What am I to say when I'm asked what I'm doing in Berlin with the son of my boss at Bank Leu? And what about how he got there – won't they spot that he did not come into Germany with me?' Henry sounded annoyed at the fact that no one had questioned this yet.

'Turn to the third page the passport please' said Hedinger. 'This is where my relationship with the passport clerk at the German consulate paid off. I asked him to stamp the passport showing that Andreas entered Germany this coming Monday – the 24th. I explained that this was a treat for Andreas. As ever, he was most obliging: given the way that the bank looks after him, he ought to be. In this envelope is the train ticket for Alfred to use from Berlin to Zurich. It is a return, showing that the outward part of the journey – from Zurich to Berlin – was on Monday 24th February. There is no reason why the German border guards should question this and the Swiss ought not to be difficult about allowing a Swiss boy to re-enter his country.'

'And the story, Herr Hedinger?' asked Remington-Barber. 'We always need to have a very good story.'

'A reward! Andreas has done so well at school that I promised him a visit to Berlin. I was planning to take him myself but have been unable to arrange it because I am so busy, so I asked one of my couriers to do so. Andreas is fascinated by everything he sees about Germany, the marching – everything. He is so excited.'

Henry sat very still with his head in his hands. Edgar raised his eyebrows high and looked at Remington-Barber who shook his head.

'Henry, any better ideas?'

'None that I can think of at the moment.'

'Basil.'

Remington-Barber shook his head. 'It's a bit thin, to be honest, but then very few cover stories are quite as watertight as we'd like them to be. We have to rely on no one probing too deeply. I suppose it does at least have the merit of being relatively simple. As long as no one pushes too hard on why a mere courier would be entrusted with taking his boss's son to Berlin. Perhaps we could say that actually Henri is also a close family friend of yours: maybe your wife could write a letter thanking him for putting himself out and all that?'

'That is a good idea, Basil' said Remington-Barber. 'Herr Hedinger, you will need to give Henri some important information: your address, what Andreas likes and doesn't like, all about his school, sports – that kind of thing. Alfred will have to learn all that in case he's questioned.'

Edgar sighed loudly, stood up and paced around the room, a trail of cigarette smoke following in his wake.

'Let's be frank. If the Gestapo pull in Alfred and interrogate him, the whole thing will fall apart. We have to hope, as Basil says, that we don't get to that point; that no one probes too deep. If none of us can come up with a better legend, I suppose that is it. Herr Hedinger, you had better get back to the bank. Can I suggest that you invite Henry round to your house at the weekend? That way he can familiarise himself with Andreas and your family. Basil, I think you ought to go too.'

Chapter 19

Berlin, February 1941

Henri Hesse arrived at the Kaiserhof hotel on Wilhelmstrasse a few minutes after six o'clock on the evening of Monday 24th February. It was only his second ever visit to Germany's capital, the first being in 1934 or 1935 – he could not remember for sure – when he had accompanied his mother as a late replacement for his stepfather who had pulled out 'because of business.' He remembered his mother being charmed by Berlin, in a rather naïve way. Utterly oblivious to the politics, she was much taken with what she saw as people's enthusiasm and the enormous swastikas draped from the buildings. She admired the dramatic colours and way that they swayed very gently even in the absence of a breeze. For Henry, the visit was simply an affirmation of what he believed in: he could not wait to get out of the city, vowing never to return.

And now he had returned. The hotel made a fuss of him, assuring him that Bank Leu were most valued clients and would he like to make a reservation for dinner? There were numerous forms and cards to fill in, which he did with the utmost care. He had spent the weekend going through the trip in detail with Remington-Barber and Edgar and he had been warned about the hotel cards. They were destined for the Gestapo, which had a special office in Berlin where every night the cards of newly arrived foreigners would be carefully examined against the Gestapo's meticulous records.

Remington-Barber had been quite candid. 'If they've got anything against you from last year's Stuttgart trip, then alarm bells will go off. They'll either haul you out of bed that night or first thing in the morning. That's the bad news, Henry. Good news is that if they have nothing adverse on your file – and there is no reason why they should – then you're in the clear and that should make the rest of the trip that much easier, relatively speaking.'

Henri Hesse ate little for dinner that night and slept badly, alert to every sound on the corridor as he waited for the Gestapo to come and arrest him for the murder of the owner of the perfume shop in Essen. At four in the morning he was convinced he could hear footsteps in the corridor and finally decided to unlock the door and have a look, but the long corridor was deserted, apart from neat pairs of shoes outside a number of the doors.

He felt a bit more relaxed and drifted asleep, only to be visited during it by the familiar face of Roza – her image far more in focus and its presence remaining far longer than usual. She spent much of the night asking questions but every time he tried to reply he found that he could not form the words. When he woke on the Tuesday morning he was exhausted, but as he lay in bed his mood lifted. It was a quarter to eight and in the corridor he could hear the chambermaids gathering. At least, he decided, he had passed the scrutiny of whichever Gestapo clerk had been scrutinising the hotel registration cards overnight.

This upbeat mood continued as he went down to breakfast, notwithstanding having to walk down corridors and stairs adorned with a gallery's worth of framed photographs commemorating Hitler's various visits to the hotel, of which there appeared to be many.

He knew that he was likely to be in Berlin until the Friday. According to Hedinger, it was not unusual for the bank's couriers to have to wait a few days to collect the return documents, and Edgar and Remington-Barber were clear that a few days would be essential for Alfred to prepare for the journey to Switzerland.

'If all goes to plan,' said Remington-Barber, 'you and Alfred will come out on Friday morning. After that it depends on your journey. With a very fair wind you could be in Zurich late Friday, but more likely Saturday. Make sure you send Hedinger a telegram from Stuttgart when you know what train you're going to be on.'

He was due at the Reichsbank at ten o'clock and his instructions were to go by taxi: it was not done to walk the streets carrying important papers. Henri Hesse from Bank Leu entered the Reichs-bank through the enormous doors on Französischestrasse. It was ten o'clock and he had been warned to expect delays and he was not to be disappointed. First he was searched, and then he had to report to reception, which was a tall, polished oak desk behind which a row of serious-looking receptionists peered down. After that he was given a form and sent over to another desk to fill it in. When he returned to the main reception desk, the form was carefully checked and only then did the receptionist deign to telephone Gunter Reinhart's office. 'Herr Reinhart will be with you in due course. Please wait over there.'

'Over there' was a small waiting area where half a dozen other people were sitting quietly. The man sitting opposite was clutching a Swiss passport and a padlocked briefcase. He told Henry he was a courier, from the Basler Handelsbank. He was surprised not to have seen Henry there before, he said: sometimes there could be as many as half a dozen couriers at the Reichsbank from the different Swiss banks.

The man got up and sat himself next to Henry. He was no more than five feet tall and was wearing a dark, formal suit that seemed to be a size too large for him. He stretched up to whisper in Henri's ear.

'I don't know who needs the other more – us or the Germans. I used to work for the SBC in Basel: I cannot tell you how much work they were getting from the Germans. Basler Handelsbank has recruited five of us in the past couple of months. From what I understand it has been even busier for you lot in Zurich, is that right?'

'Indeed.' Henry shifted to his left, away from the man, whose breath reeked of stale tobacco.

'I don't want to know where the Germans are getting all this gold and cash from – but what I do know is that if it wasn't for us they'd be stuck with it. We're doing them a big favour – and we are making a lot of money in the process. How are things with Bank Leu?'

'Yes… very good thank you.'

'So, where are you staying? Maybe tonight—'

At that point a secretary appeared in front of them, a gold swastika the only touch of colour on her dark suit.

'Bank Leu?'

Henry stood up.

'Come with me.'

Five minutes later Henry was in the small, deeply carpeted office of Gunter Reinhart. Reinhart had assured his secretary that they would not be needing coffee and yes thank you, he had all of the papers he needed. *That would be all, thank you.*

It was silent in the office apart from the ticking of a clock that Henry couldn't see. He and Gunter Reinhart eyed each other carefully. Reinhart waited a moment and then walked over to close the door which his secretary had left ajar. He gestured for Henry to sit down and held up his hand – *wait*. A minute later he walked softly over to the door again, opened it, looked around, closed it again and came to sit at his desk.

'My secretary is – how can I put it tactfully… is very efficient but nosey. She is the kind of person who likes to know everything. That is bad enough, but in these times – that can be quite a problem. Recently she joined the Nazi Party and she is forever telling me about how her husband has become some kind of party representative in the street where they live. That means they spy on their neighbours so naturally I assume that she spies on me. I am very careful with her.'

Gunter had relaxed a bit now and his manner had now become noticeably friendlier. He reached across the desk and held out his hand to shake Henry's.

'I'm Gunter Reinhart by the way, as you've no doubt gathered. I'm pleased to meet you. You have the documents? It is important that they are here and in order. We don't want people questioning why you came!'

Henry handed over the envelopes containing the Bank Leu documents. Reinhart opened them carefully with a dagger-like letter opener. He glanced over the documents and then put them to the side of his desk.

'I'll deal with them when we have finished. The documents for you to take back to Zurich will not be ready until late Thursday, you realise that?'

'So I understand.'

'It is not unusual for a courier to hang around Berlin for a few days.' He had left his desk now and come to sit next to Henry, speaking more quietly.

'Most couriers seem end up at the zoo, I have no idea why – I suppose they get bored. It is not as if they can go to a library, not now that we've burned most of the books worth reading! As far as you are concerned, you won't get bored: we have plenty to keep you busy.' Gunter Reinhart paused and coughed. He hesitated before he resumed speaking, this time in an even lower voice. He gestured for Henry had to lean closer.

'I cannot tell you how grateful I am...' Gunter Reinhart looked as if he was overcome by emotion. 'My family situation... has been a source of great stress. It has been explained to you I take it?'

'Yes.'

'I should never have divorced Rosa. We thought it was for the best. We assumed it would be a short term measure and that maybe the Nazis would change their minds or go away. How could we have been stupid as to think that? Once we realised that was never going to happen our plan was that Rosa and Alfred would move to another country and that I would be able to join them in due course, but it did not turn out like that. We both remarried. At least I believed that they would be safe once they moved to Paris, but to find that they had returned to Berlin... madness. It was a terrible shock. Now they are trapped here and I have been desperate to find a way of getting them out. For a while Rosa wanted the three of them to remain together, but once she found out about Harald's death she agreed with me that, at the very least, we must get Alfred out. Once he is in Switzerland then I can see what can be done with Rosa and of course Sophia too, even though she is not my daughter. But for now, getting Alfred out of Germany is the priority. That is what I pray for.'

'Does Alfred know about the plan?'

'Not yet. You are going to meet him this afternoon. You will obviously need to spend some time with him. Rosa knows there is a plan and she knows that something will happen this week, but she does not know the details — neither, for that matter, do I. Tell me briefly what the plan is: if you stay too long then my secretary will become suspicious.'

Henry took Andreas Hedinger's passport out of his jacket pocket and carefully placed it on the blotter pad on Reinhart's desk.

'The plan is for Alfred to accompany me back to Zurich using this identity — Andreas is Michael Hedinger's son.'

Reinhart nodded. *I know.*

'This passport is two years old, so anyone looking at it would not be surprised that the person in the photograph has changed. Also, I have with me the very spectacles that Andreas is wearing in this photograph. You can see that Andreas has quite a distinctive hair style...'

Reinhart had picked up the passport and put on his own glasses. He turned on his desk lamp and studied the passport carefully under it, his face impassive.

'Andreas's hair is much darker than Alfred's. As far as his hair is concerned, Alfred inherited my Aryan genes rather than his mother's. I had always thought that would be an advantage.'

'We thought of how to deal with the question of his hair colour. I have brought some black hair dye with me: it's back in the hotel. If we can use it on Alfred and then style his hair to look like Andreas, then it may work: especially with the glasses.'

'It is certainly feasible; there is no doubt about that. But how come you will be accompanied back to Zurich by the boy?'

Henry drew a long breath, anxious to betray any of his own scepticism as possible. 'The story will depend on us not being questioned too much, but in a nutshell it is that as well as being a courier for Bank Leu I am also a family friend of the Hedinger's and that I brought Andreas with me to Berlin as a treat.'

Gunter Reinhart said nothing but stared at Henry for a good few minutes.

'That's it?'

Henry shrugged his shoulders. *Yes, I know... don't tell me.*

'You think it will work?'

'Hopefully. On the positive side, the passport is a genuine Swiss one. As long as they're not suspicious, they will probably not push Alfred too hard.'

Gunter Reinhart snapped the passport shut, handed it back to Henry, turned off his desk lamp and walked over to the window. He looked out over the Spreekanal and then turned to face Henry.

'The alternative is to smuggle Alfred out and that is too dangerous. This plan will have to work. And you know that document will be released only once I know that Alfred is safe in Zurich?'

Henry nodded.

'Good. You are to meet Franz Hermann at one o'clock. He will escort you to the house where they are all hiding. Let me give you your instructions: you'll need to listen carefully. Incidentally, Henri, are you fond of flowers?'

–

Henri Hesse went from the Reichsbank back to the Kaiserhof where he sought out the concierge. 'I have an unexpectedly free afternoon. I wonder if you could suggest anything I might do?'

The concierge smiled obligingly. *Please could he have the guest's details?*

Henry recalled what Gunter Reinhart had told him that morning. 'Anything you discuss with them could be reported back to the Gestapo, they like to keep tabs on foreigners – so your plans will need to appear plausible: use them to create an alibi.'

'And what would you be interested in doing, sir?' the concierge asked. 'The cinema maybe? Or shopping?'

Henry shook his head.

'I have been spending so much time indoors that I wouldn't mind some fresh air.'

'The zoo perhaps? It is within the Tiergarten so you could combine the two.'

Henry shook his head. 'To be honest, I'm not very keen on animals. They make me nervous.'

'I quite understand, sir. Do you want to stay in the city?'

'I think so, it will be dark soon.'

'That is true, I was going to suggest a visit to Potsdam, but perhaps that is for another day. Are you by any chance interested in plants and gardens?'

'Yes, I am actually.' He managed to sound just the right side of enthusiastic.

'Well, we have an excellent Botanischer Garten down in Dahlem. It is a quite wonderful haven of peace and quiet in the city and the gardens are most beautiful.'

Henry managed to look as if he was having second thoughts. 'In Dahlem you say: isn't that far away?'

Not at all sir' said the concierge, 'it is no more than six or seven stops on the S-Bahn from Anhalter. The gardens are just a few minutes' walk from Botanischer Garten station. Here, let me show you how to get there.'

–

'Every minute of your visit will be laced with danger, but no moment will be more dangerous than the one when you drop your guard.'

Edgar's parting words had been menacing enough, but they hardly began to describe what Henri Hesse encountered at Anhalter. The station was busy, but unnaturally quiet apart from the noise of dogs barking in the distance. Quite a number of the people were exiting the station as he entered it, looking over their shoulders and seeming to be relieved to be in the open air. He noticed that there were a large number of troops milling around, dressed in the black uniform of the SS rather than the grey of the Wehrmacht. He purchased a return ticket to Botanischer Garten, making sure to ask the clerk behind the tiny window if he knew how long it would take for him to walk to the gardens from the station.

Continuing to feel pleased with how things had gone he headed for the platform, which was when he saw them. His first impression was that it was a lot of people waiting for one train, especially at lunchtime. *Maybe an outing?* They were two platforms away from the one he was waiting on, crowded together and hemmed in by the SS men in their

224

black uniforms. Some of the SS had Alsatians with them, holding them on a short leash but allowing them to rear up at the people on the platform and all the while the non-stop barking, which every so often orchestrated with the sound of a train's whistle or a station announcement.

Henry moved along his platform, trying to get a better view. The crowd of people was very mixed: men, women and children, old and young. They all seemed to be quite well dressed and all of the people were either carrying suitcases or clutching bundles. From what he could see, the SS men were checking what the people had with them and a few of the bundles ended up being strewn on the platform, with some clothing spilling over onto the track.

He was still trying to make some sense of it when his train pulled into the platform and there was a scramble to board it. Henry positioned himself by a window looking out onto the crowded platform. The window was dirty and it was harder to make out much detail through the screen of soot and grease. With his sleeve he tried to clean his side of the window and as he did so he caught the eye of a woman who had sat down opposite him. She followed his gaze across the track and then looked down, intently studying the rail ticket she was clutching in her gloved hands. He leaned forward to get a better view, but then the doors of the train slammed, a guard called out and the train lurched forward. Within seconds the crowd of people on the opposite platform became a blur and soon they were out of Anhalter.

'Do you know who they were?' he asked the lady.

She looked around her before answering. 'You don't know?'

He shook his head.

'Jews. They've started to take them away,' she said in a matter of fact tone.

'Where to?'

A ticket inspector had appeared next to them and they both silently handed him their tickets. She glanced up at him. *Keep quiet.* Over the crackly speaker the driver announced the next station: 'Grossgorsen-srasse'.

The lady stood up, smoothing her elegant coat as she did so. Before moving into the aisle she bent down and barely pausing, whispered into Henry's ear. 'Wherever it is they take them to, they don't come back.'

He got off the train at Botanischer Garten, crossed the Unter den Eichen and entered the gardens. He did his best to appear every bit the interested visitor and made leisurely progress to the Italian Garden, which was actually quite beautiful and, in other circumstances, would have been an ideal place to relax.

If you are not approached by him within ten minutes of entering the Italian Garden, walk back to the station and travel back to Anhalter and then to the hotel. Just act normally. Just because he does not turn up does not necessarily mean something is wrong.

He had been in the Italian Gardens approaching ten minutes when a smartly dressed man with a broad brimmed hat came up to him and spoke in an educated Berlin accent.

'Excuse me, sir; could you point me in the direction of the greenhouses?'

'I am sorry but I am not very familiar with the gardens. I can tell you that the lake is in that direction though,' said Henry, sticking carefully to his script.

The man held out his hand and shook Henry's. 'I'm Franz. I am pleased to meet you. Everything appears to be in order. We will spend another few minutes separately in these gardens and then I will head out. Follow me at a safe distance. We will exit through Königin-Luise-Strasse. If at any stage I remove my hat then that is a signal that something is wrong. In that case, keep on walking and make your way back to the station, for which you'll need to take a circuitous route. Assuming that everything is in order, you will see me enter a house – no more than five minutes from here. Allow two minutes from when I enter the house before you approach it. There is a small window above the front door. Only approach the house if the curtains in that window are open. If they are closed, head back to the hotel. Have you got all that?'

Henry nodded.

'Good. Now point me in a northerly direction. I am sure no one is watching us, but just in case they are, they will see you directing me.'

For the next few minutes they strolled apart around the Italian garden. Henry did his best to appear fascinated by the plants. A group of young Luftwaffe officers were also walking around and he wondered if their presence might cause a delay, but then he noticed the lawyer head out of the gardens. He followed him until he entered the white house on the corner of Arno-Holz Strasse.

'*Allow two minutes from when I enter the house before you approach it.*'

He had slowed his pace right down and allowed himself one quick glance behind him. The area appeared to be deserted. In a house across the street a maid had come out to put something in a bin and was looking at him. He bent down to tie his shoe laces and a glance at his watch told him that a minute and a half had elapsed since Hermann had entered the house. He would head over now.

The curtains in the small window above the porch were open and as he walked down the path the front door opened. Hermann was in the hall, gesturing for him to go upstairs. The landing was dark; he could only just make out two doorways in a corridor. One of them opened and at first the person in the doorway was only in silhouette, with the light flooding in behind them. It was a woman and she gestured for him to come into the room. It was a small lounge with two sofas and a table in the corner: a boy and a girl were sitting on the sofa. By now, Franz Hermann had joined him in the room and made the introductions: 'Alfred and Sophia,' – the boy and the girl both stood up and shook his hand, the girl only after being prompted to do so by her brother. 'Herr Hesse is a friend of the family from Switzerland, from Zurich.'

Alfred looked younger than his twelve years: he had a pleasant face that showed signs of beginning to turn handsome and the fair hair that his father had described. He was thin and slightly gaunt looking, with a pale, unhealthy complexion that no doubt owed much to having been confined indoors for so long. He had a natural smile, but it did reveal a set of yellow teeth.

Henry was unable to gauge whether Alfred's sister looked older or younger than five, but Sophia did share her brother's unhealthily pale complexion. She seemed to hold her head down and stare up at whoever she was looking at with enormous dark eyes which managed to appear both innocent and knowing at the same time. She had a head of thick, dark hair that fell over her thin shoulders and was a clutching a dirty toy rabbit close to her.

'And this is Rosa.'

Rosa.

Roza.

With long, dark hair that flowed over her slim shoulders and dark eyes that sparkled this Rosa looked too much like the Russian Roza. In a lesser light she could easily be mistaken for her. And although it was ten years since Henry had last seen Roza, in truth he had seen her image most nights since then, far too stark and far too lifelike to have allowed her to fade from his memory. This Rosa was uncannily like the one in whose murder in Interlaken he had been complicit. She was as he imagined Roza would have grown up to be: the face slightly more lined, the breasts that had been small but perfectly formed now fuller under the blouse and cardigan, the eyes having lived that much longer and experienced that much more. He fully expected her to gently touch his wrist and then, as she was wont to do in the dreams, grip them tightly and then admonish him. 'You were the one person I thought understood me. You were someone I trusted,' she had said then, certain in the knowledge of the fate that awaited them. It was what she repeated most nights to him in his dreams.

Roza.

Rosa smiled and shook his hand and then asked the children to leave the room.

'Go upstairs. I will call you down later. And remember, be quiet!'

The children silently shuffled out of the room. When Rosa spoke again Henry noticed that she did so in such a soft voice that it was barely above a whisper.

'This is the house of Franz's mother. She is very elderly and very infirm and I look after her. In fact, I am a doctor, but as far as she is concerned, I am a nurse. She has no idea that I am Jewish and nor does she have any idea that the children are here, which is why we have to be so quiet. In fact her hearing is very bad, but we are very careful nonetheless. The children never go downstairs. We have been here for well over a year and life is barely tolerable. The children have to live in silence: we cannot risk putting the lights on when it gets dark. We are so grateful to Franz, but life is very difficult: we have limited food, despite Franz's generosity: Gunter helps too but he has to be careful as his wife knows nothing. We live in constant fear that someone will find out about us. Apparently Jews can still technically leave Berlin but, in reality, it is now almost impossible to do so and we would not stand a chance: we have to stay hidden. Gunter feels that at least we should try and get Alfred out, he is insistent about that and I have come round to accepting that, even though it breaks my heart. I understand that you have come to help; I am so grateful. Please tell us everything.'

Over the following hour Henry went through the plan in detail. Rosa was impassive, perched on the edge of the sofa, straight backed and occasionally asking him to repeat what he had just said. Once, Rosa placed her hand on his, allowing her long, thin fingers to brush his wrist. It was too close to what Roza would do and Henry must have showed his emotions because Franz Hermann leaned forward.

'Are you all right, Henri?'

'Pardon?' He felt as if he had just woken up, momentarily unsure of exactly where he was.

'Are you all right? You look worried.'

'No, no… I am fine. I was just thinking about what we have to do. There is so much detail to think about.'

They both agreed that if Alfred's hair could be dyed and styled like that of Andreas in the photograph, then along with the spectacles then he would have a reasonable resemblance to the Swiss boy, especially given that the passport photograph was taken two years previously. Even the most rigorous person inspecting it would have to acknowledge that Andreas had aged.

'Alfred is an intelligent boy' said Rosa. 'I know that most mothers would say that, but he is. I am sure that he will be able to remember the details of the cover story, but how he will act under pressure is a different matter. We simply don't know, do we? He is well aware of how much danger we are in. He knows that he may never see us again.'

Henry only realised that Rosa was crying when he saw that Franz had moved closer to her and had a comforting arm round her shoulder. Henry looked first at the floor and then at the window, awkward and unsure of what to say. At first he slid along the sofa towards Rosa, thinking that it was his place to comfort her too, but then he checked himself. It would not do too appear too familiar. How could he begin to explain himself?

'In many respects, we are well prepared' said Franz. 'You have the passport and the rail ticket and you said something about the Swiss side of the border being potentially the hardest part of the journey. From what I have also heard, that is probably correct: the Swiss are very strict about who they let in: one of their own citizens ought not to be a problem. The Germans will more be concerned with someone who has a German passport trying to leave the country. The priority now is to start work with Alfred.'

Rosa stood up and walked over to the window, drawing the curtain.

'I had better go and check on your mother, Franz. Then let me have some time alone with Alfred. I would like to tell him myself. How long can you stay, Herr Hesse?'

'I suppose I have a few hours?'

'No, no,' said Hermann. 'It will look suspicious if you arrive back too late at the Kaiserhof. There is no question there that they will be keeping a note on your movements, which happens with all foreign visitors. You can have one hour with Alfred and then come back tomorrow, when you will have all day.'

–

It was the Friday, the last day of February and as the train pulled out of Potsdam station Henry noticed that Alfred, who he now could only think of as Andreas Hedinger, was crying.

It was a very private cry, the silent type where a few tears trickle down the cheek and any sobs are suppressed by a cough and biting the lip and fingers clasped firmly to the cheek as the hands are also deployed to shield the face. Andreas had shifted in his seat so that he was looking directly out of the window and neither of the other passengers in the carriage could possibly see his face. Henry caught glimpses of him in profile, along with the reflection of his face on the window.

Andreas had held himself together so far that morning and over the previous two days. Ten minutes previously, he had passed his first major test. Security at the station had been lighter than they had expected, with the main check being to ensure that the tickets were in order. But Henry knew that sooner or later they would be questioned and that had happened during the wait at Potsdam station when a Gestapo officer had entered their compartment, with two Wehrmacht soldiers waiting in corridor outside.

'*Tickets. Identity documents. Quick.*'

The Gestapo officer's eyes darted from Henri to Andreas and back again and then to the other two men. Both of them appeared to be travelling on business: one to Jena and the other to Würzburg. The Gestapo officer seemed satisfied with their papers. Then it was Henry's turn.

'Your ticket is to Stuttgart'.

'Yes: then we are travelling to Zurich.'

'Let me see those tickets.'

He studied them and then said to Alfred, 'You are travelling together?'

'Yes.'

'You are related?'

'No,' Henry said, quickly. 'Andreas is the son of a friend and colleague. He has been in Berlin visiting while I was on business in Berlin. His parents asked me to look after him'

'What is your business?'

'I work for a bank: Bank Leu. Here is my letter of accreditation.'

The Gestapo man read every word and then turned to Alfred. 'You: your papers.'

Alfred handed over the passport.

Say as little as possible and when you do, don't speak too clearly: the Germans will obviously expect a Swiss person to have an accent.

'What is your date of birth?'

That was no problem. They had been working very hard over the past couple of days.

Two more questions and I'll begin to worry.

'And where did you visit in Berlin?'

Which is when Henry did begin to worry. Surely the Gestapo man would spot that Alfred was speaking with a Berlin accent, certainly not a Swiss one.

'Pardon?'

'I said, where did you visit in Berlin?'

The carriage door opened and one of the Wehrmacht soldiers came in.

'Otto wants your help in the front – there's a problem.'

Too easy. Every minute of your visit will be laced with danger.

But that was that. Henry wanted to tell Alfred how well he had done, but all he was able to do was smile.

–

Alfred had been a model student, carefully writing down the details he needed to remember to pass as Andreas Hedinger from Zurich and memorising the story about how he had come to be in Berlin and how Herr Hesse was such a good friend of his parents and he was so good to have agreed to take him to Berlin with him.

'My father is so busy, I hardly see him these days! He kept promising to take me to Berlin and was always cancelling. Herr Hesse has been so very kind!'

That was the agreed line that they would take if anyone questioned why he was in Berlin with Henry. In an effort to persuade Alfred to believe it the story they all kept up the pretence of how plausible it was. The adults knew that the first line of their defence lay in the paperwork: if that in any way failed to convince then the story would be probed and Henry knew that it would not stand up to a lot of scrutiny. Their displays of confidence in the story must have worked because by the time they got on the train in Berlin, Henry had even come to believe in it himself.

Henry had gone to the Reichsbank first thing on the Wednesday morning – the briefest of trips, just enough to be able to show the hotel where he was going. From there he travelled down to Dahlem and spent the whole day with Alfred. Gunter Reinhart had joined them for an hour in the afternoon: when he left it was to say farewell to Alfred. He followed the same pattern on the Thursday. Franz brought Alfred to the station on the Friday morning. Alfred's hair had been cut and dyed, and along with the wire-framed spectacles, the passage of time and the relatively poor quality of the photograph, he presented more than a passing resemblance to Andreas Hedinger. Alfred stood on the platform clutching his small knapsack with a few clothes and one or two other innocuous items in it. In the pocket of his jacket was the Swiss passport – his lifeline. Franz shook hands briefly with both of them and disappeared into the crowd.

–

After Potsdam there had been a long wait in Leipzig and when the train finally left the city it moved very slowly through Saxony, meaning that they were more than two hours behind schedule when they arrived in Jena. Henry spent the long hours alternating between staring out of the window and closing his eyes, but when he did so Roza was staring at him as always.

By now Henry knew that their chances of getting into Switzerland that night were remote. By the time the train crossed over from Thuringia into Bavaria the rain that had accompanied them since Jena had become incessant. Alfred sat quietly in one position: he had eaten very little apart from a sausage and milk that Henry had bought on the platform at Leipzig. Since Potsdam he had appeared composed.

There was another long wait in Würzburg and they were joined in their carriage by three new passengers: a woman with a pinched face accompanied by a pretty teenage daughter and a Waffen SS *Obersturmführer* who was one small glass of something short of being drunk. Henry saw the boy tense as the SS officer stumbled into the carriage. At the sight of the girl, who could have been no more than seventeen, the *Obersturmführer*'s eyes lit up. For the next half hour he did his best to impress her, but the girl did her best to ignore him, helped by the clear disapproval of her mother.

Then he turned his attention to the boy. 'Where are you from? ... Switzerland? ... I LOVE Switzerland! ... The Swiss are our friends! ... YOU are my friend ... Where have you been in Germany? ... Tell me what you saw in Berlin.'

Henry struggled hard to conceal his amazement as Alfred confidently enthused about everything he had seen in Berlin, not least the soldiers – he loved seeing the soldiers and the marching –it was so exciting, far more exciting than anything we have in Zurich or indeed anywhere in Switzerland for that matter. He would love to return to Germany, maybe when he was older he could even...

Fortunately the SS man seemed to be oblivious to Alfred's apparent lack of a Swiss accent, helped by the contents of flask which he had finished since joining the train. Within minutes he had insisted on being called Karl and was showing Alfred his Mauser automatic and describing how he had captured Paris single-handed. 'When you are old enough to meet girls, Andreas, the first place you go is Paris! Which football team do you support Andreas? ... FC Zurich? ... Ah, Grasshoppers! A good team.'

Just outside the city, still in the blanket darkness of the countryside, the train pulled to a noisy halt. It was seven o'clock. Silence for a few minutes, then shouting and the sound of dogs barking. It took an eternity for the commotion to work its way down the train. When it reached them a Gestapo officer who seemed to be wider than he was tall squeezed into their compartment, breathless and with sweat dripping from his brow. He was wearing a leather raincoat that was so tight that it remained unbuttoned. He looked around and then shouted at Alfred.

'You: get up... now!'

Henry clutched the seat to stop himself swaying. The boy was so terrified he did not move one muscle, but all the blood had drained from his face.

'Did you not hear me? Come with me now.'

The SS *Obersturmführer* rose slowly and slightly unsteadily, standing directly in front of the Gestapo officer and very close to him. He was at least a foot taller than the other man and used every inch of that to ensure he looked down on him with the maximum effect.

'What is the problem?'

'We have had reports that some Jewish boys got on the train at Würzburg. The police discovered some of the vermin hiding in a cellar and had been chasing the gang: they last saw them in the vicinity of the station. We are checking all youths on the train.'

'Well, Andreas is my friend and it is impossible that he is Jewish.'

He was shouting at the Gestapo officer, flecks of spit spraying onto the other man's reddening face. When the Gestapo officer replied, it was in a much more uncertain voice.

'And how do you know that?'

'Because he is Swiss!'

The big man wiped his face with his sleeve, clearly puzzled by the *Obersturmführer*'s logic.

'I still need to check his papers and question him though...' He held his arm out towards Alfred, beckoning him to join him. The *Obersturmführer* grabbed hold of the Gestapo man's arm and pushed it down.

'You won't need to be doing that.'

'How come?'

'Because I got on the train at Würzburg and Andreas was already on it, so stop wasting your time.'

The Gestapo officer appeared reluctant to argue. By now a pair of Alsatians were barking outside the open door of the compartment. 'Let me have a look at your passport,' he said to the boy.

Andreas passed it to him. Henry noticed that the Gestapo man's hands were trembling as he quickly flicked through the passport, before handing it back.

'That is all in order.'

'Next time, try and serve the Reich in more useful ways,' the *Obersturmführer* spat at him as he left the compartment, defeated.

It was nine o'clock by the time the train arrived in Stuttgart. Henry knew he could have gone to the nearby Hotel Victoria, where he imagined that Katharina Hoch was still the night manager, but it would be too risky. He decided instead that they would stay overnight in the station, where there was a large air raid shelter. The first train to Zurich was at eight twenty in the morning, which meant that he would also have an opportunity to send a telegram to Hedinger.

The air raid shelter where they slept was crowded. The boy was still in a state of anxiety and stress from the events of the day and Henry had to whisper to him how well he had done; how proud his parents would be of him. *We're nearly there now, you'll be safe.* They found a corner of a wide bench at the back of the shelter into which they wedged themselves. Henry put his arm round the boy and gradually he felt him relax and within a few minutes he was fast asleep, on what he both hoped and feared would be his last night in his homeland.

Chapter 20

Stuttgart, Zurich & Berlin, March 1941

For the first few hours in the air raid shelter in Stuttgart station, Henry hardly slept. The spot they had found turned out to have a noisy pipe running directly above it and every time he dropped off he was soon woken by clanging or the sound of air hissing. And then when he did drop off, Roza would appear: her admonishing eyes fixed on him, telling him what he knew all too well. For a full hour she haunted him: she was there if he shut his eyes tight and still there when he opened them wide and there when he held his head tight in his hands.

But then the strangest thing happened: Roza stared at him in her familiar fashion, her eyes full of sadness and hatred. But then her face began to dissolve and when it came back into focus the dark brown eyes were there as was the dark hair flowing over slim shoulders, but now the features belonged to Rosa and with that, an unexpected calm came over Henry. Rosa was no less sad but there was the faintest of smiles on her face and a look of pleading in her eyes. And as the very beginnings of an idea began to emerge in Henry's mind, a calm that he was quite unused to came over him and the few hours he slept between then and when he woke up were the deepest he'd slept for years.

People began to leave the shelter from six in the morning and by half six it was almost deserted. Henry had hoped to stay in it until nearer to eight o'clock, but when they ventured up onto the main station concourse they spotted that a cafe was open and they were able to remain there for the next hour and a half. At eight o'clock the telegram booth in the station opened and Henry sent a message to Michael Hedinger, who he knew would have gone into the bank that morning as arranged.

Departing Stuttgart 8.20 stop Arriving Zurich 2.40 stop Papers all in order stop

Papers all in order: Andreas is with me, a successful mission… so far.

The train left Stuttgart at eight thirty but then was held at a red light on the outskirts of the city to allow a military train to pass, its open trucks carrying dozens of tanks. By lunchtime the train had made its steady progress through Swabia towards the border town of Singen, the last stop in Germany before Switzerland. They were held at an isolated platform, where they were told by a loudspeaker announcement that any passengers wishing to travel on into Switzerland should remain in their compartments: all other passengers should leave the train forthwith.

For half an hour there was no sign of anything. There was just one other passenger in their compartment, an immaculately dressed German man with the long elegant hands of a pianist and the complexion of someone who rarely ventured outdoors. He had spent most of the journey reading sheet music and attending to his nails, occasionally removing a watch from his jacket with a flourish, studying it with some fascination, tutting and then returning it to his jacket. Eventually, the delay in Singen was too much for him. He was going to see what was going on, he told Henry, and left the apartment, leaving Henry and Alfred. Henry leaned over to Alfred, who he had noticed looked considerably more relaxed than yesterday. 'Don't forget, this is the most dangerous part of the journey. The Swiss border police will be watching for anyone trying to get into Switzerland who shouldn't. Don't make any mistakes. Soon you'll be able to relax. You have done very well, my boy. But be careful now…'

Alfred looked worried and Henry was not sure he had said the right thing. *Maybe I should have just kept quiet.*

Their fellow passenger returned to the carriage. 'They have to wait for the Swiss police to arrive,' he told them. 'I thought the Swiss were meant to be efficient. Ridiculous'.

Ten minutes later the Swiss border police arrived on the platform, where they and the German officers greeted each other like old friends. Working in pairs, one Swiss, one German, they went through the train compartment by compartment.

The Swiss officer who came into their apartment looked no more than twenty. He checked the passport of the pianist, asked to see his return ticket and then handed both to the German policeman. Both appeared to be satisfied.

The officer then turned to Henry. '*Passport.*' It was only when he saw the Swiss passport and said *grüezi* that a fatal flaw in their plan that they had overlooked until now hit Henry hard in the face.

The Swiss border policeman had used the traditional Swiss German greeting, '*grüezi*'. If he was going to speak in Swiss German then the boy would not understand. He and his story would unravel very quickly.

'Where have you travelled from in Germany?' he asked, in Swiss German.

'I have been in Berlin, on business for Bank Leu. Here is my letter of accreditation.' Henry made a point of replying in standard German.

The young policeman took it and read it carefully. 'So how long have you been in Germany for?' Still in Swiss German.

'Since Monday.' Standard German. It had become like a surreal game.

'The boy: is he with you?'

'Andreas is the son of friends. He has been visiting Berlin.' Henry had tried to avoid looking at the boy, but caught a glimpse of his worried face as he mentioned him. He must have feared that he was about to be spoken to in Swiss German, which he would barely understand.

'And you stayed where in Berlin?'

'Jan, I keep telling you! Speak proper German; don't confuse me!' It was the German policeman, standing in the doorway of the carriage and clearly impatient.

His Swiss counterpart shrugged and took the passport of Andreas Hedinger. He checked the visa, looked up at Alfred and back again at the photo, repeating this three or four times, his bright blue eyes darting up and down.

'How old are you?' He spoke in standard German. Alfred gave Andreas's age and date of birth.

'Did you enjoy Berlin?'

'Yes sir, thank you. But I am looking forward to going home.'

-

He was in Zurich for less than forty hours.

They arrived in the city at three o'clock on the Saturday afternoon and were met at the station by Herr and Frau Hedinger. Alfred had shown no signs of relief as they had crossed the border into Switzerland and by the time they arrived at the station he was in a state of shock, seemingly overwhelmed by what was happening to him. The fact that he was free and safe did not seem to occur to him as he was warmly greeted by the Hedingers. Frau Hedinger led Alfred over to the station cafe for a hot chocolate while Michael Hedinger and Henry found a quiet bench. Henry handed over the papers.

'Everything was in order?'

'Yes, thank you. Your arrangements were very good; faultless in fact.'

A tall man in a trilby was strolling purposefully towards them: it seemed that he had appeared from nowhere, Henry had looked carefully around when they left the train and certainly hadn't seen any sign of this man then. It was only when he was close to them that it was apparent who he was. He removed his leather gloves and shook Henry's hand.

'So that's Alfred, eh?'

'I wondered when you might show up, Edgar.'

'You didn't imagine that I'd miss this, did you? I trust there were no problems?'

'No. Nerve-wracking but we have arrived in one piece.'

'As I can see. Hedinger, have you sorted your wretched documents out?'

Hedinger took the sealed envelopes from Henry and handed him a few more in return. 'You're returning to Berlin on Monday,' he said as he stood up. 'Edgar will tell you all about it. He has your tickets.'

'You're going to be all right with the boy?'

Hedinger nodded.

'And you'll send the telegram to Reinhart?'

'First thing Monday morning, as we arranged.'

'Won't Reinhart want to know sooner that Alfred's arrived safely?'

'I'm sure he would but this all has to look proper,' said Edgar. 'It will be odd for an official of the Reichsbank to receive a telegram from an official of Bank Leu on a Saturday acknowledging safe receipts of papers. It will have to wait until Monday. By the time you see Reinhart on Tuesday morning he will know that Alfred arrived safely and he can hand the other document over to you. Go on Hedinger, you'd better take Alfred off. Henry, perhaps you want to go and say goodbye?'

Alfred had relaxed by the time Henry met up with him and Frau Hedinger in the station cafe. He had been drinking a hot chocolate and was devouring an enormous cream pastry. He had a big grin on his face.

'Alfred was telling me that he loves dogs but has never had one. He is so looking forward to meeting Mitzi! And guess what, Herr Hesse? She is expecting puppies! I have told Alfred that he can choose one of them to be his very own pet.'

Henry embraced Alfred and promised he would come and visit him. He mustn't worry; everything would be fine. When he released the boy from his embrace he noticed that Alfred's eyes were moist. He kept saying 'Thank you' and, as he disappeared out of the station he turned round and gave Henry a nervous little wave.

–

They spent what remained of the weekend in the apartment above the hardware shop on Basteiplatz. When they arrived there, Basil

Remington-Barber was making up a camp bed in the lounge. The three of them sat around the table.

'You're booked on the six o'clock train on Monday morning. That got you into Berlin that evening, didn't it?'

'Yes: I was fortunate with the connection in Stuttgart. Coming back yesterday was a different matter. True, we left Berlin a bit later, but whether it was bomb damage or something else, I don't know, but it was a much slower journey: hence the reason why we had to stay over in Stuttgart.'

'I trust that you did not go anywhere near the Victoria?' asked Basil Remington-Barber.

'No, we stayed overnight in the station – in an air raid shelter.'

'Let's get down to business. Here's your ticket for Monday. We want to get you and the document back here as quickly as possible so the plan is that you go to the Reichsbank first thing on the Tuesday morning, hand the Bank Leu's envelopes to Reinhart and he will give you the ones to be brought back here. One of the sealed Reichsbank envelopes will contain the document – he will let you know which one. According to Hedinger, neither the German nor the Swiss police have ever tried to open a sealed envelope from any of the banks. I imagine that would be bad for business. I can see no reason why you should not be able to leave Berlin by lunchtime. I know the couriers often hang around for a few days, but we need to get you back here so we will risk it. You won't make it into Switzerland that night, but go to Stuttgart and then take the first train out on Wednesday morning. Does that all make sense?'

'Yes… but shouldn't the document be concealed?'

'We thought of that,' said Remington-Barber. 'If they decide to search you then they'll probably find it anyway. As Edgar says, they don't touch bank envelopes, especially if they are properly sealed. You're booked in the Kaiserhof there – here's the telegram confirming it. You still have the letter of accreditation from the bank? Good. And of course your passport has the correct visas. Tell me, Henry, what is Gunter Reinhart like?'

Henry shrugged. 'He's a German banker, which seems to be rather like a Swiss banker and I daresay British bankers: efficient enough, but what do you want me to say? I'll doubt we'll become close friends, if that is what you mean. Very tall also, for what this is worth.'

'What I think we mean,' said Remington-Barber 'is what kind of a chap do you think he is? Is he trustworthy? After all, we have used one of our few agents able to travel in and out of Germany to help his son escape. How do we know that this document he is promising us is genuine? Maybe it is a trick…? Has he been just leading us along as ruse to get Alfred out?'

'I really have no idea,' said Henry. 'He seems genuine enough. I suppose that if the document turns out to be either a fake or not to exist at all then he runs the risk of upsetting us and that could have implications for his own safety – and that of Rosa and Sophia.'

Edgar and Remington-Barber looked at each other, partially reassured.

'You see, he still wants to help Rosa escape and obviously that means little Sophia too.'

'I can see why Reinhart wanted to get his son out, but why his ex-wife?'

'He obviously cares very much for her and to be frank with you, I can see why. She really is the most marvellous woman, you know. She has been holed up in that house in Dahlem for well over a year now. Poor little Sophia can barely speak; she is so terrified of making a noise. It would be marvellous if we could do something to help them.'

'I beg your pardon?' Edgar was staring at Henry as if he had completely misheard him.

'I was just saying that I thought it would be marvellous if we could help Alfred's mother and sister.'

Edgar sat there open-mouthed. It was Remington-Barber who spoke next.

'Help in what way, Henry?'

'Possibly help them to leave Germany.'

'Has Reinhart asked you to raise this?'

'No.'

'So it is not a condition of his handing over the document?'

'No.'

'So why on earth are you raising the matter then?'

'Don't forget I've just come back from Berlin, Edgar. It's like a bloody prison camp, uniforms everywhere. It can only be a matter of time before they are caught. If there was any way we could help get them out before that happens then we would be doing the decent thing.'

Edgar slammed the table with his hand. 'Are you stark raving mad? Who the hell do you think we are – the Red bloody Cross?'

'I was only thinking—'

'Well don't. What has got into you: have you fallen in love with this woman or something?'

Henry hesitated as he realised that was exactly what he had done. He could feel his face reddening. 'No, not at all. I just feel awfully sorry for them.'

'Well don't,' said Edgar, who was no longer shouting. 'In our profession, we simply cannot afford to have those kinds of feelings. Do you understand?'

Until they saw him off early on the Monday morning at the station, Henry was never alone. Either Edgar or Remington-Barber was always near him. When he got up in the early hours of the Sunday morning to go to the bathroom, Edgar was awake in the lounge, sitting in an armchair that he had angled round to face the open lounge door. Henry wondered whether talking about Rosa had caused them to distrust him. He had learnt his lesson.

He was woken at four o'clock on the Monday morning for his final briefing. 'When you get here on Wednesday go straight to Bank Leu on Paradeplatz; hand the envelopes over to Hedinger apart from the one for us. Understood?'

'Yes.'

'Use the telephone in Hedinger's office to call this number. Both Edgar and I will be in Bern. One of us will answer. Tell us what train you are catching from Zurich and I will meet you at Bern station. You'll be back home in Geneva that evening.'

'Assuming everything goes well,' said Edgar, 'we will put a further 500 pounds into your Credit Suisse account. Two trips in and out of Germany – you'll have deserved it.'

Henry told them how grateful he was. 'Just one thing though' he said. 'Seems to be the most enormous effort to go to Berlin, bring the boy out and go back again to collect this document.'

'Only way of doing it, Henry. Gunter will only release the document once he is sure that his son is safe in Switzerland. We've already told you that.'

'Must be a damn important document then.'

'That, Henry, is for us to decide. Oh… and one other thing,' said Edgar as they prepared to leave the apartment. 'That Rosa woman: don't be tempted to go anywhere near her. Forget about her. Understand?'

Henry assured them that he understood.

–

Gunter Reinhart had left home just after seven o'clock on the Monday morning and as luck would have it, the U–Bahn and the trams were all running so smoothly that he was concerned that he would arrive at work too early. It would not do to be noticed. So he got off the tram early on the Unter den Linden and walked the rest of the way and by the time he turned onto Französischestrasse it was twenty to eight, which although was still early but hopefully not so early that he would draw attention to himself. He tried to appear as casual as possible as he entered the Reichsbank on Werderscher Markt but as he found himself alone in the corridors leading to his office his pace quickened.

He waited until five past eight until he picked up the telephone that he had been staring at since he had arrived in his office and dialled an internal number.

'*Yes, Herr Reinhart: a telegram has indeed arrived for you. I beg your pardon? Yes, from Zurich. From Bank Leu. Our messenger starts at half past eight. I will ensure he brings it straight to you.*'

Gunter Reinhart could not bear to wait even for half an hour, so even though it was unusual for him to do so he went down himself to the telegram bureau in the basement. He did manage to restrain himself from opening the telegram until he was back in his office.

Documentation all in order stop Courier with you again
Tuesday stop All well stop Hedinger stop

He read the telegram twice before folding it up carefully, slipping it into an envelope and placing it in the bottom of his briefcase. He felt he a wave of emotion overwhelm him for a minute or so. Alfred was safe in Switzerland. Now he had to keep his side of the bargain.

He telephoned Funk's private secretary at a quarter past nine.

'Why do you need to see it, Reinhart?'

Funk's private secretary was an unpleasant man who had a habit of following his master around like a dog, his hands held in apparent supplication before him, an admiring smile on his face. He took considerable pleasure in controlling people's access to the Minister and generally making life more difficult in an effort to make himself seem somehow important.

'Because Herr Funk has asked that I prepare a paper on dealing with assets that may come under our control should certain events happen and to complete that paper to the Minister's satisfaction I need to see the document once more.'

'When?'

'This morning.'

'This morning? Impossible: I need to accompany Herr Funk to the Reichstag. In any case Reinhart, you know that you need to put your request in writing.'

'Very well. Perhaps you would inform the Minister that I will not be able to let him have that paper by the end of today.'

There was a long pause, during which Gunter could hear the Private Secretary's worried breathing at the other end of the line.

'Very well, you can come up now if you promise to be quick.'

He waited in the secure room behind Funk's office while the private secretary fussed around; making sure the document was in order and signed for. He stood behind Reinhart as he opened the document on the table in front of him. There was a distinct smell of mothballs from the secretary's three-piece suit with a Nazi Party badge on one lapel and a swastika on the other.

'How long will you be?'

'Maybe half an hour, possibly a bit longer.'

'I am meant to remain with you but I have to prepare for this important meeting at the Reichstag. I will return in twenty minutes. Remember; do not write on the document!'

Gunter Reinhart had practised in his locked study at home over the weekend and he reckoned he could photograph the whole of Directive 21 in ten minutes. He waited for five minutes and then walked over to the door, which the private secretary had left ajar. Through the gap he could see the private secretary busy at his desk at the other end of the outer office. He waited another minute and then pushed the door a bit more, so that it was still open, but only just.

The camera that Franz Hermann had given him was tiny and he had been warned that it was very sensitive, so he had to concentrate on remaining as still as possible as he photographed each page twice. He had placed himself with his back to the door, which would give him a second or two to react but the danger of being caught was still acute.

It took twelve minutes to complete the task and he allowed a further five minutes to check the document was in order, that he had made some notes and to compose himself. When the private secretary returned he was able to announce he was ready.

'Would you like to check my notes?'

The secretary glanced at them and then checked the Directive carefully. He seemed to be slightly disappointed that everything was in order.

–

Henry Hunter arrived in Berlin slightly later than he had the previous Monday and the staff at the Kaiserhof seemed to be pleased to see him again. The concierge enquired whether he required advice on any trips during his stay, but Henry assured him that this was a much shorter visit: he expected to leave Berlin the next day. He noticed the concierge making a discreet note as he walked away from his desk.

He was in Gunter Reinhart's office by ten past ten on the Tuesday morning. Reinhart carefully opened the sealed envelopes from Bank Leu and signed a receipt for each one, making a note in a ledger on his desk as he did so.

'Please sit down, Herr Hesse. You are making me nervous standing there; this will take a few minutes more.'

Gunter Reinhart quietly walked over to his office door and opened it, checking that no one was outside it. When he came back in, he silently slipped a lock down. He gestured for Henry to move his chair nearer to the desk.

'Everything is in order,' he was speaking quietly. 'I received the telegram from Herr Hedinger this morning: he told me the package arrived safely. Thank you. Tell me, how was the journey?'

Henry told him that the journey was fine. So was the package.

'It goes without saying that I am indebted to you, but I am now about to repay that debt in full. There are four envelopes here,' he pointed to a pile of bulky envelopes on the desk in front of him, 'for you to take from Reichsbank to Bank Leu. You will sign for these in a moment. This one...' Reinhart pointed to the third envelope in the pile 'is the one that is to go elsewhere. You understand – I don't need to be more explicit, do I?'

Gunter Reinhart held up the packages, which as far as Henry could see was identical to the other three. 'You will see that there is a tiny tear on the flap of the envelope here, can you see? And on the front, this corner of the label has come slightly loose. There is one final way of distinguishing this envelope: the others have a full stop after the word "Reichsbank" – before our address. On this one, there is a comma. In all other respects, it is identical to the other three envelopes. Tell them I had to photograph it: obviously I could not possibly take the original. The document is on film in here.'

—

It was a quarter to eleven when he left the Reichsbank: he would need to be at the station by two thirty, giving him a shade under fours to do what he had planned. He was cutting it very fine; he would need to hurry.

He walked, neither too fast nor too slowly, down by the canal as the far the Spittelmarkt U-Bahn station. He passed one or two shops on the way, but he didn't want to go into one until he was further away from Werderscher Markt. The journey to Gleisdreieck took twelve minutes; it was a quarter past eleven. He changed lines, heading west to Wittenberg Platz where he changed onto another U-Bahn line, now heading south. By the time he arrived at Podbielski Allee it was a quarter to twelve. The last leg of the journey had taken him much longer than he had expected. It would take at least another ten minutes to get there and he needed to find a shop first.

He came across a parade of three shops: one with a collection of ladies' dresses hanging forlornly behind a dusty window, another appeared to be some kind of bookshop with more pictures of Hitler than books and the third was a grocers. He was annoyed to see a queue of a dozen or so people waiting outside the shop: he was not sure that he had the time to wait.

'How long will I have to queue for?' he asked the man at the front of the queue. The man was wearing a suit and a smart overcoat, but his posture was stooped and he had a sallow expression. He looked as if he had not understood the question: Henry repeated it. The man said nothing but pointed to a handwritten sign stuck to the inside of the shop's glass door.

Jews may only shop here between four o'clock and five o'clock.

Taped beneath it was a cartoon cut-out from a newspaper showing a Jewish man with a long nose stealing food from angelic-looking children.

'I am sure you can go in now', said the man. 'It's us who have to wait.'

The shopkeeper had tiny eyes and an enormous belly that appeared to rest on the counter-top. His face was heavily pockmarked and there was a growing layer of perspiration on his forehead.

'I feel like having a bath every time those rats come in here,' he said, gesturing at the queue outside the window. 'Some of them start queuing first thing in the morning, you know? There's not much they can buy these days: not even white bread or vegetables! Good thing too. I'm happy to take their money though, better that I have it than some others: I joined the party before thirty three, so I reckon I'm entitled to it. Now, how can I help you sir?'

'I need to buy some food but I am afraid that I have no ration book.'

'No ration book?' The man's tiny eyes narrowed. *A problem.*

'I am from Switzerland, you see. I am visiting friends for lunch and would like to take them some food as a gift. I'd be happy to pay in Swiss Francs, if that helps.'

The shopkeeper's little eyes lit up. *No longer a problem.*

He indicated for Henry to move to the back of the shop, where it was darker and further away from the prying eyes of the people queuing outside.

'Of course,' he whispered. 'You understand that it is hard to charge you the exact rate, because of difficulties, you understand?'

Henry understood. He would be very generous, he assured the shopkeeper.

Five minutes later he left the shop, unable to look at the people waiting until four o'clock before they could enter the shop. The queue seemed to have grown since he had gone in.

Within ten minutes he was knocking gently at the door of the white house on the corner of Arno-Holz Strasse. The interior of the house was dark and he could not hear a sound. He waited a minute and then knocked again. A lady being pulled along by two yapping dogs watched him carefully as she passed by. Still no reply. He knocked once more. It was now past midday and he was beginning to worry. He became aware of a slight movement to his right, where the curtains were drawn on the window of the front room. A few seconds later he heard Rosa's worried voice from behind the still closed front door.

'Who is it please?'

'It is me, Henri!' The door opened quickly and a hand poked out, gesturing for him to enter. *Quickly.*

Since he had begun to formulate this plan he had imagined that Rosa would be overwhelmed with gratitude to see him. She would be relieved. Instead, she looked horrified.

'It's me, Rosa. Henri!'

'I know it is you. You must keep your voice down. What on earth are you doing here? What is the matter? What has happened to Alfred?'

Her dark brown eyes were just like Roza's but now they were red around the lids, as if she had been crying.

'Everything is all right Rosa. I came to visit you and Sophia. I have brought food.'

'But what about Alfred? Please tell me.'

'Alfred is safe, Rosa,' Henry moved closer to Rosa as he spoke, placing a hand on her shoulders. She backed away. 'He is in Zurich. I managed to get him there safely. You don't need to worry.'

'You shouldn't have come here. It is so dangerous. Go upstairs quickly. You cannot stay long. I have to give Frau Hermann her lunch. Go upstairs and let me settle her. I'll be a few minutes.'

In the small lounge upstairs there was no sign of Sophia. When she finally came upstairs, Henry asked Rosa where she was.

'In bed: she has been there almost all the time since Alfred left. She misses him so much that it is making her ill. He was wonderful to her, her only companion. I don't think that she has uttered more than half a dozen sentences since he left.'

'Well, perhaps these will cheer her up.' Henry triumphantly emptied the content of his bag on the rug. He placed a pack of sweets and some chocolate to one side and handed Rosa a large cheese, a long sausage, a bag of fruit and another of vegetables. Rosa looked embarrassed.

'I don't know what to say.' Tears were streaming down her face. She knelt down beside him and gently touched his wrist with her fingers, holding them there for a few seconds before busying herself sorting the food. 'Of course I am very grateful, but you coming here is so dangerous. Our only hope is to stay here with no one finding out. Franz does his best to ensure that we get as few visitors as possible, but neighbours spy on each other and watch out for comings and goings.

My real fear is that Frau Hermann will die or have to go into hospital and then we won't be able to stay here.'

'Come with me, Rosa – you and Sophia – come with me.'

She looked at him as if she had misheard what he had said.

'Come where?'

'Back to Switzerland, Rosa.'

She burst out laughing. 'Henri – do you think we haven't thought about how we can escape ever since we got here? It is impossible: we have no papers other than our own and they are useless because I am wanted by the Gestapo. I know you are trying to be kind but...' She held up her hands in a gesture of helplessness.

'But you cannot stay here forever, Rosa. As you say, what if something happens to the old lady? And what about food? People say that it is becoming scarcer. And then the neighbours... someone could inform on you. I could help you. I could get papers.'

Rosa was looking at him as if she had misheard him again.

'How can you do that?'

At that moment there was a weak shout from downstairs.

'I must go, Henri. Frau Hermann wants her lunch.'

Henry grabbed her by the arm and moved towards her. 'I will get papers, Rosa, I will be back. Trust me.'

As she stood up, Henry did too, positioning himself immediately in front of her.

'Henri, please. I have to go to her. You must leave now. In any case, sometimes an old friend comes to see her on Tuesdays. Please let me get through.'

He hesitated for a moment, wondering whether it would be wrong to embrace her. He had expected her to be more grateful. She pushed past him and headed downstairs, beckoning for him to follow her, a finger pressed to her lips for him to keep quiet.

–

He eventually left Berlin on a train for Nuremberg just before three – only a few minutes late – and the journey was much quicker than the one to Stuttgart just a few days earlier. He arrived in Nuremberg at seven o'clock and it felt like a garrison town, troops everywhere. The concourse of the station was a seething mass of grey uniforms, with a sprinkling of black. He could see few other civilians. He joined a long queue of soldiers at the ticket office and had enough time to observe that most of them belonged to the Seventeenth Infantry Division: a gift for Edgar. When he reached the window he found out that the first train to Stuttgart was at eight twenty the next morning – 'All being well,' added the ticket clerk as he carefully stamped and then initialled Henry's ticket.

Henry calculated that he could be in Stuttgart sometime late morning and Zurich by mid-afternoon. *All being well.*

The ticket clerk told him that he would find the hotels if he turned left coming out of the station and walked over to the next block. There he found a selection of grey buildings, each seemingly reflecting the ubiquitous uniforms milling around on the street. He went into the first three hotels, each more miserable than the previous one and settled on the fourth only because it was now teeming with rain and he was exhausted.

As the manager laboriously completed the paperwork that would allow him the privilege of being a guest there for one night, Henry had an opportunity to have a look into what the manager called the dining room. If pushed, Henry would have described it as a workhouse, a memory from Dickensian novels read out loud at the end of dark autumn afternoons at school in England.

'You had better go and eat now, the dining room closes in twenty minutes,' the manager said in what Henry thought could be an Austrian accent.

'I am all right thank you,' said Henry, the smell of grease and tobacco settling already at the back of his throat. 'I may eat elsewhere.'

'You'll be lucky: there is no "elsewhere" these days. Leave your case here and go in and eat.'

He reluctantly went in to the dining room, having passed up the offer of leaving his case with the manager. There were two long tables in the dining room and each one had six or seven men – only men – hunched around it, all eyeing each other suspiciously and spooning black coloured stew into their mouths in apparent unison.

Henry found a small space at the end of one table and the man next alongside him very reluctantly moved along no more than an inch or two. No sooner had he sat down than a filthy hand deposited a bowl of the stew in front of him. The thumb and one finger of the filthy hand were dipped in the stew. Henry moved his gaze up the hand and the frayed sleeve just above it: both belonged to a hunched body and pale face flecked with red sores, a woman in her fifties who looked as if she were about to collapse.

A plate of black bread was pushed in front of him, along with a glass of watery beer. No one was speaking to anyone else around the table and Henry was grateful for that.

His night did not become any more comfortable: the room had bare floorboards and just one small threadbare rug by the bed. There was a wash basin with a stained sink by a window that had a crack in the glass and Henry doubted that the sheets had been changed since the last guest but one. As there was no functioning lock on the door he wedged the single chair in the room against it and lay on the bed fully clothed, his briefcase containing the sealed envelopes under the pillow that smelt of sweat. In the distance he could hear the muffled sound of explosions: he could not tell whether it was bombs or anti-aircraft fire but when he went over to the window and peeled back the blackout curtain he could see flashes far to the north.

He left the hotel at seven in the morning, the manager and the woman from the dining room confused as to why he declined their offer of breakfast – 'But you have paid for it sir!'

For the next hour the station cafe provided a welcome refuge from the all-pervading odour of the hotel. The Stuttgart train left on time and the connection from there to Zurich was good and he arrived at ten past two. He was under pressure now. There was a train to Bern at ten past five, which was the one he would need to catch if Edgar and Remington-Barber were not to be too suspicious about his late arrival. It ought to give him enough time, but only just.

He needed to get to Bank Leu as soon as possible, but only after he had made the phone call. There was a bank of phone booths on the main station concourse, but they felt too public so he left the station and walked across to the Bahnhofquai, where he found a cafe with phone booth at the rear, well away from the few customers. He rang the number Viktor had given him.

'Yes?'

'Peter is coming round for dinner.'

A pause and a muffled noise at the other end of the line, which sounded as if the person had placed their hand over the receiver and was talking to someone else in the room.

'And will you be bringing wine with you?'

'Yes.'

With that, the line went dead. He checked his watch: it was two twenty five: according to the Viktor's instructions he was to be at the station exactly one hour after the phone call. That would leave him just over an hour and a half to catch his train: he would need to hurry. He left the cafe by the back door and caught a taxi to Bank Leu's head office on Paradeplatz.

Michael Hedinger was apparently in a hurry. He came down to the reception and took Henry up to his office on the top floor. He checked the three envelopes from the Reichsbank for Bank Leu.

'And the fourth envelope is for your friends?'

'Yes.'

'When do you see them?'

'I'm going to Bern now. May I use your phone to tell them what time I'm likely to be there?'

Hedinger gestured at the phone: *be my guest*.

Edgar answered: '*Welcome home. What kept you?*'

'I'm catching the train at ten past five. I ought to be in Bern by eight at the latest. Where shall I meet you?'

'Don't worry, old chap, we'll meet you.'

That was that. It was now a quarter to three, he had plenty of time. He could even afford to stroll back to the station along Bahnhofstrasse, which would at least give him time to compose himself.

'And all went well?' asked Hedinger.

'Yes... yes, thank you.'

'And I presume you wish to ask me a question?'

Henry had no idea what the Swiss was on about.

'I'm sorry?'

'Alfred! Do you not want to know how he is?'

'Of course, of course! How is Alfred?'

'My wife and the children and the dog make such a fuss of him: it is as if he has been released from prison. He is such a sweet boy and very considerate. We will take good care of him. He is obviously sad though. At night we can hear him sobbing in his room. He must miss his mother.'

—

Arriving too early for a rendezvous is as dangerous as being late for one.

He had arrived outside the Hauptbahnhof at a quarter past three, ten minutes early. Without thinking properly, he had continued into the station, assuming he would find a bar and then go out onto the concourse ten minutes later. This is what he did, but no sooner had he stepped out onto the concourse than he was aware of two men either side of him, marching him out of a side exit. One of them was Viktor, his face impassive but his voice not disguising his fury.

'We said be at the station one hour after the phone call, not fifty minutes. What do you think you are up to, *synok*?'

Henry shook himself from Viktor and the other man, who had now stepped back into the shadows.

'Learn to do as you are told Henry, you understand? Now, follow me — stay behind me. I will go into a shop and through to the back. You are to do likewise. Sergei will be behind you.'

The shop was a narrow tobacconist in a warren of alleys behind the station. The countertop was already open when Henry arrived. Viktor was in a room at the back, along with a shrivelled-looking man half the size of the Russian. The man was dressed in a faded pinstripe suit and peered up at Henry through thick glasses that sat unsteadily on the bridge of a badly misshapen nose.

'Have you spoken with Edgar?' Viktor sounded impatient.

'Yes.'

'Where is he?'

'In Bern: they're expecting me to be on the train that leaves here at ten past five. I have no excuse for not being on that one.'

'Don't worry, you will be. You have it?' Viktor looked anxious.

Henry took the sealed Reichsbank envelope out of his briefcase, but held on to it while he spoke.

'I do, Viktor, but it is sealed. How are you going to open it without Edgar and Remington-Barber realising?'

Viktor passed the envelope over to the man, addressing him in German.

'Arnold, what do you reckon?'

The man took the envelope and held it under the light, turning it very slowly one way and the other, moving it close to his eyes and then running his fingers along its every surface. He nodded and replied into a squeaky, high-pitched voice.

'This should not be a problem. Give me an hour, but I want everyone out of here.'

'Apart from me' said Viktor.

'Of course, apart from you Viktor' Arnold said obediently, half bowing as he spoke.

As Henry left the room he could see the man they called Arnold arranging a large camera, a lamp and various tools on a bench. He was about to operate. Henry spent the next fifteen minutes standing silently in the alley behind the tobacconist with the man called Sergei. When Viktor called Henry back in he was clearly finding it hard to contain his excitement. Little Arnold was packing away his equipment, the surgery over. The envelope was handed to him. 'Examine it, please. See how perfect it is?'

Henry looked at it carefully. It was impossible to see how it could have been opened. With a huge arm around his shoulder, Viktor shepherded Henry to a corner of the room and whispered into his ear.

'We have made a copy: you have no idea how important it is, *synok*. We will transmit the entire text to Moscow tonight. You have forty minutes before your train, so tell me everything that you can about this man who supplied the document. It is so important that Moscow will ask me many questions about it: I need to have the answers.'

'Before I do that, Viktor, I need to ask a favour of you.'

Viktor looked at him puzzled: a favour? *Henry did not ask favours of them. They asked favours of him.*

'What is it?' he asked, hardly managing to hide his irritation.

Henry looked at the Russian, wishing that he was more sympathetic at times. Even some gratitude wouldn't have gone amiss.

'I don't want to sound like I'm going soft or anything, but I have coped very well in Germany so far and I have this worry that they could send me back there, sooner or later, I—'

'Why, have they said anything about that, *synok*?'

'No, but I get the impression that they don't exactly have a team of agents queuing up at the border waiting to be sent into Germany. I feel exposed when I am in Berlin and I was wondering: do you have anyone I could contact in Berlin – in an emergency?'

Henry shrugged, eager that Viktor should not think the request an unusual one. *What I am I to do – tell him that I am determined to go back there anyway?*

Viktor looked at Henry, suspicious at first but then more understanding.

'Let me see what I can do, Henry. There's the embassy, but I don't trust anyone there. I do have some people, I'll let you know. Now, tell me about how you got this document.'

Chapter 21

London, March 1941

Edgar arrived at Whitchurch Airport just after twelve thirty on Monday the 10th of March on BOAC flight 777 from Lisbon. A black Humber Imperial with military plates was parked close to the bottom of the aircraft steps and three hours later it deposited an exhausted Edgar outside the building overlooking St James's Square where Christopher Porter was waiting for him in his office on the top floor.

Edgar handed over the film of Directive 21 to Porter, who promptly left the room, returning five minutes later.

'We'll have that developed straight away and sent off to the analysts tonight. They've all been told to deal with it as a matter of priority. We'll meet here tomorrow afternoon to hear what they all make of it. But well done, Edgar: something of a coup to get our hands on that. How is our chap Hunter?'

Edgar leaned back in his chair, barely stifling a yawn. 'Turns out to be rather good at his job actually. Not someone you would automatically think of as spy material, but I suppose that's the whole point, isn't it? I remember that Classics don who trained Hunter saying that he looks for people who are slightly apart from the crowd but not so much so that people would notice them. He said that he had never come across someone who fitted that bill quite so well as Hunter. He's survived three missions into Nazi Germany now: if he looked or acted like a spy he wouldn't have lasted more than an hour or two.'

'And his other masters… would they have seen the Directive?'

'I certainly hope so. We allowed him enough time in Zurich between going to Bank Leu and catching the train to Bern. One of

Basil's men spotted him with Viktor leaving the station, so I think we can assume that they have the document. There is one concern, though…'

'With Hunter?'

'No, with our Portuguese friends actually. When I came back through Lisbon Sandy was in a bit of a flap about Telmo. He's been rather elusive and Sandy is worried that he may be getting cold feet. Telmo seems to think that the PVDE may be on to him, though there doesn't seem to be any evidence for that. Personally, I think he is just getting twitchy; agents get like that from time to time, as you know. There is what appears to be well founded a concern about Dona Maria though.'

'The lady in Berlin?'

'Correct.'

'Telmo says that Dona Maria has been transferred within the Portuguese Legation there: she's no longer working for the military attaché, now she's with the First Secretary.'

'And is that a demotion?'

'Not as such, but it gives her less access to the kind of intelligence we are interested in and also less access to the diplomatic bag. Apparently the First Secretary is quite high up the hierarchy at the Legation, but his role is more ceremonial. She is worried that they may be watching her: she is certain that her desk was searched recently and she thinks that she has been tailed on a few occasions.'

'By whom?'

'Not the Germans – security people from the Legation. Also, her home leave has been brought forward to 24th March: which is two weeks on Monday. She is worried that once she returns to Lisbon she will not be allowed back again. Telmo is demanding an absolute promise from us that the minute Dona Maria arrives in Lisbon we put both of them in hiding and bring them to the UK as soon as possible.'

'And you said…?'

'Yes, of course. I told Sandy to agree to whatever he asks for. I told him to say that once they get to England they will be given money, a house and new identities. I hope that is in order?'

'Oh, I'm sure the Service will be happy to find them some love nest somewhere or the other.'

–

The following afternoon Edgar and Christopher Porter were in a large map room in the basement of the St James's Square office, along with a number of colleagues from the Service and a few men in uniform. Copies of Directive 21 were handed by a lanky Brigadier from Army Intelligence who cut a colourful figure with his florid face and a large moustache that appeared to comprise of black and grey stripes. When he spoke it was with a Welsh accent.

'These are English translations, as you will see. The document itself is astonishing, quite astonishing. Let me quote: "The German Armed Forces must be prepared, even before the conclusion of the war against England, to crush Soviet Russia in a rapid campaign." That last bit – crushing the Soviet Union – is underlined. The Directive says that preparations for the invasion "will be concluded by 15th May 1941".'

There was murmuring around the room, people looking at each other with raised eyebrows and barely concealed surprise.

'They even have a code name: Operation Barbarossa. However, we must be cautious. The most important question that we have to address is whether the document is genuine because there is no point in us acting upon it if we feel that on a balance of probabilities it is not what it purports to be. We have had all types of experts studying this ever since we got our hands on it.'

The Brigadier removed a pair of reading glasses from a case in front of him and glanced at some handwritten notes.

'First of all, we have had the Directive subjected to something called text analysis by a German expert. What he does is compare one text with others, to see if they are from the same source. He believes that this document is very similar to other ones released by Hitler. I quote from his report: "It feels identical in terms of tone, syntax and vocabulary to other documents released by Hitler. The mixture of rhetoric and military detail, the constant reference to himself in terms of orders being given and decisions being made – all that is very familiar. Then there is the question of how feasible it is that Germany would consider breaking its pact with the Soviet Union. The consensus is that this is perfectly likely. The Nazis hate Communists, Russians and Slavs almost as much as they hate the Jews. In fact, they tend to see them as one and the same thing: when they think of a Russian they see a Jewish communist. So the pact was a surprise in one respect, but not in another – Hitler was being shrewd. He was buying time, ensuring his Eastern Front remained quiet while he conquered Western Europe and attempted an invasion of the British Isles. So, breaking the pact would not be a surprise, it was only ever a short term ruse."'

The Brigadier walked over to a large map on the wall behind him.

'So if we accept that this document is most probably a genuine one then we need to analyse its feasibility from a military point of view. It is an extremely ambitious plan: one which depends on co-operation from the Finns in the north and the Romanians in the south, which may be a problem as they are unlikely to be as committed to an invasion of the Soviet Union as the Germans are. It also depends on two other critical factors: a significant element of secrecy and surprise and the Red Army being utterly ill-prepared for it. We do know that the Red Army is not in a good state, but even so...'

The Brigadier was looking at the map and then at the Directive. He peered closely at the map and pointed to a spot around the Polish-Russian border.

'He seems to be talking about concentrating the main German thrust here, around the Pripet Marshes. He talks about having two army groups operating north of the Marshes and one army group south of it. The key objects of the southern army group looks like the Ukraine, with all of its agriculture and industry. The aims of the northern army group, it says here, are Leningrad and Moscow. This is what he says about Moscow: "The capture of this city would represent a decisive political and economic success and would also bring about the capture of the most important railway junctions".'

A colonel wearing the insignia of a guards regiment walked noisily over to the map, his boots echoing on the floor. After studying it for a while he turned round and spoke unnecessarily loudly, each syllable carefully enunciated. 'Personally, I cannot see the Germans attempting this with less than one hundred divisions – talk about putting all your eggs in one basket. If he thinks he's going to get as far as Moscow the only advice I can give him is that he had better get a move on. Once that Russian winter starts even the greatest army in the world doesn't stand a chance. From a logistics point of view this would appear to be almost impossible.'

For the next two hours the men crowded into the map room weighed up the pros and cons of Directive 21. All the participants took it in turn to play devil's advocate at every opportunity, but the discussion kept coming back to a point of agreement: on the balance of probabilities, the document was a genuine one.

It was ten o'clock that evening when Porter and Edgar went up to the office on the top floor. Porter pulled back the blackout blinds and turned off his desk lamp, allowing the light from the full moon to fill the room. For a while they sat in silence, picking at the plate of stale sandwiches on the desk between them.

'And what happens now?'

'Number Ten will be informed first thing in the morning,' said Porter. 'I am told that the Prime Minister and Eden discussed the matter this morning once they knew the Directive had arrived. They agreed that if this meeting concluded that the Directive is genuine we would not waste any time. We would get a copy of it over to Moscow as soon as possible and Cripps himself will take it to the Kremlin. So, well done, Edgar – you've done an excellent job. The Soviets can hardly ignore Directive 21 now, can they? It corroborates the copy Hunter showed Viktor.'

The two men left the office together and walked as far as Pall Mall.

'You look exhausted, Edgar.'

'I've booked two weeks' leave, sir.'

'Splendid. I expect your family will be pleased to see you. Heading down to Dorset, are you?'

Edgar carried on walking in silence, apparently oblivious to what Porter had been saying. They had now reached Waterloo Place, from where each would be going in different directions.

'Probably not, sir. As far as my family are concerned, I'm in the Far East: it's easier that way. I shall probably sleep for a week and then go walking on my own in Scotland.'

Porter slapped Edgar on the back. 'Understood. Five have an interesting case on at the moment and have been asking for your help, but first, have a good rest. Remember, I don't want to see you for a fortnight, that's an order.'

–

Edgar had gone straight to his small apartment in a mansion block behind Victoria Street and slept most of the next day and a good deal of the day after that, and by the Thursday he felt rested and even slightly bored. He visited the dentist, had his hair cut and began to suspect that two weeks off may be a week too long. He decided to wait until after the weekend before deciding whether to go to Scotland, stay in London or go back to work. The decision was made for him by a ring on his doorbell early on the Monday morning. It was a driver he recognised from the offices in St James.

'Very sorry to bother you, sir. Mr Porter would like to see you, sir. Now, sir, if you don't mind coming with me. There's a car waiting outside, sir.'

Christopher Porter was pacing up and down his office, managing to look both angry and embarrassed. He told Edgar to shut the door and sit down.

'I thought I was under orders not to see you for a fortnight?'

'You were, Edgar, but those were my orders and I consider that I'm allowed to break my own orders. I'm not going to beat about the bush: there's been a change of heart. It's all Winston's fault – and the bloody Foreign Office. Wouldn't be surprised if Five haven't tried to queer our pitch too.'

'I'm not sure I am following you, sir.'

'Let me lay the cards on the table and please listen carefully. As you know, we agreed that the copy of the Operation Barbarossa directive that Hunter brought back from Berlin is genuine. It was sent in code to Moscow and Stafford Cripps took it to the Kremlin and handed it to

264

Molotov personally on Thursday. Cripps said that Molotov appeared to be angry, but he couldn't tell whether he was angry with him or the Germans, or more likely it was just his usual demeanour. Then last night I was summoned to Downing Street. Apparently they have been having second thoughts.'

'Second thoughts about what?'

'About what we should be telling the Soviets after all. Their thinking – and one has to acknowledge that it does have a certain logic to it – is that the whole business could rebound on us. As things stand at the moment, Hitler's priority is still to invade Great Britain, even though we seem to be doing a rather decent job of defending ourselves. If this Operation Barbarossa turns out to be true then it will take an enormous pressure off us: Hitler will be diluting his forces by fighting on two fronts and it makes the chances of even an attempted German invasion of these shores – let alone a successful one – very remote indeed. I can hear the tinkle of teacups approaching, Edgar – shall we pause for a moment?'

Five minutes later, fortified by surprisingly strong cups of tea, Porter resumed. 'If the Soviets finally choose to believe the Barbarossa Directive and other intelligence and accept that the Germans do have hostile intentions towards them, then they will stop trusting the Germans, shore up their defences and reinforce the border. That would make a German invasion of the Soviet Union significantly less likely. The question that Number Ten have been asking themselves is this: would such an outcome be in our best interests?'

Edgar leaned back in his chair and removed a cigarette from a silver case. He was halfway through smoking it when he replied. 'So you're saying that there is now a feeling is that it is actually in our interests for the Germany and the Soviet Union to go to war?'

'Absolutely: if they go to war with each other then the chances of an invasion of Britain significantly diminish and, at the same time, Germany risks a dangerous war in the east which they could well lose.'

'So when you say that there's been a change of heart…'

'What I mean by that is that they now want us to play down the fact that Germany has plans to invade the Soviet Union. They think we should switch from doing the decent thing and telling the Soviets about the German plans to actually misleading them, telling them quite the opposite. I—'

'Bit bloody late for that isn't it? For Christ's sake! I'm sorry sir, but it has been one of the intelligence coups of the war thus far to get hold of that Directive and make sure the Soviets see it and now you're saying it's all been a bloody waste of time. Jesus…'

'Don't shout, Edgar, please. Remember that I am only the messenger. I…'

'And you said something about them now wanting *us* to play down the reports about German intentions and even misleading them. How on earth are we going to do that?'

'I am afraid, Edgar, it means we now need to provide the Soviets with another report courtesy of your man, Hunter, one which reflects serious German concerns about Operation Barbarossa and talks of its postponement at least, possibly even its cancellation. I have to say that is not entirely unfeasible: you yourself said that Hugo's general admitted there were serious concerns in the army high command about invading the Soviet Union. This report would simply reflect those concerns.'

'And how do *we* get hold of such a document?'

'Please don't be so sarcastic. Naval Intelligence are apparently rather good at this kind of thing. This morning I have asked our people to talk to their people and see what they can come up with. I have told them I want it to be ready by the end of the week.'

'And how do we then get it to the Russians?'

Porter heaped another spoonful of sugar into his tea, sipped it and then stood up and walked over to the window, looking out of it as he spoke.

'You said that Dona Maria do Rosario has to leave Berlin on 24th March, which is a week on Monday – correct? This report needs to be taken to Lisbon, where Telmo is to get it into the diplomatic bag to Berlin. In her final act of service for us in Berlin, Dona Maria will pass the report on to Hugo. Hunter can then go back to Berlin to collect the report so that he can let the Soviets see it when he returns to Switzerland – as before. I grant you that is a complicated route by which to get it to the Soviets, but hopefully it is one that they regard as at least plausible.'

'By the sounds of it, Porter, the Hon. Anthony Davis is about to return to Lisbon.'

'Correct, Edgar: and thereafter to Switzerland.'

Late on the afternoon of Sunday 16th March, Edgar was back in Christopher Porter's office. Edgar noticed that Porter was looking uncharacteristically confident. He had a broad grin on his face. On the desk between them was black leather-bound book, with an ornate cross on the padded front cover.

'Contemplating the priesthood are you, sir?'

'Now, now, Edgar. You may remember that when we met last Monday I said that we would need to concoct a report purporting to show that the Germans were now having second thoughts after all about invading the Soviet Union?'

Edgar nodded. 'And you want this report to fall into Soviet hands?'

Porter rubbed his hands and tenderly picked up the black leather-bound book and passed it over to Edgar. The words 'A Bíblia Sagrada' were etched on the cover in gold leaf. Edgar gently picked it up and turned it round in his hands.

'Careful, Edgar. The team that put this together want us to know how much trouble they went to to get hold of a Bible in Portuguese. They've done a pretty impressive job though. Here, pass it to me.' Christopher Porter took the Bible over and opened it at the inside back cover. The thick paper on the inside of the back cover was loose and Porter very carefully peeled it away to reveal a gap, folded into which was a document which he carefully removed and opened: three pages on brown paper, typed in German with some scrawled handwritten notes.

'This is the Rostock Report: it is a note on a meeting supposedly held a couple of weeks ago in Rostock, on the 3rd and 4th of March. If you look here, it lists the various participants...' Porter turned the page.

'And on this page it describes the purpose of the meeting: "To review plans for proposed campaign against the Soviet Union – Operation Barbarossa". The next section is essentially a summary of what was in Directive 21.'

Porter was checking the document against a typed sheet in English. 'It makes the case for the invasion of the Soviet Union and repeats pretty much what was in Directive 21. Then we have a rather clever link from the Hitler Directive to the fake report. We already know that, at the end of the Directive, Hitler said "I await submission of the plans of Commanders-in-Chief on the basis of this directive. The preparations made by all branches of the Armed Forces, together with timetables, are to be reported to me through the High Command of the Armed Forces." What follows is, in effect, the Commanders-in-Chief appearing to do just that.'

Again Porter was consulting his typed sheet, the English translation. 'There is a rather long section detailing the submissions of all the different services, I don't propose to go into detail. But then there is a paragraph concluding thus: "It is the unanimous view of the OKW, OKH, OKL, OKM" – those being the High Commands of the Armed Forces, the Army, the Air Force and the Navy – "that for the reasons summarised below, Operation Barbarossa should be postponed until the spring of 1942 at the earliest." It then goes on to give those reasons: are you happy for me to read them out to you?'

Edgar nodded. He was leaning back in his chair, his eyes half shut as if to fully absorb what was being read to him.

'"Number one – we are of the opinion that our intelligence services may have seriously underestimated both the size and the strength of the Soviet forces. The ability of Stalin to motivate the Red Army is significant. Number two – we consider that our own planners may have overestimated our ability to supply our forces adequately if the advance through Soviet territory is as rapid as it will need to be. There is a serious danger that our forces could be dangerously exposed by shortages of ammunition, fuel and food. Number three – Operation Barbarossa depends on the co-operation of Finnish and Romanian forces. We are of the opinion that this co-operation cannot be taken for granted and could leave the northern and southern sections of our front vulnerable. Number four – the Russian winter presents a very severe risk to our forces. To achieve our objective of capturing Moscow before the onset of the winter, we would recommend that Operation Barbarossa is launched by early May. At present, factors such as the Yugoslavia campaign mean that this is highly unlikely. The risk of maintaining an offensive during the winter is unacceptable. Number five – Great Britain is proving to be far more resolute that we had expected. We had been of the opinion that either they would have surrendered by now or would have been weakened to the extent that an invasion could be launched. That is not the case and therefore we have to take into account the fact that we would be fighting on two fronts." There's a bit more about future meetings and such like, but that is the gist of it. What do you think?'

Edgar said nothing but asked to look at the report. As he read through it he nodded approvingly, once or twice allowing a knowing smile to cross his face.

'It's good enough to make the Soviets pause at least. Depends on what mood Stalin is in. That line about his ability to motivate the Red Army is a clever touch – does no harm to appeal to the man's ego. My feeling is that at the very least it will confuse the Soviets.'

'And at the very best?'

Edgar glanced again at the report and turned it round in his hands, as if checking its weight. 'At the very best, they'll believe it: it's good.'

'Provided we can make sure they see the damn thing,' said Porter. 'The plan is that we seal the report in the bible – I have even been supplied with special glue for that purpose – and you take it to Lisbon: you have a seat on tomorrow's flight from Bristol. Telmo will have to get the Bible in the diplomatic bag to Dona Maria and she will pass it on to Hugo. All being well, that will happen on Thursday or Friday. Meanwhile, Basil Remington-Barber has been told to make sure we get Hunter out to Berlin for a week on Monday, where he will collect the report and bring it back to Zurich. Naturally we are counting on him showing the report to Viktor first.'

Edgar nodded approvingly. Porter picked up some other papers on the desk.

'These are for Sandy to show to Telmo. They're the carrot that we're dangling in front of him and Dona Maria. This photograph here...' he handed a photo of a very pretty cottage, with a broad expanse of wisteria across its front and a thatched roof. 'This is the place we can tell Telmo we have rented for him and Dona Maria to live in once they get here. And this is a statement from Barclays Bank in the Strand confirming that accounts have been opened in each of their names to the tune of 500 pounds each. And then there are various other bits and pieces, all amounting to what we hope is a demonstration of our positive intent towards them.'

Chapter 22

Portugal, Switzerland & Berlin, March 1941

'And what if Telmo refuses? He is so nervous at the moment, he's hardly communicating with me. To persuade him to send this on to Berlin is going to be extremely difficult, Edgar.'

It was late in the afternoon on Monday 17th March and Sandy Morgan was far from his convivial self. In front of him was the Bible that Edgar had told him to get Telmo to put in the diplomatic bag to Berlin as a matter of urgency.

'Tell him it's an order.'

'Yes, yes – I understand that, Edgar, you don't need to keep repeating it. All I can say is that we're pushing our luck. Remember, he is under no obligation to obey our orders.'

'Look, Sandy, you have to make him realise that this is in his best interests. Show him the picture of the pretty cottage the Service has sorted out for him, show him the bank statements and all the rest of it. In short, promise him the earth – anything to make sure he sends the Bible over to Dona Maria and impresses on her to hand it over to Hugo. If he says he wants to play cricket for England at Lords, tell him it's no problem. If he wants tea with the King and Queen at Buckingham bloody Palace, ask him how many sugars he takes. Promise him that the minute Dona Maria arrives back in Lisbon, you will spirit both of them into a safe house – tell him that, Sandy, he needs to hear it.'

'And what about if he's still difficult?'

'Tell him that unless he co-operates you'll go straight to the Rua Victor Cordon and tell the PVDE all about him and Dona Maria. And make sure he knows that we mean it.'

On the Wednesday morning the telephone rang twice in the space of five minutes in the apartment that Henry shared with his mother just off Quai du Mont Blanc. On the first occasion his mother answered and after a minute said 'Pas de problème,' in a somewhat resentful manner, as if her being disturbed was indeed a problem. *Wrong number.*

When the phone rang a few minutes later Henry answered. A lady was speaking very quickly in French.

'Monsieur Hesse this is Madame Ladnier at Credit Suisse. I need to see you urgently here at the bank: two o'clock this afternoon. Now, please respond to this call as if I have called the wrong number again. Two o'clock.'

'No, it is not,' replied Henry, aware that he was sounding rather aggressive. 'You have the wrong number. Please do not disturb us again.'

At two o'clock he was ushered from the reception in the Quai des Bergues branch of Credit Suisse by Madame Ladnier, through a warren of corridors at the back of the bank and up a staircase to the first floor. She unlocked the door to a small office and then opened an interconnecting door. Lounging on a leather sofa in the room on the other side was Basil Remington-Barber.

'When you have finished ring me on this telephone. I am on extension eighteen,' said Madame Ladnier.

'Henry, Henry – how nice to see you. Do come in, sit down. Sorry I cannot offer you a drink but it seems that Swiss banks are not very good on that score. Apologies too for all the subterfuge: I needed to contact you urgently and had to rather prevail upon Madame Ladnier to make the calls. Ah well, all's well that ends well, eh?'

Henry had sat down on a more formal chair opposite Basil Remington-Barber.

'Look, Henry – little bit awkward this: I know that we promised you a nice long rest but something urgent has cropped up.' Remington-Barber stood up and walked over to the window and then paced around the room, at one stage slapping Henry jovially on the shoulders.

'Rather annoying really but I am afraid that we need to send you back to Berlin somewhat sooner than we had envisaged. We thought that there was an outside chance of that but we didn't imagine it would be quite so soon.'

Basil Remington–Barber had returned to the sofa and seemed a bit less hesitant now that he had passed on the message.

'When would this be?' Henry sounded casual, even rather keen.

'Monday, I'm afraid: Hedinger is sorting things out from the Zurich end, but Edgar wants to see you in Zurich on Saturday. I have to return to Bern this afternoon but I'll travel over with you on Saturday morning. Apparently some of the Swiss banks have started to fly their couriers in and out, seems less risky if they carrying important documents and he thinks that he can find some top level papers for you to take in. Plan is for you to fly in via Stuttgart on Monday morning and out the next day by the same route – means you should be back in Zurich early Tuesday evening: hand over the bank papers to Hedinger and then hop on the last train to Geneva, where I'll meet you. With any luck you will be in your own bed by midnight.'

Henry did his best to affect a tone of mild annoyance. 'And what is it that is so important now?'

'Another document, nothing to do with Reinhart this time: this one is even more important than the last one. Hermann will pass it on to you and you bring it back to us.'

–

Friday lunchtime and Henry had just arrived at the luxury villa high above Lutry. He waited for twenty minutes in the magnificent lounge, watching the ferry that had brought him to Lausanne that morning heading along the lake towards Montreux and another ferry steaming in the opposite direction towards Geneva. It was a clear day and he had a good view of Évian-les-Bains on the French side of the lake.

Outside there was a slamming of car doors followed by the sound of men talking in Russian in the hallway. Viktor did not so much walk into the room as storm into it, slamming the door as he did so. He was wearing a long black coat, gloves and a black Homburg hat. '*Get me a coffee,*' Viktor shouted at whoever was outside the room. 'This is urgent, is it, *synok*?'

'Of course, otherwise I would not have contacted you.'

'I was in Vienna,' Viktor said, as if being in Vienna was a reason why he should not have been contacted. The door opened again and one of Viktor's men came in with a tray of coffee and sandwiches. Still wearing his coat and hat, but having removed the gloves, Viktor sat down and began to devour the sandwiches. He indicated to Henry that he should join him. Viktor ate most of the sandwiches and finished two cups of coffee before he removed his hat, tossing it onto a chaise longue on the other side of the room. He was still wearing his overcoat and from one of its inside pockets he removed a leather notebook. A knife emerged from another pocket and the Russian began to sharpen his pencil in an aggressive manner.

'Moscow is very satisfied with the material you brought back two weeks ago by the way. Very satisfied indeed.'

'Good. I think I may have more.'

Viktor stopped sharpening the pencil and blew the shavings from it off his coat onto the floor.

'Really... from the same source?'

'I am not too sure, it sounds like it is from the lawyer this time, rather than the Reichsbank. But Remington-Barber did say that "this one is even more important than the last one".'

'He told you that?'

'Yes, two days ago.'

'They tell you a lot, Henry.'

'Maybe they trust me.'

'Maybe they do, maybe that is how the British operate. We tend not to be so forthcoming. What are the travel arrangements this time?'

'They want me in Zurich on Saturday – apparently Edgar is going to be there –and then I'm to fly to Berlin on Monday, via Stuttgart. Back the same way on Tuesday. I still have to deliver bank documents over to Hedinger, that's my cover after all, and then catch the late train from Zurich to Geneva, where I give the document to Remington-Barber.'

'All right, Henry. We make the same arrangement as before. When you return to Zurich on Tuesday you go straight to Bank Leu and then to the station. From there we will meet you and we will go to have the document copied. Are you sure they were not suspicious last time?'

'I'm sure. They seemed to be very pleased with how things had gone.'

Viktor had stood up, slowly hauling himself out of the chair and walking over to the window before turning to face Henry. His enormous frame appeared as a silhouette, with the sun behind him.

'Let me tell you, *synok*, it is possible to be pleased and to be suspicious at the same time! But I think that that if Edgar is here again, it must mean that the document is at least as important as the last one. But I still find it odd that they don't meet you in Zurich to collect the document'.

'The British don't like Zurich, I keep telling you that. Everyone speaks German there, or their version of it. They feel safer on this side of Switzerland.'

'All right, Henry, you go back to Geneva now and we will see you in Zurich on Tuesday.'

'There is one thing...'

'What is that, Henry? You want to ask me again if I'm still a believer?'

'In Zurich I asked a favour – if you could give me the details of any comrades I could contact in Berlin, in an emergency.'

Viktor nodded his head: yes, *I remember*. The Russian walked back to sit in the chair opposite Henry.

'I used to run networks in Berlin, Henry. To be honest, it was a surprisingly easy city for us to operate in: even after Hitler came to power in thirty three I am convinced there were still more communists in the city than Nazis – and many committed ones at that, very ideological and very disciplined. That is what I realised about Germans, they like to have an ideology, whether it is Communism or Socialism or Nazism or Catholicism. It is a few years now since I operated in Berlin and most of my networks have either been arrested, switched over to the Nazis, left Germany, or the few that remain have been taken over by the NKVD or the GRU boys at the embassy. But I have kept a couple: I am going to tell you how to contact one of them, listen carefully.'

Henry leaned forward in his seat; he was just inches from the Russian and could smell stale coffee on his breath.

'There's an agent called Kato and I have no reason to believe that they are not still in Berlin. Kato was my prize agent; I was never going to give them up. Do you know Wedding?'

'I have heard of it, but never been there.'

'Just north of Charlottenburg, not far from the centre. The important thing about Wedding is that it was always a communist stronghold and even now I understand that it is a more amenable part of the city for us, which does not mean that it is safe. Catch the U-Bahn line that goes north through Friederichstrasse and Oranienburg and get off at Leopold Platz. From there walk north along Müllerstrasse and turn into Wannitz Strasse. If you come to Amsterdamer Strasse you will have gone too far. Have you got all that so far? On Wannitz Strasse you will see a row of five or six shops under a large apartment block. One of those shops sells items for the kitchen – pots, pans, plates; that kind of thing. Go in there and ask if you can leave something for a Frau Schreiner in apartment twelve. Tell the person you have come from Dresden to deliver it. The reply that you should expect is that they will say their sister lives in Dresden. You will know then that you are dealing with Kato: hand them the envelope. In it will be a message from me: I will write it now. Once they read it they will give you their full co-operation. You don't need to worry about the message by the way, there will be nothing incriminating in it: it will look like a shopping list.'

'And how will I know that the man in the shop is Kato?'

'You will, don't worry. In any case, Kato is a woman.'

—

That same day, at the Portuguese Legation in Berlin, Dona Maria do Rosario had to wait until the First Secretary left the office at five before she could open the Bible which had arrived in that day's diplomatic bag.

Telmo's message the previous day had told her exactly where to look and how urgent everything was. She carefully removed the Rostock Report from the Bible and placed it inside an envelope which she then slipped into her handbag. After that, she stuffed some blank paper into the gap where the document had been and glued the card back in place before placing the Bible in one of the drawers.

She delayed leaving the Legation until half past five, timing her departure to coincide with that of a number of the other secretaries. She walked with them for a while and then quietly peeled away from the little group and headed for Opernplatz and the vast sanctity of St Hedwig's.

She knew that Father Josef was not due to be taking confession that night, but he would be assisting at the Mass. She would sit towards the front and wear her red scarf: he would know then that she needed to see him urgently.

Father Josef was one of a number of priests on the altar during Mass and not once did Dona Maria notice him looking at her. When it was time to take Communion Dona Maria chose to join the small queue in front of Father Josef. He bent down when she took the communion and whispered in her ear, 'go to the undercroft; wait for me there.'

The undercroft was deserted and she sat quietly on a narrow wooden bench set back in the shadows. After a few minutes she heard gentle footsteps echoing towards her. Without acknowledging her but looking all around him Father Josef walked to the furthest chapel and beckoned her to follow.

'Are we safe here?' she asked him when they were alone in the chapel.

'For a few minutes, with any luck. I rarely see people down here after evening Mass. What is the problem?'

'I have something urgent for Hugo.'

'Very well: I will send a message for him to come to confession tomorrow: then you can meet him on Friday.'

'No, Father! I cannot wait that long, it may be too dangerous. I am returning to Portugal on Monday and I fear for my safety. After today, I cannot do anything else.'

'So what do you want me to do?' Father Josef looked terrified. *A messenger, I'll be no more than a messenger.* That is what he had said in the beginning. Now they wanted him to be more than a messenger.

Dona Maria removed the envelope from her handbag and pushed it into the priest's hands.

'Here, please give this to Hugo, Father.'

'No, I cannot do that.'

'You have to, Father.' At that moment there was the sound of heavy footsteps walking towards them. The priest started to say something and then slipped the envelope into the folds of his cassock and sunk to his knees in prayer. By the time he had finished, Dona Maria had slipped away.

Chapter 23

Berlin, March 1941

Henry Hunter arrived in Zurich on the Saturday afternoon and throughout that weekend was briefed by Edgar and Remington-Barber on what was expected of him in Berlin. If all went well, he was assured, he would be in the city for little more than twenty four hours.

Henry tried very hard not to show that he was pleased he was to be returning to Berlin. He felt more relaxed than he had been for over ten years: he was going on his own mission, as well as theirs.

He left Zurich airport on the first leg of the journey early on the Monday morning and by the time they landed in Stuttgart it was a clear day. It was a year and a month since he had last been at the airport and this time the plane taxied to an even more remote section, well away from any buildings or Luftwaffe planes, a few of which he could make out in the distance. The Swissair plane came to a halt by an anti-aircraft battery and alongside a Deutsche Lufthansa plane. When all the passengers had left the plane they were counted on the tarmac and then divided into two groups. Those remaining in Stuttgart were to board a bus that would take them to the terminal building; those flying on to Berlin were to transfer to the waiting Junkers Ju 52 plane.

The flight for Berlin took off half an hour after they had landed in Stuttgart and within two hours and twenty minutes they had landed at Tempelhof: getting through security took almost as long.

For the first hour after he landed he was kept in a small room with the three other non-German passengers. One by one they were taken into a room to be questioned and he was the third one to go in. He was in there for just under an hour, during which time he was searched, as was his case and then he was thoroughly questioned. 'How many times have you been to Berlin? ... What do you do when you are here? ... Where do you eat? ... Do you meet anyone not connected with your work? ... Why have you flown into Berlin on this occasion? ... What views do you have on the policies of our government? ... Have you met any Jews while in Germany? ... Or communists? ... Please tell me again, how many times have you been to Berlin? ... What do you do when you are here?'

Then another wait, this time on his own at the end of an over-lit corridor, followed by a few more questions and finally he was able to leave the airport and on Edgar's advice walked over to Flughafen station, from where he took the U-Bahn north for three stops as far as Koch Strasse. From Koch Strasse station it was a short walk across Wilhelm Strasse to the Excelsior on Askanischer Platz, where a room had been reserved for him. It was an enormous hotel, with well over five hundred rooms and, as far as Henry could tell, eight or nine restaurants. Both Edgar and Remington-Barber felt that the anonymity of the hotel may be more suitable for this visit.

It was two thirty by the time he checked into his narrow room on the third floor, overlooking Saarland Strasse. The room was over-heated, but when he opened the window the noise of the city flooded in and he found himself unable to think properly.

'Stay there until the next morning,' Edgar had told him, which was all very well but that left no time for anything. Tuesday was going to be very tight as it was: meeting Hugo at nine o'clock to collect the document and then to the Reichsbank to exchange papers with Gunter Reinhart. After that he was supposed to go to Tempelhof in good time to catch the twelve thirty flight to Stuttgart.

Maybe.

He managed to stay in the hotel room for twenty minutes, pacing up and down, still not fully decided on his course of action. There were too many flaws to his plan; it depended too much on chance and it meant ignoring everything he had been trained to do over the past ten years or more. He was truly caught between a rock and a hard place.

His mind still unresolved, he left the hotel through a side entrance and from Stadt Mitte caught the U-Bahn north as far as Leopold Platz. He was in Wedding and he was about to use up the favour he had asked of Viktor. Depending on how that went could help make up his mind.

Carefully following Viktor's instructions he turned into Wannitz Strasse and spotted the small parade of shops with the hardware shop in the middle. He walked past it from the opposite side of the road and when he noticed a woman leaving crossed the road and entered.

The shop was empty: behind the counter was a well built woman, perhaps in her late thirties, possibly older. She had untidy hair that was turning grey and a face that was noticeable for the thick mascara around her bright green eyes and the dark lipstick that was closer to black than red. On the wall behind her was a small, framed photograph of Hitler, next to a shelf full of white candles. They smiled at each other and he spent a minute or two showing undue interest in a copper saucepan. He checked the inside pocket of his jacket: Viktor's note was there, in an envelope from the hotel. '*You don't need to worry about the message by the way, there will be nothing incriminating in it: it will look like a shopping list.*'

'Can I help you?' The woman had come round from behind the counter and was alongside him. She pointed to the copper saucepan he was holding. 'This is best quality: a company in Magdeburg manufactures them.'

'I have come from Dresden,' said Henry, aware that his voice sounded uncertain. He was trying to speak quietly. 'I have something for Frau Schreiner in apartment twelve: please could I leave it here?'

The woman glanced anxiously towards the door and then edged slowly back towards the counter. 'Of course. My sister is from Dresden.'

Kato.

The woman casually walked back behind the counter, smiling at Henry, who smiled back at her. Silence, as she looked at Henry, waiting for him to say something.

'You have something for me, maybe?'

'I am sorry, yes I forgot.' He handed the envelope to her.

She removed the note from the Hotel Excelsior envelope and momentarily gasped as she began to read it. The hand holding Viktor's note was shaking, her other hand was steadying herself on the counter. He heard her quietly say 'Viktor'. When she had finished reading the note she indicated for him to wait and went to a room behind the counter. There was a brief smell of burning. She back came out with two lit cigarettes, and handed one to Henry.

'No, thank you. I don't smoke.'

'Smoke it please: in case anyone comes in. It is better to disguise the smell. So, you are a comrade?'

Henry nodded. *A comrade.*

'I never thought that I would hear from Viktor again, never. I know I am not supposed to ask any questions, but just tell me this – is he well?' Her eyes appeared moist and the hand holding the cigarette was shaking, so much so that she used her other hand to steady it.

She loved him. She still does.

'Yes.'

She looked at him quizzically, hoping he would say more about Viktor, but he just smiled and nodded his head.

'He says you are to be trusted, I am to help you,' said Kato. 'I have heard nothing from anyone for over a year. There were five of us, all loyal to Viktor. He told us not to trust anyone at the embassy. Two comrades managed to escape to Sweden, another was arrested and died at Sachsenhausen and one disappeared: she is a Jew and I suspect she has gone underground. I am fortunate that none of our cell went over to the Nazis: that happened with a number of comrades. What do you need? Somewhere to stay? Some money?'

'Is it safe to talk here?'

'Of course! Do you think I'd be doing that if it wasn't? There is no one in the back and I can see whoever comes in. Take the saucepan from the stand and one or two others – we can make it look as if you cannot decide which one to buy: men never can anyway. Tell me what you need.' She was clearly nervous, her hands still shaking while she inhaled deeply on the cigarette, but her bright green eyes danced with a mixture of fear and excitement.

When he had finished telling Kato what he needed he expected her to say it was impossible, but she acted no more surprised than if he had ordered a new dining set.

'You want this for tomorrow morning, you say?'

'Yes, please.'

'What time in the morning?'

'Around eleven o'clock, possibly a bit later but certainly by noon. From here?'

'No, most certainly not. When you leave here, we will never see each other again. You should avoid Wedding anyway, the Gestapo have too many people around here. What you want will be ready from eleven o'clock. Will you be around the centre of Berlin?'

'Yes.'

'Do you know Ku'damm?'

He shook his head.

'It is actually called Kurfürstendamm, but everyone knows it as Ku'damm. It is a very well known street in the south of Charlottenburg: before the war it was very fashionable. Now, nowhere is fashionable. Go to Uhland Strasse U-Bahn and come out on the Kurfürstendamm exit, then cross the road and head west, for just two or three blocks – not very far. On the corner of Kurfürstendamm and Bleibtreustrasse you will see a kiosk set back in the wall; it sells newspapers, cigarettes; all that kind of thing. Don't be put off by the swastikas and the pictures of Hitler all over. Tell the old lady in the kiosk that you have come to collect Magda's cigarettes: she will hand you a pack of Juno. What you need will be inside the packet, but put it straight in your pocket, buy a newspaper and leave. Carry on up Bleibtreustrasse and take the second left – Niebuhr Strasse. Open the packet when you get into Niebuhr Strasse, there will be a note there telling you which one to go to. Now, I need to check that you have remembered all that.'

–

At six o'clock on the morning of Tuesday 25th March, Henry finally gave up trying to force himself back to sleep, as he had been attempting to do for most of the night. They had all come to visit him during his brief spells of sleep: Roza, of course, but also her brother, the man in the perfume shop in Essen and even Foxi the dog – all shouting at him. Then Rosa had appeared and, for a brief while, she seemed to sit on the end of the bed alongside Roza. He had a bath and then sat on the floor, with maps spread out before him. He had been absorbed in these maps since returning to the Excelsior late the previous afternoon.

He could see the routes; there was no doubt about that. He wandered over to the window. Down on Saarland Strasse a group of Waffen SS were happily chatting away and slapping each other on the back. Not for the first time since he arrived in Berlin, he felt real fear. His chest tightened and the maps shook as his hands trembled.

I don't have to do this. I am not committed to anything. If I abandon my plans now, no one will know anything.

Back to the maps. During his training by the British he had been told that he was a natural map reader. He could study a map and its contents would come to life. He was immediately able to picture the area as if they were observing it from above and could envisage different routes and varying permutations of those routes.

First of all there was the map of Berlin and then that of Germany. It all appeared to be straightforward, he knew where he had to be and how to get there but he could not foresee the hazards and he knew that there would be plenty of those.

He checked out of the Excelsior at half past eight that morning, assuring one of the over-attentive managers on duty that he had indeed enjoyed his stay, everything had indeed been to his satisfaction and he would most certainly consider staying at the Excelsior when he returned to Berlin.

There was a light drizzle as he walked to the Opernplatz, where the expanse of St Hedwig's Cathedral rose before him. He reminded himself of Edgar's instructions:

Do not enter the cathedral before five to nine.

He paused at the entrance to Opernplatz. It was ten to nine and realising that it was too early he found a stone bench to sit on, despite the rain. He waited, steeling himself to go into the cathedral. He had a passionate dislike of churches, buoyed by a fear that he had first encountered in his childhood – that churches were the one place where secrets weren't safe; even the statues and gargoyles seemed to know all about him.

Five to nine.

'*Enter the cathedral through the main entrance*'.

A few people were coming down the steps after the eight o'clock Mass.

'*And don't forget to cross yourself. Find a seat about half way along between the entrance and main altar.*'

The cathedral was enormous and there must have been no more than two dozen people dotted around it, sitting alone or in pairs, all in silent prayer.

'*If he has seen that all is clear, Hugo will appear on the same row as you and sit two or three seats away. Do not expect to see him before ten past nine. However, if he has not appeared by twenty past nine, leave the church and walk back to Unter den Linden. Do not look around for Hugo.*'

Ten past nine. The cathedral was much emptier now as the last Mass worshippers had left and people made their way to work. He tried very hard to close his eyes and hope that some spiritual feeling would come to him, something to assure him not to worry, that everything would turn out right. Nothing, but at least the ghost of Roza did not appear. He became aware of a scrape of chairs alongside him as someone moved down his row towards him.

'*Do not look directly at him but do look in his direction so you can be sure it is him.*'

It was Hugo, dressed in a long black coat and clutching a hat and his briefcase.

'*If he places his briefcase on a chair either side of him then that is a sign of danger. Leave immediately. If the briefcase remains on the floor, all is well.*'

The briefcase was on the floor. He saw Hugo remove a Bible from the small wooden receptacle on the back of the chair in front of him and slip something into it.

'*Remain where you are until Hugo has finished and left. Then you know how to retrieve the document.*'

After five minutes Hugo finished praying. He put the Bible where he had taken it from, stood up and left.

'*The document will be folded in the middle of the Bible. Remove it as soon as you can.*'

He stood up and straightened his coat and when he sat down again it was in the seat next to where Hugo had been sitting. He picked up the Bible Hugo had left and opened it. The document was indeed in the centre, folded as if ready to be inserted into a narrow envelope. He glanced around, but no one was close to him or looking in his direction, apart from a reproachful medieval saint or two. Within seconds, the document was inside his jacket pocket.

'*Once you have retrieved the document, remain in your seat for another five minutes. Remember to pray.*'

He thumbed through the Bible and stopped randomly. It was psalm 130 – 'Waiting for the Redemption of the Lord'. 'Out of the depths I have cried to you O Lord. Lord hear my voice!' A shiver ran down his spine and he looked up to see if anyone was watching him now. He looked back at the psalm. 'For with the Lord there is mercy, And with Him is abundant redemption'.

He found himself shaking and he was so hot that the sweat from his hands was staining the page. He glanced up and saw that a stone angel on a pillar near him looked like Roza. He had never been a religious man; it was alien to his ideology. But he was quite clear now. What he had just read decided him. He was certain. He had to concentrate very hard now to remember Edgar's instructions.

'*Put the Bible back behind the seat and leave the cathedral. Do not forget to kneel and to cross yourself. There is a chapel just before the porch from where you leave the cathedral. Hugo will be in there: if he gets up to leave as you go past and his coat is folded across his arm, you know all is well. He will follow you but do not look round. Leave through Opernplatz and then walk down Oberwallstrasse: if Hugo is certain that you are not being followed he will approach you before you go into the Reichsbank to check that everything is in order.*'

As he walked past the chapel he glimpsed Hugo beginning to follow him out, his coat folded across his arm. He walked through

Opernplatz back into Unter den Linden and after a block turned right into Oberwallstrasse, which was a long narrow street leading down to Französischestrasse and the Reichsbank. About halfway along the road was filled with rubble from what appeared to be a bombed building. He paused to look up at it, allowing Hugo to catch up with him.

'Everything appears to be all right. I will walk with you as far as the Reichsbank. You have the document safe?'

'It's here in my pocket,' said Henry.

'Good. Make sure that you get a proper envelope from Reinhart to put it in, along with some other Reichsbank papers – and don't forget to get him to seal it. It is essential that it looks like a normal letter from the Reichsbank to Bank Leu, I am sure you realise that. Then go straight to Tempelhof.'

'Franz!'

A smartly dressed man was striding towards them. Hugo muttered, 'Oh no,' and then under his breath said, 'Give me a minute; I need to get rid of him. I'm giving you directions to the Reichsbank, remember that.'

'What are you doing down here, Franz, you should be in the office. I am on the way there myself.'

Henry had a feeling that he knew the man, but could not place him. He was wearing a formal suit and spoke with a Berlin accent. He had begun to stare at Henry, as if recognised him too.

'Yes Alois, I too am on my way to the office. I had been at Mass and this gentleman asked me to direct him to the Reichsbank.'

'I think we may have met.' The man Franz Hermann had called 'Alois' had now turned directly to face Henry, positioning himself uncomfortably close to him. Henry was convinced that they had met, but had no idea when or where.

'Are you from Switzerland, by any chance?'

Henry replied that he was. He could now remember the man. Franz Hermann was standing behind him and looking worried.

'Alois – I do need to get to the office. Perhaps you will join me? I am sure our friend now knows his way to the Reichsbank.'

The man called Alois ignored Hermann. 'I remember now! Bern, last June – we met at the Schweizerhof. My name is Alois Jäger. I told you that you should contact me if you were ever in Berlin. Do you recall our meeting?'

Henry noticed the Nazi Party badge on Alois Jäger's lapel. 'Yes…' he said hesitantly, appearing to recollect their meeting from the back of his memory. 'I do remember. Of course I do.'

'You name is Henri, correct?'

Henry nodded.

'And what brings you to Berlin?'

'I am here on business.'

'For whom, may I ask?'

'Bank Leu – I work for Bank Leu in Zurich. I have business on their behalf at the Reichsbank.'

'Ah – a Swiss banker! I am most impressed. I have some good friends at the Reichsbank. Perhaps you know Herr—'

'I should explain, Herr Jäger – I am just a courier. My dealings with the Reichsbank are limited to delivering and collecting documents, I am afraid.'

'Do not worry, my friend. It is all very important. I am told that the support we are getting from the Swiss banks is proving to be a lifeline for Germany: such discretion – we are so grateful. And you are from Zurich, a most charming city, so… proper. But I am confused, Herr Hesse: when we met in Bern you said you were from Geneva? You were travelling to Stuttgart I think, on business. I recall that because I remember wondering why such a good German speaker was from Geneva.'

Henry could see Franz Hermann's eyes shine with fear. 'Geneva, you say? Ah yes! For a while I did live there, but now I live in Zurich and work for Bank Leu.'

'So you are no longer in business?'

'No, no longer.'

'I see,' said Alois Jäger, sounding unsure. 'And what a remarkable coincidence that not only should I encounter you today in Berlin, but that you should also be talking with my good friend and colleague Herr Hermann. You looked like you know each other – it shows what a hospitable city Berlin has become under the *Führer*. Perhaps we could have dinner tonight – the three of us?'

Henry explained that he was leaving Berlin that day. 'In fact, I have a flight from Tempelhof at twelve thirty.'

'Well, I want you to promise that the next time you are in Berlin, you will contact me? We shall have a meal together. What do you think, Franz?'

All three men agreed that this was a most agreeable idea as they walked together to the end of Oberwallstrasse, where they enthusiastically shook hands. Alois Jäger and Franz Hermann were turning right towards their office in Friederichstrasse. Henry turned left towards Werderscher Markt.

Henry was shocked. Alois Jäger was clearly suspicious and the fact that he was wearing a Nazi Party badge and that Hugo looked so horrified was a worry. He would have had even more cause for concern had he looked round just before he entered the Reichsbank and noticed the formal figure of Alois Jäger watching him from the side of the road.

–

When Henri Hesse presented himself at the Reichsbank reception his heart was racing, his chest felt tight, he was perspiring heavily and beginning to feel quite unwell. It was ten thirty. His options were still open: he could exchange documents with Reinhart, go to Tempelhof, return to Switzerland and please both his masters. But the chance reading of the psalm in the cathedral had made up his mind: he would take a much harder option, but one that he knew would give him peace.

Gunter Reinhart appeared to have aged ten years in the short time since Henry had last seen him and, other than thanking him once again for taking Alfred to Switzerland, said very little. He took the envelope from Bank Leu, signed for it and handed over the sealed envelope for him to take back to Switzerland.

'I need you to give me another envelope, perhaps with another document in it?' asked Henry. 'I would then like to put something in myself and then ask you to re-seal it.'

The German looked uncomfortable.

'I said to Hedinger, this has to be the last time. I cannot risk this anymore. You took Alfred to Switzerland for which I am deeply grateful and in return I supplied the Directive. Now I have done you this one other favour. Life is getting too dangerous: if I give any cause to suspect me then not only will I be in danger but so will Rosa and Sophia, not to mention my wife and children of course. You must promise me this, don't ask me to help again. Don't come back to Berlin. You understand? It is too dangerous, far too dangerous.'

He took another envelope from a drawer, found a few sheets from a tray on his desk and slipped them in. Henry carefully inserted the papers he had taken from the Bible in-between the sheets and handed the envelope back to Reinhart to seal it.

He promised Reinhart that they would never meet again, which was not difficult as he had every intention of keeping it. It was unusual for him to make a promise that he intended to keep.

After leaving Werderscher Markt he travelled by U-Bahn to Uhland Strasse. Kato's instructions had been clear enough. He came out on the Kurfürstendamm exit, crossed the road and then headed west as far as the corner with Bleibtreustrasse.

Sure enough, there was a kiosk set back in the wall, with narrow swastika banners hanging down from either side of a large advertising sign: 'Berlin Raucht Juno' – Berlin smokes Juno. Lucky Berlin.

The old lady in the kiosk appeared to be wearing two coats and had a scarf wrapped round her head with a woollen hat on top it. Behind her was a large picture of Hitler at a slightly jaunty angle and in front of her a small queue of people in a hurry. He courteously allowed a woman in a fur coat to go first so that, by the time it was his turn to be served, there was no one else waiting.

'I have come to collect Magda's cigarettes.'

The old lady glanced up at him and held eye contact for a moment before she scanned the street behind him. He wondered whether he was meant to say anything else: had he forgotten something? He added 'Please' and smiled.

She bent down and from under the counter produced a white packet of Juno cigarettes, which she pressed into his hands, no longer looking directly at him. As he slipped the packet into his pocket he could tell that there was something heavier than twenty cigarettes in it. By now he had been joined at the front of the kiosk by two Waffen SS officers. He picked up a copy of the *Völkischer Beobachter* and placed two Reichsmarks into the old lady's mittened hands. By the time she had pocketed the money she had already turned her attention to the SS men.

Niebuhr Strasse was a quiet street, in marked contrast to the bustle of the Ku'damm. He stood in the doorway of a dress shop and removed the packet of Juno from his pocket. There were only four or five cigarettes in it and he placed one straight into mouth and lit it – it could have looked too suspicious to do otherwise. Tucked into the packet was a car key attached to a small metal disk with the word 'Opel' engraved on it. Inside the Juno packet was a folded slip of paper, which he unwrapped: 'UTM 142'.

He looked down the street. There were few cars parked on it but he could not see the one he was looking for. He walked down the block and the last car on the corner before Schlüterstrasse was an Opel Super 6 sedan – UTM 142. It was a handsome car; four doors, dark green, white wall tyres and neither too clean nor too dirty that it might stand out.

He unlocked the door and settled into the driver's seat. The car had a musty smell to it, a mixture of damp and old leather. 'I will do my best to get hold of the various papers you want, but it will not be easy,' Kato had told him the previous afternoon. 'Whatever I can get will be in the glove box, inside the log book.'

He reached across to the glove box in front of the passenger seat and removed the black leather log book, with the word 'Opel' in faded silver on the cover. The back cover of the book formed a sleeve and within that was what he had asked for: identity cards and a form showing that the owner of UTM 142 was entitled to buy petrol. Tucked behind the log book was something hard, wrapped in a thick, grey cloth.

'The car has been hidden in Weissensee since before the war began,' Kato had told him. 'A mechanic who was a secret Party member has been looking after it. He now works in an SS garage, so he has been able to obtain the correct documentation. I have kept the paperwork up to date. I was keeping it for an emergency, but if Viktor says... The identity cards will not be easy, not with so little time. It is possible to purchase these things though; the black market is very active at the moment. Do you have money I can use, by any chance?'

He had handed her a substantial sum of Swiss Francs and her eyes lit up. 'That should make it much easier,' she said. 'I will do what I can.'

A policeman had walked past the car and now in his rear view mirror he could see him turning around and heading slowly back in his direction. He needed to move, but first he removed from his pocket a tightly wrapped piece of paper, from which he produced the Nazi Party membership badge he had taken from the perfume shop owner in Essen. He pinned it carefully to his lapel and checked in the mirror that it was at a proper angle. The car started first time, if rather noisily and lurched forward as he selected the gears. He drove slowly down the side streets to get a feel of the car before turning into Kurfürstendamm.

'*Create a commentary: decide your route, write it down and then memorise that route in the spoken form. When you are driving along, keep reciting the commentary, it means you can avoid using a map and drawing attention to yourself.*'

East along Kurfürstendamm, then right into Joachimstaler Strasse, which becomes Kaiser Allee. There was surprisingly little traffic on the road, though he had to be careful of the trams. The Opel was a heavy car but a powerful one and he had to concentrate hard to keep his speed under control.

'*Through Wilmersdorf and Friedenau. Kaiser Allee leads into Rein Strasse. At the end of Rein Strasse you will see the Botanischer Garten signposted. Turn right into Grunewald Strasse: you will know where you are from there.*'

It was twenty past eleven. The journey had been quicker than he imagined and the Opel now handled beautifully: he had little doubt that once it got out on the open road it would perform well, assuming they got that far. In Kaiser Wilhelm Strasse he eased the car slowly to a halt in a position where he could see the house on the corner of Arno-Holz Strasse.

At various stages since he had arrived in Berlin he had been telling himself that he did not need to do this, that he could pull out now. No one would know if he did, with the possible exception of Kato. He could drive on towards Tempelhof, abandon the car and still have time to catch the 12.35 flight to Berlin – there was just about enough time – and for a brief moment he hesitated.

Then the image of Roza appeared again, smiling this time and the sense of calm that he had first encountered in the air raid shelter in Stuttgart station returned.

He left the car and walked over to the house, knowing that there was no going back.

Chapter 24

leaving Berlin, March 1941

Henry Hunter's career as a secret agent ceased the moment he knocked on the door of the house near the Botanischer Garten where Rosa Stern was hiding.

He had been a Soviet spy since 1930 and a British one for a year and half. Serving first one and then two masters had required him to be constantly on his guard and to be in control and exercise caution all the time. Despite sometimes affecting an air of detachment and possibly coming across as a bit too questioning, Henry knew that he had survived because he had actually always done what he was told.

Now, he was doing the opposite. From this moment on he was ignoring all of his training and turning his back on the obedience which had dictated his life for previous ten years. He had no intention of forgetting all his training, but would exploiting that in his own interests.

When Rosa opened the door she looked as if she had seen a ghost.

'What on earth are you doing here? I told you it was too dangerous to return: you must leave now! Oh my God, Henry, this is so dangerous. Please go. Please!'

'Let me in, Rosa. I need to explain. You will understand when I tell you why I am here. You know that it is dangerous for me to stand here. Please.'

So she had let him in and hurried him upstairs while she settled Frau Hermann. When she came up to the small lounge on the first floor she look flustered and stood by the closed door, her arms folded.

'What is it, Henry? And how come you're still in Berlin? My God – what is that?' She was pointing at the Nazi Party membership badge on his lapel, its black swastika stark on a white background. 'You're not…'

'Don't worry Rosa; it is to stop me looking suspicious.'

She laughed sarcastically. 'A Swiss citizen walking round Berlin wearing a Nazi Party badge: you think that doesn't look suspicious?'

'Listen to me, Rosa. You are in danger, you and Sophia.'

'Thank you for telling me that, Henry. Don't you think I am already very well aware of that?'

'No, no… what I mean is that you are in immediate danger. You have to leave the house now!'

She gasped and moved away from the door, moving to the sofa opposite Henry.

'What do you mean?'

'I saw Franz this morning. He told me that he has heard through a contact that the Gestapo have been informed that you are hiding in this area: they have been told that you are in a house in one of the roads just north of the Botanischer Garten. They are planning to search every house. The search could begin at any time!'

'But Franz was here yesterday, he never said a word about this. I would have known if something was wrong, surely?'

'I saw him early this morning: he had only just heard.'

'Are you sure?'

'Of course I am sure. Why else do you think I am here?'

'But Franz had a plan that we would use if we are ever in danger: he would telephone and use a code word and then Sophia and I would go to Pankow, where a friend of his has a shop and we would be able to hide in the attic. He—'

'There is no time, Rosa. I am sure Franz made all these plans but maybe he panicked. I told you, they could start the house to house search at any time. We have to leave now.'

'We?'

'Yes. I have a car. I am going to take you and Sophia, but we need to leave now.'

'This is madness, Henry. We have no proper papers and what about Frau Hermann? I can't just abandon her.'

'I have papers, Rosa, here – look.'

He handed her the identity cards that Kato had left for him in the car, hers in the name of 'Dagmar Keufer', Sophia's in the name of 'Gisela Keufer'. Rosa studied them carefully.

'The photographs, Henry – they are even not of us!'

'No, of course not – there was no time. But they *could* be of you: they ought to be good enough for a basic check, they're not too bad and I have a card in the name of Erich Keufer, so we will be able to pretend to be a family. You see that our address is in Frankfurt: we can say that we are driving there.'

'To Frankfurt? Are you mad? We will be lucky to get out of Berlin. And what do we do when we get to Frankfurt – buy a house, join the Nazi Party?'

'We are not going to Frankfurt, Rosa. We are going to Switzerland. I also have Swiss papers for you and Sophia, I had these prepared only last week. They are very good, but I think we can only risk using them when we are much closer to the border.'

Rosa was pacing around the room, almost in a circle, shaking her head and running her hand through her hair. 'I am sorry, Henry but this doesn't make sense to me. You seem to have got hold of these papers very quickly – I thought you said that it was only this morning that Franz told you he heard that we were in danger?'

'Can be honest with you, Rosa? When I first visited you here it was apparent that your situation was too dangerous. I thought that something like this would happen but I didn't want to voice my fears to Franz as he has been so good to you. But I was so worried that I had these identity cards prepared: just in case.'

Rosa sank back in the sofa, looking overwhelmed and confused. She clearly thought that Henry's plan was crazy, but so would be remaining in the house if there really was a chance it was about to be searched by the Gestapo. Henry was sure she was far from convinced but he was counting on her not risking her life and that of her daughter by ignoring him.

'And Frau Hermann?'

'Make her comfortable and tell her that you will be back later. Franz will come round after work. Rosa, we need to move fast – you need to get Sophia ready. Pack a few things, but nothing that identifies you or Sophia. We also need to take food and some blankets; we may not be able to stop.'

Rosa was back by the door now, her hand on the handle and peering at Henry in a sceptical manner.

'Perhaps I should contact Franz? We have an agreed system to use in an emergency – I telephone him pretending to be a secretary from another law firm.'

'No, Rosa! Under no circumstances! Franz said he thinks they will be listening in to all telephone calls in this area – maybe that is why he has not contacted you himself. If you phone him at his office it could reveal your location and bring him under suspicion. You must do nothing that would draw attention to this house, do you understand?'

Once Rosa decided that she had no alternative but to go along with Henry, she moved fast and decisively. She gave Frau Hermann her lunch early and told her that she would be back later. She packed a small suitcase for her and Sophia, telling the little girl they were going on a long journey and – if she was a very good girl, did everything she was asked to and told anyone who asked that her name was Gisela – then she would see Alfred. *'But only if you are good. And only if you remember that your name is Gisela.'*

He decided to bring the car right outside the house rather than risk Rosa and Sophia being seen crossing the road with a suitcase.

–

Although Henry had ceased to be a spy the moment he entered the house, he had no plans to dispense with all aspects of his training. He had excelled at what the British called a 'clandestine driving' course and was now about to put what he had learnt into action, though not to quite the same effect that the British had intended.

'Always see a car journey in the same way as one on foot – as a series of short journeys: a car trip from London to Edinburgh, for example, should be broken down into a series of shorter stages – London to Northampton, Northampton to Nottingham, Nottingham to Sheffield et cetera. These are

much easier to explain if stopped, as long as you have a very feasible story ready to explain that journey.'

All that and more was racing around in Henry's mind as they left the house in Arno-Holz Strasse at noon. They were just ahead of the schedule he had in his mind when they pulled into a lay-by just outside Potsdam forty minutes later. He turned off the engine and removed a road map from the side of the seat.

'Here, let me show you our route.'

'Where to?'

'To Switzerland, I told you.'

'You're serious, aren't you? How are we going to get that far?'

'Let me show you, I have it all planned.'

Henry opened out the map, allowing it to rest on the dashboard and their laps. He moved towards Rosa as they looked at the map. As he got closer he caught the scent of a delicate perfume. She flicked her hair out of her eyes, looking carefully at the map as he pointed at the Swiss border.

'I do know where Switzerland is.'

'There are two possible routes, Rosa. This one here – I've called that the "east" route. It's a more direct one, we'd go due south west in a more or less a straight line: Leipzig; Bayreuth; Nuremberg; Ulm. The plan would be to cross the border around Lake Konstanz—'

'*Attempt* to cross the border, Henry.'

'Attempt to cross the border then. I understand that the Lake Konstanz part of the border can be a bit less dangerous than some other crossings. However, that would take us through Bavaria and very close to the border with the Protectorate, where apparently security is especially strong.'

Henry had to lean over Rosa to expose more of the map, her hair brushing his face as he did so.

'This is what I call the "west route" – it's much more circuitous. We'd drive to Brunswick and then down towards Stuttgart before crossing the border round Singen, with an option to go over the mountains. It has the advantage of taking us close to Frankfurt and that is where the identity cards say we are from.'

Rosa studied the map for a while, frowning as she did so.

'I suppose your west route is the lesser of two evils. With all this planning, do you know how long it will take us?'

'From here to Brunswick is just over 110 miles, but I am planning to come off the main roads and stick to the side roads as much as I can. If anyone asks why, just say that you get car sick on main roads. I think we will get south of Brunswick – maybe as far as Göttingen before it gets dark. We can then look for a wood to drive into and hide for the night. We'll be 200 miles from Stuttgart: we can be there by Wednesday night and then drive to Switzerland on the Thursday.'

Rosa said nothing, but shrugged as if in reluctant agreement. Henry re-started the Opel and they pulled out into the road.

'You must drive slower, please – and not so close to the centre of the road. You had this all planned, didn't you?'

'What do you mean?'

'You are too near the kerb now, just slow down a bit. Are you seriously telling me that you saw Franz this morning and since then you have sorted all this out, including working out how long it is going to take?'

'Yes and no. I told you, Rosa, since I first met you I had been so concerned at the danger you were in that I had given some consideration to this, but when Franz told me this morning I had to move fast.'

To the surprise of both of them, the journey to Brunswick was uneventful. Where they could they dropped off the main road: the Lower Saxony countryside seemed to be suited for this kind of driving with plenty of small narrow roads leading off the larger ones. On the occasions that they passed police or military vehicles no interest was paid in them: a husband and wife and their daughter out for a drive. A few miles to the north of Göttingen, with the light beginning to fail, they came across a wood with a track leading into it from the road. Henry stopped the car and managed to open a creaky wooden gate at the top of the track and then drove as deep into the wood as possible. When he walked back to shut the gate it was impossible to see the Opel from the road. It was when he returned to the car, feeling quite pleased with himself and almost relaxed that Sophia started crying. It was a soft cry at first, almost a series of sobs, but then it became louder.

'What is it, darling?' Rosa asked.

When Sophia replied she spoke so quietly that her mother had to lean across the front seat to hear her.

'I can't hear you, darling. You'll need to speak up.'

'But I can't, Mama' she whispered. 'You told me always to whisper. You said people mustn't hear me speak.'

Rosa turned round and stroked her daughter's face.

'It's all right now darling. You don't need to whisper here in the car: only if there are other people around. Now, what were you trying to say?'

'I'm frightened', each word punctuated by a noisy sob.

'What are you frightened of?'

'The goblins! There are always goblins in a forest.'

'There's no such thing as goblins,' said Henry impatiently. 'And in any case, this is not a forest, it's a wood.'

This only seemed to make things worse and Sophia's cry turned into a wail. Rosa left the front seat and went to sit next to Sophia in the back. After a long cuddle, the little girl calmed down.

'Where are we going?'

'You should rest now, darling.'

'But where are we going?' Sophia sounded as if was pleading with her mother, begging her to answer the question.

'Somewhere safe, darling. Now, please rest.'

'If we are going somewhere safe, does it mean that we will see Alfred there?'

'Yes, darling, I told you we would, especially if you are a good girl. You should rest now.'

'Will we also see Papa in this safe place we are going to? Why don't you tell me?'

Rosa did not reply. Henry glanced back at her, her head had dropped and she was tapping her teeth with her knuckles as her eyes filled with tears. Sophia was sitting with her legs hunched up to her face, her enormous dark eyes unblinking as they looked up at him from behind her kneecaps. In the gloom her pale skin now appeared chalky white. She gave him the beginnings of a smile and waved one of the paws of the dirty white one-eared rabbit she was clutching at Henry, who waved back awkwardly.

'If you are very quiet, Sophia and behave very, very well then I promise you that when we get to this safe place you will get a present. But you have to be quiet.'

'What kind of present?'

Henry shrugged. 'Chocolates.'

The little girl said nothing but pulled a face.

'What about a new rabbit? That one looks very old – it only has one ear.'

'But I love Mr Rabbit! You cannot take him away!'

The little girl started crying again. Rosa pulled her close.

'No one is going to take Mr Rabbit away darling. Henry meant that we will buy you a friend for Mr Rabbit.'

During the long silence that followed the light dropped dramatically and when Sophia spoke again it was almost dark.

'It will be nice for Mr Rabbit to have a friend, won't it, Mama?'

'Yes darling. You try and rest now.'

'Because we don't have friends anymore, do we?'

'What do you mean, darling?'

'Alfred told me that, he said that the reason we had to be so quiet in the house and not make a noise and not go anywhere near the window is because no one is our friend. Is that true?'

Rosa said nothing, but busied herself arranging a blanket around Sophia, allowing the rabbit's head to poke out of the top of it.

'Here are some biscuits, darling. Eat those and then you must sleep.'

She munched at the biscuits, her eyes looking around the car, apparently unblinking.

'Why is no one our friend, Mama?'

'Don't keep asking questions, darling. Where we are going, everyone will be our friend.'

'Is Henry our friend?'

In the rear-view mirror Henry caught Rosa's face as she hesitated very briefly before replying.

'Yes, darling. Sleep now.'

Henry watched through the mirror, waiting for Sophia to fall asleep. When she finally did so he cleared his throat and turned round to talk. Now was the time, he had decided, to be a bit more honest with Rosa and maybe then she would see him in a better light.

But when he turned round Rosa was fast asleep too and the moment had passed.

–

On the Tuesday morning, before the Opel had even left Berlin, Franz Hermann was becoming increasingly worried. He had been unnerved by the encounter with Alois Jäger in Oberwallstrasse and even more so by the way his colleague had behaved since then. First of all Jäger had only walked with him part of the way to the office, then had suddenly stopped and said he needed to go back and check something. Back at the office he had come in to see him.

'If you had not told me otherwise, Franz, then I would have thought that you and that Swiss man knew each other. You looked like you were acquaintances, rather than one stranger giving directions to another.'

He assured Jäger that he was mistaken: he had been to morning Mass and as he left the cathedral the man had asked him for directions. He had even gone somewhat out of his way to make sure the man went in the right direction.

'And fancy the coincidence of me having met him in Bern last year!'

Franz agreed with Jäger that it was indeed a coincidence. 'It's a small world, as they say.'

'But so strange. When I was in Bern he was about to travel to Stuttgart on business and I even helped him with his visa at our Embassy there. He was staying at the Schweizerhof, which I tell you, Franz, is a very expensive hotel. And now look – he is a mere courier.'

'Perhaps he fell on hard times, Alois?'

'Perhaps.'

Both men continued to be uneasy about the encounter. As was the custom on Tuesdays, the senior lawyers at the practice lunched together and the two men eyed each other suspiciously throughout the meal. Franz Hermann was worried that Alois Jäger did not believe him and Jäger was convinced that Hermann appeared to be nervous. When they went back into their respective offices, each man closed his door and made a phone call. Alois Jäger made his first, telephoning a good friend of his who was in charge of the Gestapo office in Treptow.

'Tell me, Lothar,' he said after a brief exchange of pleasantries, 'you must have good contacts with your colleagues at Tempelhof, no? You are practically neighbours…? Good, I thought as much. Do me a favour will you, Lothar? I am sure it is nothing, perhaps just me being suspicious, but could you discreetly check whether a Swiss citizen called Henri Hesse travelled on a flight from Tempelhof to Stuttgart at around twelve thirty today?'

Lothar asked one or two questions. 'We are very thorough in the Gestapo you know, Alois!' Both men laughed. Lothar checked the exact spelling of the man's name. 'And could you describe him?'

'Perhaps mid-thirties; average height, possibly slightly overweight. Pale complexion, darkish hair as far as I could tell, but he was wearing a trilby hat.'

'I will see what I can do, Alois.'

At more or less the same time in his office one floor below Jäger's, Franz Hermann was pacing up and down. Something was not right, but he had no idea what he could do about it. He picked up the telephone and dialled his mother's number in Dahlem. At least he could be reassured that all was well there.

–

Captain Edgar and Basil Remington-Barber had travelled to Geneva after spending the weekend with Henry in Zurich. They based themselves at a perfectly decent if somewhat anonymous hotel within sight of Cornavin railway station, where they hoped to meet Henry late on the Tuesday night.

The hotel had been chosen carefully. Apart from its proximity to the station they had been able to book two rooms on the top floor, set apart from the other rooms on that corridor. Each room had a telephone and they made sure that from the moment they arrived in Geneva, one of them would always be beside it. They did not expect to hear anything until four thirty at the earliest on the Tuesday afternoon, when Henry Hunter's flight from Stuttgart was scheduled to land at Zurich. Rolf would be waiting at the airport to watch Henry arrive and check that he travelled onto Zurich; one of Rolf's men would then be at the station to watch Henry meeting with the Russians and then catching the train to Geneva. Edgar and Remington-Barber ensured that they were both waiting by the phone in Geneva from four o'clock on the Tuesday afternoon. At a quarter past four Remington-Barber observed that the Henry's flight ought to be landing and at four thirty he mentioned that they should be hearing from Rolf at any moment.

'It's a tight schedule we've allowed him, Edgar. He has to go to Bank Leu, then meet up with his Russian chap, allow them to copy the document and still make that last train to Geneva.'

'He'll be fine, Basil. Why don't you sit down and relax? Hedinger will stay on as late as he needs to and the last train to Geneva leaves at a quarter to eight. Please stop worrying. You can pour us another drink if you think that will help.'

By five o'clock Edgar, if pressed, would have described himself as concerned. Five minutes after that the phone rang and both men jumped. Basil Remington-Barber answered it. 'Yes, hello Rolf... I see... Yes... No... Are you sure...? And you have checked there...? Do so again please, Rolf... Yes... Probably... Call us back in ten minutes.' As he replaced the phone his hands were shaking.

'Well?' asked Edgar.

'Henry was not on the flight.'

'Are you sure?' Edgar's face was just inches from his colleague's.

'You heard what I said, Edgar. Rolf Eder is no fool, he is one of the best men I have ever had in the field, doesn't miss a thing. He said that there were twelve passengers who came off the Swissair flight and Henry Hunter was not one of them.'

'Maybe he missed the connection at Stuttgart? After all, there was only a twenty minute gap between the Berlin flight landing there and the Zurich flight taking off?'

'Yes, but they are connecting flights. If the Berlin flight is late they hold the Zurich one. It is possible that he missed the flight from Berlin, but it's unlikely: he had ample time to meet Hugo, go to the Reichsbank and then get to Tempelhof.'

When Rolf called back ten minutes later he said that he had been able to check the flight's manifest with a Swissair contact: although a 'Henri Hesse' had been booked in he had not been on the connecting flight from Berlin. Edgar snatched the phone from Remington-Barber.

'Rolf? It's me— Edgar. Look, your best bet is to get to the station in Zurich as soon as possible and join your man there. See if you can spot Viktor and his chaps. If Henry's not going to show up they'll probably get worried at some stage and break cover. Just see what they up to. If we see them looking for him then at least that tells us something.'

'Jesus Christ,' said Edgar, slamming the phone down and pacing the room. 'Basil… you telephone Hedinger and ask if his courier has arrived from Berlin. I cannot imagine that he will have done, but there is a very distant possibility that he may have heard from him or from Reinhart. In fact, ask him to send a telegram to Reinhart asking if all went well with the courier and then tell Hedinger to stay on until at least seven. Jesus Christ.'

By eight o'clock they knew little more. Michael Hedinger told them he had neither heard nor seen his courier and promised to send a telegram to Reinhart that night. Rolf reported that he had managed to get to the station by six o'clock, where he was joined by three of his men. At seven o'clock they spotted Viktor prowling around the station, looking anxious. There was no sign of Henry Hunter boarding the last train to Geneva or any of the ones before it. Viktor had been waiting by the ticket barrier, his face creased in anger as the train departed.

'At least he's let them down too.'

'What do we do, Edgar?'

Edgar continued to pace the room angrily, cursing under his breath. 'It's that bloody woman, I'm sure it is. Jesus Christ. We'd better get on the first train in the morning to Zurich.'

–

The mood in a dingy rented apartment in a narrow side street between the railway tracks and the river in Zurich was scarcely any better. Each of the four men who had been with him at the station were brought in one by one and questioned by Viktor, but as he had been there himself there was little point in it. Henry had not come anywhere near the station.

'He seems to have disappeared,' said Viktor.

'When we met him last week he said something about having asked you for the details of any comrades he could contact in Berlin, in an emergency,' said one of Viktor's men.

'So…?'

'So, I was thinking that if you did give him details of any comrades in Berlin then possibly they would know what happened to him.'

Viktor said nothing for a while, thinking how little he could trust even those closest to him.

'You are mistaken: I have no comrades left in my network in Berlin: they've all gone – either escaped, disappeared, dead or become Nazis. I told him to contact the Embassy.'

'Really? I thought you didn't trust anyone there?'

'I don't,' said Viktor. 'I don't trust anyone.'

–

Back in Berlin that Tuesday evening Alois Jäger finally heard back from his friend in the Gestapo, Lothar. It was six thirty and Jäger had remained behind in his office awaiting the call.

'You say that his name is Henri Hesse and he is a Swiss citizen?'

'Yes,' said Alois Jäger.

'Well I not only contacted Heinrich at Tempelhof but I actually went over there to his office so I was able to look at all the paperwork.

There were three Swiss nationals on the Deutsche Lufthansa flight that left for Stuttgart at thirty five minutes past twelve but none of them had that name. The officer in charge of checking the papers as the passengers boarded the plane said that, as far as he can recall, one of the Swiss was a woman and the other two were men in either their fifties or sixties.'

'He was obviously not on that flight then.'

'However,' said Lothar, 'he was *booked* onto that flight, he just did not turn up for it. And furthermore, there is a record of him having arrived at Tempelhof yesterday, on the flight from Stuttgart. What is it that concerns you about this man, Alois?'

Alois thought long and hard.

'I'm not sure, Lothar. Something about him doesn't quite add up. And now missing his flight like that.'

Very odd, they both agreed – so much so that they decided to meet up the next day to discuss the matter.

–

Franz Hermann had telephoned his mother's house in Dahlem five times on the Tuesday afternoon and each time the call went unanswered his anxiety increased. By five to five he decided he had to go down to Dahlem to check but he was wary of Alois Jäger; he decided it would be unwise to leave the office before him. Normally his colleague was so preoccupied with Nazi Party meetings in the evening that he invariably left the office no later than five o'clock, but that day it was six thirty before he left.

As soon as he did so Franz Hermann made his exit too. It was nearly quarter past seven before he arrived at his mother's house on Arno-Holz Strasse. He knocked on the door but there was no reply, so he used his own key to let himself in. The house felt empty and there was no reply when he called out. The lights were on downstairs but the upper floors were dark. Certain that he was walking into a trap he headed for the room at the back overlooking the garden, where his mother slept and spent her days.

He found her propped up in her armchair, swathed in blankets with a tray next to her and her eyes red from crying.

'I've been calling her for hours, Franz!' she said in a hoarse voice. 'She said something about going out but that you would be here later. What does she think she has been up to? I have been on my own all this time. I am desperate to go to the toilet and I haven't had my evening meal yet. The telephone was ringing but I couldn't reach it!'

Setting aside his fear, Franz Hermann acted swiftly. He helped his mother to the toilet and then settled her before going upstairs. There was no sign of Rosa and Sophia, and within half an hour he had gathered up any items belonging to them or that could even be associated with them. He bundled everything into old laundry bags and carried them into the attic, where he locked them in an old trunk, which he then covered with old tennis rackets, a cello case and other reminders of when life was more normal.

When he came downstairs he telephoned Gunter Reinhart at his home. He knew was a big risk, but he had no alternative.

'Did your courier visit today?'

'Yes – why?'

'And was he acting normally?'

'I think so, hard to tell really. Is there a problem?'

'No, no, no – of course not. I was just checking what time he left you?'

'I'm not too sure, I would say by half past ten. Something like that.'

'Perhaps we will meet tomorrow for a chat?' said the lawyer, hoping the other man would recognise the urgency in his voice.

'Yes, perhaps that would be a good idea,' said the banker.

After that Hermann telephoned his wife and told her that he would stay tonight at his mother's house as the nurse had been called away. He telephoned his sister with the sad news that the nurse who cared so well for their mother had been called back to Bremerhaven because her husband had been killed at sea. *It was terrible* they both agreed. The poor nurse had no idea how long she would be there, but in the meantime they needed to sort out their mother. Franz Hermann's sister paused for a while and then said that if he could look after his mother until Thursday, she would then come over and bring her back to Brandenburg. She can stay with us for a week or so.

'I imagine the nurse will be back by then.'

'I am sure she will,' replied Franz.

–

It was some time after dawn on the Wednesday, before enough light to wake them had penetrated the dense canopy of the woods just to the north of Göttingen. Sophia was upset again when she woke. The tall trees frightened her and she wanted to know whether, if there was no such thing as goblins, what about witches? Hardly reassured by her mother's promise that there were no witches in the wood she then wanted to know when she was going to see Alfred.

'Soon, darling.'

'When is soon, Mama?'

Henry had been out of the car for a few minutes and had just returned.

'The sooner we can leave this place – the better,' he said. Sophia must have sensed her irritation, but she was glaring at him.

'Give us a few minutes, Henry,' said Rosa.

'Sophia, eat these biscuits and drink the milk, then we can be on our way,' she said softly.

'And see Alfred and Papa?'

'Maybe not today, but hopefully soon. And remember, darling, if anyone asks, your name is Gisela: Gisela Keufer. We will all play that game until we meet Alfred, do you understand?'

Henry checked the map and tried to show the route to Rosa, but she seemed to be barely interested.

'It is amazing that we have got this far, Henry. Our luck cannot hold out much longer.' She spoke quietly so that Sophia could not hear, but there was no disguising the annoyance and fear in her voice.

'I don't see why not, especially if we keep to the back roads.'

'What if they are looking for us?'

'How would anyone know? Franz is unlikely to report us, is he?'

They waited until seven o'clock before starting off, first heading south through Göttingen and then keeping to the patchwork of smaller roads until they reached Würzburg at lunchtime. They needed to stop for petrol which was risky, but Würzburg was just seventy miles west of Frankfurt and, according to their identity cards, that was where they were from. They drove slowly through the town centre, looking out for a petrol station. The first one they found had a police van waiting at one of the two pumps, so they drove on. Just before the river they came to a garage with a solitary pump and an elderly owner sitting outside on a bench with a large dog sitting next to him and less than an inch of a lit cigarette protruding from his lips. He asked to see the documents entitling them to petrol.

'If I was minded to be difficult,' he said in a gruff Bavarian accent, 'then I would say that you are only entitled to half a tank.' He smiled, revealing a mouth with no more than half a dozen nearly-black teeth in it. The cigarette stub appeared to be stuck to his lower lip. The man's eyes focussed on the Nazi Party badge on Henry's lapel and swiftly his mood became less hostile. 'But fortunately for you, sir, I am not minded to be difficult. I had a delivery of petrol yesterday – the first for over a week. I will fill you up but you don't need to tell anyone that. Come inside. It takes longer these days to do the paperwork than it does to repair a car... maybe even longer than it takes to build one.' The man's throaty laugh echoed around the workshop before breaking into a violent cough.

They went over to a counter at the side of the garage. The owner checked the paperwork painfully slowly: he checked the identity card in the name of Erich Keufer and the documents showing that Opel Super 6 sedan registration number UTM 142 was entitled to petrol every ten days. Henry glanced out of the garage and saw Rosa looking worried: this was taking a long time. The owner wrote slowly in a large ledger.

'So tell me, are you returning to Frankfurt?'

'No, we are just on our way from there. We are visiting my wife's family in Nuremberg.'

'You sound like you may not be from Frankfurt?'

'Very well spotted my friend: I have lived all over Germany, which explains my accent!'

The owner nodded and handed back the paperwork, which was now covered in grey grease marks. 'Odd that your petrol entitlement document was last stamped in Berlin.'

When he returned to the car Sophia was asleep on the back seat and Rosa looked pale and tense.

'Why did that take so long?'

'Paperwork,' he said, thinking it best not to mention the apparent flaw in petrol entitlement document.

–

The garage owner, Jürgen Neumann, was a worried man as he watched the Opel Super 6 pull away awkwardly from the forecourt of his garage not far from the banks of the River Main in Würzburg.

He was not a political man by any means and nor was he any good at keeping his mouth shut, and that was his problem. In recent months he had rather too openly complained to his decreasing number of customers, about the infrequency of his deliveries, the cost of food and the lack of business. This had led to a series of visits, the first from a Würzburg police officer who happened to be a friend of his, and lastly a visit from the deputy head of the local Gestapo, who was no friend at all.

'This complaining has to stop. If you are out to make trouble then be assured we can make plenty of trouble for you. It is about time you were more co-operative with us.'

And that had been followed by a noticeable drop in business and in the delivery of fuel. So now Jürgen Neumann had decided that enough was enough. Unless he went out of his way to ingratiate himself with the powers that be, he would have to close down his business. He picked up the telephone and dialled the number of the deputy head of the local Gestapo, the man who had recently given him his final warning.

'It is probably nothing, sir, but I did promise to contact you with any information.'

He explained about the car that had come from Frankfurt but whose petrol entitlement document was last stamped in Berlin and whose driver said they were heading for Nuremberg but had driven off in the other direction. It all seemed rather... odd.

'Do I have the registration number sir? Of course I do!'

–

Only three hours before the garage owner in Würzburg contacted his local Gestapo office a lady in Berlin rang her local police station and began in a similar manner.

'It is probably of little consequence and I was unsure whether to trouble you, but I thought I would pass on this information in case you were interested.'

The officer who took the call at Dahlem police station was well used to this. These days he seemed to spend half his time taking calls from people eager to inform on neighbours, work colleagues, friends and even family. This one sounded little different and he took down the details. The lady – a Frau Werner – said that she lived in Arno-Holz Strasse and, although she was minding her own business and was certainly not the kind of person to spy upon her neighbours, she could not help to notice something unusual the previous morning.

'Yes, Tuesday. There is an elderly person who lives opposite me: a Frau Hermann. I hardly ever see her these days, she is virtually housebound. She has a nurse, I understand, who also hardly ever leaves the house. But yesterday, it must have been at around twelve noon, I happened to notice a man leave the house and walk over to a car parked just across the road. He then parked immediately outside Frau Hermann's house. Within two or three minutes, no more than that, I saw the man come out of the house along with Frau Hermann's nurse and with them was a young girl. They all seemed to be rather nervous, looking around. I have never seen a child going in or out of that house before: never. How old, do you say? Four or five, I'm not sure. They were in a hurry. Do I think they saw me? No. I don't want you to think bad of me, sir, but I was kneeling down on the floor, peering through a gap in the net curtains... As it happens, sir, yes I did. Are you ready? It was an Opel – I am not sure what model, but it was dark green and the registration number was… do you have a pen ready? UTM 142.'

Up until a couple of weeks previously the policeman in Dahlem would have been more annoyed than he was now by this call, as it would have meant hours of work just to satisfy the whim of a nosey neighbour.

But recently the rules had changed. After one or two unfortunate incidents, the Gestapo had realised that criminals and other people they were interested in were finding it too easy to move around the Reich by car. As these people drove from one town or district to another, there was no proper system of keeping track of them. So the Gestapo brought in a new system: the details of any cars that the Gestapo or other sections of the police were interested in would be passed on to a central control in Berlin.

Suits me fine: more work for them, less for me, thought the officer. He filled in the form and took it upstairs to the Gestapo liaison office in the station. *Still*, he thought, *they will be pleased enough with this one.*

Not often we get a registration number.

Chapter 25

The Black Forest, March 1941

Franz Hermann woke early on the Wednesday morning, checked on his mother and then walked around the house he had grown up in, preoccupied with the thoughts that had played around in his head all night. He needed to move fast.

Once his mother was settled he left the house through the back gate. From there it was a swift ten minute walk to his own home. He explained to his wife what he was planning to do. Before leaving the house, he telephoned his sister and then the office, telling them he would be slightly late as he needed to see a client on his way in.

He rarely used his car these days but the Daimler started at the third attempt and within two minutes he was back at his mother's house, parked by the back gate he had departed through barely half an hour previously. He told his mother that she would be coming to his house for a day or two and then his sister would collect her and she would go and stay with her in Brandenburg for a week or so. Hopefully after that the nurse would return and everything would be back to normal. His mother was confused but there was no time to argue.

Once she was settled at his house he left for work, but not before stopping once again at his mother's house, where he spent an hour checking again that there were no signs that anyone had been there for at least a day or two.

He made a point of leaving the house though the front door and boldly walking over to the house opposite, from where the lady carefully observed all the comings and goings in the street. As he approached her door he noticed the net curtains in the front window twitch. A moment later the door opened, a split second before he had knocked on it.

'Frau Werner, I just thought I'd let you know in case anyone asks that there will be no one at my mother's house for a few days. In fact, she has not been there since Sunday – she is staying with my wife and me. Her nurse has had to return to Bremerhaven suddenly – a death I'm afraid. Her husband was in the navy, he died in the cause of the Reich.'

The woman was very grateful to be told. She told Franz that she had wondered about Frau Hermann because only the previous day she had seen the nurse leave the house with a man... and a young girl. They had been carrying a case and some other things which they put in the boot of a car parked outside the house and then driven off.

'Oh really?' He was trying his best to sound confused rather than shocked. 'Could you describe the man?'

With unerring accuracy she described Henri Hesse. Franz Hermann did his best to look none the wiser. 'As I say, Frau Werner, my mother has been staying with us since Sunday. I have no idea about this man; it is possible that he was taking her to Bremerhaven.'

'And what about the girl?'

'As far as I am aware no child has been in the house for a very long time. How old would you say she was?'

'Perhaps four or five, hard to say. I did not get a perfect view, you understand. She was such a slight thing.'

'And are you certain they came from my mother's house? Maybe they were just passers-by.'

She was certain. She just happened to be cleaning the windows at the time – by coincidence.

'I don't suppose you saw what car it was, by any chance?'

'I do, Herr Hermann: it was an Opel, a dark green one. And not only that: I even wrote down the registration number. But don't worry; I have given all the details to the police.'

–

315

When they left Würzburg they headed south. Henry announced that they would head south west, into the Black Forest.

'The Black Forest!'

'Yes, Rosa, the Black Forest.'

'You are crazy! Do you still read fairy tales?'

Sophia started to cry in the back seat. She didn't want to go into a forest. She was afraid of witches. Henry turned round and snapped at the little girl.

'I told you! There is no such thing as witches, or goblins. Or fairies, for that matter.'

Sophia's crying became louder.

'Don't shout at her: she's a little girl. She is frightened and she is not the only one.'

'Trust me, Rosa, the Black Forest stretches down to the Swiss border – it almost goes as far as Basle!'

'I am aware of that but do you really think we can just stroll over the border? Maybe the SS or whoever is guarding it will help us carry our cases?'

'Listen to me, Rosa: our Swiss papers our very good, far superior to the German ones. I am using my own papers and I managed to get papers showing you are my wife and she is our daughter. They are hidden in the boot. When we get near the border we can use them, but we will need to abandon the car first.'

They stuck to the side roads and lanes and, at four thirty, emerged from a long lane onto the main road at Heilbronn, before taking the road to Pforzheim and from there into the Black Forest.

–

Edgar and Remington-Barber arrived in Zurich on the Wednesday afternoon and were met at the station by Rolf, who took them to another of their safe houses, an apartment above a bar on Predigerplatz. On the way up he collected a bottle of whisky.

'I think it may be a bit early for that,' Edgar said once they were in the small apartment.

'Not when you hear what I'm about to tell you,' said the Austrian. 'I went to see Hedinger this morning, he had just heard from Reinhart. Apparently Henri did come to Reinhart's office at the Reichsbank yesterday morning and collected the documents. Last night Hugo called Reinhart to ask whether Henri had been to his office and they arranged to meet up today, which they did at lunchtime. It seems that rather than heading for Tempelhof Henri headed for Hugo's mother's house in Dahlem.'

In the shocked silence that followed Remington-Barber looked confused, as if he had not properly heard what Rolf had said. Edgar had heard clearly enough and looked furious.

'No!'

'Yes, I am afraid so. Hugo knows this because he was telephoning his mother's house all Tuesday afternoon and when there was no reply he went round there after work. His mother was all alone; there was no sign of Rosa or her daughter. This morning he spoke to a neighbour who had seen Rosa leave the house along with a young girl and a man who seems to match Henri's description. They drove off in a green Opel.'

Edgar had declined the offer of whisky until this moment but now leaned over to the bottle and poured himself a measure that, in other circumstances, would be described as excessive. He drank most of it, repeating 'Jesus Christ' quite a few times.

'How on earth has he managed to get hold of a car?' Basil asked.

'Your guess is as good as mine, Basil. The fool probably stole it. Carry on, Rolf.'

'Reinhart is in a terrible state, according to Hedinger. He thinks the Gestapo are about to knock on his door and of course Hugo is worried sick too, not least because when he was with Henry on Tuesday morning after they left the cathedral they bumped into a colleague of his who is not only an active Nazi but also claims he had met Henry in Bern a year ago.'

Remington-Barber was watching Edgar very carefully, expecting him to explode at any moment, but he remained calm. Edgar drank the whisky remaining in his glass, removed his jacket, loosened his tie and walked over to the window. 'Thank you, Rolf. By the sounds of it, Henry decided that rather than return to Switzerland as he'd been instructed, he'd turn his return journey into some kind of adventure: a rescue mission.' Edgar was speaking very calmly, as if everything he said had a perfect logic to it.

'But he is carrying the Rostock Report, Edgar. That is meant to be falling into the hands of our Soviet friends!'

Edgar turned from the window. 'Thank you, Basil, I had realised that.'

By March 1941, few people in Germany would have been foolish enough to accuse the Gestapo of inefficiency. When the deputy head of the Gestapo in Würzburg was informed by the garage owner about the 'odd' dark green Opel Super 6, he simply followed procedure. He sent a telex giving the details of the car to his regional headquarters, where, in turn, the duty officer also simply followed procedure and passed on the details of the car to the new central control room in Berlin. Around three o'clock that Wednesday afternoon an officer at the control room in the Gestapo headquarters in Prinz-Albrecht-Strasse was reviewing the 'alerts' received since his lunch break. When he spotted that a dark green Opel, registration number UTM 142, had been added to the watch list he thought there was something familiar about it, so he checked that morning's alerts. Sure enough, the Gestapo liaison office at Dahlem police station had passed on details of that same car: a woman who lived in Arno-Holz Strasse had observed a man, woman and a young girl leaving a neighbour's house and getting into the car. They seemed – according to the neighbour – 'nervous'.

The officer wrote up his notes: the car was seen in Berlin at noon on the Tuesday and just over twenty four hours later was in Würzburg. It would certainly be worth putting this one out for national alert. He should have been less sceptical about this new system, maybe it was working after all. And thank heavens for frightened business owners and nosey neighbours, what would the Gestapo do without them?

At four o'clock that Wednesday afternoon officer Reinhard Goetz left the police station in Pforzheim for a routine patrol, briefed – among other things – to keep an eye out for the dark green Opel. 'Berlin is interested and it was last seen in Würzburg,' he had been told, 'heading south – so you never know. It's the Gestapo who are in interested, so keep your eyes peeled.'

The traffic policeman headed east on his BMW motorbike and after a while changed direction – south into the Black Forest. At five o'clock he decided that he had earned his first cigarette break so, just before the small town of Tiefenbronn, he pulled into a clearing in an area where the forest started to become dense. He would be able to enjoy his cigarette in peace but, as he turned into the clearing, he noticed that a car was already there. A dark green Opel Super 6. He parked his motorbike so that it blocked the path back to the road and walked over to check the registration number of the car.

Henry was on his own in the car when Goetz pulled into the clearing, Rosa having taken Sophia down into the trees to go to the toilet. He watched as the officer parked his bike and headed towards the car. Henry glanced to his left, but there was no sign of Rosa and Sophia. Watching the policeman all the time, he leaned over to the glove box in front of the passenger seat and removed the bundle wrapped in a thick grey cloth from behind the log book. The policeman smiled at him from a distance and Henry smiled back as the policeman moved in a wide arc to the front of the car. Henry held the bundle below the steering wheel and slowly unwrapped it. By now, the officer was at the front of the car, peering down at the registration plate. He looked up at Henry and made a motion with his fingers to unwind the window.

Officer Goetz bent down by the window, his face inches from Henry's.

'Is this your car?'
'Yes.'
'Where have you come from today?'
'Frankfurt.'
'And where are you going?'

'We are just out for a drive – to see the forest.'

'We?'

'My wife and daughter – they have gone to the toilet down there.'

'Have you been in Berlin in the past day or so?'

'Berlin? No, of course not!'

'Or Würzburg today?'

Henry hesitated for too long. He had no idea how to respond. 'Maybe… we stopped at a town for petrol. I don't know what it was called.'

'Right, get out of the car now, I want to check your papers.'

He noticed the policeman's right hand moving towards the holster on his hip and he knew he had just seconds to act. The policeman stepped back as Henry opened the car door and at that moment he heard the voices of Rosa and Sophia emerging from the trees. As the policeman glanced up in their direction Henry pushed the revolver into his stomach and fired. It was a muffled shot and the man staggered back before collapsing to the ground. He was still conscious and trying to remove his own pistol from its holster. Behind him, Henry could hear Rosa and Sophia screaming. He stepped towards the prone body of the policeman. A large pool of blood was forming under him as he tried to lift his own revolver, but did not seem to have the strength. Henry held his gun no more than a few inches from the man's head and pulled the trigger. In the ensuing seconds, his world slipped into slow motion.

He was aware of a chunk of the man's head flying away, of gore splattering all around him, of the sound of the shot bouncing off every tree in the forest and what appeared to be thousands of birds swarming in every direction, and then Rosa and Sophia standing in front of him, their mouths wide open in silent screams. By now he had sunk to his knees, the gun still in his hand, staring at the body of the third person he had killed.

For a time he could not hear anything other than the ringing of gunfire in his ears. When his hearing began to return Sophia was shouting at him.

'What on earth have you done? You have killed a policeman!'

'Calm down and get Sophia into the car. We need to sort things out.'

Rosa bundled her daughter into the back of the Opel and came back over to him.

'He was looking for us. He checked the number plate and then asked whether we had been in Berlin or in Würzburg today. He told me to get out of the car and I could see he was reaching for his gun. He was distracted when he heard you so I knew I had to do something. We need to move him and his bike – quickly.'

It took the two of them ten minutes to carry the man's body as deep into the forest as they could manage, covering it with undergrowth. While Henry wheeled the motorbike far amongst the trees in another direction Rosa did her best to clean up the ground where the man had been shot.

'What do we do now?' They were both standing by the car, breathless and filthy.

'We need to get away from here as quickly as possible.'

'Even I could have worked that out. Which direction do we head in? Towards the Swiss border?'

'No, not now – it's too late and he will be reported missing soon. We don't want to be stuck in the forest or even near the border when that happens.'

'So where do we go then?'

'We'll go to Stuttgart and ditch the car.'

Rosa sniffed. 'And what do you propose we do then – check into the best hotel in Stuttgart?'

'Something like that – yes.'

Chapter 26

'Basil, without in any way wishing to appear rude, may I suggest that you pause, take a deep breath and then start again?'

It was the evening of Friday the 28th of March and Edgar and Basil Remington-Barber had been stuck in the apartment above the bar in Zurich since Wednesday. They had heard nothing further about Henry since Hedinger's report that he had last been seen in Berlin on Tuesday. The circumstantial evidence that he had possibly left Berlin with Rosa and her daughter was bad enough: the fact that he had the Rostock Report with him rather than it being in Soviet hands was disastrous.

Now, Basil had received a phone call from the embassy in Bern – *some news*.

'I am sorry, Edgar; the tension does rather get to one at times. They're in Stuttgart.'

'Who?'

'Henry, Rosa and her daughter.'

'Jesus Christ: I knew it. What on earth does he imagine he is up to? Is he safe?'

'For the time being, yes, although I would say that considering their circumstances, "safe" is a very relative word.'

'And how do we know this?'

'You remember Milo, the Night Manager at the Hotel Victoria? Well, we've heard from her. She contacts us in code by telex to a travel agent in Bern, one with which we have an understanding. It is a safe form of communication– a hotel confirming bookings with a travel agent, terribly routine stuff – if a bit cumbersome. It rather relies on the travel agent passing the messages on to us quickly though, and although Milo sent the telex on Thursday night the travel agent did not see it until this morning and for reasons that are not entirely apparent, waited until this afternoon before informing my office at the embassy. They in turn seem to have taken their time before thinking of letting me know. I shall be having harsh words with them about this, I can assure you.'

'So how does Milo know about them?'

'Because they are in her hotel, Edgar.'

–

By the time they left the Black Forest it was five thirty on the Wednesday evening and it took them another two and a quarter hours to reach Stuttgart. It was a quarter to eight when Henry parked at the northern end of the Schlossplatz, as near as he dared get to the railway station. As they parked, a squadron of Heinkel fighters flew low overhead.

'You are sure this is going to work?' Rosa asked him, not for the first time since he had explained his plan.

'No, Rosa, I am not sure. But it is our best hope. They are bound to find the car and I just hope they will assume that as it is so close to the railway station we must have caught a train, so with any luck they will look for people leaving Stuttgart rather than staying in it. And when we walk away from the car, we will look like travellers who have just arrived by train.'

It took them five minutes to walk from the Schlossplatz to the Hotel Victoria, Rosa carrying an exhausted Sophia. Instead of going to the main entrance on Friedrichstrasse they walked into Keplerstrasse at the side of the hotel. It was quiet, the night was drawing in and there was no movement in the street. In a room above them in the hotel – possibly the restaurant – they could hear people laughing and glasses clinking. Henry moved Rosa and Sophia into a concealed doorway.

'Wait here and keep an eye on me. If I can get the door open then watch out for my signal and then hurry along but don't run.'

'And if you can't?'

Henry hesitated. 'Don't worry. I'll think of something.'

Keeping as close to the wall as possible Henry edged towards the door that led to the basement of the hotel. He had last been there with Milo on the morning of his journey to Essen the previous year. He had no idea whether Milo was still working at the hotel. For all he knew, she could have been arrested, but it was the only plan he could think of.

The door to the basement was stiff, but started to give after a few pushes and when he used his shoulder it sprung open. He descended the steep concrete steps: the basement was warm and dimly lit. Beyond the machinery he could make out a laundry area. After that was a door that he seemed to remember led to the stairs into the main part of the hotel. There was no sign of anyone down there.

He climbed back up the stairs and gestured for Rosa and Sophia to join him. Once they were safely in, he shut the door and whispered to Rosa.

'We will find somewhere in here to hide and after midnight I will go up into the hotel and see if she is there.'

'You say this woman is on duty at night?'

'Most nights, but not every night. But I have to tell you, Rosa, that it is nearly a year since I saw her, I cannot even be sure she is still here.'

They found a corner of the basement that was dark and warm, and huddled together. They gave what little food they had left to Sophia and soon she fell asleep in her mother's arms. At midnight, Henry decided to go up into the hotel.

'How do I look?'

'Terrible! Here, let me see what I can do.' Tenderly, Rosa wiped his face and brushed his clothes down and took a brush from her handbag to tidy his hair.

'That's better. You have your Swiss papers with you?'

Henry patted his jacket pocket. A few minutes later he was on the ground floor of the hotel and walking across the deserted foyer to the reception desk, where a young night porter was on his own.

'Can I help you, sir?'

'Yes, I had some dealings before with a most helpful manager. I wondered if she was on duty tonight? Her name was Katharina Hoch, I seem to recall.'

'Fraulein Hoch? Indeed she is, sir. May I ask your name?'

'Herr Hesse – from Switzerland.'

'Thank you sir. And which room are you in?'

'I beg your pardon?'

'Which room shall I tell her you are staying in?'

Before he could think of what to say, Katharina Hoch emerged from the office behind the reception desk. It was a good job that the night porter had his back to her because her eyes were wide open in fear as she saw Henry. She steadied herself against the doorframe and wiped her brow before regaining her composure.

'Herr Hesse! How good to have such an honoured guest back with us. Please do come through to my office.'

She took Henry down a corridor at the back of the reception and into another office.

'What the hell are you doing here?' she said after making sure no one had followed them.

'Hiding.'

She stared at him for a minute, slowly shaking her head.

'Well you can't. It is too dangerous. Everything is so dangerous now that we do nothing other than pass the odd bit of information on to Bern. As for helping agents and hiding people, that is a thing of the past. You have no idea how much of a risk it is for you to be here. You must leave.'

'I can't.'

'You have to, please. Since you were last here, the situation has got so much worse. Everyone informs on everyone else as a matter of course.'

'But I cannot leave.'

'You have to, I told you. I can give you some money and something to eat and then you go. How did you get in here?'

'Through the basement, you remember you took me there the morning I went to Essen?'

'You must leave that way then.'

'I can't, I'm not on my own. And I killed a policeman today.'

\-

Katharina Hoch said nothing as Henry told his story. By the time he had finished she was running her fingers through her long hair. He noticed that she was now wearing a bright red lipstick, which managed to make her lips look less sensuous than before.

'I was foolish enough to imagine that we may be safe,' she said.

'What do you mean?'

'My brother, Dieter – you remember you used his identity when you travelled to Essen – he even joined the Nazi Party after you left, the situation has become that bad. We thought that may help us if there was any suspicion. Now what happens? You kill a policeman and turn up here with two Jews. What do you expect us to do?'

'Help us get to Switzerland. I was hoping to drive to the border, but I cannot use the car now. It is too risky. They are obviously looking for it.'

'And how do you propose to get to the border? They'll be searching for you: hide in the basement tonight, but no longer than that please. I will have to send a message to Bern but I will wait until tomorrow night, I must to talk to Dieter first.'

'Why are you sending a message to Bern?'

'At least we can let Basil know that you're here. He may have an idea.'

\-

'Is the only way we can communicate with Milo through this travel agent?'

Edgar was chain smoking now and sitting close to Basil Remington-Barber, as if he were interrogating him.

'It is not the only way, Edgar, but it is by far the safest way. The problem is that it is now Friday evening and the travel agent does not reopen until Monday morning. In the meantime, we could send a telex direct to the hotel, but that is not without risks. At least we know that Milo is on duty tonight and over the weekend so the chances are that she will be the only person to see it.'

Edgar stood up and walked slowly around the room, a trail of cigarette smoke following in his wake.

'The first time I met Henry was in August 1939, at Croydon Airport. I had to remind myself that appearances can be deceptive, that he may have looked and even acted as something of a nonentity, but there was clearly more to him than that. I recall saying that he was actually rather impressive. No hint whatsoever who he was really working for and there was a danger that we could underestimate him. God knows what we're to make of him now.'

Remington-Barber started to speak but Edgar held up his hand. *I'm thinking.*

'What telex machine would you use from this end?'

'One of Rolf's contacts works in a hotel here in Zurich. We can get a message out through her tonight. It's open I'm afraid, but needs must.'

Another pause while Edgar paced the room, deep in thought.

'You ready to write this down, Basil? Tell Milo to tell Henry that he is to leave Stuttgart and get back to Switzerland as soon as possible. He is to come on his own. Under no circumstances should he attempt to bring that woman and her daughter out with him. He's already been told that we're not the Red Cross. That last bit is not part of the message.'

–

Katharina Hoch had come down to the basement in the early hours of the Thursday morning. It was not only for reasons of humanity that she realised she could not turn the three of them out onto the street. It was likely that they would be arrested within minutes and one of them was bound to say something about the hotel. She realised she would have to hide them until at least she had spoken with Dieter.

At the back of the basement was a narrow corridor, no more than five feet high. It led to a room behind the main boilers and had been used to store equipment. Now the room was empty and never visited. She led the three of them into it. The room was dark, with no lights, a rancid smell and the scuttling sound of mice. Its saving grace was that it was warm and safe, for the time being. Once they were in the room she brought down blankets and some food, and told them to remain there until her next visit – she would come down when it was safe.

It was three thirty on the Saturday morning before they next saw her, holding a torch and carrying a bag with some food in it. She asked Henry to come out with her.

'I cannot stay long. There is a problem with the plumbing on one of the floors and I really need to be around to supervise things.'

They were at the end of the corridor, back in the main part of the basement.

'We have heard from Bern. You are under orders to return to Switzerland.'

'Good! I told you that is where we want to go.'

'Just you: the message is very clear. You are to go back on your own.'

'What – and leave them? Of course not, they're coming with me. What did your brother have to say?'

'According to him, the police at the railway station are searching for all of you. They have your names, but no photographs, which I suppose is something. They found the car naturally and the fact that it was so close to the station means that they realise you may not be in the city, but that is not the point: as soon as you leave the hotel you will be at risk. The only chance you have is for Dieter to drive you south of the city on Sunday, which is his day off. He may be able to get hold of a van from the railways, so that ought to be safe. He will try and get you as close to the border as possible. You stand a chance if you try and cross at night: alone.'

'But I told you, I'm not going anywhere without Rosa and Sophia.'

–

The next time Edgar and Remington-Barber heard from Stuttgart was on the morning of Monday 31st March. Milo had sent a telex overnight to the travel agents in Bern and this time the message was passed on promptly.

'According to Milo,' said Remington-Barber, following Edgar as he paced around the room, 'Henry absolutely refuses to leave the basement of the hotel without the others. Dieter turned up on Sunday with his van, but Henry would not budge. Milo and her brother are at their wits end. They know that they can't turf them out of the basement because the three of them together are bound to be caught within minutes. But she's convinced it's only a matter of time before someone finds them. If the Gestapo haven't found them elsewhere they'll assume they must still be in Stuttgart and she's worried they will then search the hotel.'

'Tell her to hold on then. Keep them in the basement and we'll sort something out. Do you still have that cache of German identities?'

'Yes, but I'm down to three, possibly four that I would say I could totally trust.'

'Where are they?'

'In the safe in Bern.'

'Better get them sent here as soon as possible. What about good Swiss identities, do you have many of those?'

'A couple that are watertight, Edgar. I'll get them to send those.'

'How much do you trust Rolf, Basil?'

'I've told you Edgar, he's one of our best, no question about it: type of chap you'd want to open the batting with.'

That's Basil's world, thought Edgar. *Judging people on whether you trust them enough to open the batting with you.*

'And on the train you mentioned something about him having been across the border before – into Germany, I mean.'

'Yes, late thirty nine it must have been. We needed to get some cash to an agent I was running in Freiburg. We sent Rolf in over the mountains and he came back the same way.'

'You'd better get him up here.'

When Rolf joined them Edgar gestured for him to sit down. Edgar leaned back in the sofa, opposite the Austrian. Rolf was only slightly shorter than Edgar. With his blond hair and blue eyes he was far closer to the Aryan ideal than Adolf Hitler, his fellow Austrian. Rolf's undoubted good looks were marred by one characteristic though: large, protruding ears which gave him a slightly comical appearance. But he was slim and sprightly-looking, the kind of person who was always moving, but in an energetic rather than nervous manner. He invariably had a pleasant smile on his face, as he did now.

'I understand that you are familiar with Germany, Rolf?'

'I have been many times, though of course not recently.'

'And, excuse me asking, but do you sound like an Austrian when you are there?'

'A good question: I can sound like a Swiss when I am in Switzerland, an Austrian in Austria and a German when I am in Germany. I try to suppress my Viennese accent in Germany, it is too distinctive. Why do you ask?'

'Because you and I are going to Germany.'

To Edgar's surprise, he noticed that Rolf's smile was wider than before.

–

They crossed the border late on the morning of Tuesday 1st April. The German identity papers had arrived from Bern late on the Monday afternoon and yet another of Rolf's contacts had worked through the night to turn Edgar and Rolf into impeccable German citizens. Rolf Eder had become Ludwig Kühn, an engineer from Landshut, just north of Munich. Edgar became Karl Albrecht, a businessman from Hanover, a city he was not only familiar with after having spent a year at university there, but for which he could also manage the correct accent.

'I hope this chap of yours is reliable' said Edgar as they drove towards Lake Konstanz from Zurich. Both Rolf and Basil Remington-Barber looked at each other, unsure of who should answer.

'All I can say that he has not let us down so far' said Remington-Barber.

'And how many times have you used him?'

A long pause. 'Once.'

Edgar said nothing but slowly shook his head.

'At short notice he is our only option,' said Rolf. 'We are paying him a lot of money and he is running an enormous risk.'

They pulled off the main road between the small towns of Rorschach and Arbon and, after a while, the track they had turned onto petered to a dead end and they found themselves surrounded by trees, with the lake just visible through them. They waited for five minutes and once Remington-Barber was certain that they had not been followed nor were being watched, they set off through the small wood. When they emerged they found themselves at a small jetty, with the black water of the lake lapping high against it and the shorelines of both Germany and Austria clearly visible. Rolf removed a pair of binoculars from his jacket and scanned the lake. He handed the binoculars to Edgar and pointed to a tiny shape in the middle of the water.

'That's her. She will be with us in maybe fifteen minutes. We will wait in the trees until she arrives.'

Twenty minutes later the fishing boat had pulled up alongside the jetty and the three men were scrambling across it. The skipper had a deeply tanned face and a heavy moustache and snatched the thick envelope that Remington-Barber handed to him. He gestured for Rolf and Edgar to go below deck, where despite the noise of the idling engine they could hear the conversation going on above them.

'Don't worry, Paul, it's all here: Swiss Francs and Reichsmarks.'

'And those two – they're not going to cause trouble are they?'

'Of course not.'

'And promise me they're not Jews.'

'Are you crazy, Paul? What Jews would want to escape *from* Switzerland *into* Germany?'

'Ones who have money hidden there. They still control many businesses you know.'

'No, Paul, I promise you they are not Jews. You had better get a move on. Your brother knows what to do? Don't forget that is why we are paying you so much. It's for the whole journey.'

'Don't worry, he knows what to do. You are getting us on the cheap. I am thinking of putting my price up.'

As the boat pulled away from the jetty and accelerated into the main body of the lake Edgar realised that they had not properly said goodbye to Remington-Barber, which was probably just as well. Sending agents into enemy territory was always the worst part of the job, not so different from pronouncing a death sentence.

They remained in the hold throughout the crossing. They briefly caught sight of the two other crew members, a boy who looked as if he should be in school and a giant of a man who had a permanent grin and seemed to communicate through sign language.

'We have been lucky so far today,' said the skipper when he came down into the hold for a minute. 'The Swiss and German patrol boats are all near Konstanz – there's been some row there about fishing rights at the other end of the lake. The Austrians are lazy: they are just putting out one patrol boat a day at the moment and they seem to prefer to stay around Bregenz. There's a small landing just outside Nonnenhorn – Johannes will be waiting there with his truck. If it's all clear, we will pull in there. If not, we'll continue into port and we'll have to get you off the boat later on, when it is quiet.'

On the first pass there must have been a signal that all was well, because the boat suddenly cut its speed and turned sharply to the shore. Once the boat was tied up, they were called up to the deck, where the skipper had been joined by a man who looked like his identical twin. *Johannes*. Some quick shaking of hands and they were hurried along to a narrow road and into the back of a van waiting there. There was just enough room for the two of them between the crates of fish. Once he was in the driving seat, Johannes turned round.

'I can't pretend this will be anything other than a very uncomfortable journey, but I will get you to Munich in good time, don't worry. And we should be fine if we are stopped: all my papers are in order. You're staying at the Hotel Bayerischer Hof, yes?'

'I am,' said Edgar. 'My friend is staying at a smaller one by the station'

'That is good.'

'Why is that?' asked Rolf.

'Because I am delivering the fish to the Bayerischer Hof!'

They arrived in Munich just before five o'clock and during the journey Edgar and Rolf talked through their plans. They would have no contact with each other while they were in Munich or on the journey to Stuttgart, so if one was caught there was a chance the other would make it.

'I am not terribly sure why we are taking this route to Stuttgart: it's hardly the most direct way,' said Rolf.

'True, but when we arrive in Stuttgart it will be as travellers from Munich. That should make us far less suspicious.'

Johannes dropped both Rolf and Edgar off in a side street by Munich Hauptbahnhof. It was only round the corner from the station hotel where the Austrian would be staying and for Edgar the ten minute walk to the Bayerischer Hof on Promenadeplatz not only meant that he would not be seen getting out of a van delivering fish at the hotel, but also gave him the opportunity for a bit of fresh air and the chance for the smell of the van to evaporate.

On the Wednesday morning both men were on the eight o'clock train from Munich to Stuttgart. They had stood close to each other on the concourse at the Hauptbahnhof, as arranged, but did not exchange a word nor make eye contact. Both men were carrying their small suitcase in their left hand and holding their hats in their right hand, the signal that all was well. They purchased seats at opposite ends of the same carriage so that they could spot if there were any problems, but the journey was straightforward. Their papers were checked as they boarded the train and then once during the journey just after the stop at Augsburg, but each time they seemed more bothered that their tickets were in order.

Both men had bought copies of that day's edition of the *Münchner Neueste Nachrichten* and they made sure they were prominent as they arrived in Stuttgart, where security was far more noticeable. Their papers were searched but neither man was pulled out of the queue for their bags to be searched. They took different routes to the Hotel Victoria, Edgar arriving fifteen minutes after Rolf.

Milo had reserved rooms for the two men close to each on the second floor and just across the corridor from the back stairs that led down to the hotel basement. Hidden in an enevelope taped to the underside of the wardrobe in Rolf's room was a key to the basement and note as to where to find Henry, Rosa and Sophia. It was one thirty in the afternoon when Edgar reckoned it would be safe to knock on Rolf's door. The two men stood in the tiny bathroom, the tap running to mask their voices.

'You have the key?'

Rolf dangled it in front of Edgar. 'She says that they are hiding in a room at the rear of the basement – here, she has drawn a sketch.' Rolf handed the piece of paper to Edgar.

'I don't like the fact that she took such a risk, putting it down on paper like that.'

'What else was she meant to do? You need to decide. When do we go down? And do we go together?'

'Just let me have another look at that note.' Edgar read it carefully, nodding his head, formulating a plan. 'She says that she comes on duty at eleven o'clock tonight and that we're to wait in our rooms. She will come up to us between half eleven and midnight, apparently. I don't think that we can risk waiting until then, they've been here almost a week already. You have Henry's new identity papers?'

Rolf gestured towards his small suitcase.

'Good. Let me tell you the plan and then you go down and bring Hunter up here.'

Rolf was impressed with Edgar's plan; it was not without considerable risk and would require nerves of steel, but it was clever. He then left the room and went down the back stairs that led down to the basement. It took him ten minutes to check the basement was clear and then navigate his way through to the room hidden behind the boiler. When Rosa heard him she cried out in fear.

'It's me, Henry, Rolf. You remember me from Zurich?'

Henry clasped Rolf by the arms.

'It is all right, Rosa – don't cry, Sophia. Rolf is a friend. He's come to rescue us. Are you here on your own, Rolf? When can we leave?'

Rosa had lit a candle in the room and Rolf glanced around, it was cramped, with rusty equipment against the walls and blankets and an old mattress on the floor. The heat was oppressive and there was a foul smell.

'Yes, we have a plan, don't worry. First you need to come with me, Henry, just for few minutes – don't worry, Rosa, he won't be long.'

–

There was only enough space for the three men to stand more or less shoulder to shoulder in the Rolf's bathroom, which meant that Edgar and Henry were facing each other. When Edgar finally spoke, after a minute of looking Henry up and down with the makings of a sneer on his face, his voice could only just be heard above the noise of the tap which had been turned on to cover the sound of their voices.

'As much as I am a reasonable man, Henry, and am prepared to give you the benefit of the doubt, I struggle to see how you can possibly manage to come up with a satisfactory explanation for all this.'

'For all what, Edgar?'

Edgar inched closer to Henry, clenching and unclenching his fists as he did so.

'For what? You were supposed to fly from Berlin to Zurich last Tuesday morning and then meet myself and Basil and in Geneva. What happened?'

An embarrassed smile on Henry's face and a shrug of the shoulders. *What can I say?*

'I bent the rules a little bit and decided to rescue Rosa and Sophia at the same time. I thought that if I did so then Gunter Reinhart would be better disposed towards us and provide us with more intelligence.'

'Oh really, Henry? I have never regarded myself as particularly naive, but I would be bordering on the certifiable if I were to believe a word of what you are saying. You've set yourself up as some knight in shining armour rescuing a damsel in distress—'

'I thought there would be no harm...' Henry shifted uncomfortably, his face now a bright red.

'No harm?' Edgar's voice was raised for a split second before Rolf nudged him. 'You have seriously jeopardised this mission, the purpose of which – in case you have forgotten – was to collect a document from Hugo and bring it back to Switzerland. Do you have that document?'

Henry coughed and stepped away as far as he was able to from Edgar.

'I am afraid not. I know this is going to sound dreadful, Edgar, but after we left Berlin it dawned on me that there was a possibility that we could be caught. I thought that the worst thing that could then happen from a British point of view was that the documents would fall into German hands, so I burnt them.'

'Where?'

'In some woods where we were hiding on the Tuesday night. I am so sorry, I know that I failed in my mission, but I felt that the alternative would be far worse.'

Edgar turned around, facing the frosted window. 'Jesus Christ,' was all that he could say and repeated those words a few times.

'We need to get you back to Switzerland as soon as possible. We cannot risk you being caught by the Germans, as tempting as that may be in some respects. Heaven knows what you'd say to the Gestapo—'

'Now, look here Edgar—'

'No, you look here, Hunter. Rolf and I are putting our lives at risk by attempting to rescue you. The very least that you can do is co-operate, you understand?'

'I will, but I am not leaving without Rosa and Sophia. I am adamant about that.'

'So I am told, and we understand that. We will get them out too. Don't worry, we have it all worked out. We have very good German identity papers for you: your photo and everything. We also have new Swiss papers for you as you can hardly re-enter as Henri Hesse – not after all the fuss you've caused.'

'But what about Rosa and Sophia?'

'We have papers for them too, but you cannot leave together as they will be looking for the three of you together. If you travel separately it will be less conspicuous. You will leave first with Rolf and take the train to Switzerland: your documentation is good enough to risk that kind of journey. We cannot risk Rosa and Sophia being stopped and questioned, so I will drive them to the border myself.'

Henry stared at Edgar, his face full of scepticism.

'Really? You are sure this will work?'

'It's the best way, Henry, believe me. Dieter is sorting out the car: we will be able to hide Sophia under the rear seat and Rosa and I will look like a married couple.'

'But how can I be sure that you will follow on?'

'I am hardly likely to stay on in Stuttgart, am I?'

'You promise me this, Edgar – on your life: that you'll bring Rosa and Sophia out with you?'

'I promise you, Henry. You can trust me. Now we need to move fast. You and Rolf must leave this afternoon. Dieter will bring the car tonight so I will follow with Rosa and Sophia in the morning. All being well, we will meet up in Zurich either tomorrow or Friday.'

Rolf accompanied Henry back to the basement, where he explained the situation to Rosa. He could tell that Henry was uneasy, he had his head in his hands and kept shaking his hands. When Rolf had explained everything, Henry turned to Rosa.

'What do you think?'

'I am not sure what you mean?'

'Should we go along with this? Do as they ask?'

'But what else can we possibly do? They are right: the three of us will never make it anywhere near the border on our own, let alone cross it. Nor can we stay here: it's only a matter of time before we'd be caught. We have to do as your friends suggest.'

There was a brief goodbye, hurried along by Rolf. A few minutes later they were back in Rolf's bedroom.

'It's a quarter to three' said Edgar. 'There is a train from Stuttgart leaving at three thirty, the last one to cross the border tonight. You and Rolf will catch it, but first you need to have a shave and a bath and get changed: you look a mess and smell like you haven't had a proper wash for days. You'd better get undressed in here while Rolf runs the bath for you.'

As soon as Henry went into the bathroom Edgar whispered urgently to Rolf. The Austrian positioned himself by the bathroom door while Edgar frantically searched Henry's clothes and case. It took him five minutes before he found what he was looking for. He then meticulously replaced everything as he had found it and beckoned Rolf over. Through the bathroom door they could hear the sound of splashing. Edgar was holding three sheets of brown paper with German type on them.

'The Rostock Report!' he announced, waving it triumphantly at Rolf.

'Are you sure?' Rolf was close to Edgar, the pair whispering to each other.

'Of course I'm sure: I saw it in London,' replied Edgar.

'Where was it?'

Edgar was holding a pair of thick, dark trousers. 'Inside the lining, look – that's why I made him get undressed in here, so that I could check his clothes.'

'But how come you knew he had it? He told us he'd burnt it.'

'Keep your voice down, Rolf. When I was talking with Basil the other day I told him how one could very easily underestimate Henry. I simply did not believe what he told us and my instinct was correct. He may have embarked on this mad mission to rescue Rosa and Sophia but, despite everything, he can't risk upsetting his Soviet masters by not delivering this report back to them. All the more reason to get him back to Zurich as soon as possible.'

Through the bathroom door the sloshing noise of Henry getting out of the bath.

'Are you going to be long?' Edgar asked, as he carefully replaced the envelope.

'Five minutes, no more I promise'.

'And what do I do with him when we get to Zurich?' Rolf whispered.

'Check him into a hotel, one of the smaller ones around the station. Tell him to stay there while you make contact with Basil. Then leave him, make sure he thinks he is on his own for a while. Have one your boys keep a watch, but it is vital that he is left alone for a while.'

'Not long now – mind if I use both towels?'

Edgar assured him he could use as many towels as he wished.

Chapter 27

From the window of his room Edgar had watched Rolf and Henry as they left the hotel, both seemingly relaxed and chatting away. They gave the appearance of amicable colleagues: a small group of men in the black uniform of the Waffen SS walked towards them, but there was no hesitation in the step of either Rolf or Henry, and the SS men politely parted to allow the two men to walk on through. Edgar continued to watch as the pair walked down Friedrichstrasse towards the station, eventually disappearing as dots into the distance.

He would have to remain in the hotel that evening. Rolf – Ludwig Kühn – had explained to the receptionist that he had been called back to Landshut. 'So inconvenient, I am so sorry. I insist on paying for my room.'

Edgar had been discreetly watching this as he scanned a nearby notice board. The receptionist had insisted this was not necessary – 'These things happen, Herr Kühn' – but Edgar knew that if two guests checked out within hours of their arrival it could arouse suspicion. In any event, he needed to see Milo. He would stay the night and slip away in the morning: ahead of the hounds, with any luck.

Edgar ate early in the hotel's ornate but largely deserted dining room and retired to his room. He would wait until Milo came on duty at eleven o'clock.

–

Because he had been in his room on the second floor since eight o'clock Edgar was unaware of what was happening below him.

The police had turned up at nine: the manager was asked to gather all the staff together in an office. They wanted to know if a family of three – a man and woman in their mid to late thirties and a girl, perhaps four or five years old – had been staying at the hotel. Unfortunately, the police told them, they had no photographs but they had names and descriptions.

'Please think *carefully*. Remember they may have used different names. The man is Swiss; the woman and child are Jews. It is possible that they may have split up.'

They passed around the sheets with the names and descriptions on them. No one recognised them. But at the back of the room was the young night porter, who had just come on duty. He stared at the sheet; gripping it tight in the hope that no one would notice his hands shaking. He looked up and around the room then back again at the sheet of paper, hoping he had misread the name on it the first time he had looked at it. It was still there: 'Henri Hesse, Switzerland.' And then the description: unmistakably that of the man who had turned up the week before asking to see Katharina Hoch.

Even though he had said nothing about it at the time, the night porter had thought there was something odd about the situation. When Fraulein Hoch had taken the man to an office well away from reception he had checked the register. There was no one staying at the hotel called Hesse. It was not his place to say anything to Fraulein Hoch and he had thought no more of it, until now.

'You are all certain then that you have not come across these people – these criminals?' The police officer in charge looked as if he were in a hurry. 'We need to move on, you are not the only hotel in Stuttgart, you know. Look once more, but remember: withholding information from the authorities is a serious crime.'

At the end of the month he was leaving the hotel, the time had come for him to join the army. What had his father told him even the before the war started? 'Keep your head down. Don't get involved. Don't express an opinion, never volunteer and do as you're told.'

That was his instinct, to keep his head down and say nothing. But then what would happen if they caught this man and they found out that he had spoken to him that night and he had failed to mention it? *A serious crime.*

The police decided they were going to get no help from the staff at the Victoria and told the staff to go back to work. One of the officers brushed past him as he left the room.

'Please could I have a word with you, sir?'

'Is it in connection with this matter?'

'I think it may be, yes.'

The officer called one of his colleagues over and the two policemen shepherded the night porter to a quiet corner. '*Tell us.*'

'I am not sure how relevant this is, sir, but a week ago I was on duty at reception. Sometime after midnight a gentleman appeared at reception and asked if Katharina Hoch was on duty.'

'Who is she?'

'She is the night manager.'

'He said his name was Hesse, from Switzerland. I asked him which room he was staying in but before he had a chance to tell me, Fraulein Hoch appeared from her office behind me and greeted the man, who she appeared to know. She then took him down a private corridor to an office well away from reception.'

'Which day was this?'

'Wednesday, so really it was in the early hours of Thursday morning.'

'You have seen the description of the man – Hesse – does it match that of the man you saw?'

'It does, sir, very much so.'

'And what happened after that?'

'He must have been with Fraulein Hoch for a while – I didn't see him again.'

'And is he still staying here?'

'Well, that's the odd thing, sir. I checked his name on the hotel register and there was no record of him staying here that night.'

The officer signalled to the other policemen with him to wait. He spoke kindly to the young night porter, who looked terrified. 'We're not the Gestapo, you know!'

'And Fraulein Hoch – when is she next on duty?'

The young night porter glanced at his watch, the one his grandparents had bought him for his last birthday. 'In just over an hour, sir – at eleven o'clock.'

–

Edgar spent the evening in his room, alternating between resting on the bed and almost relaxing to getting up and pacing around the room, peeking out into the street through the thick curtains or pausing by the door in case anyone may be approaching.

He became aware of a lot of activity below his window, cars pulling up and people entering the hotel and a fair amount of talking. It was, he decided, what one might expect from a busy city centre hotel and in any case, he was not minded to look out of the window and draw attention to himself. He would wait in his room until Milo came up, as she had promised. He waited patiently, even when eleven thirty had gone, with midnight soon after. *Who knows how busy she may be? Another half hour.*

There was no sign of her by half past midnight, when he allowed himself to open his door as quietly as possible and glance up and down the corridor. It was empty and there was no note on the floor. An hour late was worrying, there was no denying that. Edgar stood with his back to the door, surveying the room. He tried to imagine how it would look to someone coming in to question him. It looked ordinary enough but he was more concerned about his false identity. The papers for Karl Albrecht from Hanover were good enough, but he was not sure how long he could sustain his story if anyone suspected him.

By one o'clock he decided to go down to reception. He would ask if they had any aspirin for a headache. *For some reason I was unable to get through on the telephone!*

He took the main stairs down to the reception. He opened the glass doors onto the landing before the final flight of stairs swept down to the entrance lobby, only to be pushed aside by a uniformed policeman running past him.

Edgar paused and then edged slowly towards the staircase, just able to see into the lobby while still hidden in the shadows of the landing. The area was crowded with police and Gestapo, and in the middle of them was a young woman. She towered above a man in an ill-fitting suit was standing in front of her.

'Fraulein Hoch, you have spent two hours refusing to give a satisfactory explanation as to why this Herr Hesse came to see you.'

'Look, I keep telling you, why do you not believe me?' She sounded annoyed – exactly as Edgar would expect her to do in such circumstances. *Don't come across as defensive: the more aggressive you are the more they may believe you.* 'Look, I keep telling you, I know nothing about him. He was a guest who had stayed here last year. He asked to see me because he said he was staying at the Marquardt on Schlossplatz and wanted to see if he could transfer here, but he did not want to make a fuss about it.'

'At midnight?' The short man in the ill-fitting suit looked confused, unsure whether to believe her. Edgar took a step back into the shadows. He could now hardly see what was going on, but he could still hear clearly.

'Very well,' said the man. 'Remain in your office Fraulein Hoch. Oberg, seal the hotel; make sure there are guards on every floor. No one comes in or out. First thing in the morning we shall thoroughly search this place.'

–

Edgar crept back to his room on the second floor. They clearly knew that Hunter had been at the hotel, but he had no idea how they knew. Had he and Rolf been arrested before they reached the border? If that was the case then it was possible that Hunter would not only have told them about being in the Hotel Victoria in Stuttgart but would also have said something about him – but then if that was the case, they would be looking for him now and rather than waiting for the morning.

Edgar went into the bathroom, undressed and washed his face in cold water. Speculating on what may have happened merely served to stop him thinking about more important matters like what to do now. He changed into his pyjamas and pulled back the sheets and blankets on the bed – if they did come to his room it must look as if he had been asleep.

There was no question now of his going down to the basement, even to warn Rosa. What would be the point? Unless Rosa had heard the commotion and decided to escape they would be found in the morning.

Edgar dozed off in a series of fifteen, twenty minute spells during the night. Each time he woke up he lay still in bed, listening for any hint of a sound. Then he would roll slowly out of the bed and crawl along the floor to the door. By lying flat he was able to look through the inch high gap at the bottom, but not once could he see anyone near his room.

At six o'clock he decided he could not risk dozing off again. Seven o'clock, he decided, was the earliest he could risk leaving the hotel without it looking too early. He checked his small case. There was nothing in it to give him away, apart from his Swiss papers and they were so skilfully concealed in the lining that they would pass any routine search.

At seven o'clock he did a final check of the room, emptied all of his pockets, looked over his papers for what felt like the one hundredth time and left the room.

The lobby was beginning to fill with police and Gestapo: it was obvious that the search had begun. All around was the sound of doors slamming and boots moving heavily across corridors and rooms.

'Can I help you, sir?' It was a manager, his face pale and drawn, his fingers nervously intertwining with each other. Next to him was another man, his arms folded, looking Edgar up and down.

'Yes,' said Edgar, placing his room key on the desk in front of the manager. 'I wish to check out, please. If I may settle my account?'

'Most certainly, sir,' said the manager, scanning the hotel register. 'Your name, please?'

'Karl Albrecht.'

'From Hanover, I see.'

'Are you returning to Hanover now?' It was the other man. As he spoke he stepped forward, holding out his Gestapo identity badge. 'Your papers, please.'

Edgar handed over the papers for Karl Albrecht. The Gestapo man looked at them carefully. 'Please can you confirm your address?' Edgar confirmed it, hoping that he was not overplaying his Hanoverian accent. The other man looked over to the register, which the manager was still holding. 'Just a short visit then?'

'Indeed. Thankfully my business here went well.' *He is now going to ask me about this business.* Edgar glanced at his watch. 'Are you in a hurry, Herr Albrecht?'

'Well, there is a train to Frankfurt at seven thirty which I would like to catch if at all possible; it has a good connection to Hanover.'

'Indeed. Come over here and I will examine and search your case.'

Edgar moved over to a table by the side of the reception desk. As he placed his case on the table there was a noise to his right, beyond the reception desk. It was just a shout at first, followed by the commotion of people running and then more shouting.

'Quick, we've found them!' It was a policeman, running past reception. The Gestapo man who was about to search Edgar looked up and around, clearly eager to join in. He ruffled through Edgar's suitcase, looking up for most of the time in the direction that the noise was coming from.

'Empty your pockets, quickly.' Edgar placed the contents of his pockets on the table. The man shuffled them around, finding it hard to disguise his haste. The noise was getting closer now. Edgar turned round, in time to see a woman and young girl being manhandled across the reception area; they were both blinking and look terrified. *Rosa and Sophia.* The policemen and Gestapo who had found them brought them to a halt in front of the reception. They were just yards from Edgar. He turned round and looked at the Gestapo man.

'Am I able to leave now?'

The other man was already moving from around the table. 'Yes, yes. Go.'

The senior officer and the short man in the ill-fitting suit moved over to Rosa and her daughter.

'We found them hiding in a room at the back of the basement, sir.'

'What about the man?'

'It was just them, sir.'

'You are certain?'

'Yes, but we are continuing to search the basement.'

'We must search every inch of this wretched hotel. What is your name?'

Rosa clutched Sophia, but a man dragged the child away. As he did so a toy rabbit the little girl had been holding fell to the floor. A policeman kicked it out of the way.

'Dagmar Keufer, from Frankfurt. I have papers. This is my daughter, Gisela.'

The Gestapo officer held his hand out for the papers. He looked them over and snorted, passing them to a colleague.

'A joke! Not even good forgeries – the photographs look nothing like you! You, little girl. What is your name, come on?'

He had bent down in front of Sophia, his hands resting on his knees. Sophia's eyes were wide with fear as she tried to look at her mother.

'Go on, your name!'

'I don't know.' Tears were streaming down her face.

'You don't know! What girl does not know her own name, eh? It's Sophia, isn't it? Sophia Stern?'

'Yes,' she said, almost sounding relieved. Edgar took his time in picking up everything he had removed from his pockets and putting them back. They were still searching for Henry: he must have got away after all.

'So,' said the Gestapo man, standing directly in front of Rosa. As he shouted, his spit covered her face. 'If this is Sophia Stern, you must be Rosa Stern. I am pleased to meet you.' Rosa said nothing.

'Where is the Swiss man?'

'I don't know.'

'He was here with you?'

She nodded. 'Yes, but he left.'

'When?'

'Yesterday.'

347

'Where did he go.'

'I don't know.'

'Was he on his own?'

There was a long pause before Rosa replied.

'Yes.'

The Gestapo officer hit Rosa so hard that Edgar could clearly hear the crack of bone. *Leave now, go* a policeman was indicating. *Go. None of your business.*

'I am not going to tell you anything!' Rosa's voice was defiant, even confident.

'I think you may now!' Edgar straightened his coat and had moved towards the door. He turned round to see the Gestapo man holding a revolver against Sophia's head, the barrel buried in the girl's thick hair. An officer stepped back and another one held out a hand, as if to restrain the man with the gun.

'You tell me exactly where he is and who is helping you!'

'But I don't know!' Rosa sounded panicked, no longer defiant.

Because he was holding the revolver directly against Sophia's head, neither the sound of the gun nor its echo was nearly as loud as Edgar would have expected, especially in a relatively confined space. Then there was the silence that one would expect, partly caused by the noise of the shot and partly by the shock. Edgar stepped closer to the hotel exit, not certain he could avoid being sick. He noticed a horrified look on the face of a policeman and broad grins on the faces of others. And then the scream came. It was restrained at first, like someone calling from a distance. By the time Edgar reached the hotel entrance it had turned into a wail, so loud that people in the street stopped to see what it was.

By now he had turned into Friedrichstrasse, pausing to compose himself before attempting to quicken his stride as he walked towards the station. With every step that took him away from the hotel, the scream became louder. He turned into a small alley, crouched behind a large dustbin and threw up. The noise drowned out the scream, but for no more than a second or two. He waited a minute and then hurried to the station.

During the short walk, something died inside Edgar. He felt tears welling in his eyes and his pulled his hat down low to hide them. He had never experienced anything quite as dreadful as this and was quite unprepared for the impact it was having on him. He continued to hear the scream long after he entered the station, the noise of the trains failing to muffle it. The scream was still ringing in his ears as he asked the clerk for a ticket; he heard it above the sound of the train that took him south.

It was the last sound he heard as he slipped out of Germany that night and the first sound he heard as he entered Switzerland.

Chapter 28

Zurich, April 1941

Edgar arrived back in Zurich on the morning of Friday, 4th April. He had started out from Stuttgart the previous morning well aware of how perilous the journey could be, but throughout it he was accompanied a sense of almost surreal detachment, brought about by the shock of what he had seen at the hotel and the consequences of his own failure to do anything.

He had been forced to deceive Henry: he knew that promising him that to help Rosa and Sophia escape was the only way of ensuring he would leave the hotel with Rolf. Trying to bring Rosa and Sophia with him back to Switzerland was always a risk he could simply not contemplate; they would never have stood a chance. Even going into the basement to warn them would have been too great a risk to consider.

But the sight of little Sophia being shot in cold blood had utterly overwhelmed him. For a few hours, his defences were down and his normally pin-sharp judgement was blunted. When he looked back on that day in the months – and indeed years – that followed he realised that for much of it he hardly cared what happened to him. It was not just Sophia: he did not want to contemplate what fate awaited Rosa, and he imagined that Milo and, no doubt her brother, would be unlikely to survive. For all he knew, poor Rolf and Henry may even have been caught after all. It had been an utter disaster and what would bother London most was that the Russians would not get to see to the Rostock Report. For a few hours that day, it did not bother him at all.

Edgar's trance-like state continued as he broke all the rules by not taking the first train out of Stuttgart. Instead, after buying his ticket he sat in a corner of the draughty station buffet, sipping at an ersatz coffee he had allowed to get cold and nibbling a sausage. By half past eight, a sense of reality slowly began to return to him as the initial shock thawed and he began to think more clearly. Rolf and Henry would have tried to cross the border after Singen and he decided to try a different route, just in case. He chose to wait for a train that would give him other options and caught one heading south at half past nine. The train was crowded, with a large number of soldiers on board. About ten minutes out of Stuttgart a woman brushed past him as she pushed her way down the carriage. Even from behind there was something familiar about her and as she turned to open the door at the other end of the carriage Edgar caught a glimpse of her face. Had he not thought that at that moment she was in the hands of the Gestapo then he would have sworn it was Katarina Hoch.

He did not spot the woman again and left the train at Tuttlingen. It was a quarter to twelve and according to the timetable on the wall of the deserted forecourt there was a train to Waldshut-Tiengen leaving at twenty past two. Waldshut-Tiengen sat on northern bank of the Rhine, with Switzerland on the other side: it would be safer place to cross the border.

The ticket office was closed, so Edgar walked into the town and ten minutes from the station he came across an inn. The innkeeper was leaning against the bar, seemingly intent on avoiding serving anyone. Edgar had to position himself directly in front of the man and cough loudly to attract his attention. When the man did deign to look at his new customer it was with a pair of eyes that never stopped blinking.

'Yes?'

'I'm looking for a room please, just for a couple of hours.'

The eyes blinked even faster and then narrowed. 'A couple of hours? What kind of a place do you think we are?'

'I am sorry, there is a misunderstanding. I have been travelling for a long while and I am just looking for somewhere to have a bath and change my clothes before I return home to Geneva. I am catching a train in a couple of hours.'

The innkeeper leaned closer to Edgar. 'But the journey from here to Switzerland will take you just two hours.'

'I realise that, but then I have to travel on to Montreux, which means I will arrive home late. Look, I am happy to pay the full daily rate for the room if that helps.'

Edgar peeled a generous amount of Reich marks from his wallet and slipped them into the innkeeper's hand, whose eyes lit up and stopped blinking for a moment. He smiled briefly, allowing a glimpse of a mouthful of dirty yellow teeth.

'No problem, sir, use room four. Here's the key. Can I send some food up?'

Edgar said that would not be necessary, he would eat later. Once in the room he locked the door, jammed a chair against it and placed his small suitcase on the bed. It took him ten minutes to carefully unthread the lining just far enough to extract his Swiss papers. He was now Marc Rassier from Montreux. What remained of Karl Albrecht was torn up into little pieces and then burnt in an ashtray, the ashes flushed down the toilet. Once he had washed and changed, Edgar went back to the bar and ordered lunch, leaving the inn as soon as he felt it was reasonable to do so.

The two twenty train arrived on time to take Marc Rassier to Waldshut-Tiengen, arriving at the station in the north of the town at half past four. An elderly policeman checked his Swiss papers as he left the station.

'Are you taking the bus across the border?'

He had saved him from asking the question. 'Yes. When does it leave?'

'An hour: you need to register for it though. They have to check everyone who gets on. Wait over there – those ladies are going on it too?'

Edgar waited with two Swiss German women, who were thankfully as reserved as he would expected them to be, especially when they realised he was French speaking. At five thirty, a noisy blue bus pulled in front of the station, by which time another four people were in the waiting area. A police car pulled up and a young officer, wearing a smart raincoat and leather gloves checked everyone's paperwork.

'What has been the purpose of your visit to Germany, Herr Rassier? I need to know where you have visited in the Reich.'

Edgar affected broken German. 'I am sorry, my German is poor. Do you speak French perhaps?'

He didn't. One of the Swiss German ladies explained to the officer that this was typical. 'They make no effort. They expect us to speak French but you never hear them speak German!'

She spoke to Edgar in slow French. 'He wants to know where you have been in Germany.'

Edgar launched into a lengthy travelogue, covering as much of Germany as he could manage and speaking quickly. The Swiss German lady clearly did not understand too much of what he said.

'I am not terribly sure, sir,' she told the police officer. 'They speak so fast. He seems to have been in Munich and elsewhere in Bavaria, as far as I can gather. He says he has many documents if you want to check them.'

Behind them the queue had lengthened. The officer checked the papers for Marc Rassier again. 'And you entered Germany where?'

Edgar managed to look irritated and took back his passport. 'Look, it says here – Munich; by train, one week ago.'

'I see. You may board the coach now.'

It was approaching six o'clock when the bus pulled away from the station, driving slowly through the town and over the bridge crossing the Rhine. Once they were on the Swiss side they pulled alongside a narrow building, where their papers were checked by the Swiss police. Half an hour later the bus had arrived in Baden. It was seven o'clock and he was back in Switzerland, but felt little sense of elation.

'What time is the next bus to Zurich?' he asked the driver.

'A quarter past seven.'

'And do I catch it from here?'

'Yes.' The driver had turned off the engine and was locking up the bus, anxious to leave.

Edgar put his suitcase down and settled down on the bench inside the small bus shelter. The bus driver set off, turning round after he had walked past Edgar.

'I wouldn't make yourself too comfortable. It leaves at quarter past seven in the morning.'

–

It was half past eight on the Friday morning when Edgar walked slowly across Basteiplatz to the small apartment above the hardware shop. He knew that Basil Remington-Barber would be waiting there. He had thought about telephoning him from Baden the previous night or when he arrived in Zurich, but he decided against it. His few hours' sleep in the small inn in Baden had cleared his mind and now the enormity of what had happened was hitting him hard. He needed time to consider quite how to explain this disaster to London. A 'debacle', they would call it, these people whose only experience of danger was dodging the traffic around Trafalgar Square on the way to their clubs. He would probably end up in Wales looking after munitions, if he was lucky.

Remington-Barber answered the door, looking as if he had seen a ghost. If he had, Edgar was the first because in the lounge Rolf and Henry were sitting around the table. It was a while before anyone said anything.

'Well, this is quite some reunion,' said Remington-Barber finally, sounding quite jolly.

'When did you two arrive?' Edgar asked.

'Yesterday,' said Rolf, who had now come over to Edgar and was shaking his warmly by the hand. Henry was now half-standing, half-sitting, saying nothing and peering beyond Edgar, looking to see if anyone was behind him.

'Plain sailing?' asked Edgar, as he removed his hat and coat and dropped them on to the armchair.

'Surprisingly so,' said Rolf. 'When we arrived at the station in Stuttgart I saw that the train to Singen was delayed until four o'clock, but there was one to Ulm leaving almost immediately. When we arrived there we found there was another training leaving soon for Friedrichshafen. We booked into a hotel overlooking the lake and yesterday morning we took a bus to Konstanz. We crossed the border there using our Swiss passports and then took a train to Zurich.'

'Where are they, Edgar?' Henry had stood up now and walked past Edgar into the small hallway. He opened the door of the apartment, came back in and walked over to the window overlooking Basteiplatz.

'You promised me you'd bring Rosa and Sophia with you. Where the hell are they?' His voice had an urgent tone to it, louder and more broken than usual.

Edgar signalled to Rolf to stand by the door. 'Sit down, Henry.' He led him over to the sofa and sat him down and placed himself in the armchair.

'I am afraid they are not here. I am sorry.'

'Where are they?'

Edgar hesitated: he had rehearsed various versions of what to say in answer to this inevitable question and he was quickly deciding which one to use.

'I am sorry, Henry, I really am… but they were arrested before I had a chance to get them out of the hotel. I—'

'Arrested by whom?' Henry had stood up from the sofa and only sat down again when Remington-Barber guided him down with a firm hand on his shoulder.

'Don't shout and please do sit down. I promise you this is something I regret just as much as you do, but it was the Gestapo, I am sorry to say. They must have come to the hotel late on the Wednesday night. I am not sure what happened, but because Milo had not made any contact with me I decided to go down and find her at around one in the morning. As I went down I spotted that she was being questioned in the reception area and I heard them say that they were going to search the hotel in the morning. There were police everywhere. I went back to my room and remained there until seven in the morning. If there was any way I could have gone down to the basement I would have done, but every time I looked out of the door there police patrolling the corridor. When I went down to check out I saw Rosa and Sophia being led away.'

'And you didn't try and warn them or anything?'

Henry was shouting so loudly now that Rolf quickly shut the windows and Basil Remington-Barber closed the lounge door.

'I told you, Henry, I just didn't get a chance, I promise you. The Gestapo were over the place. I was worried if I went down into the basement then I could be caught and that would alert the bastards to search down there. I...'

Henry had begun to cry. It started as a gentle sobbing but within a minute had turned into uncontrollable weeping, with tears streaking down his cheeks. Remington-Barber stood awkwardly in front of him holding out a handkerchief, while Rolf sat next to Henry and placed an arm round his shoulder, but nothing would console him. He was grief-stricken and everyone in the room knew there was nothing to be said that could be in any way reassuring.

Henry did nothing other than weep for five minutes. By now, Remington-Barber had taken Edgar's place in the armchair. He held a glass of water and in his open hand were two large white tablets.

'Take these, old chap. They'll help you rest and when you wake up it will be with a clearer head.' Henry looked at the tablets and took them one at a time. Within five minutes he was stretched out on the sofa, fast asleep. They waited another five minutes and then carried him into the bedroom, which Rolf locked from the outside.

'He'll not wake up for most of the day.'

'Well, before he does, we need to check something,' said Edgar.

They emptied all of Henry's possessions on the floor and searched them carefully, paying particular attention to the pair of thick, dark trousers they had last seen in the hotel room in Stuttgart. The envelope they had found there was missing. It was nowhere to be found. As far as the Russians were concerned, he would have served his purpose.

'Well, that's a relief,' said Edgar. 'only told him half of it, you know, Basil?'

'Well, whatever you do, better not to tell him the other half,' said Rolf. 'In the hotel in Friedrichshafen last night we got talking: I was telling him about Frieda, my fiancée in Vienna – about not having any idea of what has happened to her and all that. Henry opened up a bit: I can tell you he was absolutely set on rescuing Rosa and the child. He regarded it as his mission, the most important thing in his life. I don't think love or romance comes into it, he kept going on about how if he saved Rosa then he could save himself. He said something about saving her was a way of making up for something terrible he'd done in the past. I asked him to tell me more, but he said it was too terrible to talk about it. It tortured him to even think about it, he said. He said that he hoped that, once we'd rescued Rosa and her daughter, he would find some sort of peace. He clammed up after that.'

'Were they killed?'

'The little girl was, Basil. Shot in cold blood, just yards from me. God knows what they have done to Rosa. In the…'

'Are you all right, Edgar? You seem a bit choked up yourself. Would you like a couple of these pills?'

Edgar had moved over to the table, his back to Remington-Barber and Rolf. For a while he said nothing. When he did, it was in an unusually quiet and faltering voice.

'Better not, we need to talk. I'll help myself to this Scotch, if you don't mind, Basil. Rolf, you tell me what happened when you got back here. That's the most important thing right now.'

Rolf and Remington-Barber joined Edgar at the table, both sitting opposite him.

'I did exactly as you said, Edgar. As soon as we arrived in Zurich I booked us into a small hotel on Löwenstrasse. Once we were in the room I told Henry to wait while I went back down the reception and from there I was able to call Basil and he alerted my watchers. I stayed in the room with Henry for an hour, by which time I reckoned my men would be in position, so I told him I was going out for a couple of hours to find out where Basil was and to see when it would be safe for us to come here. I said he could go for a walk if he fancied, but not to go far and certainly be there when I got back. I walked off down Löwenstrasse. My watchers say that he left the hotel five minutes later and went into a bar across the road to use the phone. He stayed in the bar for about fifteen minutes and was doing his best to see if he was being watched. Then he left the bar and walked up to the station. He met up with Viktor by one of the suburban platforms and my watchers say that they are sure they saw Henry hand an envelope over to him. They spoke for about five minutes and then Henry made his way back to the hotel. When I got back I told him I had made contact with Basil and that we were to come here and wait for you – and here we are.'

Edgar leaned over and patted the Austrian on the arm. 'Well done, Rolf, well done. Maybe London will not see this as quite the total disaster that I feared they might.'

'I suppose that means that everything has worked out rather well in the end, eh Edgar? Rather against the odds I must say, but the going turned out to be in our favour. I have lost my cell in Stuttgart, which is a damn shame, but then they did last somewhat longer than I thought they would.'

'Can't you see that we still have a serious problem, Basil?'

'Not sure I'm with you, Edgar. Tragic about the little girl and one would not rate the chances of her mother or Milo and her brother very highly, but surely in terms of our—'

'Think Basil: think. Henry. Henry is the problem.'

'But he handed the document over to the Russians and—'

'Indeed, but consider this Basil: the Germans were clearly after a "Henri Hesse" from Switzerland. They knew he was the man who had taken Rosa and Sophia from Berlin, and who had turned up at the hotel in Stuttgart and somehow escaped from it. Rest assured that they would have informed the Swiss, who will take a very dim view of this indeed. The last thing they want is one of their citizens using Switzerland as a base from which to cause trouble for the Germans: they are not keen on biting the hand that feeds them, are they?'

'No.'

'Henry entered Switzerland yesterday on false papers, which buys us some time – but that is not a long-term solution. Either he stays hidden for the rest of the war, which to me is not feasible, or he returns to Geneva under his proper identity.'

'I see, Edgar… and get arrested by the Swiss, no doubt.'

'No doubt indeed, Basil. Just think then of the implications for all our work here if he starts to spill the beans. The Swiss will know what we're up to, so will the Germans and quite possibly the Soviets too, undoing all the good work.'

'*If* he starts to spill the beans, surely.'

Edgar stood up, brushed himself down and loosened his tie.

'I fear that we are not going to be able to take that risk Basil.'

They left Zurich in the middle of the afternoon of Monday seventh of April. Rolf had borrowed a Citroen TUB van from another of his apparently endless stream of contacts and he was driving, with Edgar and Basil Remington-Barber next to him in the front. They headed south out of Zurich and then through Luzern, Sarnen and the valleys of Unterwalden.

They drove slowly: they were in no hurry, had no desire to draw attention to themselves and in any case the van made worrying noises when it felt it was being pushed too hard – 'rather like a woman' Basil had said, but none of them were in much of a mood for humour.

It was only seven o'clock when they arrived in Brienz and despite everything, it was still too early. They would need to buy some time. They found a small inn with enough space for them to park the van at the back, in the shadows and hopefully away from anyone else. They took it in turns to go into the inn, one by one. Although none of them would admit as much, no one fancied being left in the van on their own.

Edgar and Remington-Barber were in the van together at around eight o'clock. The older man attempted to break the silence.

'Rum business this, Edgar.'

The silence continued, although Edgar did nod his head. *Rum business, no question of that. A messy one too.*

'Lord knows what will happen if we are stopped.'

'I told you, Basil. You are a British diplomat: you have your papers. You are on Embassy business. They cannot touch you or the van. Please stop worrying.'

'But if… if… anything goes wrong, all hell will break loose. Heavens know what London will have to say.'

'Basil,' Edgar had turned round to face the other man, 'whatever happens will be more acceptable than the alternative. And in any case, nothing is going to go wrong. Pull yourself together.'

They left Brienz at half past eight, when it felt like it was getting properly dark and drove along the north shore of the lake, stopping in a side street in Interlaken for another hour for it to get even darker and ensure there was no chance they had been followed.

It was ten o'clock when they pulled out of Interlaken, driving along the track across the north shore of Lake Thun. It was only a few days past the new moon and that, along with the thick banks of trees on either side of the track, ensured they were now driving in near total darkness. Rolf brought the speed of the van down to just ten miles an hour, the headlamps fighting hard to pick much out in front of them. Shortly after they had passed a sign for Steinbruch they spotted a clearing to their left and Edgar told Rolf to pull in.

'Wait here.'

Edgar checked his torch and revolver and disappeared into the trees. He was only gone for five minutes.

'This will do. The lake is just through the trees and there is a decent slope which will help us. Rolf, reverse as far as you can into the trees and then we can take the dinghy down first.'

Once they had placed the dinghy by the shore they walked back to the van.

'How far out will we need to go?' asked Remington-Barber.

'Thun is supposed to be one of the deepest lakes in Switzerland: five minutes rowing should get us as far out as we need to.'

They struggled from the moment they hauled it out of the back of the van, the three of them manhandling and dragging it through the trees. They paused twice for Basil Remington-Barber to throw up and once they reached the dinghy they had to return to the van for the ropes and the weights. By the time they pushed the dinghy into the seemingly solid lake it was half past eleven and the world was completely silent. Edgar and Rolf rowed, in the end for ten minutes until they felt they were far enough out.

'You do your best to hold the boat steady, Basil: Rolf and I will do the rest.'

'Shouldn't we… I don't know… say something?'

'Like what, Basil?'

'A prayer perhaps? Seems like the decent thing to do.'

'If you must, Basil. Be quick though.'

Basil Remington-Barber muttered his way through Psalm Twenty Three – pausing after the words 'still waters' and struggling with the walk 'through the valley of the shadow of death' – sounding decidedly tearful by the end.

And then the deed was done. It took them less than five minutes to row back to the shore and once they reached the town of Thun they were less than an hour from Bern. No one in the van said a word until they saw the lights of the city ahead of them.

'I didn't know you were the religious type, Basil.'

'I'm not, Edgar. Church every so often and all that, but nothing serious. Why do you mention it?'

'Knowing the whole of that psalm, off by heart.'

An ironic laugh. 'Forced to learn it at prep school. The chaplain would beat the living daylights out of you if you got one word wrong. Never imagined I'd have cause to use it, not like that at any rate. I was thinking while I was reciting it, you know. That reference to the "presence of mine enemies" – who would you say his enemies were?'

It was a long while before Edgar replied, so much so that it seemed at first that he may have ignored the question.

'Everyone, Basil. Everyone was his enemy. That, I am afraid, is a consequence of serving more than one master.'

–

It had taken two days for Henry Hunter, who body they had consigned to the depths of Lake Thun, to die.

Once Edgar had persuaded Basil Remington-Barber that they had no alternative, they came up with a plan. They woke Hunter up at two o'clock in the afternoon, when he was still drowsy, and made him drink some water, into which they had dissolved seven of the tablets. They were convinced that he would not wake up, but one of them still remained in the room with him all the time. Although his breathing became more shallow and at times he appeared to be on the verge of slipping away, he held on through the Saturday and by the Sunday morning his breathing sounded stronger. They crushed a dozen tablets into a saucer and turned it into a paste with a bit of water which they spooned in his mouth, but struggled to get much of it down him.

But Henry hung on. By the Sunday evening they were convinced that they needed to do something else. Remington-Barber was in a terrible state, red-eyed, shaking and pacing around the apartment. He had convinced himself that something was bound to go wrong and they would all be arrested, creating a diplomatic incident in the process. Rolf suggested he went out for a walk. Edgar and Rolf stood at the window watching him cross Basteiplatz and then nodded to each other. *We need to get on with it.*

Edgar removed his jacket and rolled up his sleeves and the two men entered the bedroom. Henry was now he was stirring, tossing and turning and making noises as if he were trying to speak. As Edgar approached him, Henry half opened his eyes and his mouth moved.

'Come on, Rolf, quick.'

'He's trying to say something, Edgar.'

'Exactly. Let's get on with it.'

There was an indistinct sound coming out of his mouth now, although just before Edgar put the pillow over his face and Rolf held him down, there was one word they could both clearly hear. *Rosa.*

There was a very brief and one-sided struggle, but they both agreed afterwards that it was probably painless. *He would have been too drugged up to have an idea of what was going on*, they assured each other.

'He couldn't have known a thing,' said Rolf.

Edgar was straightening his sleeves as he turned to reply to the Austrian.

'He knew too much'.

Epilogue

Rosa Stern was taken to the Gestapo headquarters in old Hotel Silber building on Dorotheenstrasse, just south of the Schlossplatz and not very far at all from the Hotel Victoria. She was in such a state of shock that she did not utter a word. She sat very still in her cell, staring at the wall, her hands crossed neatly on her lap and her mouth slightly open, occasionally breaking into the slightest of smiles. A psychiatrist brought in by the Gestapo assured them that she was not putting anything on. It was, he told them, one of the most extreme cases of catatonia he had ever seen. *Could she, by any chance, have been subjected to a serious trauma recently?*

'So she's gone mad then?' the Gestapo officer asked.

'You could put it like that: I find that it is much more common these days.'

They tried for a fortnight, convinced that when she did speak she would have plenty to reveal. Who was helping her in Berlin? Where had Hesse gone?

But Rosa said nothing, sitting quietly, occasionally swaying very slowly as if listening to a piece of soothing music and once in a while mouthing something silent to the wall. In the end, a Gestapo officer stormed into her cell and held his revolver in front of her, but there was still no reaction whatsoever. When he hit her hard around the face she didn't make a noise and stayed in the same position as she had landed on the floor. When he knelt beside her and released the safety catch she did not blink. He shot her four times, only stopping when his gun jammed.

-

Rosa Stern's first husband, Gunter Reinhart, managed to avoid suspicion. He was questioned on two occasions during that April, but was able to persuade the Gestapo that the man, Hesse, was a mere courier from one of the many Swiss banks he dealt with and his contact with him was confined to the handing over of documents.

'I wish I could help, but I really remember little about him... he was such an inconsequential little man.'

Reinhart assured the Gestapo that he had not had any contact with his first wife since their divorce in 1935 and that it had been many years since he had seen his son. The last he had heard, Alfred was in France. The Gestapo officer assured him that this was one of a number of unresolved aspects of this case.

–

Franz Hermann also managed to avoid coming under suspicion. Because he knew that the woman who lived opposite had already contacted the police, he decided to risk taking matters into his own hands. With his mother safely at his sister's in Brandenburg he went to his local police station in Dahlem and reported that the nurse he had hired to look after her had disappeared.

'She mentioned something about her husband being killed and having to return to Bremerhaven, but now I am not sure... and a very helpful neighbour told me that she saw the nurse leave the house with a man and a young girl and drive off in an Opel. I hope that I am not wasting your time, but I am becoming very suspicious...'

The Gestapo officer in charge of investigating the whole business of Henri Hesse, Rosa and Sophia decided that he believed Franz Hermann's account – after all, had not the lawyer reported the matter himself to the police?

Franz Hermann's good fortune only lasted until July 1944 when he was one of many thousands of people arrested after the attempt on Hitler's life. Although the Gestapo never suspected him of being a British agent, there was enough circumstantial evidence to link him with the resistance to Hitler and he was sent to Sachsenhausen concentration camp, where he was murdered in November 1944.

Edgar and Basil Remington–Barber agreed that, as Marlene Hesse had been unaware of her son's intelligence activities, any contact with her would be counter-productive. She had waited until the second week of April before reporting her son missing to the police in Geneva. They could tell her nothing, but appeared to be very interested in what she could tell them Could Herr Hesse have perhaps travelled to Germany? Could she provide a list of his associates in Switzerland? She insisted she knew nothing and promised to let them know if she heard from her son.

Marlene Hesse's income disappeared along with her son. Edgar was adamant that it would be too suspicious if any money was transferred from Henry's account at Credit Suisse.

'The last thing we need. What if she tells the Swiss police and they try and track the money? They're good at that type of thing.'

Madame Ladnier was prevailed upon to close the account and ensure there was no trace of it having ever existed.

Her reduced circumstances meant that Marlene Hesse had to move to a drab bedsit in a block in between two railway lines, earning a living as a cleaner.

–

Viktor was not altogether surprised that Henry had disappeared after he handed the Rostock Report over to him at the railway station. He had long wondered when the British would discover that the man they had recruited as an agent in 1939 had been a Soviet spy for many years before that. Moscow seemed to be pleased with the Rostock Report: it reassured them that a German invasion was unlikely and Stalin used it as vindication of his conviction that reports of invasion plans were just the British being mischievous. Viktor was well aware that Henry's disappearance could cast doubt on the veracity of the report, so he decided to say nothing to Moscow. If they were pleased, why upset them?

As far as Henry was concerned, he assumed Edgar had killed him, which was what his service would have done in the same circumstances. It was a shame: he quite liked *synok* and he had been a good agent and he had lasted far longer than Viktor had expected him to. In early June he told Moscow that Henry had been recalled to London.

Viktor Krasotkin's encounters with British Intelligence resumed in early 1944 when he turned up in Vienna, where he remained there until at least the end of the war.

–

Rolf Eder continued to work for British intelligence. Edgar had been so impressed by him that when he became involved in plans for a clandestine mission inside Austria he had no hesitation in recommending Rolf. He slipped into Vienna in early 1944 and was still operating there when the Red Army liberated the city in April 1945.

–

Captain Edgar returned to London soon after Henry Hunter's death. The mission was deemed to have been a success by those who pronounced on such things, although they acknowledged it had not been without its more unfortunate aspects. Operation Barbarossa meant that Germany had committed itself to fighting on two fronts in Europe and British military chiefs were convinced this was a fatal error. Edgar was credited with having run a successful intelligence operation, helping to ensure that the Soviet Union was, at the very least, confused as to German intentions and, at best, – thanks to the Rostock Report – convinced there would be no invasion.

Author's note

The Swiss Spy is a work of fiction and, with the exception of a few obvious people referred to in passing, such as Churchill or Hitler, all the characters in the book are fictional and should not be confused with anyone in real life. Having said that, the book is based on actual historical events and in that respect I have endeavoured to be as authentic and accurate as possible.

There was indeed a high level meeting of senior German military figures in the Bavarian town of Bad Reichenhall in July 1940, where plans to invade the Soviet Union were first discussed, notwithstanding the fact that the two countries were supposedly bound by a non-aggression pact at the time. Hitler's Directive 21 referred to in the book is genuine and was released on 18th December that year and outlined plans for Operation Barbarossa, the invasion of the Soviet Union. The Rostock Report featured in the book is a work of fiction.

Operation Barbarossa began on 22nd June 1941 and Hitler expected it to have been successfully concluded within just a few months. In the event, it ended in disaster for Germany. They failed to reach Moscow by the time the Russian winter took hold, allowing the Red Army to regroup and push the Germans back. The Germans suffered a crushing defeat in the Battle of Stalingrad in February 1943 and Operation Bagration in June 1944 was the start of Germany's defeat on the eastern front.

There is a good deal of evidence to show that the Soviet Union ignored dozens of credible intelligence reports about the planned German invasion. Many of these came from their own intelligence services, including a copy of a handbook to be used by German troops in the Soviet Union which was passed on to the Soviet Embassy in

Berlin by a German Communist printer. As for the British intelligence, Stalin was convinced that these reports were disinformation, designed to provoke a war between the Soviet Union and Germany. He described them as 'English provocation'. So, although the missions at the core of *The Swiss Spy* are fictional ones, the idea of British intelligence using other sources to inform the Soviet Union would be quite in keeping with what was happening at the time.

I have done my best to ensure that details such as street names, the locations of embassies, railway stations, airports and other named buildings and places are accurate.

Many of the hotels referred to in the book existed and in some cases, still do. The Adlon in Berlin seems to be the preferred hotel in most Second World War espionage novels, but in fact both the Excelsior and the Kaiserhof, where Henry Hunter stayed, were prominent Berlin hotels during the Second World War. Both hotels were destroyed in Allied bombing, as was the Hotel Victoria in Stuttgart, which had been the main hotel in the city.

Readers may wonder whether it really was possible to fly on commercial routes in Europe during the Second World War. The answer is that it was, most commonly if the departure or destination airports were in neutral countries. Muntadas Airport in Barcelona was a major hub for travel around Europe, as was Portela Airport in Lisbon and Zurich Airport. During the war, Whitchurch Airport in Bristol replaced Croydon Airport as Great Britain's main commercial airport: the site is now a housing estate. In June 1943 a BOAC flight from Lisbon to Bristol was shot down by the Luftwaffe over the Bay of Biscay. All four crew and thirteen passengers were killed, including the famous British actor, Leslie Howard. It was one of very few attacks on a civilian flight in Europe during the war. The names of the airlines, the type of aircraft used and the flight details in the book are, to the best of my knowledge, accurate.

The Roman Catholic cathedral of St Hedwig was destroyed in an Allied air raid in March 1943 (it has since been reconstructed). Although Father Josef is fictional, a priest at St Hedwig, Bernhard Lichtenberg, was arrested for publicly protesting at Nazi policies towards Jews and the euthanasia programme. He died while being transported to Dachau in November 1943.

This is probably not the place to go into detail about the considerable complicity of the Swiss banks in the Nazi war effort. However, it is well established that there was an active relationship, to say the least, between the Reichsbank and most of the major Swiss banks, including Bank Leu. Bank Leu was an independent bank until it became part of Credit Suisse in 1990.

To save fellow football fans the effort I had to go to, I can assure you that the match between Sporting Lisbon and Barreirense that features in Chapter 15 did actually take place on the 9th February 1941 – and Sporting did indeed win 2-0.

I would like to thank my agent, Gordon Wise at Curtis Brown and his colleague Richard Pike for their help, encouragement and sound advice. Gordon rightly has an outstanding reputation as an agent and I realise how fortunate I am to be one of his clients. I would also like to thank Rufus Purdy and Alice Lutyens. Rufus first saw *The Swiss Spy* when I mistakenly thought it was the finished article: the fact that he has contributed so significantly to its current state is a testament to his editorial brilliance.

And finally, my thanks and love to my daughters, Amy and Nicole, and my wife, Sonia. It cannot always be easy living with a writer, not least one who wonders aloud how to kill someone and who at times may give the impression of living in a world that existed seventy years ago. As a teacher, Sonia is a very astute and frank reader: draft chapters are returned with plenty of annotations in red biro, the occasional tick more than compensating for the more frequent exclamation marks.

About the Author

Alex Gerlis was a BBC journalist for more than twenty-five years before leaving in 2011 to concentrate on his writing. His first novel, *The Best of Our Spies* (2012), is an espionage thriller set in the Second World War and like *The Swiss Spy*, based on real events. He is also the author of *The Miracle of Normandy*, published in 2014 as a non-fiction Kindle Single. Alex Gerlis lives in London, is married with two daughters and is represented by Gordon Wise at the Curtis Brown literary agency. He is a Visiting Professor of Journalism at the University of Bedfordshire.

www.alexgerlis.com

Spy Masters

The Best of Our Spies
The Swiss Spy
Vienna Spies
The Berlin Spies